Edited by Kristi Yanta and Nancy Sway.

Proofread by Melissa Martin, Brooke Lindenbusch, Nevia Brudnicki, Nicole Chiem, Laura Albert, Kellie Porth-Bagne, Janice Owens, and Karen Boehle-Johnson.

Cover by Victoria Cooper.

PRAISE FOR MELANIE SUMMERS

A fun, often humorous, escapist tale that will have readers blushing, laughing and rooting for its characters.

~ Kirkus Reviews

A gorgeously funny, romantic and seductive modern fairy tale.

~ MammieBabbie Book Club

The Royal Treatment is ... perfect for someone that needs a break from this world and wants to delve into a modern-day fairy tale that will keep them laughing and rooting for the main characters throughout the story.

~ ChickLit Café

I have to HIGHLY HIGHLY HIGHLY RECOMMEND *The Royal Treatment* to EVERYONE!

ALSO AVAILABLE

ROMANTIC COMEDIES by Melanie Summers

The Crown Jewels Series

The Royal Treatment

The Royal Wedding

The Royal Delivery

Paradises Bay Series

The Honeymooner

Whisked Away

The Suite Life

Crazy Royal Love Series (Coming in 2020)

Royally Crushed

Royally Wild

For Lori,
A truly lovely soul, a wonderful source of support to those who are lucky enough to know her, and a great reader. You've loved well and lost, yet you still walk along the shore every day to look for the magic in life.
Thank you for sharing your magic with me,
Mel

AUTHOR'S NOTE

Dear Reader,

For those who have read my other books, you may be expecting something funny and upbeat, so fair warning: this is NOT a romantic comedy. In fact, the happily ever after is not guaranteed this time around. Just as in life and love, you'll have to enter at your own risk and trust that the journey's worth taking.

I started work on Abigail's story way back in early 2016. After two months of furious writing, I had to set the book aside and give it a few weeks to breathe. A few weeks turned into two years, and then I came back to it and changed much of the story. Then left it again. Turns out, it took close to four years for me to figure out what it all meant and feel it was ready to share. I hope I'm right.

Wishing you all the best in life and love,
Melanie

CHAPTER ONE

> ❝ *If love is the answer, could you please rephrase the question?*
>
> ~ Lily Tomlin

Every love story ends the same way—in misery. 'They lived happily ever after' is just code for 'they eventually realized they weren't compatible and got a divorce, they grew tired of each other but were too lazy to do anything about it, or, they truly loved each other for eighteen years until one of them died, leaving the other one gasping for air as endless swells of grief crashed over her for the next forty years.'

Fairy tales end with the aforementioned lie for two reasons: a) it's much quicker and more poetic, or, b) no one wants anyone to think it through, in case we all come to the conclusion that loving anyone is utterly pointless (which it most certainly is). This would be a dangerous shift in the zeitgeist, because not only would it be the end of the human race, but without all those wedding registries being filled every year, it would also be the demise of Bed, Bath and Beyond.

Those are the cold, hard facts of love.

Here's another fact: I'm ninety-nine percent certain I'll never have a moment's pleasure again. Well, maybe ninety-eight percent. I was mildly pleased when Starbucks brought back the peppermint mochaccino a few weeks back. But other than that, nothing interests me. It's been over a year now, and I'm still asking myself how long this terrible pain will remain lodged in my chest.

Forever? I'm pretty sure it will be forever.

But life moves on. That's what everyone tells you. Move on. Get out. See people. It's the only way you'll start to feel better. The truth is, they only want you to move on to absolve them of the guilt they feel about being happy. To them I say, go forth and enjoy your Saturday date nights. Just leave me the hell out of it, because I'm done.

CHAPTER TWO

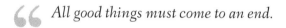 *All good things must come to an end.*

~ H.H. Riley (1857)

Isaac and I are at the beach. We're spending the weekend in Maine to celebrate our anniversary. It's a chilly fall day and we're both wearing fleece jackets and jeans. The wind whips my hair around and smacks me in the eye. Tucking the errant pieces behind my ear, I shiver and try to convince myself that it isn't actually cold outside, but refreshingly crisp. Soon I feel the warmth of the sun on my skin as the clouds move out of its way.

Isaac is telling me about a new student of his. She is particularly bright and is someone he refers to as a 'sensual' reader, devouring the likes of Dumas, Wharton, and du Maurier.

Irritation scratches my chest. I mentally resist his account of her brilliant reflection on Kincaid's *See Now Then*, threatened by the look

3

in his eyes as he talks. I hate it when he does this. How does he not know that this scares me, considering how we met?

I smile and nod and say things like 'Really?' and 'Oh, I never would have looked at it that way,' hoping to sound confident. Part of me marvels at the fact that I've managed to hide my insecurity from him for so many years. It's an ugly side of my personality I've never admitted to out loud.

I convince myself that he feels safe to tell me these things because we are so secure in our relationship. Only a loyal husband who's madly in love with his wife would talk about an especially bright young woman in this way. If he were considering leaving me for her, he wouldn't tell me all about her. He would keep her very existence a secret until the last possible second, when he would have to admit the awful truth because she was outside our building in a convertible wearing a push-up bra that matched the French-cut panties under her mini-skirt. She'd honk the horn so they could beat the weekend traffic up to the Poconos, and it would all come spilling out at once in a tumble of apologies and reassurances that the entire thing was neither planned nor my fault.

He takes my hand and gives it a gentle squeeze. "How's your book coming along?"

I inhale the sharp, salty air, then exhale the imaginary drama out of my lungs. No need to harbor such ridiculous thoughts, not while I'm walking along hand-in-hand in the sunshine with my husband of twelve years. He's not some rogue from one of my books. He's the gentlemanly duke who would lay his overcoat on a puddle for a lady to cross.

A buzzing sound interrupts me as I am just about to explain I've had to stop writing for the last year and a half to research seventeenth-century lace patterns. Pausing, I look out to the sea to locate the source of that incessant buzzing sound. "Isaac, do you hear that?"

"Hear what?"

My eyes open. I'm on the couch, not on the beach. Isaac is dead. It's the middle of the afternoon, and whoever is at the front entrance of the building seems determined not to leave without invading our romantic walk.

I stumble to the front door while rubbing the sleep out of my eyes. "Who is it?"

"It's me." Lauren's voice is all business.

"Oh, hi. Are you here as best friend Lauren or literary agent Lauren Duncan?"

"Which one will you let up?"

"Neither," I say, putting on a British accent so as to sound very well-to-do. "I'm afraid I'm not taking visitors today."

"Then why'd you ask?"

Good point. She's tricky. "You know us writers, we're a curious bunch."

"And you know where all that curiosity got the cat, don't you?" Lauren asks, sounding annoyed.

"But do I care?"

"Jesus. Just buzz me in already. It's freezing out here and I've been sent to check on you."

Shit. "My mother?"

"Yes." There's a strain in her voice that makes my entire body feel fatigued.

"Fine, you can come up, but only because you had to talk to Helen." I push the button to open the front door, unleashing a sense of panic in my chest.

Glancing around the room, I try to discern what to clean up first. The layer of grime I've accumulated on my body will take at least ten minutes to scrub off in the shower, so that's out. The empty takeout cartons on the coffee table are closest, so I collect and deposit them in the garbage. I pray that the elevator is stuck on the top floor as I plug the kitchen sink and squirt in some soap, then open the hot water tap to full force, hoping the bubbles will hide the pile of dishes. Scurrying around, I gather cups and forks and plates covered with dried-on food, drop them in the sink and shut off the water. Walt Whitman, my Siamese cat, is watching me from atop the back of the couch, looking

5

thoroughly confused. He hasn't seen me move this fast since ... well ... maybe ever.

The knock at the door makes my stomach drop. Lauren is about to become privy to my current reality, which means I'm in for a lecture and some very disapproving and pitiful looks—my least favorite kind.

Tightening the sash on my bathrobe, I pull open the door. "Ma'am, Private Sloth ready for inspection." I salute and clap my heels together, but they don't make a satisfying clicking sound because I'm wearing fuzzy slippers.

Lauren chuckles and I step aside to let her in. She's dressed in a black suit and the timeless camel-hair coat I've admired on many occasions. She can pull it off because her complexion is warm brown instead of recluse white like mine. Also, she's tall, so she doesn't look like she's playing dress-up in her father's clothes when she puts on a long coat. Lucky bitch. I could also hate her for being wonderfully fit—like I used to be—but since she's not responsible for the year-long binge I've been on, I'm going to give her a pass on that.

"When did you have to suffer through a call from my mother?" I make my way to the kitchen, keeping my distance in hopes she won't notice how long it's been since I bathed.

"Last night."

"Sorry. I'll ask her to stop doing that," I say, rolling my eyes. "Tea?"

"Please." Lauren puts her briefcase on the floor and shrugs off her coat, hanging it neatly on the rack. "She's not that bad, Abby. She's just worried about you. And by the looks of things, her concern isn't exactly unfounded."

"What?" I ask, looking around the room. "Oh, I know it's a bit messy today, but I had a rough night last night, so I was feeling a little lazy."

She is standing on the other side of the island now. "Bullshit."

"Seriously, I'm fine."

She tilts her head to the side and raises one eyebrow. I know that look. She gives it to her husband, Drew, and it never fails to break him.

6

Well, it won't work on me because *I'm* not hoping to have sex with her later.

I turn and open the cupboard where we keep the tea.

I. Where *I* keep the tea.

"Your mom is concerned that you might try to ... maybe ... take your own life."

That gets my attention. I whirl around with my mouth hanging open. "What?"

"She's worried that you're deeply depressed, and if you don't get help, you might do something drastic."

Instantly, my cheeks burn and my eyes prick with humiliation, but I draw on my considerable store of anger to bring my emotions in check. I force an icy smile. "Well, that is not going to happen. That's ridiculous."

"Prove it."

"What?"

"Prove. It." She's playing hardball literary agent Lauren Duncan.

"Fine." I huff and fold my arms across my chest. "For starters, I'm too lazy to kill myself. Do you know how much work that would be?"

Oh, that was appalling. My gut clenches at my words, but since she's now the one gaping, I continue, even though I wish I could stop. "I'd have to figure out what to wear, what to do with Walt, and then there's the whole letter thing. I can't even begin to imagine how many drafts I'd need. I'm a writer, so the last thing I write had better be spot-on perfect." I shake my head and give a careless little shrug. "That all sounds like way too much work. Plus, I wouldn't find out how *A Hand-maid's Tale* ends." I give her a 'see, I told you' look.

Lauren snorts then laughs. "Oh my God, you're terrible."

"You probably shouldn't say things like that. I'm in a very delicate state," I say, fighting a smile.

"Abby, stop it," she says, covering her smile with both hands. "It's not funny. This is very serious."

I sigh. "Tell her my sense of humor is intact, so you take that as a solid indicator that there's no need to worry."

She narrows her eyes at me. "How can I be sure you aren't just trying to throw me off?"

Giving myself a moment to think, I stare at the ceiling before answering. "Because I haven't done it yet. If I were going to do it, it would have been months ago, when I couldn't stop crying for more than a five-minute stretch. Not now, when I'm comfortably numb."

"See, when you say it that way, it doesn't exactly sound reassuring."

My shoulders drop. "I can't believe we're even talking about this."

The kettle whistles and I turn to the stove. When I finish filling the pot, I take it over to the island and set it down. "Look, I'm just taking a little time out from life right now. It's all good, though, I promise. I'll be venturing out into the world soon enough."

"Starting when?"

"I don't know. Soon." I cross the room and take two mugs out of the cupboard. "Next Wednesday at three fifteen p.m. Eastern Standard Time." I turn back to her with an impish grin that I hope will work.

She doesn't return my smile. "I'm holding you to that. You're on notice, Abigail Carson."

"Okay, boss lady." My tone suggests that she really doesn't have control over me, even though deep down I'm a little scared of her and she knows it.

Her face softens as her eyes pass over my fleece frog-print robe. "Not today, but when you're ready, I need to talk to you about your contract with Titan."

My stomach tightens. Even though I knew this was coming, I was hoping it would be longer in getting here. "I'm pretty sure I already know what you're going to say. When do they want the advance back?"

She sighs and says, "This can wait."

"I can tell by the look on your face that it can't. How long do I have?"

"Thirty days to start making installments unless you can come up with the entire forty-five thousand at once. Or maybe ..." She pauses and gives me a hopeful yet terrified look. "You managed to write an entire novel without mentioning it?"

Thirty days. My entire body goes numb and I want to sink into the couch and pull a blanket over my head. Instead, I give her a confident nod. "No problem. I can write them a check." I think.

"They've been at me for almost six months now, and I've held them off as long as I could," Lauren says. "I'm sorry."

"No, I'm sorry. I just can't seem to ..." My voice is barely audible, even in my own ears.

"Erica said that when you start writing again, she'll look at anything you do. Of course, they want you to finish the Duchess series, but if that's too hard right now and you want to write something else, they'll read it. She said to tell you she's sorry, but accounting is on her ass about it."

I stare out the window for a moment as I let this information sink in. "The thing is, Lauren, it's kind of hard to write lighthearted historical romance when nothing is remotely funny anymore, and after you figure out there is no such thing as happily ever after."

Nodding, she says, "So maybe try something new. Just keep the historical part and write, I don't know ... horribly depressing drama."

I manage to curve my lips upward for a second, then let them drop. "There's just no part of me that wants to create anything. I honestly don't know if I'm a writer anymore."

"Oh, Abby, don't say that. Maybe you're not ready to go back to it at the moment, but you can't give up. It's who you are." She rests her hand on mine. Her palm is warm and soft and the feeling of another human touching me brings an unwelcome swell of emotion.

"Maybe you could try something else—just for a little while—until you feel inspired again. Work in a flower shop or a bookstore or something. Anything so you'll have—" She stops herself when she sees the glare on my face.

"A reason to get up in the morning?" I quip, pulling my hand away. "He's gone."

Lauren sighs, and the look on her face says she's as defeated as I intended her to be. Her cell phone buzzes and she glances at it. "Shit. I need a new assistant. The one thing I needed her to do was reschedule my three o'clock, but it looks like she hasn't managed it."

"You were going to take the afternoon off for me?"

Lauren nods.

Don't I feel like a total bag? "That's really not necessary. I'm doing fine."

"This isn't healthy, Abby," she says, standing and picking up her briefcase. "You need to get out and be around people."

"I have Walt. He's people."

"The other kind of people—human beings with opposable thumbs who can hold up their end of a conversation," she says as she starts for the door. "I don't know. Maybe you should try getting a little wild and having some fun for once."

"I have fun all the time." Spying my plate from breakfast, I pick it up off the coffee table and lick Pop-Tart crumbs off it. "See? That was wildly wonderful."

She slides on her coat. "I'm serious, Abby. You can't go on like this."

"Oh, I'm pretty sure I can."

"You're going for a late lunch with me this Friday. I'll be here at one-thirty to get you."

"I won't go with you, but I promise I'll be alive."

She laughs reluctantly. "You're such a shit."

"You love that about me."

"I do, and you are leaving this apartment on Friday, even if I have to drag you out by your ankles."

"I'd like to see you try."

"Oh, I can do it, lady. Just make sure you shower and put some clothes on."

"Nah, I'd rather make you take me out like this," I say, opening the door for her. "But I insist we go to the Russian Tea Room."

She walks out into the hall and turns to me, her face full of the pity I've grown to hate. "If you need help with paying back the advance—"

"That's very kind of you, but I could never allow that." I shake my head at the notion. "I can manage it."

The elevator bell dings and the door slides open, allowing Mr. Puente, the co-op board director who I've been artfully avoiding to catch sight of me. Son of a bitch.

"Abby, finally," he says with a loud sigh. "I've been trying to reach you for weeks."

"Let me guess, someone wants to re-open the great welcome mat debate of 2016," I say, giving a discreet eye roll in Lauren's direction. She gives me an 'oh brother' face and winks before she hurries to catch the elevator.

"Those mats were a tripping hazard." He rushes toward me with his perfectly straight posture. He's dressed in tan slacks, a starched white button-up, and a pea soup green sweater vest I'm sure he spent twenty minutes ironing this morning. "Have you been away? I've tried emailing, calling, and stopping by repeatedly."

"I've been very busy."

His eyes travel to my slipper-clad feet, and when he looks back up at my face, it's with sympathy. "I see. Can we step inside for a minute? I'm afraid I have bad news."

"Perfect, because it's bad news day at Casa de Carson." I gesture for him to come in, then start toward the kitchen. "Tea?"

"No, thank you. I'm wondering if you've read any of the letters the co-op board has sent." When I turn back to him, he's staring at the toppled pile of envelopes on the counter.

"I've gotten behind on my paperwork lately."

Mr. Puente takes a deep breath and closes his eyes for a second. "As you may or may not know, we're up for another major rent increase later this year. The board has been pulling together the funds to purchase the land from Killborn. All the co-op owners either need to pay their share or sell."

Shock vibrates through my bones, followed by a sick, panicky feeling. I should not have been ignoring things for so long. "How much?"

"For your unit, it would be a four-hundred-and-eighty-thousand-dollar buy-in."

My knees grow weak and I suddenly wish I were sitting down. "Who has that kind of money?"

"Some have it. Some have managed to get financing. It's a great investment if you can swing it." He glances at my slippers, then continues. "If not, we found a realtor who offered to drop his commission for anyone who needs out."

"But the market is ..."

He nods. "Yes, you'll be lucky to get three-hundred-thousand out of it."

"How long do I have to figure this out?"

"That's the thing. You need the money by next Friday." The way his face twists shows that he's torn between pity and irritation. I've put him in this incredibly awkward position by ignoring what surely must have been the only thing my neighbors have thought of for months now. "I'm very sorry, Abby. I really did try to reach you."

"No, it's okay. It's not your fault." I shake my head, and, much to my horror, tears spring to my eyes without my permission. Oh, perfect.

He stiffly makes his way over to the coffee table, returning with a tissue box. "Here."

I take two and hold them up to my face, trying to cover the evidence of having actual feelings. "Thanks."

"I can only imagine how hard this past year has been for you, and I know this won't make it easier."

I nod and blow my nose, which is now running at record speed. *Not very dignified, Abby.*

Mr. Puente digs in his pocket and hands me a business card. "This is the realtor I mentioned. He's quite good. He'll take care of everything for you."

And just like that, a ball has begun rolling down a steep hill, and there will be no catching it. No ignoring it. Only chasing.

CHAPTER THREE

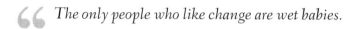 *The only people who like change are wet babies.*

~ Mark Twain

"Now what?" I sit on the couch with my laptop in front of me. My eyes are burning from spending the last four hours scrolling through pages of condos for sale. Despite what Ben, the opportunistic realtor, tried to tell me, I held onto a shred of hope that I could somehow find the one remaining apartment in the city I can afford. But there is nothing. Not for someone who isn't willing to share a space with a roommate or forgo the luxury of a window. And certainly not for someone without a solid job. This city demands ambition, something I've always loved about it, until I lost mine. I have to leave New York, my home of twenty-one years.

The apartment sold yesterday, after fourteen days on the market. Now, I have eight weeks to find a cheap place to live. I shut my laptop and lean back, closing my eyes as desperation rockets up my spine again. I don't want to do this, and I definitely don't want to do it alone. The mountain of work ahead of me is so high, I can't see the top from down here. I slide my thumb through Isaac's wedding band, which hangs from a gold chain around my neck. The smooth gold doesn't magically transport him here from the netherworld when I need him most, not that I held any hope it would.

Why can't you be here now, you bastard?

Isaac would know what to do. He'd have thought of the perfect solution by now, and instead of feeling like this is the end of the world, it would feel like an inconvenient-yet-somewhat-exciting new adventure.

But this is not 'the fresh start I might need,' as Lauren gently put it on the phone this morning. This is my life spiraling out of control without my permission.

I suppose that's the thing about life, it never asks for permission. It just thunders along, taking horribly sharp, random turns, and you're strapped in for a ride you never agreed to take.

Isaac appears as soon as I close my eyes. We're on our annual school-is-out road trip, this time up through the Canadian Maritimes. He's driving, and I'm sitting in the passenger seat. I caress the back of his neck with my fingertips, taking in the delicious warmth of his skin.

He smiles over at me. "You happy?"

"I am." The tall cliffs to the left whip by at a violent pace, but inside the car, I hear the overture from Mozart's Lucio Silla playing through the sound system. I look out at the ocean to my right and watch the waves slamming against the rocky shore below. The sun on my shoulder has a hypnotic effect and the brilliant blue sky is full of possibilities. "I think this is my favorite place on earth."

He chuckles. "You say that about every place we go."

"I know, but this time I really mean it." I let my hand drop down to his thigh. "We should move here when you retire. It would be perfect. We can buy a nice little cottage for next to nothing. Somewhere overlooking the sea, where I could write and you could—I don't know—take up gardening."

Isaac lets out a low growl. "Gardening is for old men."

I twist my face into a grin. "Well in twelve years, you'll be an—"

"Do not say it." He laughs as he grabs my knee and squeezes it.

Instinctively, I cover his hand with mine, lacing my fingers through his. "Don't worry. I'll be old by then, too."

"Liar," he says, his eyes shining with laughter.

He looks so relaxed and happy, I'm suddenly desperate to convince him. "Fishing, then. You could get a little wooden boat and go out on days when the water is calm."

"Fishing, hey?" Isaac tilts his head as he considers it. "I could bring a cooler of beers and stumble home with our supper."

The image makes me feel almost giddy. "If we could live here, I'd even gut and clean the fish while you shower."

Isaac lets out a loud laugh. "You really are full of shit today."

"Am not. I just love it here *that much*."

Looking at me from under his eyebrows, he says, "So much that you'd be willing to gut a fish? With a knife? Your delicate writer's hands getting all bloody as you reach in and pull out—"

Holding up one hand, I stop him. "Okay, okay. To be completely honest, I may have been too hasty with that offer," I say, my mouth twisting to one side. "But if it's a deal-breaker, I'm willing to let you *think* I'll do it."

It takes Isaac half a second to sort out what I've actually said and his chest starts to shake with laughter. I join in, hope rising as we revel in our amusement.

When the moment passes, he nods once. "Okay, deal. In twelve years, we'll find a place here."

"Really?" I ask, tingling with delight all the way through to my bones.

"Really."

Reaching up, I pull his head closer, furiously planting kisses on his cheek while the orchestra swells to a joyful crescendo. When I let him go, I turn up the music and lean my head against the seatback, utterly content and already dreaming of our new life as I gaze out at the sailboats in the distance.

"Make sure you don't forget, okay?"

"What?" I ask, sitting up and turning to him.

He turns to me with an expression so piercing, it wipes the smile off my face. Letting go of the wheel, he swivels his body to face me. "You need to remember this when you wake up."

"What are you doing?" I ask, glancing from him to the approaching curve in the road. My heart speeds up, outpacing the racing bows of the sinister violins. "Isaac, you're driving!"

He takes no notice, reaching for me instead of the wheel. I push his hands away, furious that he's risking our lives. "Stop it. This isn't funny."

"It's fine, this is more important."

The curve is coming fast. Beyond it is a steep drop. I choke out a sob as my entire body freezes solid. But Isaac is stupidly calm. He leans toward me and takes my cheeks in both hands, turning my face to his. "Listen to me, Abby. This is where you belong."

The clanging of a garbage truck in the alley below wakes me. My heart pounds and I bolt up, panting and trying to slow my breath. When I open my eyes, the sun disappears, replaced by a dark gray winter morning. "It's okay, it's okay," I whisper, clutching for the comfort of my duvet. *This* is real. That wasn't.

The dream fades quickly, but the unsettled feeling lingers. Reaching for Walt, I pull him onto my lap and run my hands down the length of his body. I had the answer. I know I did. But to what? After another few moments, I accept that whatever brilliant revelation I thought I had is gone forever. "I'm sure it was just nonsense anyway, right?" I say, sliding Walt back over onto Isaac's pillow.

He answers by opening one eye for a second, then curling himself into a tight ball.

16

"Exactly. We have more important things to worry about than some stupid nightmare. In a matter of weeks, we're going to be homeless." My gut hardens at the thought, and I throw off my covers and get up. As I pad across the cold hardwood to the en suite, my brain still wrestles to remember where I was before I woke up, while my raw nerves fight to forget.

I splash some warm water on my face, and as soon as my palms touch my cheeks, my mind flashes to Isaac holding my face and his earnest eyes pleading with me to understand. Suddenly, it comes to me. *This is where you belong.*

Not bothering to dry my skin, I hurry back to my bed where my laptop waits on the night table. "I figured it out, Mr. Whitman. The perfect place for us to live. It's cheap and safe and lovely, and it'll be just like Isaac is there with us because we were going to move there anyway."

Walt lifts his head as though intrigued, and I give him a quick scratch behind his ears. "And best of all, nobody will bother us there."

CHAPTER FOUR

 Story of my life. I always get the fuzzy end of the lollipop.

~ Marilyn Monroe as Sugar Kane Kowalczyk, *Some Like it Hot*

Two Months Later

"Where are you, pumpkin?" I can tell by his voice that my dad is trying to sound supportive and I love him for it.

"Nova Scotia. I just passed a little place called Antigonish."

"So, are you almost to Cape Breton Island then?"

"About another hour. I should reach South Haven sometime around three."

"What's it like to drive again?"

"Like riding a bike."

"That's what worries me. You never were that good at bike riding."

A small laugh escapes my lips. "Thanks for the encouragement."

18

"Any time. But seriously, you're okay hauling a trailer behind that little Honda?"

"It's not that small, it's a CRV. Getting out of the city was sketchy, but now that I'm on the open road, I'm fine."

"Did you get the oil changed before you left? And check the tire pressure?"

"Yes, Dad," I say, sounding like an annoyed teenager. "I had it serviced when I took it out of storage."

"You know you have to give yourself twice the distance to come to a stop with all that weight behind it."

"I know. I'm going slow, giving myself lots of room."

"Okay, well, I'm glad to hear you're not flipped over in a ditch somewhere."

"You should have been the writer."

"What's that? You're really quiet." Despite a mountain of evidence, my dad seems utterly unaware of the fact that he's losing his hearing.

"I said I think Walt is having a worse time than me. He'll definitely be glad to be out of his carrier when we get there."

"Walt?" He pauses. "Oh, right, the cat. Okay, I better hand the phone over to your mom. She's been pacing around waiting to hear from you for hours."

"Oh, no, that's—"

"Hello? Abby? Is that you?"

I squeeze my eyes shut for a split second when I hear her voice. "Yes, Mom."

"Are you on speakerphone?"

Isaac and I would have shared a knowing glance just now. The thought instantly tortures me, and I silently gasp to make it stop. "Yes, of course."

"Good. Is it safe to drive there? I've heard the roads can be very icy in Canada. Did you get winter tires? I read that you need special tires there."

"I think that's only in the winter. It's almost eighty degrees today."

"Oh, I didn't realize that." Her words come out short, their undercurrent hinting at the strain I've always been on her. Well, the feeling is mutual, Mom.

She sighs heavily. "This is very hard for me, you know. You just pick up and move to a foreign country. What if it's not safe for a single woman there?"

"It's Canada, Mom, not a war zone in the Middle East. A tiny little village with less than three thousand people too polite to rob you. Besides, I ran a check on the Internet, and South Haven has been certified to be completely free from gangs and thugs." I'm not proud of how sarcastic I sound, but somehow, I can't seem to stop myself.

"Ha ha." She adds extra emphasis to each 'ha' as proof of my lack of wit.

"Sorry. It really is lovely here though. The sky goes on forever, and the rest is just a lot of trees and fields." I hope my false bravado is convincing because I refuse to let her know I'm locked in a relentless battle against my urge to make a U-turn and go back to New York. "Every once in a while, I catch a glimpse of the ocean. It's really lovely." Damn, I said that already.

"You already said that."

I suppose I can't blame her for not being enthusiastic. She was hoping I'd move home, and instead, I've added thousands of miles to the distance between us.

"It was a smart move, Mom. You know there's no way I could afford a place anywhere near Portland. Here, I already own my house outright, and I have enough money left over to write for the next year or so without worrying about how I'll pay for groceries." And I can be alone.

"Well, you wouldn't have to—" She stops herself from finishing, but I know the end of the sentence. You wouldn't have to pay for food if you came home.

Trying to control the edge in my voice, I say, "I need to stand on my own two feet for once."

"You need to be with the people who love you most in this world."

I sigh loudly in lieu of an answer, knowing any attempt at trying to make her understand will fall on deaf ears.

Neither of us speaks for a full thirty seconds, which is an eternity in a conversation. As much as I want to hang up, I know I can't just yet. We've both grown accustomed to the tight wire that holds us together and the way it threatens to snap at any given moment. A small token of peace must be offered so we'll have an inroad the next time we speak. "How is everybody there?"

"Fine. Same as usual. We're going to Medford on Saturday. Kaitlyn has a gymnastics competition, so that should be nice."

"Oh, great. You'll enjoy that."

"Yes, I will. She's so talented, and she works very hard. It's really something to see." Meaning that it's really something I should see.

"Good for her. Well, wish her good luck from Aunt Abby."

"I will."

"And hello to everyone."

She swallows before she speaks again, and I know it was a lecture about staying in touch with my family that she's just ingested. Switching gears, she goes from guilt to my other favorite, doubt. "I just can't believe you bought a house sight unseen. What if it's a scam? Or it's completely run down and it costs a fortune to fix?"

"It's fine, Mom. Seriously. I'm not an idiot." Probably.

"I've never once thought you were an idiot. Stubborn, yes. Stupid, no."

"Gee, thanks."

"What if it's overrun with rodents? Or cockroaches?"

"It's not—can you just give me some credit, please?" I grip the wheel harder than necessary, then remind myself that when this conversation ends, it'll be weeks before I'll be reproached for whatever my next horribly disappointing decision might be.

"Well, it's hard for me to understand how you can sound so sure if you haven't seen it for yourself."

"Yet, I am." Or at least I was until she got on the phone.

"Abby—"

"I should go. I don't know how much this call is costing me."

"Fine."

Silence fills the line again, and it is so much louder than any of our words have been. Countless arguments that will remain unheard. In her mind, I haven't done even one thing right since the day I met Isaac. She'll never understand me, and I'll never bend to her will and become the daughter she wishes she had. Nothing will ever change, and we both know it.

"Drive safely, Abby. I love you." Her voice cracks and I suddenly wish for the uncomplicated, easy love we shared when I was a child. I can see her smiling down at me and feel my hand wrapped in hers as we walk home from the playground.

She clears her throat, and when she speaks again, her voice breaks the spell. "Call me when you find the time."

My tone mirrors her tension. "I will. Love you."

"Love you too."

I let the phone disconnect on its own. Our conversation knocks around in my brain, letting every shot she took hit me again. If Isaac were here, he'd tell me I'm not stubborn but determined, and that I have good reasons for not being close with people who choose not to understand me. He'd follow it up with the fact that it's their loss, not mine. I'd pretend to feel better until I actually did, not wanting to let him fail at his attempt to rescue me from my toxic relationship with my mother. Not having to pretend is maybe the best part of being alone, because right now, I don't want to be soothed. I want to feel indignant and misunderstood and hurt. I want to wallow in it so I don't have to face how fucking terrified I am.

Even though I'm bone-tired, I drive on without stopping. The past two months have drained me. Cleaning out every drawer and cupboard. A thousand decisions a day, each one a punch to the gut. Violent sobs shook my body as I bagged up Isaac's clothes and hauled them to the door for Goodwill. There was a reason I avoided it for hundreds of days.

It was the unexpected things that destroyed me. The sight of his carefully polished shoes lined up in his closet, waiting. The box stuffed to the top with every card and note I'd written him over the years. I had no idea he was saving them. I just assumed he tossed them out.

In the end, I kept very few of his things and brought only slightly more of mine. His desk is with me, along with as many of his books as I could fit in one box. The rest has been given away. I only have his slippers and his favorite scarf—a gray, white, and red plaid cashmere strip of fabric that he wore everywhere in the colder months. It sits somewhere in the back of the U-Haul, still carrying a hint of his aftershave. I sold nearly all our furniture, including our bed, the couch, and the kitchen table. Everything I own—other than my house, I suppose—is with me as I put mile after terrifying mile between myself and my old life.

As brave as I like to sound, I've been second-guessing my decision to move to Canada since the moment I made the offer on the cottage. Other than a road trip Isaac and I took to the Maritimes over a decade ago, I haven't spent any time here at all. Everywhere I look, I see a world that is the polar opposite of Manhattan. There are no traffic jams, skyscrapers, or crowded sidewalks. No busy streets lined with restaurants, nightclubs, and clothing stores that make it easy to hide.

If this were one of my novels, I'd be a lady in the eighteenth century who was being sent to live with a distant relative after losing my husband. I wouldn't be driving down a smooth highway, but riding in a carriage along a bumpy dirt road. Instead of a black hoodie and comfy faded jeans, I'd be in a Brunswick gown and a straw hat meant for traveling. I'd describe the view as 'meadows of tall grasses and delicate wildflowers stretching on for miles, only interrupted occasionally by stands of pine and maple trees that seem pleased by their good fortune to have taken root here.' And I'd suggest that 'if they can be happy here, maybe I can too.' I'd take note of how the ocean appears more often to my left now, shimmering under the bright sun, hinting at what lies ahead.

What a load of horse shit. It's empty, uninhabited land, and that ocean is probably littered with trash, or at the very least, riddled with microplastics. It's so much better to live in reality than to believe in fairy tales. Once you accept reality, it won't disappoint you like romantic fantasies will. Fantasies will make you weep. It suddenly occurs to me that, for the first time in weeks, I haven't cried today, but that's only because I'm completely frozen with fear.

When I glance down at the passenger seat, Walt glares at me from behind the bars of his cage.

"I know, Walt. This has been a tough trip, but I promise, the worst is over." Maybe.

Just after three in the afternoon, I see a sign that says,

Welcome to South Haven,
The Little Village with a Big Heart.

"Oh, gross."

The empty highway runs along Bras d'Or Lake to my left and the town to my right. The speed limit slows enough to allow me to properly take it all in. So far, it doesn't look any different than it did when Isaac and I spent a day exploring the town before moving on to Sydney (where the best hotels on the island are) for the night. First is a wharf with sailboats and fishing vessels bobbing up and down. Shops are next —the quaint bakery where we ate quiche and sipped tea is still there, as is the used bookstore where Isaac found a second edition Thoreau. I fight the squeezing of my heart at the memory and instead focus my attention on the cozy cafés and souvenir shops with wooden storefronts that speak of a simpler time.

The sidewalks are sprinkled with retired tourists clad in sunglasses and hats, cameras slung around their necks. A long stretch of grass leads down to a rocky beach. Next to it is a large playground with preschool-aged children running and climbing while their stylish moms sip coffees and study their cell phones. The shops and restaurants grow closer together as I continue on, and soon, the road veers away from the lakeshore, and there are two-story office buildings on either side of me.

After a few blocks, houses appear—small, older homes with slanted roofs and flower boxes spilling over with colorful blooms. A large brick schoolhouse sits on a hilltop, and I imagine how, if I'd had that view as a girl, I'd have sat in class staring out the window and daydreaming.

I drive on through town and slow to a crawl when the GPS tells me it's time to turn left onto Shore Lane. My heart pounds as I take in the wide, tree-lined street. My eyes search greedily for house number five. Up ahead, a 'for sale' sign swings in the breeze with a 'sold' sticker cutting across it. "I think we made it, Walt."

Another sign catches my eye, belonging to the property next to mine.

Sea Winds Bed & Breakfast & Pub
Kitchen Parties Every Thursday Night.
Rooms Available.

"A bed-and-breakfast and a pub? That's too many ands," I say, signaling to indicate to no one that I'm turning into my driveway. "What the hell is a kitchen party, anyway? It better not be loud or they're going to find the police at their door every Thursday night."

As soon as I'm facing my property, my heart thrums in my ears and I forget about all the 'ands' next door. A thick screen of trees and over-grown shrubs line the property, and I can't see the house until I've gone several feet up the long gravel driveway. Pulling to a stop, I feel like an intruder even though it's mine.

Once I shut off the engine, I allow myself to take it all in. It's the faded blue two-story clapboard I found myself drawn to on my computer screen (mainly because the price was right), but the house from the photos looked much nicer than this one. This one is all boarded up. Both of the large main floor windows have empty flower boxes fixed to them with sparse, curly strips of white paint threatening to drop at any second. The yard is overrun with knee-high grass and jumbled weeds that seem to have broken through the sidewalk blocks in their quest for world domination. The white gutter on the detached single-car garage has come loose and hangs in the way of the rusted overhead door.

Eunice Beckham, the realtor, told me the photos were taken 'a while back' and that the place was 'a little worse for wear but still loaded with potential.' Apparently, her version of 'a little' and mine are not at all the same. My stomach feels suddenly heavy and my skin tingles. "Fuck," I whisper. "Why did I do this?"

My mom's words come back to me. Scam. Rodents. Oh my God. This is the perfect place for rodents. And spiders. In fact, it looks like it's been abandoned long enough for the spiders and rodents to have mated, creating some sort of super rat-spider mutant. The thought sends shivers up my spine.

Groaning, I look at Walt again and open his kennel door. "So, listen, I'm going to need you to become a mouser and a spider-hunter right away. Do you think you can manage that?"

He springs out of his kennel onto the floor, then looks up at me with a glare that says, 'no way in hell.'

"Spoiled city cat," I say, finally forcing myself to open the car door and step out. I stand and stretch, feeling the relief of a few pops in my spine, then look back at him. "Come on, Mr. Whitman. Don't make me do this alone."

He's crouched motionless on the rubber mat, his ears sideways and his eyes wide.

"Isaac should have gotten me a dog."

He doesn't budge.

"Fine. Be that way. I'm going."

Here we go. This is home, whether I like it or not. Oh, I am so not going to like this.

I walk gingerly up the sidewalk, keeping my eyes peeled for rats or spiders or spider-rats. A gust of wind ripples through the tall grass and causes a bright yellow army of dandelions to nod their heads at me. I flinch in response, waiting for something nefarious to jump out at me, but nothing happens. If Isaac were here, he'd walk ahead while we laughed about my imaginary enemies, and it would all seem amusing rather than sinister. A flash of anger passes through me, as it sometimes does. How dare he die on me? We were supposed to do this together.

Guilt is next.

Then nothing.

Walking around to the backyard, I'm relieved to find the property is surrounded almost entirely by tall, full pines and aspens that part in the south to give a clear view of the water. At least that's the same as the pictures. Now that I'm back here, I feel slightly less positive that this was the worst idea anyone has ever had. I can picture myself sitting at a small wrought-iron table with a mug of tea and my journal, listening to the waves lap against the shore. If Walt the Wimp ever gets out of the car, he may even enjoy hopping through the grass to hunt bugs.

It's not his fault he's scared. He's never been outdoors in his entire life. Not free, anyway. Isaac brought him home a few days after he found out he was sick. Walt was ten weeks old at the time. Since then, he's lived exclusively in the five rooms that made up our apartment, only to go outside in his cage to the vet a couple of times. But here, he can be free. And maybe so can I.

I make my way over to the large glass greenhouse. Several of the panes are smashed, but the white frame seems sturdy enough when I push on it. An old wooden shed is tucked in the back corner of the lot. According to Eunice, it has every gardening tool needed to get this place back into shape, not that I know what to do with them.

As I wind my way around to the front yard, I expect to find Walt waiting in the car. My muscles tense up at the sight of an older woman standing by the U-Haul holding my cat.

"Hello, you must be Abigail Carson." Rather than having a Maritime accent, she sounds Irish.

The New Yorker in me is immediately suspicious of a stranger calling me by name. "Yes, I am." I hurry to take Walt from her.

"I live next door. Nettie O'Rourke. Well, Annette, actually, but everyone calls me Nettie. This lovely boy must be yours." She smiles and instantly her face looks younger by a decade. Her gray hair is swept up in a messy bun, and from the looks of her clothes, she's been out gardening for some time. Maybe years.

"His name is Walt."

"I hope you don't mind me picking him up. He was meowing so loudly that I came by to see what was going on."

"No, it's fine." It is *so* not fine.

"Eunice told me you'd be arriving today. Welcome to South Haven." Nettie reaches out and touches my arm.

"Thank you," I say tightly, pulling my arm back as an indicator that I'm not here to make friends.

Seeming not to notice my attempt at being standoffish, she continues to smile at me. "It'll be grand to have a nice new neighbor around."

Might as well set the boundaries right off the bat. "Well, I'm not that nice."

Instead of scurrying away like I hoped, Nettie laughs. "You've got that fast New York wit about you. How fun!"

"Listen, Nettie, I think it's important for me to be clear. I'm more of a cat person than a people person," I say firmly.

"Don't worry, we'll change that," she answers with a wink.

I'm just about to tell her not to bother when she snaps her fingers. "Oh! I almost forgot. Eunice gave me the keys so you won't have to wait for her. A retired couple from the city came to town today to look at a few houses." She digs around in the front pocket of her jeans and produces my house keys.

I take them from her and stare at the dull metal in my palm. "This is not how we do real estate transactions in Manhattan."

"I imagine not," Nettie says with a chuckle. "Eunice said to tell you she'll be by around four o'clock to check on you and bring you the paperwork."

"Okay, great. Thanks." I close my fingers around the keys and my heart thumps in response. I'm about to unlock the door to my first house.

"I'll let you get to it then. It's wonderful to meet you, Abigail." She pats Walt on the head and immediately his motor starts up with a purr.

Traitor.

She turns to leave, then stops. "Come by anytime to get the key to your room and have a bite of supper. And let us know if you'll need any help bringing your luggage over."

"Umm, I'm staying here tonight." I point to the house with one thumb. "Thanks anyway."

"Didn't Eunice tell you? None of your services are hooked up, so you could stay here, but you'd have no power, water, or electricity."

I purse my lips together, holding in the string of curse words on the tip of my tongue. "She didn't mention that, no."

"Oh, dear, yes. It usually takes Gus about a week."

"A week?" Are you freaking kidding me? "Is there no one else who can do it?"

Shaking her head, she says, "Nope, just Gus Nickerson. He's the only one in the area who has the permits."

"But, that's ridiculous. Isn't it just a quick flip of some switch or something?"

"I suspect so, but Gus isn't one to rush anything. He doesn't believe in being in a hurry," she says. "If you ask me, a lot of people should take a page out of his book."

But I didn't ask, and I really don't care about Gus the gas guy's beliefs, so ... "Right, sure," I answer, wanting to return to the real issue. "So, is there any way I can get a hold of Gus to ask him to hurry just this once?"

Instead of answering, Nettie chuckles softly. "We've got a lovely corner room with a big soaker tub reserved for you and Walt here. Fifty percent off your stay since you're a neighbor," Nettie says, turning to leave.

Fifty percent off? When I shouldn't have to pay for anything because I should be staying in the house I just paid for? "I'm assuming the utility company will pay since they're failing to provide timely service."

"That's considered timely here." She calls over her shoulder, "Dinner's served from five 'til seven. Tonight is lobster bisque, Caesar salad, and biscuits, followed by roast chicken and mashed potatoes with gravy."

I fume silently as she disappears down a path through the trees that separates my lot from hers. I am clearly in need of a tall fence around the property to keep Nosy Nettie out. But first, I'm going to call up the gas company and give them a piece of my mind. "Gus doesn't believe in rushing," I mutter. "This is insane. *I'm* the customer and *I* believe in rushing so he better damn-well rush."

I try to put Walt down, but he resists, digging his claws into my shoulder. "Ouch, all right," I say, straightening up.

First, go inside. Then put the cat down. Then call the utility company. Or fight the spider-rats, then call them.

My skin feels prickly as I make my way over to my front door, trying to convince myself there's no such thing as a cross between a rat and a giant spider, but only managing to invent spider-riding rodents instead. "Oh, Abby, what were you thinking?"

Walt makes opening the ancient screen door a sweaty affair, but there's no point in trying to put him down, not unless I want him to take long strips of skin with him. I prop open the screen door with one foot while I fiddle with the lock. "It's okay," I tell him. "There's nothing to be afraid of ... except whatever's living in there."

Turning the handle, I draw a deep breath and open the wooden door. It feels stiff and creaks loudly, and I can't decide if it's welcoming or warning me. When I step inside, I'm greeted by beams of light that shine through the cracks in the boards on the windows. Thick layers of dust hide the true colors of the home, and when I move, tiny particles dance and swirl in the light. Standing perfectly still, I hold my breath, listening for scurrying or scratching sounds, but there's only silence.

"Do you smell or see any tiny poops?" I ask Walt as I scan the floor of the small foyer. He doesn't seem like a cat who's just picked up the scent of something delicious to chase, so I continue on.

Once inside, I'm given three choices—up the stairs in front of me, through the wide opening to my right, or through the door to my left. Deciding to go right, I find myself standing in the living room with a high, sloped ceiling held up by dark wooden beams. There is a stone fireplace with a thick, wooden slab for a mantle. Floor-to-ceiling book-shelves line one wall, and if they aren't rotten, they'll be filled soon. Other than that, the room is bare. A cheap green carpet covers the floor, and I wonder if it's too much to hope for beautiful wood plank floors under it. Of course it is.

I lean forward and Walt hops out of my arms onto the floor. "Seri-ously? You're terrified of grass, but you'll happily wander around on a filthy, stained carpet? What does that say about my housekeeping skills?" I say. "Don't answer that."

I follow the carpet through a wide opening in the far wall where a long, wooden table fills up most of the space. There are no chairs, but the table appears to be handcrafted and is what the host of *Antiques Roadshow* would call 'a find.' Upon closer examination, I realize the table is not only dusty, but is also sprinkled with dead flies. Yuck. Turn-ing, I see the kitchen on the other side of the dining area. It's a modest galley-style setup, but it's more than enough room for me to toast Pop-Tarts.

Once I'm standing in front of the sink, I peer through the crack in the boarded-up window that overlooks the backyard. I glance at Walt, who has followed me. "What a pleasant view we'll have when I don't do the dishes."

A few minutes later, I've ventured as far down into the basement as I dare without electricity. Using the flashlight on my cell phone, I stop on the bottom step where I scan the room for wildlife or dead bodies, my heart in my throat the entire time. But instead of anything rabid or rotting, I find a furnace, a hot water tank, and an ancient washer and dryer sitting on a disappointing dirt floor. The cement walls are broken up only by one small window so covered in grime it barely allows in any light. I used to hate my tiny laundry/storage room back in Manhat-tan, but compared to this dungeon, that seems like a positively luxu-rious place to hang my unmentionables.

The top floor is much less spooky and by the time I've walked through the three small carpeted bedrooms and one bathroom, I'm almost confident that the house isn't overrun with things that leave trails while they scurry about. Having set that fear aside, I return to my original goal, which is to call the utility company and give them a piece of my mind. We'll see if a little New York attitude can light a fire under Gus the Zen Gasman's ass because there is no way in hell I'm staying at that B&B tonight.

CHAPTER FIVE

> *I don't know if you've ever noticed this, but first impressions are often entirely wrong.*

~Lemony Snicket

So, apparently, I *am* staying at the Sea Winds tonight. It's either that or in my car because there is no way I'll be getting my services hooked up today. In fact, I was robbed of the pleasure of yelling at someone because when I called the gas company, instead of a real person, I received a voicemail informing me they are 'closed for a family celebration, but they'd be back bright and early Monday morning to take my call—unless the party gets out of hand in which case, it'll be closer to noon.'

A family celebration? Since when is *family* a reason to close the gas company? I left a long, terse message, then looked up the number for the water company, which as it turns out, is the same place. Ditto for the electrical company. So, there's that.

I'm now hunting around in the trunk of my car to find a box of full-sized Snickers bars to take the edge off my hunger. It won't fix the problem, but it will soothe me for a good minute or two. The sound of a vehicle coming up the driveway interrupts my search for sustenance. When I look up, my retinas are assaulted by a brilliant white Ford Fiesta sporting a huge image of Eunice Beckham's grinning face on the side. A word bubble covers the side window that says, 'If I can't sell it, no one can!'

Makes sense. She's the only realtor in town, so ...

She offers me an open-mouthed Barbara Walters smile as she unfolds her lanky body from the car. "Abby, welcome to South Haven! I'm so sorry I wasn't here to greet you when you first pulled in."

Eunice is wearing a cotton candy pink pantsuit and is coming toward me at an alarming speed. She claps her hands together and then holds her arms out wide, moving in for a—oh dear God, no—she wants a hug?

A second later, I'm being choked by a pink cloud of White Diamonds perfume. Every muscle in my body tenses up and I stand perfectly still, trying not to breathe until it's over.

When she finally releases me, she takes my cheeks in both hands. "Oh, how fun to have our very own New Yorker in the village! You'll bring such a sassy spice to the place." She is beaming at me. Literally beaming. Or is that the makeup? Are those sparkles? Yes, yes they are.

"Thank you?" I say, allowing my tone to rise in that way that says I'm not at all sure about being the new resident New Yorker in the village.

"Oh, silly me. I haven't introduced myself! It's me! Eunice Beckham. And if you're wondering if we're related to a certain rock-hard soccer player who doubles as a Calvin Klein underwear model, yes, *he's* a distant cousin of my husband, Dennis Beckham, mayor of Cape Breton County." Her voice goes up when she says mayor as though she's announcing a prize at the ham bingo. "It's easy to remember. Eunice and Dennis. Dennis and Eunice. Beckham. But now I don't want you to feel at all intimidated by us, love. We're just like everyone else here. I still put my pantsuit on one leg at a time." She laughs gaily at her down-to-earthiness.

Before I can respond, she slides the strap of her briefcase off her shoulder and holds the case up with one hand so she can open it. It's pink and matches her suit perfectly.

"I have never seen a pink briefcase before," I remark.

"Isn't it fun? I have every color of the rainbow. When you're in my business, appearance is everything. People need to know you have an eye for detail."

You can't argue with that logic. "I never would have thought of that."

She pulls out a pink clipboard bearing a stack of forms and a pen neatly inserted in the slot at the top. "So, I need you to sign these, and I'll take care of the rest. How do you like the house so far?" She's talking and moving so fast I'm having trouble keeping up.

The pen is thrust into my hand, and she holds up the clipboard. I take it and begin signing next to each of the Post-it arrows. "Well, to be honest, it's in a lot worse shape than I thought. You said it was 'a little worse for wear' but this looks really bad."

Shaking her head, she says, "That's just because the yard's over-grown and the boards are on the windows. Trust me, this house is solid as a rock. It's survived four hurricanes over the past ninety years and hasn't moved a centimeter."

"I hope so."

"I *know* so. You're going to love it here."

"There's also another pretty major problem. I expected to have services hooked up today and when I called about it, no one is there."

"Yes, it's Clara McTavish's ninetieth birthday today."

Well, that explains it. "And everyone who works there has to attend?"

Eunice looks at me like I've sprouted gills. "Of course. Both her daughters run the utilities office. But truth be told, even if they were working today, they wouldn't be able to get you hooked up. Gus is up in Dingwall."

Oh, Dingwall. Wherever the hell that is.

"Did Nettie come by and tell you I've arranged a room for you next door?"

"Yes, she—" I stop because, apparently, Eunice was only pausing for a breath.

"You'll love it there. They have the best bisque in all of Cape Breton—but don't tell my mother-in-law I said that. And every Thursday night, they have a big kitchen party." As she talks, her hands move swiftly, taking the documents and tucking them into her brief-case. "Such a fun time. The mayor and I are there as often as our sched-ules allow, but not tonight," she says, shaking her head. "Tonight, we're at a fundraiser for the Breton Abilities Center. Which reminds me, I must run so I can stop at the office in time to process your land title before my updo appointment."

And she's off, teetering down the gravel driveway in her pink heels. "Tootles! Call me if you need anything!"

Dear God, please don't let me need anything.

———

I squeeze out my wet hair with a towel while I stare out at the view from my third story corner room at the Sea Winds B&B. Bras d'Or Lake—an enormous body of water in its own right—meets up with the ocean directly in front of the property. The late-day sun shimmers off the water while a sailboat drifts lazily along with a few passengers sunning themselves on the deck. A curious seal bobs his head out of the water, then, seeming to decide the boat is of no concern, lies on his back, exposing his sleek, black tummy to the sky. The sight of it calms my irritation, but just the tiniest bit.

I'm really here. I have actually done this.

I just moved to Canada on a whim.

Oh shit. I just moved to Canada, and it's too late to change my mind.

At this very moment, a couple is moving into my apartment back in

New York, and I doubt very much that they'd allow me to move back in with them. "Son of a bitch."

Grabbing my cell off the nightstand, I dial Lauren's number.

She picks up on the fourth ring, her breathing loud and jagged. "You made it?"

The sound of her voice makes me emotional. I try to stuff in how much I miss her and how scared I am. "I did. You at the gym?"

"Yes. Just finishing up on the treadmill." I can picture her there, her long legs working at a furious pace. We used to go together three times a week back when I cared about that type of thing. "How's Nova Scotia? You bored yet?"

Terrified is more like it. "Ha ha. Nova Scotia is exactly how I remembered. So far, I've arrived, signed the final papers, and done a walk-through of my new old house."

"And? Tell me everything."

"It's ... old, which I obviously knew. And ... rustic." I say, not wanting to admit the shape of it. "Oh, and I found out I won't have water, lights, or gas for a few days, so the realtor booked me at the B&B next door."

"A B&B? Your favorite place to stay—in someone's home where you get to share a bathroom with a bunch of strangers," she says.

"I have my own bathroom actually, and according to the sign at the front desk, there's no such thing as strangers. Only friends you haven't met yet."

Lauren bursts out laughing. "Oh my God, I wish I was there."

"Trust me, you don't."

"Okay, that's probably true, but let's back up because I'm interested in the word rustic that you tried to bury earlier."

"You caught that?"

"Obviously. Abby, it's me. You can be honest, even if you've made a gargantuan mistake, and right now all you can think of is getting back in the car and driving home at record speed." Lauren spent the last two months trying to talk me out of leaving New York. I guess she's not done.

"No way, I love it here."

"Oh, so we're doing that thing where you pretend everything's fine even though you're ready to burst into tears?"

"Yes, and I'd appreciate if you'd go along with it."

"Fair enough," she says, "So long as you know that I know the truth."

"Deal. Crying won't change anything. I'm here and I have to make the best of it." I flop onto the bed and scratch Walt's tummy. "Besides, it'll be fine. The house just needs a good scrubbing and maybe some minor repairs," I say, trying to sound confident.

"Is this the part where I say I'm sure it'll be amazing and you're going to be so happy there?"

"Yes."

"Why don't we just skip my half of the conversation all together and you hold up both sides?"

"Perfect," I say. "Truthfully though, there could be some other things wrong, but I won't know until the services are hooked up."

"Hmm, and how long will that take?"

"Depends on when Gus, the utility guy, makes his way to the village."

Lauren laughs so hard she snorts. When she's done, she says, "Oh, you were serious."

"Unfortunately."

"What year is it there? I mean comparatively speaking? Like 1940ish?"

"All right, just because you're still in the center of the universe doesn't mean this isn't also ... a place to live."

Hope fills her voice. "You can always change your mind."

"Tell that to my bank account." What starts out as a smartass remark rings all too true when my voice cracks.

"Oh, hon, you're not okay."

"I am. I'm just tired from the drive," I say. "This will be good for me. Really, it will."

"And if it isn't, you can come back here. I'm more than happy to help you find a dilapidated place here in the city to hide out in. We can pretend you're doing it for me because I miss you so much."

Taking a deep breath, I say, "I know you're trying to help, but to be honest, I'm all filled up on people doubting my decisions and making me feel guilty for one day."

"I take it your mom called?" she asks.

"Yes."

"Sorry," Lauren says, her voice all but getting lost in the background music. "But I am proud of you, Abby. You're doing something genuinely brave."

"Thanks. That's more like it," I say, glancing at the clock. "I should go. I'm starving and dinner service ends at seven p.m."

Lauren bursts out laughing again, and this time, I find myself joining in. "Don't forget to slap on some Bengay so you'll fit in with the other seniors," she says.

"Already slathered in it. It really does ease my muscle pain. Now, I just need to slide on my orthopedic loafers and I'm all set."

"Enjoy your first night."

"That's unlikely. I may have moved, but I'm still actively anti-enjoyment."

"That's my girl."

"Hugs and shit."

"Hugs and shit back."

I stand at the entrance to the inn's lively pub/dining room with the latest Liane Moriarty tucked under my arm, scanning the room for a quiet spot at the back. Seaside views, dark woods, and cheerful lace tablecloths make it look like a scene out of *Murder She Wrote*. I half expect to see Angela Lansbury typing away in the corner.

The ten or so tables are packed with tourists eating while they remember the day they've just had. A well-shined mahogany bar sits on the opposite side of the room, and a man with a shock of thick white hair and rosy cheeks is behind it, filling a glass with red wine. My only option is the empty stool at the bar. God, I hope this guy doesn't serve up a side order of chitchat with my meal.

Seating myself, I hardly have time to read the chalkboard menu on the wall before I am greeted by the man. "Start you off with some wine, love?"

"I'm thinking of a beer, actually."

"Guinness?"

"Sounds delightful." I open my book and look for my spot on the page.

"Oh, so you're our new Yank." He's obviously Nettie's husband, based on his Irish accent. Well, and the fact that he's working here. He takes a mug from under the counter and pulls on the tap. "Nettie told me you'd checked in."

Swirls of amber liquid fill the glass, making my mouth water. "Abby Carson."

"We were hoping you might pop down for dinner, but Nettie thought you'd be too tired." He gestures with his head to the woman I met earlier today, who is returning to the bar with an empty tray.

She has cleaned up from her afternoon of gardening and is now dressed in a smart white shirt and gray slacks. "Welcome, Abby! Glad you could join us."

"Just for a quick bite while I read my book, then off to bed."

Nettie smiles at me but talks to her husband. "Abby here likes to be alone."

"We'll have to change that, then won't we?" he says, sliding the glass to me.

"No, you won't," I say, matching his cheerful tone.

He laughs and points at me. "Oh, she's a quick one."

"Quick and dangerous," I mutter, looking down at my book again as a clear sign I'm not joking.

Instead of taking the hint, he says, "We're transplants like you. Moved here from Dublin thirty years ago. Never looked back. This here's God's country."

Nettie steps behind the bar and starts loading the tray with cutlery and napkins. "So, what brings you to our little corner of the world, Abby? We were speculating last night after Eunice dropped off your key. This mug head thought you were running from the law, but I said it's more likely you're running from a bad man." She leans in and gives me a conspiratorial look.

"Now, is that any way to talk about your loving husband?" He holds out his hand to me. "I'm Peter, by the way. Just think of me as the poor bloke who fell in love with the cruel-but-beautiful Nettie when he was still wearing short pants."

I laugh in spite of myself and shake his hand. "Nice to meet you."

"So?" they both say at the same time.

"What?" I'm momentarily confused, then remember they want to know why I'm here. I give them a serious look, glancing around the room, then lean in toward them and lower my voice. "Peter's right. I'm on the run."

"I knew it!" He slaps his hand on the bar. "Ha! Took forty-two years, woman, but by God, I'm finally right about something!"

His wife gives him a disgusted look. "She's not serious, you big dope!"

His face falls, and he turns back to me, utterly dejected.

I give him an apologetic little shrug. "I'm not, but it's a much better story than the truth."

A man's voice cuts across the room. "Miss! Excuse me, can we get some more water?"

Nettie smiles at him. "Of course, love. On my way."

Peter passes off a jug to her and she's gone, smoothly making her way through the maze of tables and diners.

A bell dings from behind a door next to the bar. Peter disappears, then, before the door stops swinging, he's back, arms loaded with four plates of food. The restaurant is a swirl of activity, my hosts getting so busy they have no time to continue peppering me with personal questions. Thank God. I can be left alone for a few minutes. Although, now that I'm not talking with anyone, I feel like the girl at the homecoming dance wearing glasses, braces, and headgear. Being alone is so much more comfortable when you're by yourself.

I glance around and spot an elderly couple at a table by the window smiling at me. They're wearing matching blue sweater vests. The woman raises her wineglass to me and says, "You must be Abby. Welcome to South Haven!"

What the ...?

The man, who I assume is her husband, adds, "We're excited to have a real New Yorker among us."

I give them a flash of teeth and a quick nod, then return my gaze to my book in a way that says no small talk for this lady. But instead of reading, I try to decide how much to reveal about myself to my nosy neighbors. It's kind of nice not to be getting the 'pity face' for once. Maybe I could pretend I'm just a single woman—a novelist who travels the world for her art, breaking hearts wherever she goes. Or I could tell them the truth—that my dead husband came to me in a dream and told me I should move here. That actually might be the most effective way to go, since people tend to shy away from crazy. Or I could just be a woman of mystery who never gives a direct answer.

A lull brings Nettie and Peter both back to the bar at the same time. She sets her tray on the counter. "Well now, back to what brought you here. Let's have it."

I stare at her for a second, then hear myself say, "I lost my husband last year, and it was time to make a fresh start." So much for being mysterious.

They both look at me for a moment, but surprisingly neither of them gives me the pity face. There are no awkward glances at their feet. No pauses while they try to think of what to say. They both simply nod.

Nettie's words come out in a very matter-of-fact tone. "Well, this is a most excellent place to start over. You'll love it here."

Peter wipes a bit of liquid off the bar top. "Yup, you're in for a real treat tonight. We're havin' a kitchen party, which is a Cape Breton tradition. A bunch of locals come in every Thursday to play music and sing. Mostly Celtic tunes. I'll be getting out my accordion."

Nettie, who is making her way across the room again, calls over her shoulder, "And I've been warming up my vocal cords."

Peter covers his mouth with one hand and lowers his voice. "And by 'warming them up,' she means screeching at her loving husband all day."

Nettie shouts back. "I heard that!"

I look at him with wide eyes and stifle a laugh.

"I've no idea how she does that, but it's fecking scary, isn't it?" Peter says while he pulls another pint. "Do you play an instrument?"

"I used to play the oboe in high school band class, but I honestly don't know if I could even read a simple song anymore."

"Well, stay and listen, then. It's good for the soul," Peter says definitively.

"That it is," Nettie adds as she swings back around to the bar. "Another round for table five," she says to Peter. Glancing at me, she asks, "So, how's the house? Have you had a chance to go through it?"

"Yes, but it's hard to tell what shape it's in with an inch of dust covering everything." I have a sip of beer, then dab my top lip with a napkin.

"The electrical's in need of work." Peter nods. "And as far as I can remember, the plumbing was starting to go before Violet moved out. Isn't that right, Nettie? The toilet or something?"

"Yes, and it's been a long while since the roof was done. We had ours done at the same time, so that's going on, what, eighteen years? Maybe twenty?"

My heart drops to my shoes. My little nest egg is about to get cracked wide open.

Peter wraps his knuckles on the bar. "You'll want to call the Millhouse boys. They'll have a look and tell you what you need done."

Nettie's back at the counter, looking over his shoulder. "Not the Millhouse boys. They'll be on the water by now for lobster season. She should be asking Liam Wright." She gives him a pointed look.

Peter's face lights up. "Well, of course! Why didn't I think of Liam?"

"Because you're a little slow on the uptake." Nettie grins at Peter, and he gives her a mock scowl.

"Liam's just the bloke for the job. He should be by in a bit. Comes every Thursday. A hell of a fiddle player, that one."

Great. Because that's what I need in a contractor—a hell of a fiddle player and the guy you get when the Millhouse boys have gone fishing.

"He's not too hard on the eyes either," Nettie says, with a wink.

And ... there it is. He's obviously single, therefore the two of us are destined to fall in love. You know, because we're probably the only two single people in the village, so we must be compatible. I take another swig of my beer to stop myself from going full New-York-stay-out-of-my-business bitch on this nice unsuspecting Irish couple.

Why do I not drink more often? I'm almost through my second pint and I honestly can't remember feeling so good. I don't even care how out of place I am. Instead, I happily devour a slice of homemade lemon meringue pie. Dinner service has ended, and most of the guests have filed out, replaced by several locals bearing instruments. A new feeling takes over the restaurant. It's an easy, relaxed vibe full of inside jokes and laughter as they rearrange the tables into a large horseshoe. I rush to finish my dessert, hoping to make my exit before I attract the attention of every snoopy musician in the village.

Peter gives me a nod. "Liam's just come in now."

I turn and see a man standing at the entrance. He looks to be in his early forties. Medium height, with the sturdy build of a fisherman or maybe a miner in days gone by. He has shaggy sandy-brown hair and thick stubble that's somewhere between needing a shave and needing another couple of months to grow. His eyes, though. There's something about them that makes me stare a moment too long. They're the shade of ice blue usually reserved for wolves.

He looks straight at Nettie and Peter, and my gaze follows his. They are standing side by side with matching hopeful grins. They look at me, then back at him, and when I glance in his direction again, I'm met with a look of dread. It doesn't take me more than a second to figure out he thinks he's about to be set up and he's absolutely horrified at the thought of having any of his parts touch any of my parts.

And here I am gawking at him like a moron.

Blue sweater vest woman walks by and touches my arm. "You've got a bit of a mustache, love."

She hurries off in the direction of the ladies' room while I dab my upper lip with a napkin, confirming that I did, in fact, have a frothy white beer mustache.

Well, that's that, then. The Millhouse boys it is.

"Liam! Come over and meet Abby!" Peter calls.

No. Please don't. I swivel my stool to face the bar, and in my overly enthusiastic effort, I swing it too far and bang my left knee on the wood bracket. The force of it causes my body to jar and jerk back to my right and I plant my left hand in what's left of my pie. I'm a regular Princess Di this evening, all elegance and grace.

Check, please.

Nettie gives me a concerned look. "You all right, love?"

"I'm fine. I just remembered I have to make a phone call. Can you put this on my room?" I smile too brightly as I slide off the stool and start for the side door as fast as my legs can carry me.

"Well, come back when you're done so you don't miss the music!" Nettie calls.

"And you still need to meet Liam!" Peter yells.

"I most certainly will!" Not.

CHAPTER SIX

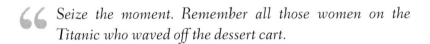 *Seize the moment. Remember all those women on the Titanic who waved off the dessert cart.*

~ Erma Bombeck

Ten minutes later, I'm lying in the tub with steam rising up around me. Mr. Whitman sits on the ledge, dipping his paw in the water, consumed by his own reflection. Poor guy. No matter how many baths I take, I don't think he'll ever figure out he's the cat who appears. "It's just you, Walt."

My mind wanders back to Liam walking into the pub, and my cheeks burn at the memory of the horrified look on his face. Why I care, I have no idea. It's not like I was looking to be the next Mrs. Wright. Or Mrs. Anything for that matter. I've got Walt, and when I sleep, I've still got Isaac to stare at me lovingly. He didn't recoil when he first saw me. Mind you, I was twenty-two and didn't have a frothy white mustache.

I try to imagine what I looked like all those years ago, sitting in the faculty lounge, a young teacher's assistant, shamelessly gazing at Professor Isaac Carson as he and my mentor, Professor Juanita Rodriguez, debated the rightful winner of the Booker Prize. I soaked in his words, not understanding the nuances of their discussion, but loving the sound of his deep voice.

He finally glanced at me, and when his eyes met mine, I knew love at first sight was not just a myth. It never bothered me that he was nearing forty, the sprinkle of gray hair and the way the skin around his eyes crinkled when he smiled making me sigh like a fool. I didn't understand those were signs that much of his time on this earth had passed by already. I was too young to think about any of that. Too naïve to understand what it would mean to be left behind.

Instead, I looked forward to Mondays, Wednesdays, and Fridays when Juanita and I would go to the faculty lounge after her office hours. I'd wake early to shower and blow out my hair, then stand in front of my tiny closet, searching in vain for something sophisticated to wear.

It took a year for Isaac to resign himself to the fact that he would actually date from within the pool of graduate students. It was my writing that did it—a short story Juanita had asked him to read that I wrote about a birdcage. Before that, he was convincingly disinterested in my fluttering eyelids. Although, after we were solidly a couple, he admitted otherwise. He confessed he had done his best not to notice me or to inhale my perfume whenever I sat next to him. It turned out Isaac had also anticipated seeing me at lunch and got up early to shave and put on something that might make him look more hip.

I smile, thinking of that time in our lives—the thrill of it all. Sneaking around so we didn't get found out. Going on dates far off campus. Making love until the early morning hours at his apartment. He would drop me off at the train station nearest the university, and we would kiss like a couple of fools before I would reluctantly peel myself from his embrace and the warmth of his car, only to see him in the hallway of the English Literature building twenty minutes later.

The passionate first few years turned into a very real and beautiful partnership. Something rich and easy and supportive. Isaac was the first to encourage me to write a novel. As soon as I finished my graduate degree, he told me to take a year and write. I didn't have to work. We could get married, and I could live off him until I made it big, then he could quit teaching and live off me. That was how he proposed. He made it sound casual, like I could take it or leave it depending on how I felt at that moment.

I took it, of course, jumping into his arms in Central Park and kissing him wildly. We were married a month later in that same spot, tucked away at the back of the Shakespeare Garden. A small ceremony under an old maple tree that stretched its arms out to shelter us from the heat of the June sun. We had two dozen guests, including my parents, who accessorized their Sunday finest with sour expressions. They expected me to come home to Portland when I finished school. Instead, I married a man nearly twice my age, intending to stay two thousand miles away from them for the rest of my life. They certainly couldn't wrap their heads around my plan to 'sit around daydreaming and expect to earn a living.'

But even worse than my career choice—'a long shot at best,' as my dad called it—they were horrified to find out Isaac and I didn't want children. He was not the man they would have chosen for me. But he's the one I chose for myself. He's the one I miss with every cell in my body.

Through the open window in my room, I hear a guitar being tuned while people chat and laugh. Soon, the talking stops and the sound of a lone, low voice wafts up from the pub. The words aren't in English, but both the voice and the tune are hauntingly beautiful and I know it's about love lost. More voices join in, then a flute. Next is a violin, and I can't help but wonder if it's Liam. Apparently, he's a hell of a fiddle player. The thought of him brings another flash of embarrassment, and I long for a third pint to distance me from it. This is why I prefer cats. They don't make you feel things you don't want to feel. Humiliation. Rejection. Longing.

This song is making me miss Isaac so much it hurts.

That's it. I'm shutting the window.

I step out of the water, wrap my hair in a towel, and slide on my robe. Hurrying to the window, I start to shut it but don't. Instead, I listen as the song builds to a crescendo, torturing myself a little longer for reasons I don't understand. I sigh and lean on the window ledge as the torment continues. The sun sinks into the sea as the first stars appear. Walt rubs against my leg, and I pick him up so I can stroke his soft head. "You're my people, Walt. Everyone else can just suck it."

The next morning, I wake having dreamed about Isaac. For a moment, I'm blissfully unaware that he's gone, because we've just been strolling hand in hand down 7th Avenue, and he's been patiently listening as I try to decide on furniture for our new house. I love the caramel leather chair, but I think the dark brown one might fit better in the room. In the end, he suggests waiting until the carpet is ripped up to see what's under it. Better to have no chair for a few extra weeks than the wrong one for a decade. I tell him he's so sensible.

I open my eyes, and the unfamiliar ceiling causes my stomach to drop. My bliss evaporates abruptly as the last twenty months of my life come rushing back at me. I don't want to get up. I want to go back to sleep, in case he's still there. Rolling over, I close my eyes, praying for sleep to come, but after a few minutes, I give up. He's lost to me again. At least until tonight. Maybe if I go to bed early, I'll find him waiting.

It's a touch before nine o'clock when I hurry downstairs for breakfast, book in hand. I'm in flannel duckie pajama bottoms and a T-shirt, and I haven't brushed my hair. As I catch a glimpse of myself in the mirror that hangs on the lobby wall, I realize I might be making myself far too at home here at the Sea Winds B&B. I second guess the pants, then decide to go for it, for fear of missing breakfast altogether. Relief fills me when I find the restaurant empty because being fed and being alone are my two main goals, and it looks like, for once in my life, I'm getting what I want.

I walk in, spot Peter, and wave.

"Good morning, Abigail," he says, holding up a coffee mug. "You never came back last night for the music."

Nodding at the mug, I say, "I had some things to take care of, but I heard it from my room."

I'm about to pick a table by the far window when Peter pats the top of the bar. "I saved your seat for you."

Great, there's really no way to turn that down without offending the man who feeds me. No matter, I can eat fast and go back to my room. "Is there any oatmeal left?"

"If there's not, there soon will be." He winks, then disappears into the kitchen, only to return less than a minute later with a plate holding a bowl of oatmeal with all the trimmings, along with a side of ham and bacon. "Here you go, love. Eat up."

I sprinkle brown sugar on the oatmeal and add milk from the tiny white jug. I'm about to take my first bite when I sense someone behind me. Out of the corner of my eye, I see a man settling himself on the stool beside mine. "Seriously? You take the spot right next to me when the entire place is emp—"

I stop talking as soon as I make eye contact with him, and I realize it's Mr. Too Good for Me.

He looks taken aback for a second, then slides off his stool and walks all the way to the far end of the bar. Giving me a small grin, he says, "How's this?"

"Better." I wrinkle up my nose at him in a way that says, 'I find you as repulsive as you find me.'

"So, Abby," Peter says, rubbing the back of his neck. "This here's Liam Wright, the fellow we were telling you about last night. I asked him to come by this morning about your house."

Oh, so he already knows I wasn't on the prowl for a taste of man-candy last night. And I've now bitten the head off the only person in the vicinity who can fix my house. Super. Turning, I give Liam a polite but restrained smile. "Oh, yes, hello. Pleasure to meet you."

"Is it?" he asks, narrowing his eyes, even though they're sparkling with amusement.

"Sorry, I just thought ..." What?

Peter rescues me from myself. "Abby prefers to be alone."

Nodding, Liam says, "Okay, well, that's good to know. I'll stay here then." He raises his voice deliberately loud. "I hear you're in the market for some repair work."

"Yes. I bought the place next door, and it needs some TLC. What do you do?"

He answers with one hand cupped next to his mouth. "Oh, a little of this and a lot of that. Whatever needs doing."

"Uh-huh, sure," I answer, nodding and raising my voice as well. "That's kind of a vague answer to give someone interviewing you for a job."

He gives me a sideways grin and hollers, "I didn't realize this was a formal interview on account of the ducks on your pajama pants."

My face burns and I roll my eyes, then give a conciliatory nod. "Okay, what if we start again? You could maybe sit ..." I reach over and point at the stool next to the one beside mine, "... here."

Liam stands and comes over. After he sits down, he extends his hand. "Liam Wright, jack of all trades."

Taking his hand, I give it a firm shake. "Abby Carson. Person in need of house repairs."

"Nice to know you, Abby."

I chuckle at the ridiculousness of it all, then say, "You, too."

"What kind of repairs are you looking for?"

"Basically, I need help with the yard, the exterior, and interior."

Liam grins. "Now who's being vague?"

I take on a slightly haughty tone. "I'm only being vague because I don't actually know what needs to be done."

He blinks a few times before answering. "You probably shouldn't admit that when you're interviewing contractors. If you hire the wrong guy, he'll try to take advantage of you."

Shit. He's got me there. I narrow my eyes. "Are you the wrong guy?"

"Nope, I'm honest to a fault," he replies, then his eyes fill with laughter. "But then again, if I were the type to take advantage, I'd have lied to you just then anyway."

I purse my lips together and look at Peter. "So my options truly are limited to Mr. Mind Games here or the Millhouse boys who have gone fishin'? There's literally no one else?"

"Afraid so, love," Peter answers. "He may be a bit of an arse, but at least he's an honest one, and he does good work."

"I should have that printed on a business card," Liam says, holding his mug out for a refill of coffee. "Liam Wright, Honest Arse. Does Good Work."

"And how long is lobster season?" I ask Peter.

"Until mid-July, but the Millhouse boys head up to P.E.I. to keep going until October," he answers as he tops up both our coffees.

Liam takes a sip, then smacks his lips together. "Guess you're stuck with me, then."

"It would appear so." I give him a long stare. "Listen, I'm not some rube. If you try to screw me, you won't like what happens next."

A wide grin spreads across Liam's face. "Nicely played. An ambiguous threat intended to create fear of the unknown."

I laugh again, even though it undermines my attempts at being scary. "Oh, I'll follow through, believe me."

"I believe you would, but you won't have to."

"Good," I say, lifting my chin. "We can't get started until the utilities are turned on, but I need to get everything going as soon as possible."

"Oh sure," Liam says, throwing a grin in Peter's direction. "I can see why you'd be in a hurry to get out of this place."

Peter pretends he's offended. "You believe this guy? Here he is, fueling his insults on my coffee."

Liam laughs, and it's a hearty, full sound. He turns to me. "Don't mind him. He's sort of a delicate flower."

Peter fixes him with a glare. "No more *anything* on the house for you."

Liam winks at me. "Fear not, he'll forgive me. He's not only delicate, he's also kind."

Ignoring the wink, I say, "I wouldn't forgive him."

"I won't," Peter says with a mock-scowl.

Liam taps his hand on the bar. "In that case, I best be off to the Harveys' to earn a few dollars for coffee. I'm finishing up their new deck today." He pulls his wallet out from the back pocket of his jeans, retrieves a card, and sets it on the counter. "There's my number. Call me when Gus shows up, and I'll swing by and have a look. Once I have an idea of what needs doing, I'll get you an estimate."

He slides off the stool, then holds out his hand. I take it, and we shake once more, his rough palm against mine. "Nice to meet you, Ms. Duckie Pants."

My mouth drops open, and he says, "It's only fair. You called me Mr. Mind Games."

And with that, he's gone.

When I turn back to my oatmeal, I can't help but notice Peter standing in front of me with his arms folded. "He's a good fellow. The best father I think I've seen."

Father? "How many kids?"

"One little girl. Car accident took his wife and their baby boy. The little tyke was only three months old at the time." Peter picks up a rag and wipes the counter. It's spotless, but he does it anyway. "Lovely woman, Sarah was. And that baby. The cheeks on him. A real tragedy if ever there was one."

"Oh, God, that's awful. How long ago?" A lump fills my throat.

"Coming up to six years. His daughter was in the car when it happened. She was two. People think she was so young that there's no way she can remember, but I'll tell you, she's never been the same since. She used to be full of giggles and squeals, but now, she seems lost in her own world."

"Wow, that's just ... shitty," I mutter as the melancholy of Liam's story sinks in.

Peter and I are quiet for a few minutes. I'm sure his mind is on Liam's family, judging by the shift in his demeanor. The corners of his mouth have turned down and his eyebrows furrow together. My mind races as I digest the information. It feels strange to know something so intimate about a stranger—one who seemed utterly carefree just now. I suppose this is how people react when they find out I'm a widow. Sad. A little shocked, maybe. It also occurs to me that there are people who have it much worse than I do. I've just met one, and he seems to be surviving.

CHAPTER SEVEN

 It is far better to be alone than to wish you were.

~ Ann Landers

Well, I have solved the mystery of why it took Gus so damn long to show up. It's because he feels compelled to regale everyone he meets with his entire life story. Gus is the third of the seven Nickerson boys, of the famous Nickerson clan who settled here on Cape Breton over one-hundred-fifty years ago. He's been married for twenty-eight years, and it only feels like a century—hardy har har. He and his wife, June, have three children, two of which were accidents—the first attended their wedding as a fetus, and the last one was the cause of him getting the old 'snip snip,' which is not necessarily something I need to know about the utilities guy. Oh, and he'll bare-knuckle fight anyone who says Sidney Crosby isn't the greatest hockey player who ever lived.

After close to an hour of inane chatter, he finally wanders to the basement to turn whatever dial or switch is required for me to have running water and natural gas. He tests the kitchen sink first and we both stare until it sputters to life.

"Oh perfect. Thanks so much, Gus," I say, shutting off the tap.

I'm about to say how lovely it was to meet him when he settles himself against the kitchen counter, clearly with no intention to leave just yet. "So, Eunice says you're from New York City, but you don't have that accent."

Shoo. Get out. "I grew up in Portland actually," I say as I take a few steps toward the front door.

He doesn't take the hint. "Oh, so you're a long way from home."

"Uh-huh." Please leave now.

"Yeah, yeah, yeah." He does a sucking-in-air thing while he says yeah. It's a thing I've noticed the people here do when they run out of things to say. Does it mean the conversation is ending? Dear Lord, I hope so.

"This here place has been empty for quite some time. It's been about three years since I shut everything off. After Violet McMasters had to go into the old folks' home." Gus gives me a nod as though we both remember that day well. "She was hoping one of her kids'd take over the house, but you know the young folks. They all move out west to find work."

The young folks? How old does he think I am?

"Violet's in a home in Halifax now. Must be going on ninety. Tough old bird. Seen some hard times but always managed to come out okay," he says. "Actually, you remind me of her in a way."

"I remind you of a tough old bird?" I ask, raising one eyebrow.

He laughs, pointing one finger at me and nodding. "You're a feisty one. Liam's going to have his hands full with you."

Oh, sweet Jesus, Gus the water guy is getting in on the matchmaking? Time to nip this in the bud. "I'm not sure what you heard ... or where, frankly ... but I'm really not interested in any sort of romantic entanglement, so whoever is doing the talking, please tell them to stop."

He tilts his head in confusion. "I meant when he's doing your house. Didn't you hire him?"

"Oh, right," I say, as my cheeks heat up. "That."

He gives me a thoughtful expression. "Are you a fan of Shakespeare?"

Okay, where is he going with this? "I'm familiar with his work."

"Me thinks thou doth protest too much," he says with a chuckle, and the smug air about him irritates the shit out of me.

"Actually, the line is 'the lady doth protest too much, methinks,' and trust me on this one, I'm not secretly pining for a boyfriend."

"I think you'll change your mind about Liam when you hear he lives on a yacht during the warm months." Gus lowers and raises his eyebrows. "Eh? He'll take you on lots of romantic adventures on the sea. What woman wouldn't want that?"

"This one."

The sound of a vehicle approaching saves me from whatever Gus was about to say in response, and I'm filled with relief that he's finally following me to the front door. We step outside in time to see Liam getting out of an ancient red pickup.

I make my way down the three steps leading to the sidewalk and start toward him as he shuts the creaky door.

He nods in our direction. "Hello, Abby. Gus."

"How's Olive these days?" Gus asks.

"Growing like a weed," Liam says, lifting a large toolbox out of the truck bed. "And yours? Keeping out of trouble?"

"I wish they'd get in trouble. At least they'd have a spark of life in 'em," he says with a disgusted shake of his head. "June has spoiled them rotten. I doubt any of them'll ever get off my couch."

Turning to me, Gus says, "The youngest is twenty-one and they're all still at home."

Liam grins. "Well, there's always hope."

"Speaking of hope," Gus says, pointing at me with one thumb, "if you've got any designs on this one, you might as well forget it because she's not in the market for a fella, especially not you."

Oh, for God's sake. "Nope, that is not what I said. It's not you, Liam. I'm simply not looking."

Liam gives me a serious nod, but his eyes are dancing with amusement. "Good to know. We'll keep it strictly professional, then."

"Yes, we will. Shall we get started?" I ask, hoping Gus will take the hint.

Thankfully, he does. "I best be going. There's a new couple up by Crocus Bay who've been hounding me to get out to their place. I can still make it if I hurry."

"Well, since it's only an hour's drive, and it's eleven in the morning, I'd guess you might have a shot at making it before supper," Liam says. "Unless you spot someone you know on the way."

Gus ignores the not-so-subtle dig and holds out his right hand to me. "It's a pleasure to know you, Abigail."

Shaking his hand, I lie, "You too."

He lowers his voice, but I'm sure Liam can hear him since he's basically standing right beside Gus. "Nice job, by the way."

Against my better judgment, I ask, "With what?"

"Playing it cool. There's nothing men like more than somethin' they can't have," he says with a wink.

Liam politely ignores the exchange and busies himself putting on his toolbelt. When Gus has finally climbed inside his van and shut the door, Liam looks up at me.

"Listen, about all that ..." I say.

Liam holds up one hand. "No need to explain. It's a small town full of people with not enough to do. They've been trying to find me a wife for years and they're not about to stop now."

"Okay, good. Well ... not good. They should leave you alone. If you're not interested in a relationship, no one should push you into one." I'm rambling now. Dammit. "What I mean is, I'm glad you're aware that I'm not the one trying to ... I'm not in the market for a ..." I gesture in the air with both index fingers making little circles that apparently mean relationship. Is it hot out here? It feels hot out here. My entire body is suddenly clammy.

"Relax, Abby," Liam says with a low chuckle. "I get it. Why don't we start by getting those boards off the windows so we can have a good look at everything?"

I let out a sigh of relief, my shoulders dropping. "Perfect."

It takes us close to thirty minutes to take the boards off the windows. But now that they're off, I kind of wish they were back on because this place is so much dirtier than I thought. My muscles grow sore at the mere thought of cleaning every inch of the house. I really am going to have to stock up on Bengay.

While Liam is upstairs examining the bathroom and windows and whatever else contractors look at, I clean out the kitchen sink, then fill it with water and some lemon-scented discount cleaner so I can get started on the cupboards. The sounds of Liam moving around upstairs above the kitchen bring a tense vigor to my scrubbing. I'm filled with dread about what he'll find up there. And down here, for that matter. And outside ...

Finally, I hear Liam's heavy footsteps on the stairs. He finds me with my head in the corner cupboard.

"Well, it's not as bad as I thought, but you'd be smart to replace the insulation in the attic before winter."

"Okay." I don't even want to think about what that'll cost. "How about the plumbing?"

"So far, I can't see any sign of leaks, but you're going to need a new toilet up there. New taps for the sink and tub. I'll keep going through the house, then let's have a chat about what needs doing and what you're wanting to change just for the look of it."

By the time he's done, the phrase, 'you're going to need a new ...' brings a fresh wave of nausea. I knew it might be bad, but the truth is, when I woke this morning, a part of me was clinging to the hope that the house would just need a little elbow grease and some WD-40. Now, that hope has sailed off into the sunset, and reality is setting in. The gorgeous hardwood hiding under the carpets hasn't come to fruition. Instead, it's a slightly rotted subfloor, which of course means I'll 'need a new one.'

We move to the front yard so Liam can get the ladder from his truck and inspect the roof. On his way back toward the house, he says, "I see you've got a U-Haul to unload. If you like, I can round up a couple of fellas. We'll get it done in no time."

"No, thanks though," I say, holding up one hand. "I've already hired movers from Sydney. They should be here in two hours."

"Are you sure you want to pay for that when you could get it for free?"

"Yes, I am. Nothing's free in this world."

He gives me a conciliatory nod. "No, you're probably right. We'd have charged you a round of beers the next time we'd see you at the pub."

"As tempting as that is, I have a few old, expensive pieces of furniture that need to be treated quite delicately."

"Oh, well, in that case, it's best to leave it to the professionals," he says, extending the ladder and setting it against the house.

I stand, fiddling with Isaac's ring while Liam disappears over the peak. I tell myself everything will be okay. It seems like it won't be, but what's the worst that could happen? I sink every penny into it and end up broke. Oh yeah, that.

A few minutes later, he comes back into view, standing casually on the steep slope with one hand on his hip. My heart jumps to my throat at the thought of him falling, but it appears to be the furthest thing from his mind.

"What do you do for a living, Abby?"

"I'm a writer. Mainly novels."

"Well, you better get writing. You need a new roof."

My heart drops from my throat to my knees at his words, and tears prick my eyes but I force them back in.

He climbs down and surveys the yard. "Yeah, yeah, yeah," he says as he rubs his chin. "Great spot here. Shame the McMasters kids let it get all overgrown after their ma went into the home. She was a real meticulous gardener. Will you want help to get the yard cleaned up?"

Yes, but there's no way I can afford it. "I need to do as much as

possible myself. We may be about to stretch my budget so far it'll snap."
I try to sound casual, but those damn tears appear again. I clear my
throat and turn toward the house to hide my fear. But the sight of the
paint peeling off the window boxes brings with it a sense of doom.

"Listen, Abby, I imagine this is probably overwhelming for you. It
would be for me, if I were in your shoes."

"No, I can handle it," I say with a scoff. "Believe me."

"Sure, you're a tough New Yorker and all that. I know you can
handle it, but it's okay to admit if you're upset."

"I'm not upset," I say, taking on a business-like tone. "I'm just ... surprised at how many things need to be replaced, and I'm wondering if I
stupidly bought a total money pit that will suck every dollar out of my
bank account until I'm forced to sell it and move back home with my
parents like some thirty-nine-year-old loser. Because I really can't have
that, Liam." My voice goes up by two octaves and my face screws up in
what is about to become an ugly cry. "I already lost my husband; I can't
end up back in Portland where all my relatives will stare at me and
shake their heads at how I couldn't make it in the world without a man.
I can't do that. I simply can't."

"But you're not upset," Liam says lightly, making me laugh while
he digs a tissue out of his pocket. He unfolds it and hands it to me.

"Not at all," I answer, managing a grin while I wipe my tears. "Sort
of terrified maybe, but otherwise fine."

When I finally make eye contact with him, he doesn't seem at all
put off by my show of emotion. He nods and says, "Tell you what? Let's
make this a lot less terrifying. How about I teach you how to do
anything you can do yourself? You can save a lot of money, so long as
you're not afraid of some hard work."

"I'm not."

"Well, then you and this house will get along just fine."

CHAPTER EIGHT

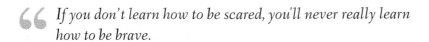 *If you don't learn how to be scared, you'll never really learn how to be brave.*

~ Simon Holt, *The Devouring*

Liam was wrong. This house and I are not going to get along just fine. Somehow the kitchen that looked so small tripled in size the second I started scrubbing out the cupboards. Suddenly, a window-less bachelor suite next to the subway tracks is extremely appealing to me. If I hadn't made such a fuss about getting out of the B&B as soon as possible, I'd be heading back there right now to have a long bath and hide under the covers instead of preparing for my first night in this hellhole. I still have at least another hour's work in the kitchen before I can move on, and my body is already going into shock. I finish the last drawer in the fridge, then open a warm can of Coke and take a long swig. Leaning against the counter, I give the oven a good hard glare, dreading the thought of tackling whatever's in there.

Maybe I could just not open it. Ever. That would save me a lot of work.

Yes, I'll ignore the oven, at least for this week. I have another overwhelming and more pressing task ahead of me in the form of a U-Haul that has to be unpacked and returned to the depot in Sydney. Checking my watch, I see that the movers should be here in a few minutes.

At exactly three o'clock, there's a loud knock on the door. I wipe my hands on the sides of my jeans while I hurry to answer it. When I swing the door open, I'm met by Liam and another man, both wearing green golf shirts and matching baseball caps.

Liam gives me a broad grin. "Hello, ma'am. I understand you booked a couple of movers for this afternoon," he says in a very formal voice. "I'm Liam Wright, and this here is James Campbell. We're here to professionally move all your delicate and expensive pieces of furniture."

"We'll move the cheap stuff, too," James says with a shrug.

I start out shaking my head and trying to look annoyed but laugh instead. "Is this the thing you do a little of or a lot of?"

"A little. We don't get many clients up here."

I rest a fist on my hip. "Why didn't you just tell me you were the mover?"

"You seemed pretty set on only letting a professional near your stuff, and who am I to argue with the client?"

James extends his hand to me and we shake. "I'm James. I live four blocks that way," he says, pointing to his left.

And I need to know that, why, exactly? Giving him a polite smile, I say, "Nice to meet you."

"I hear you're not interested in Liam, as far as dating goes."

Pursing my lips together, I glare at him, then turn to Liam, who puts his hands up in surrender. "He didn't hear that from me."

"I ran into Gus when he was on his way up to Crocus Bay."

Two hours later, the U-Haul is empty. Liam finds me standing in the middle of several boxes in the kitchen. "We're all done, Ms. Carson," he says, gesturing with a clipboard in his left hand. "I'll just need you to sign these forms saying everything was unloaded carefully and that neither James nor I damaged any of your priceless things."

I roll my eyes as I take the clipboard and sign my name. Liam rips off the top sheet and hands it to me. "There's an online survey you can fill out if you like. It'll get you ten dollars off at Weagle's Greenhouse."

"Good to know, thanks."

"All right, enjoy your new home, Miss," Liam says. "And please remember to call W.S. Movers again for all your storage, packing, and moving needs."

James walks into the kitchen and says, "Well, that's that then." He snaps his fingers. "Oh, I almost forgot, I'm heading to Sydney first thing in the morning. I can return your U-Haul for you if you like. Save you a couple hours."

I shake my head. "No, I couldn't ask you to do that. Thank you, though. It's a kind offer."

"You sure? I'll be literally a block from the rental place. I gotta go to Canadian Tire." Looking at Liam, he says, "They've got Timberline work boots on clearance. Seventy percent off."

You don't say? "I'm good, thanks. I have to head into the city for a bunch of supplies anyway."

"All right," James says. "We'll leave you to it, then."

I stand, holding Walt in my arms, feeling oddly emotional as I watch them leave. I'm about to spend my first night in my dilapidated old cottage, which suddenly feels like the last thing I want to do.

It's nearing seven o'clock as I hurry up the road to Nettie and Peter's. It was either that or dig through the boxes for some Pop-Tarts. To be honest, I'm also going in search of some liquid backbone for my first night alone in my creepy cottage. When I was turning the water off after my shower, I heard a thumping sound, which led to a quick bathrobe-clad examination of the house. It ended with me standing at the bottom step to the basement with my heart pounding wildly.

Although I found no explanation of the loud thump, I did have the awful thought that the dirt floor would be the perfect place to hide a body. Maybe the body of a certain old, single lady who used to live here.

I sprint up the steps to the B&B, only exhaling when I'm safely inside with the door closed behind me. When I walk into the restaurant, I almost want to kiss the wood floor. Never have I been so happy to see a bunch of senior citizens eating pie and drinking coffee.

"Back already?" Peter asks, as I take my usual stool at the bar and set my book down.

"I didn't have time to get groceries today."

"Oh, sure. Beer?"

"Please, and some of that lobster bisque if you've got it."

"Coming right up," he says, rapping his knuckles on the bar.

One hour, two pints, one bowl of bisque, and six homemade biscuits later, Peter walks me home. The moon and the streetlamps (which are far too spread out for my liking) light our way.

"This is really unnecessary," I say for the third time.

"Well, I wouldn't feel right letting you walk home alone at this hour."

"Eight p.m.?"

"Exactly."

I walk up the front steps to my house, key in hand. Turning to Peter, I say, "Well, thank you. I should be good from here."

"Are you feeling a little nervous about your first night alone here?"

Narrowing my eyes, I say, "Why? Should I be?"

"Nope, but I couldn't help but wonder, based on all your questions about Violet's true whereabouts."

"I just wanted to make sure she's okay. Single woman, living alone in a house surrounded by trees. Anything could have happened to her."

"Other than living well until a ripe old age, nothing else happened to her here." Peter gives me a reassuring smile. "You know what? Why don't you collect Walt and come on back to your room at our place?

You could spend your days here and your nights with us until you get to know all the noises and such."

I shake my head and make a *ppffftt* sound, spitting all over my fleece coat for good measure. "That would be ridiculous. I'm not scared of my house."

"Of course not. Would you feel better if I did a quick walk-through to make sure everything's okay?"

"No, but if that would make *you* feel better, have at it."

"Yes, I'll sleep a lot sounder knowing you're safe," he says with a wry grin.

I unlock the door, and when we step inside, I say, "I'll wait here while you check things out."

Peter slides off his shoes, then starts for the stairs to the basement, patting Walt on the head when they cross in the hall.

While he's down there, I shout, "You okay? You don't see any evidence of freshly dug graves, do you?"

He pops his head around the corner a moment later. "All fine, as you knew it would be."

A few minutes later, he walks down the stairs. "All clear. Thanks for letting me look around."

"No problem. I would hate to make you worry."

Five minutes later, Peter's gone, the doors are locked, and I'm upstairs in my bedroom with the covers pulled up to my neck as I listen for murderers. My cell phone rings and I jump, startling Walt, who zips off the mattress, then turns to stare at me from across the room.

I pick up my phone off the box I'm using as a night table. It's Lauren. Thank God. "Hey lady, what's up?"

"Just checking on you to see how the first night in your new house is going."

"Couldn't be better," I say, trying very hard not to slur but failing miserably.

"Are you drunk?"

"A little."

"Let me guess, your imagination ran away on you, so you had a few drinks to help you relax."

"Maybe. How did you know?"

"I'm your best friend and you're a writer with a gigantic imagination. You don't always use it for good."

"Right," I say, feeling slightly sheepish. "I would have been fine if it weren't for the dirt floor in the basement."

"Did you convince yourself there's a bunch of bodies buried down there?"

"No, just one. But you think there could be several?"

Laughing, Lauren says, "No, I do not."

"Okay, good. You had me worried for a second."

"Do you want to talk on the phone until you fall asleep?"

Relief sweeps over me. "Could we?"

"Of course."

CHAPTER NINE

 Drowning people sometimes die fighting their rescuers

~ Octavia Butler

I wake to a text from Liam. *I can swing by after I drop my daughter at school to go over the quote. Will you be home in an hour?*

Sounds great. See you then.

Actually, it doesn't sound great at all. As much as I have to face the reality of the renovations, I've been enjoying the last few hours of blissful ignorance. But that time is swiftly drawing to a close, just like all happy moments. *Whoa, that was dark. It's just some repair work, Abby, take it down a notch.*

I text Lauren to thank her for putting me to sleep last night and promise her I'll be fine from now on. As I look around the bright room, I feel almost sure it's true. In the light of day, there is nothing foreboding about this place.

I dress, feed Walt, then brew a pot of coffee, becoming increasingly anxious as the minutes slide by. I toast two slices of bread, but when they pop up, I suddenly realize I'm too nervous to eat. I spread butter on them anyway, then sit down on the office chair that has found a temporary purpose at the kitchen table. Taking a bite, I chew, only to find it feels like sand in my mouth. Why the hell am I so nervous? I have almost a hundred and fifty thousand left in my account. Even if the repairs cost me one hundred of that, I'll still have a nice big chunk left over while I write my next book.

My chest squeezes at the thought of writing again. That's it. This feels like a very final decision. If I go ahead with the work, it's really me saying I will write again, because I won't have a choice. I can't live off the money forever. The housing market is sloth-level slow here, so pouring more cash into this place will dramatically move up the time-line on the necessity for me to work again. Letting out a big sigh, I stare out the window into my mess of a backyard, then realize the choice was made when I signed the official offer on the house. I committed to starting over here and I'm not the type to turn back when I've made a decision. I stick to my guns. It's one of my best traits. Or worst, depending on who you ask.

Liam arrives right on time. When I open the door, I'm greeted by a freshly shaved version of him. He's dressed in jeans and a plain white T-shirt today. We exchange hellos and I step aside to let him in. As he walks past me, I catch just a hint of aftershave which draws out the memory of what it's like to touch the smooth, strong jawline of a man. I sweep the image away, trying to brush the accompanying guilt into the dustpan of my mind. "Hey, you arrived exactly when you said you would. I thought contractors were supposed to keep you waiting."

Liam turns and smiles. "I'm not a real contractor. Just a guy who does a little of this and a lot of that."

"Oh, right, I almost forgot." I chuckle. "So, men who do a little of this and a lot of that show up on time?"

"It's one of the many advantages of hiring us."

"One of many?" I ask as I start toward the kitchen.

"Yes, we also don't charge an arm and a leg. You'll see in my esti-mate that the customary fifteen percent for materials is missing."

"Oh, well that *is* a big advantage."

He follows me to the kitchen, and I can't help but feel self-conscious, wondering if he's giving my enormous behind the once over. I'm suddenly aware of how I'm walking, so I straighten up my back and suck in my gut, which is pointless because he has a view of my ass, which cannot be sucked in, no matter how hard I try. And also, I already know he finds me grotesque. And I really don't care either way. I let it out again, slightly satisfied at this tiny act of defiance.

"Can I get you a coffee before you ruin my dream of living in an affordable little seaside cottage?"

"Sure, thanks. I like cream in my coffee. It makes the dream crushing taste sweeter."

Liam leans up against the counter while I prepare his coffee. I hand it to him, then gesture to the table. "Office chair or stool?"

"I'll go stool," he says, settling himself on it. He sips the coffee, then opens a black zip-up padfolio and hands me the two-page estimate. "You'll see I've broken it down into two sections—the must-do repair work, then the nice-to-do stuff. I've priced out mid-range fixtures and materials, so that bit really depends on your taste. It could go lower, although I wouldn't suggest going too much lower because you'll only end up having to replace everything a lot sooner. You could also go as high as the clouds, if you want top of the line. Some people do that too."

Flipping to the back page first, I start with the bottom line. $87,500 if we do everything. The amount causes my stomach to lurch. I study the numbers, making little 'mm-hmm' sounds, hoping to appear cool and collected.

"It's a lot all at once," he says. "You could break it up into smaller bits. Do the musts this year, then wait a while to do more. It's really all up to you. And don't feel like you need to decide today. You can think it over and let me know later."

I lean back in my chair and look up at him. "If we did everything, how long will it take?"

"You'll be stuck with me hanging around for the better part of six months," he says, looking almost apologetic. "But it'll sure be nice once it's all done."

True. It'll be what I thought I was getting. Reaching up for Isaac's ring, I slide the tip of my index finger through while I chew on the inside of my cheek. "Screw it. I'm in it up to my knees, I might as well dive right in."

"You can always change your mind, you know. If it feels like too much."

"I won't."

"I didn't think you would. So, what should we start with?"

"My office. Definitely."

I'm out in the yard, mowing the overgrown lawn, which proves much harder than expected. First, I needed to get this ancient lawnmower started, which was a whole mysterious process that forced me to seek out Liam's help. I found him stripping the hardwood floor in my office. He came outside, quickly changed the oil, and added gas. Then he disappeared back inside, but not before giving me a thumbs up that said he believes me capable of this job.

I'm not so sure I deserve his confidence, though. I only make it a few feet before the bag is filled and I have to empty it, which is a pain in the rear because holding a big black garbage bag open while I also maneuver the mower bag into it seems to require two sets of hands and I've only got the one. I've stuffed four bags with grass and weeds already, and I'm still not even a quarter of the way done with the front yard. The sun beats down on me as I drag the latest filled bag to the edge of the driveway.

A truck pulls up and I see Gus waving at me from the driver's seat. Oh, perfect. That's what I need right now—an insanely long conversation with the utilities big mouth. A young man sits in the passenger seat, wearing headphones and staring at his cell, seemingly oblivious to everything around him. Gus shuts off his engine and gets out of his truck, leaving the door wide open. "Hello, Abby! I see you've got quite the job ahead of you."

I smile, but not so nicely that he thinks I want to visit. "Yup, and I'm hoping to get it done by supper, so I really better get on it."

He takes on a condescending tone. "By dinner time? Not a chance." Pointing to a few errant blades of grass, he adds, "You missed a spot."

"Thanks. That's just what I wanted to hear," I say with a deadpan expression.

He stares at me for a moment, then laughs. "God, you're a quick one. Listen, I got what's known as a win-win proposition for the two of us. I'm needing to get my useless son, Colton, off my couch, and you're clearly needing a lot of help with this here yard."

Holding up one hand, I say, "I'm going to stop you right there. I'm afraid I don't have the budget for another employee."

"This one's free of charge."

"I would have assumed Canadians were against slave labor."

Gus chuckles again. "It's not slave labor if he gets paid."

"You lost me, Gus. Is this some sort of riddle?"

"You pretend to hire him, June and I will pay you, then you pay him."

"This helps you, how exactly?"

"Because I figure once he's had a taste of what it's like to earn for himself, he'll want to keep going. Hopefully, right out the door. I want to turn his room into a mancave."

I lean to the left and peer at the young man who is still absorbed in whatever's happening on the screen in front of him. "Can he hear you?"

"Nah," Gus says, turning and hollering, "Bee, Colton! There's a bee in the truck!"

Colton just keeps tapping on his phone with his thumbs.

I give Gus a skeptical look. "I don't know. Why don't you just make him get a job at McDonald's or something?"

"There's no McDonald's in town. Besides, June doesn't want to overwhelm him with a real job." He rolls his eyes. "She doesn't think he can handle that much responsibility yet."

"How old is he?"

"Twenty-one."

Twenty-one? I blink a few times in response.

"So you can see why I'm desperate, yeah?" Gus asks.

"Yes, but I really don't have time to supervise someone."

"He knows how to work a mower."

Well, now, this just got interesting. "Really?"

"It's literally the only thing he can do. How about I drop him here for the afternoon and you see how it goes?"

"All right, why not?"

Without skipping a beat, Gus turns and slaps the seat to get his son's attention. Colton jumps, then slides his left headphone slightly behind his ear. "What?"

"This is Abby, the widow I was telling you about. She wants to pay you to mow her lawn."

Colton gives me a nod and says, "Hey."

"Hi," I answer.

Gus continues. "If you do a decent job this afternoon, she'll keep you on for a few weeks. She's got a ton of stuff to do around here."

"What does it pay?"

Oh, for God's sake.

Gus answers for me. "Ten bucks an hour."

"That's not even minimum wage," he answers, wrinkling up his nose.

Lowering his voice, Gus says, "It's all she can afford. She's a *widow.*"

Seriously? I clear my throat to get Gus's attention. "Yeah, this isn't going to work."

Colton looks at me again, his face softening. "Nah, it's okay. I'll do it."

"Great," I answer. A pity mow.

I leave Colton with a jerry can of gas and a box of garbage bags, then go inside to have a drink of water. When I walk through the front door, I'm greeted by the sound of a sander. Even though a sheet of plastic covers the closed door to my office, fumes of sawdust and wood stain fill my nostrils. Outside, the mower starts up, and although I'm glad to not be the one standing behind it, the reality of the next six months starts to sink in. It's going to be noisy, dusty, dirty, and sweaty—just what every woman wants.

I busy myself shopping online for kitchen chairs but find nothing that ships here. When I go out to check on Colton, he seems to know what he's doing. Fifteen bags of grass sit by the roadside now, and I smile a little at the fact that this place looks slightly less abandoned. I give Colton the 'would you like some water' gesture. He nods and shouts, "Yeah, please."

Gus pulls up just as Colton finishes the front yard, and I can't help but wonder if he's been watching from the trees or something. He gets out of his pickup and inspects his son's work. "So, Abby? Is he hired?"

I walk over to Gus. "Yup. He did well."

He slips me three tens. I tuck them into the front pocket of my jeans, then, feeling foolish, turn to Colton and take the money out. "Thanks very much. Here you go."

Colton pulls one headphone back, takes the money, and counts it. "Great, okay then," he says with no enthusiasm whatsoever.

"You should thank her," Gus says under his breath.

"Thanks." He slides his headphone back into place and gets in the truck.

"Thank you, Abby," Gus says with much more sincerity than his offspring. "We'll be back tomorrow as soon as I drag his lazy ass out of bed."

"He worked hard," I answer, feeling a little sorry for Colton.

Gus looks genuinely surprised. "Really?"

"Really." I nod. "It's actually much better than what I would have done."

Grinning a little, he says, "Well, I'll be damned. He might not be completely useless after all."

I watch as Gus pulls out of the driveway, then look around the yard. It's still full of weeds, but at least they're short, and they can't hide any imaginary rat hybrids. The screen door slams, and I turn to see Liam coming out, covered from head to toe in dust, except for a shockingly clear patch where his protective glasses and mask were. His skin and hair are damp with sweat, and he wipes his forehead with the back of his arm. "Was that Gus?"

"Yes, he brought his son here to get some work experience."

"Colton? And you agreed to hire him?"

"Only because Gus is secretly paying his wage."

Liam busts out laughing. "Christ, he's desperate to get that boy to move out."

"Apparently. He did well, though."

"So you'll keep him on, then?"

"I'd be a fool not to for those rates," I answer. "I should see if he knows how to do a little of this and a lot of that. Maybe Gus could pay for my entire reno."

Liam smiles, then says, "Speaking of which, the floor in your office has been sanded and vacuumed. I need to go pick up my daughter at the babysitter. I'll see you in the morning to start painting the walls and staining the floor. You could save yourself some money, and me some time, if you wipe them down tonight."

"Deal."

"Okay, then. Enjoy your evening," Liam says with a nod.

"You too."

I walk back inside and stand in the doorway to the office. The floor looks dull now, but by next week, it'll be a shiny walnut, and this room will be just the right space to pen a bestseller. I hope.

CHAPTER TEN

> *I don't have a short temper, I just have a quick reaction to bullshit.*

~ Elizabeth Taylor

I groan when my alarm goes off, my entire body aching from my first few days of homeownership. Colton showed up again yesterday and mowed the backyard while I started on one of the five large flower beds in the front—a kidney-shaped bed that sits at a pleasing angle next to the driveway. After hours of digging, yanking, and disposing of the jungle of weeds, it looked much better, and I looked much worse.

When I finally drag myself out of bed, I stand at the window and survey our progress. From up here, I can see the enormous garbage bin Liam had delivered is almost half full already, and I wonder how many times it'll need to be emptied before this is all done.

Liam arrives five minutes early, and I offer him a coffee while we have what we've started calling our 'morning site meeting.' He opens his padfolio and takes out his list.

"I want to give that stain three full days to set before setting that heavy desk on it. I'd like to get started on the master bedroom, so if you think you might change your mind about knocking down that wall, best to do it now."

I give him a no-nonsense look over my coffee mug. "I don't change my mind."

"I almost forgot—you get everything right the first time."

"Exactly."

"Must be nice to be perfect," he says with a grin.

Shrugging, I say, "It's not that great actually, because I'm surrounded by imperfection everywhere I go." I do my best to seem serious until I can't hold it anymore and we both start laughing.

"So, since we're definitely adding that en suite, why don't we head into Sydney today to pick out the tub, sink, and everything else you'll need? Save you a few dollars in delivery and give you a break from all the yard work."

Happiness surges through me. "My muscles thank you for the temporary reprieve."

"Tell them they're welcome. We can stop at the furniture store, too, if you like. I know a guy who'll give you a good deal on kitchen chairs and whatever else you need."

"Don't tell me you're getting sick of sitting on that stool."

"Nah, I love it," he says, with a little grin. "But since you're so clearly the type to throw fancy dinner parties, I figure you'll need to seat more than one guest."

I raise one eyebrow. "Are you making fun of the village recluse?"

"You're not a real recluse. You just forgot how much fun people can be."

"I take offense to that, Liam Wright," I say, narrowing my eyes. "The only good people are cats."

His face grows serious for a moment, then he says, "Is that because they have nine lives?"

I pause before answering, trying not to think about what he meant by that. "It's because they mind their own business."

"Touché," he says, tipping back his mug.

The drive to Sydney is over an hour, and although I was temporarily concerned about awkward silences, we're almost there and we've managed to fill them in. Liam has just been telling me about the weekend adventures he and his daughter take during the summer. They sail around to new places every Saturday or Sunday, depending on the weather.

"Gus told me you live on your boat during the summer months. Is that something you've always done?"

He shakes his head. "Not until after the accident. Olive had a lot of trouble sleeping. My mom came from New Brunswick to stay with us for the first few weeks and she'd get up in the night to rock her back to sleep, sometimes twice before morning." He pauses for a second while he passes a slow semi-truck. Once that's done, he continues, "Anyway, when my mom left, it didn't take long for it to wear me out—getting up in the night, then up early for work. At some point, I remembered how well Olive slept on the boat, so I took her down there for the night. We both had a solid sleep for once, so we did it again. And after a while, I realized it also didn't feel as lonely as the house."

"Did you ever think about moving so you can be closer to your family?"

He shakes his head. "I could never do that to Sarah's mom and dad, not after everything they've been through."

"Right. Of course," I say. "I'm just going to keep asking questions that are none of my business."

"That's okay, I'm used to it."

"Good," I say, with a smile. "Where do you live in the winter?"

"We have a small house up on Todd Hill. If you stand on a stool, you can see the ocean from the bathroom window," he says, squinting his eyes. "I rent it out for the summer months, then we move back in the fall and ride out the cold."

"Sounds like a very sensible plan."

"Yeah, it's worked out well. It's not the house I shared with Sarah, actually. I sold that one the year after she died."

"Fresh start thing?"

He shakes his head. "Money thing. I wanted to put money away for Olive's education. It's worked out well for the most part. Olive probably won't want to live on the boat when she's a teenager, but for now, it's been good for both of us."

I suddenly wish I hadn't asked. I've forced him to think about something that wasn't on his mind today, and maybe he didn't want it in there. "I'm sorry. I shouldn't have brought it up."

"No, that's okay. Friends want to know about each other." He glances at me with that same easy smile he shows the world.

Liam stands patiently beside me while I test out kitchen chairs. We're in a small shop, but the owner promises he can have me sitting at my table faster than any of the big box stores. I've tried every chair here to the point where I could reasonably say I've done dozens of squats today, but I have yet to make a decision. I wind up wishing I were curled up on my couch back in Manhattan, where the only thing I had to decide was what show to watch. Today is filled with countless choices to be made, and I'm never quite sure I'm making the right one. I also have the pressure of needing to hurry because I made such a big deal about never changing my mind, and it's been nice having someone think I always know what I want.

I sigh, staring at the antiqued black wooden chair I'm considering. "Do you mind giving this one a try?"

He sits in it, and I wait while he pretends to cut a slice of some imaginary food, then mimes putting down his knife before having a bite and chewing thoughtfully. The entire time his expression is so serious that I can't help but snort-laugh.

Finally, he looks up at me. "Well, it's sturdy, it allows free movement of my arms, and it's the right height for me to reach my steak."

"Oh, is that what that was? Steak?"

"Medium well, a little overcooked if you ask me." He grins. "But let's not blame that on the chair, which I'd give a ten out of ten. Solid choice."

I narrow my eyes at him, but I'm still smiling. "I can't tell if you're making fun of me or not."

"I'm just trying to make you laugh. You're taking it all so seriously, but at the end of the day it comes down to two things—do you like it, and can you afford it, which only you'll know."

I open my eyes wide. "But what if the future of mankind rests on which chair I choose?"

"Like some sort of butterfly effect? Pick the wrong one and a month from now, we end up in a full-scale nuclear war?"

"Exactly."

He pretends to be deep in thought. "Well, in that case, we should probably—"

"Liam? Is that you?"

I turn to see a woman behind me. She looks to be about thirty with long blond hair falling in soft curls around her shoulders. The tight expression on her face tells me she and Liam were once more than friends.

"Hannah, hi."

I watch as Liam stands and kisses her cheek, suddenly feeling very awkward. She closes her eyes when his lips touch her skin, and there is the tiniest movement of her face toward him when he pulls away.

"How've you been?"

"Great. Really happy." She doesn't mean it. Her eyes flick over to me, and she looks me up and down before returning her gaze to him. "Wow. Don't tell me somebody actually passed the Olive test."

Liam's face hardens, but almost instantly, his easy smile returns. "This is Abigail. She's new to the island, and she's hired me to fix up her house. Abby, this is Hannah."

I stretch out my hand, and she shakes it as though I have a communicable disease.

"Nice to meet you, Hannah."

"You, too." The two little words are loaded with disdain. She turns back to Liam. "Well, I should go."

"Nice to see you. Take care of yourself."

She gives him a brief nod, then turns to leave without answering.

I return to the safe topic of kitchen chairs so Hannah won't think we're going to talk about her behind her back (which I certainly hope we will do). "So, you think this one will work?"

She swirls around. "A little tip for you, Annabelle ... if you need to find out what Liam thinks, you should ask his daughter."

Annabelle? Okay, now I'm getting annoyed. "I'm sorry?"

Her words come out as shards of glass. "You need to ask his daughter if he likes the chair because he doesn't know."

I glance at Liam, completely unsure of what to say. Nothing? Probably nothing is the way to go.

He rubs the bridge of his nose and shuts his eyes for a second. When he speaks, his voice is calm. "Hannah, I'm very sorry things didn't work out. Truly. But it would've been a disaster if we'd tried to force—"

She holds up one hand. "You know something, Liam? If you keep letting her rule your life, you're going to end up old and alone."

"I should be so lucky."

Hannah shakes her head in disgust and stalks away. I watch her open the door and storm past the window.

When I glance at Liam, he seems suddenly tired. "Sorry about that."

"It's okay. I've seen worse." I shrug. "Although there was a moment when I thought I might have to fight her."

He offers me a flicker of a smile before his face clouds over again.

Liam's jovial mood doesn't return. He's quiet and clearly distracted as we make our way around the city. After four hours of driving from store to store and examining fixtures and comparing measurements until my brain hurts, I'm desperate to go back home, put my jammies on, and spend the evening in bed watching Netflix. Our last stop is at a hardware store to find a new sink for the tiny main floor bathroom. Once we're done, we need to head back to South Haven so Liam can pick up Olive from her babysitter.

I play with Isaac's ring while I try to choose between two sink pedestals.

"If you don't mind me saying, I think you're better off with that cabinet over there."

I glance up and see Liam pointing at a white bathroom cabinet with matte black cup handles.

"It'll give you some storage." He shrugs.

I grin up at him. "Sold, to the lady who wants to go home, get into her duckie pajamas, and put her feet up."

The drive back is quiet. I spend most of it crossing things off my 'to buy' list and jotting notes. When I finish, I stare out at the sea, watching the waves roll and the odd seagull fighting the wind.

Liam clears his throat suddenly. "About that business with Hannah ..."

"Oh, you don't have to explain that to me."

"I know, but I'd like to. I told her it was because she and Olive didn't warm up to each other—which was true. But it was more of a timing thing. I had some personal stuff come up that I didn't want to drag her into, and I knew if I told her about it, she'd insist on sticking around, which wouldn't have been fair to her ... or Olive."

I nod even though I don't really know what the hell he's talking about.

"Anyway, I just didn't want you to think Olive is some sort of tyrant who runs my life, because she's actually a very sweet little thing." He glances over with a sheepish grin. "And I know every dad thinks that of his daughter, but in my case, it's true."

"Okay, thanks for filling me in because I was worried about that—as people usually are when they hire a contractor."

Liam's playful grin comes back. "I'm not a real contractor though."

Chuckling, I say, "Right, so I needn't have worried."

"Exactly."

We drive along for a few more miles in a comfortable silence, then Liam says, "I worry all the time. A little girl growing up without a mom —it's a lot harder than I would've guessed."

"I bet."

"It's the little things, you know? Like, she inherited her mom's naturally curly hair and I don't have the first clue what to do with it. And I'm not exactly oozing with fashion sense, so even though I try to help her pick out nice clothes, most of the time she ends up looking like some feral seven-year-old who lives on her own in the woods. Except she's always clean," he adds, sounding just on the verge of defensive. "I make sure of that."

"I'm sure you do." I know he needs to talk, but part of me really doesn't want to hear any of this. I have my own sad shit to deal with.

"Half the time, I'm worried I'm screwing it all up, and the rest of the time I know I am. And to be honest, when I think of her teenage years, I break out in a cold sweat."

"Sure, I can see that. Teenage girls are widely considered the most terrifying sub-sect of human beings on the planet. You should definitely find a very brave woman to marry before she turns twelve." There, I've lightened the mood. Let's stay here, shall we?

"Or by next week. It's the Mother's Day Tea at her school. Every year it just guts me. Everyone dresses up and the teachers bring in china tea sets. Sarah's mom goes, and Olive makes a nice card to give her, but the truth is, I'd rather the school would abandon the whole thing. There are already so many reminders for the poor kid that she doesn't have a mom. But that one ... Jesus."

My nose prickles and an unwelcome swell of emotion rises. I

mentally swipe it away and tap into the injustice of it. "That's a stupid tradition. Olive can't be the only one who doesn't have a mother. That's just rubbing it in the kids' faces!" I make a *tsk*ing sound that reminds me very much of my own mother. "Fucking morons. They should know better."

Liam's eyes grow wide and he looks slightly taken aback. "I didn't mean to upset you."

"You're not the one who upset me. It's the thoughtless idiots of the world who prefer to forget that other people out there don't have perfect lives." I allow my righteous indignation to flow through me. "You know what you should do? Take her out of school when they have that Mother's Day Tea. Just go see a movie or something and forget all about the whole thing."

"Could do, I suppose," he says, scratching his cheek. "It would upset Sarah's mom though. She enjoys it."

"Well, it's not about her, is it?" I bark. "It's about Olive."

We look at each other, and the shock in Liam's eyes suddenly makes me all too aware of how ridiculous I sound. I cover my mouth with one hand and laugh at myself, then say, "That rant was brought to you by PMS. PMS, for the times you need to get angry in an instant."

Liam chuckles and shakes his head. "I can't say I've ever met anyone quite like you."

"Then you've been lucky."

"Up to now, that is."

Swatting him on the arm, I find myself laughing, and Liam joins me.

After a moment, he starts to imitate me. "Fucking morons putting on a stupid tea."

"How dare they?" I say, mocking myself. "The bastards."

When the moment passes, Liam sighs. "Thanks for getting it, Abby."

"No problem," I say, with a firm nod. "You can't really understand unless you've been through it. Not that my situation is the same. But, in general, you know, *grieving*."

"Yes, I knew what you meant. You had it perfect for a while, and when it ends, the world is never quite the same." Liam gives me a sad smile. "But at least we both had it for a while, right?"

"Yes. Some people never even get that."

CHAPTER ELEVEN

 A ship is safe in harbor, but that is not what ships are for.

~ John A. Shedd

The next morning, Liam helps me move Isaac's desk into my new office, then he goes upstairs to start knocking the wall down between the small master bedroom and the tiny one next to it. I spend the next few hours unpacking all my work-related items and setting everything up just how I like it.

When I finish, I make a slow circle, taking in the butter-yellow walls which brighten the north-facing space, and the white sheers that frame the large window. The built-in walnut bookshelves have been scrubbed and now hold dozens of books interrupted by framed photos and the odd candle. Isaac's large mahogany desk sits in the center of the room, facing the window. My notebooks and laptop are in place, waiting for me to get started. Taking a deep breath, I inhale fresh stain.

Hmm. I better let it air out for a few days before I spend too much time in here. Paint fumes aren't exactly healthy. Plus, I should do the outside work while the weather is good. I can spend the entire long, Canadian winter holed up in here writing.

Gus and Colton arrive just as I start scraping the peeling paint off the window boxes. They get out of the truck, and Gus takes a long, skinny tool out of the back, then hands it to Colton, who looks none too pleased. His headphones are resting around his neck and he offers me a quick wave.

Gus inhales. "Yeah, yeah, yeah. You can't use weed killer so close to the water like this."

"Oh really?" I ask.

"Yup." He gives me a sideways grin. "So, Colton'll have his work cut out for him to pull all them dandelions. It'll be several days' work, maybe even a couple of weeks."

I turn to Colton and smile. "You're back for more, are you?"

"Apparently." He shrugs.

Gus eyes my handiwork on yesterday's flowerbed. "Not bad for a city girl."

"Thanks. Where are you off to today?" I ask, hoping he'll realize he should probably go now.

"Not far—Baddeck, then Iona, if I can manage it."

Although I have no clue where either of those places are, I'd feel confident betting against him getting to both places in one day. "Okay, well, happy trails."

Instead of leaving, he glances around some more. "You coming to the kitchen party tonight?"

"Not likely. I have so much to do around here."

I smile over at Colton, trying to include him in the conversation. "Are you going?"

"Nah, that's for old people," he says, then his eyes grow wide. "Not that you're old."

Laughing, I say, "Oh, I'm old. We don't have to pretend."

Gus shakes his head. "He never goes out. Just plays Fortnite every waking hour."

Colton turns a little red and looks down. "I'm trying to qualify for the big tournament in July. I could win a million dollars."

"But you won't," Gus says.

My mouth drops open and I wish I could say something to smooth things over, but then I realize it might be kinder to pretend I didn't hear that.

Gus points to the tool. "Do you remember how to use that?"

Colton glares instead of answering.

"Your ma will be here at four to pick you up."

"'Kay."

Colton slides his headphones on and trudges over to the far corner of the yard to get started while I turn and pick up my spade, hoping Gus will take the hint and leave.

Thankfully, he does. As soon as his truck pulls away, I say, "Thank Christ," under my breath.

Colton laughs, and I spin my head toward him, shocked that he heard me. "Sorry, I thought you had your music on."

"I was changing playlists."

"I shouldn't have said that. It wasn't very nice of me."

"It's okay. I'm glad, too."

It's almost six o'clock when my muscles decide it's quitting time. I've scraped and painted the two large window boxes under the front windows. They're now a soft white and I can already picture them spilling over with wave petunias. Liam is still working upstairs, but thankfully the smashing and thumping have stopped. I peek my head through the plastic sheet that has been hung over the entrance to my bedroom. The wall is gone already. "Wow! This looks incredible! I can't believe how big it'll be."

He looks up from his sweeping and nods. "Yup, I'd say you made the right choice."

"Obviously," I answer with a playful shrug.

"Say, Abby, I was thinking of hiring Colton to help me with the roof. But since it is your roof, I figured I better check with you first."

"I don't know. Is it safe?"

"Well, not as safe as being on the ground, but not as dangerous as you might think. I'll harness him up so if he falls, he won't hit the ground. His manbits'll be sore for a few days, but he won't break his neck or anything."

"What a lovely image, thanks for that."

"Anytime," he says. "It'll save my back and save you a fair bit of money if he does even a halfway decent job."

"I suppose I should pay him myself for this. And it's probably worth more than ten bucks an hour."

Liam nods. "Fifteen at least, but that's still less than half of my rate."

"Good point," I say. "Why not? What's the worst that could happen?"

Liam winces. "Ooh, famous last words."

"Let's hope not," I say, glancing out the window at the setting sun. "Hey, do you know how late it is?"

"I do. My in-laws take Olive on Thursday nights. She sleeps over there and I go to the pub. You stopping by tonight?" He continues quickly, "And before you say no, it would mean a lot to Nettie and Peter to see you there."

"No, it wouldn't."

"It would, actually. Things have been a little slow for them, and if a certain famous writer showed up once in a while, it would drum up a lot of business."

"I'm afraid you're mistaken. I'm not even the teeniest bit famous. I wasn't even the biggest writer in my apartment building."

"But here, you're a big deal."

"Nope. Forget it. Not falling for it."

"Abby, how many authors do you think live in South Haven? And of those, how many have books on the shelves at the library?" He asks. Holding up one finger, he says, "That's right. One. And I have it on good authority there's a wait-list on all your titles."

I shake my head. "That knowledge actually makes me want to barricade the door and never go outside again."

"What's the point of writing if you refuse to meet your public?"

"First of all, I don't have a 'public,'" I say doing air quotes. "Second, I write because it allows me to earn a living while avoiding real people. So, showing up at the pub every week would literally be the opposite of that."

"You don't have to go often. In fact, it's better if you only make the occasional appearance—just enough to keep everyone guessing. That way, they'll all show up every week for fear of missing out on the chance to see you."

I start to protest but Liam holds up one hand. "Trust me. You're the biggest celebrity to come to South Haven."

"What about the Beckhams?"

Liam barks out a laugh. "So, you're the *newest* celebrity, then." Before I can dispute this, he says, "Just come tonight—for your kindly neighbors that gave you a big discount on your stay."

I let out a long groan and drop my shoulders. "Really? You're going to guilt me into going?"

"Whatever works."

"Well, that is plain evil." I cross my hands across my chest.

"Oh, come on. It won't be *all* bad. They've got beer and pie. Plus, you can say you've done your good deed for the day."

"What?" I ask, wrinkling up my face in disgust. "You're supposed to do one *every day*?"

"In theory," he says with a wink. "Now, I better go home and get cleaned up. I'll see you later, then?"

I narrow my eyes at him. "Fine. But I'm not happy about it."

"You're a good woman, Abigail Carson. Don't let anyone tell you different."

CHAPTER TWELVE

> *The nice thing about living in a small town is that when you don't know what you're doing, someone else does.*

~Immanuel Kant

I can hear the music as soon as I walk out my front door, and I find myself hurrying along the road to the B&B. Not that I'm excited about going or anything. I'm only rushing so I can get this over with and go home to watch *Scandal*. In fact, I'm not even going to sit down. I'll just have one beer, maybe some pie, then leave.

I walk up the steps, then take a deep breath as I open the door. I give myself the once-over in the lobby mirror. Not awful. I'm in some cropped jeans, leather sandals, and a cute flowy V-neck blouse that hides a lot of flaws. My hair is down and I took the time to run the straightener through it. The overall look says, 'hasn't quite given up on life.'

The song ends just as I walk in, and I join in the applause while I look for somewhere to sit in the crowded room. This is one of those moments that's so much nicer when you're part of a twosome. I play with Isaac's ring, trying not to think about how much he would have loved this or how much more comfortable I'd be with him holding my hand right now.

The tables are set in a large U-shape with both musicians and their fans sharing the space. I spot Eunice, who is dressed in a glittery black sweater and pleather pants. She waves at me. "Abby, come meet the mayor!"

She puts her hand on the shoulder of a man in a sky-blue button-up shirt that needs more of the buttons done up. He has a comb-over that is three shades too dark for his eyebrows and an 'it's nice to meet the little people' smile.

When I walk over, he extends his hand. "Dennis Beckham, at your service. And yes, *he* is a close relative."

"I heard. He's quite the soccer star."

"Football!" Peter yells from behind the bar. "The proper name for it is football."

"Don't mind him, he gets a little testy about his precious football game," Nettie says.

"Well, you should use the proper name for a sport," he answers, filling a glass from the tap. "Not just steal the name for some senseless game, then rename the right one with a word that means nothing."

"Oh, come on, Peter," Dennis says, swiping one hand in the air. "Don't start that again. You'll insult our new American friend here."

All eyes turn to me, and I feel my face and neck growing uncomfortably hot. "No, you won't. I don't have an opinion on the matter. Sports, that is. Word usage, though, I do care about. And in that case, I think Peter's right. We should have come up with another name for our version of football."

Apparently, I'm on the losing side of the debate because my comments lead to jeers and muttering.

Peter glances around the room with a satisfied smile. "There you have it, folks. A professional in the ways of the English language has settled the debate, once and for all." He gestures for me to come to the bar. "Here's a free Guinness for you, love."

Beer in hand, I search for an empty chair, accidentally making eye contact with Gus, who waves to me. "Come and meet the ball and chain."

His wife sits next to him, looking all kinds of weary, and I'm pretty sure I can guess why. She has short blond hair with sprinkles of white throughout and, although she gives me a warm smile, her eyes make her look dead inside. "Hello, Abby. Thanks for hiring Colton to do your yard. It's been good for him to get out of the house."

Gus speaks up over the din of the crowd. "Did you hear that, folks? Colton's starting his own lawn services business. If you want to check out his work, stop by next door at the McMasters' place."

My head snaps back at the idea, and June, who is clearly less oblivious than her husband, says, "Gus, don't be inviting people to someone else's house. That's rude."

He gives her a pointed look. "Do you want him out of the house or not, woman?"

"Not enough to be obnoxious about it," she says.

You tell him, June.

They start to bicker, giving me an opportunity to search out a spot on the opposite side of the pub from Gus. Turning, I see Liam smiling at me, looking like he's had a few drinks already. He pats the vacant spot next to his. "Hey Miss Duckie Pants," he calls. "I saved you a seat."

This starts a buzz of gossip, and I glare at him as I take in bits of conversation about how we'd make such a nice couple and it's about time Liam found someone. I am really going to have to stock my fridge with beer because I'm not doing this again.

Nettie must be able to read my mind, because she speaks up, "Now shush, all of you. Abby here is not looking for a man, so just leave her well enough alone, or she'll never come back."

Exactly. I start across the room, raising my voice. "Thank you, Nettie. I appreciate your help, but I assure you, idle gossip has little effect on how I live my life."

And to prove it, I sit down next to Liam. This turns out to be big news because it sets off more laughter and knowing smiles from around the room.

"Well done," he says under his breath. Leaning in a bit, he says, "You look lovely tonight, by the way."

"Thanks, friend," I answer, trying not to enjoy being called lovely.

Nettie carries a tray of drinks to the table. "Now then, Abby, good that you came because Liam's had us all preparing a song for you."

What? Oh, for God's sake. My heart jumps to my throat and I turn to Liam with pleading eyes. Under my breath, I say, "What are you doing?"

He leans in with a confident smile. "Don't worry. You'll love it." Raising his voice, he says, "Shall we?"

One of the women lifts her flute to her mouth and starts up a few melancholy notes, then Nettie starts singing as she hands out the drink orders. I can't understand the lyrics, but my nerves tingle as they all join in, Liam with his violin, James with some sort of Celtic pipes, and more of the women singing. I pick up my drink and suck half of it down, glancing around occasionally. This is quite possibly the most awkward moment of my life, especially when I accidentally make eye contact with anyone. Everyone in the place is simultaneously smiling at me while they play their instruments and/or sing. Do they not know how fucking creepy this is?

I lean toward Liam and whisper, "This better not be a love song."

He just grins and continues to play.

"Seriously," I mutter. "I will kill you if this is something even remotely romantic."

When the song finally ends, silence fills the room. All eyes are on me, waiting for a response. "Thank you all ... that was lovely." Turning to Liam, I lower my voice a little. "What is it called?"

"Yes, Liam," Nettie says. "You never did tell us the name of it."

Liam is wearing an expression that is far too amused to be apologetic, although I have a distinct feeling the second emotion is the proper one. "Now, I hope you won't be offended. I thought you could use a theme song. You know, something to help get the word out that you like your privacy."

My nostrils flare and I purse my lips together. "Just spit it out already."

"Okay, but remember, I meant it in the kindest of ways," he says. "Also, for a bit of a laugh."

I fold my arms across my chest and glare.

"It's a Welsh tune called The Hermit of the Sea Rock."

Gasps and titters come from around the room. Then it grows deadly quiet as they wait for my reaction. I shake my head and start to laugh, slapping him on the chest with the back of my hand. Looking up at Peter, I say, "You were right about him. He is an asshole."

Peter holds up one finger. "I believe I said a bit of an arsehole."

"In America, it's the same thing."

Liam does his best to seem hurt even though he can't seem to stop laughing. When he finally manages to get himself under control, he says, "Now, why would you say that? I was just trying to help you set boundaries with the rest of the village."

"I'm starting to dislike you very much."

"That's odd. Most people love me," he answers before taking a swig of his drink. "Especially women."

The party ends just after eleven, and I'm still here for reasons I don't wish to explore. The mood is jovial but more subdued now as latches on instrument cases click shut, and chair legs scrape against the floor. A few of us carry empty glasses to the bar while the others put the room back in order for tomorrow's breakfast service. When everything seems to be done, I smile as I tell the remaining few people that it's time for the hermit to crawl back under her sea rock. Then, I walk out into the late evening air.

I'm slightly too warm from all the Guinness and laughter, so the cool breeze feels delightful on my cheeks. When I'm almost to the road, I hear the front door shut and Liam call my name. I turn and wait while he hurries down the steps toward me. "I'll walk you home."

"You think that's a good idea? We'll get everybody in town talking."

"That's odd. I seem to recall you saying that you're not the type to let idle gossip inform your decisions."

We fall into step with each other. "Yeah, well, that's fine for me, but I don't know if you can handle that kind of heat. A nice Canadian boy like yourself."

"I think I can take it. I've faced worse and I will again," he answers, and something about his tone bothers me, although I can't think why.

He looks down at me under the dim light of the streetlamp and grins. "Besides, Peter figured you might need someone to look around for intruders."

I wince, then let my embarrassment give way to irritation. "Good Lord, is there anyone in this town who doesn't have a gigantic mouth?"

He taps his chin a couple of times as though pondering, then says, "Umm, no."

I chuckle a little, then remember I'm mad. "No wonder houses are so cheap around here."

"Aww, it's not all bad, is it? After all, if he hadn't said anything, you'd be walking home on this dark, lonely road without an escort who'd gladly battle Norman Bates for you."

"Are you making fun of my overactive imagination?"

"Just teasing you a little. That's how we show new people we like them."

"I see. So everyone in town takes the eight-year-old boy approach— pull on the new girl's pigtails to show her you think she's cute, or in this case, mocking the new town hermit."

He stops in his tracks, gently placing his hand on my arm. I turn to see a very earnest expression on his face. "Hey, I hope I didn't upset you with that. It was sort of my way of bringing you into the group— kidding around with you so everyone would know you've got a good sense of humor—which you do."

"Oh, I'm aware of that. I'm freaking hilarious, but I don't need other people to know that," I say, continuing along the road.

"Right, on account of wanting to isolate yourself for the rest of your life."

"Precisely."

"But did I hurt your feelings? Because I'd be really sorry if I did."

"No, it would take a lot more than that to upset me. But I do have to say, don't ever do that again. I despise being the center of attention."

"Duly noted."

"Good," I say, turning onto my driveway. "To be honest, I'm more troubled that you lied to me than about the song."

"Lied to you?" he asks, then a look of recognition crosses his face. "Oh, you mean about Peter and Nettie needing a big celebrity to help bring in customers?"

"You can lay off the flattery now. The game is up and I know what you did."

"Sorry."

"Yeah, maybe in Canada an apology magically erases the past, but where I'm from, I still get to be mad," I say, walking up the steps to the front door. Liam holds open the screen while I dig my keys out of my handbag. "They're doing fine, aren't they?"

"Probably. I'd never ask them about their financial situation." He shakes his head with a mock condescending expression. "You know, it really isn't polite to ask someone how much they make."

I give him a light punch on the arm and growl. "You're impossible."

"Never said I wasn't."

"You're also a liar, Liam Wright." I raise an eyebrow at him. "What happened to 'I'm honest to a fault?' Or is that just a line you use when you need a job?"

"No, of course not," he says, sounding slightly offended. "But sometimes there's good reason to bend the truth. Like, say, to protect someone's feelings or maybe give a somewhat stubborn, yet deserving friend an evening out."

"Ah, I see. Well, the friends I keep know I don't like being lied to, and they certainly know I like making my own decisions based on facts. *And* they're smart enough to know not to guilt me into attending parties under false pretenses."

"So, I really blew it in the friend department, didn't I?"

"I'm afraid so. You're on notice."

"Won't happen again, I swear on my father's grave."

"Is your father really ...?"

Nodding, he says, "He passed twenty-four years ago. Cancer."

"I'm sorry to hear that."

"Me too. He was a hell of a guy. I'd never swear on his grave unless I meant it."

"No more lies?"

"I promise. Only the truth from here on out."

"I'm going to hold you to that," I say, unlocking the door.

"I'd expect you to," he says. "You want me to do a quick security check?"

"No, thanks. I'm fine."

"See you tomorrow morning then?"

"Umm-hmm."

He walks down the steps, then turns back. "Say, Abby? I hope you had a good time tonight, in spite of me being an ass."

Holding the door open, I say, "I did."

A slow smile spreads across his face. "So, are you maybe a little glad I talked you into it?"

"Don't push it, Wright."

"Gotcha."

I go inside, feeling sleepy and relaxed after a long day. I find myself chuckling about Liam and his stupid song while I brush my teeth. When I look in the mirror, I see a woman who looks happy and the reason for her smile shocks me a little, as does the knowledge that I haven't thought about Isaac since I walked into the pub. I wipe the smile off her face as a small act of contrition.

CHAPTER THIRTEEN

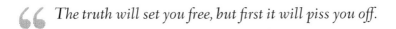 *The truth will set you free, but first it will piss you off.*

~ Gloria Steinem

Today I turn forty. Yuck. Shit. Fuck. Who wants to be forty? If Isaac were alive, he would have thrown me a lavish dinner party. He'd have invited all our friends, spent the last two days in the kitchen, and sent Lauren and me to the spa for the day while he executed the preparations to a T. I would have spent the entire day philosophizing about age and the beauty myth and gratitude and a whole bunch of other bullshit with Lauren, until I felt much better about this unwanted milestone.

But instead, other than accepting a few phone calls, I'm going to pretend it's not happening. The calls will come in this order: Lauren, who is also on Eastern Standard Time. She'll likely have sent a card in the mail, which will be a few days late. Then my parents will call so I can hear how they can't believe their daughter is the big 4-0. Yeah, because it's about *them*. My mother will lather on some 'time flies by and you should really come see your family' guilt. Yay. Happy day. My brother Chad's 'over the hill' jokes will come in around midnight via text, after his wife, Tammy reminds him it's my birthday.

Instead of a spa day, a beautiful evening with friends, followed by some fabulous birthday sex, I'm going to do some yard work, then binge-watch *Scandal* until I fall asleep.

I suppose I should be grateful that the minutes don't tick away here like they did at the apartment. Instead, they disappear like clams into the sand. I'll be spending my big day with Colton, who will have no idea I've just turned 'ancient.' He'll arrive on his bike around eleven in the morning and continue with the tedious job of ridding this entire property of weeds. After three weeks, he's still pulling weeds and his parents are still paying for it, which I have to say, I'm starting to feel a bit guilty about. (Just not guilty enough to put a stop to our arrangement because ... weeds).

Liam has made good progress inside, giving me hopes of having my little corner of the world all to myself sooner than I originally thought. This is a good thing because I'm starting to enjoy hanging out with him more than might be advisable. There's something about his easygoing nature and the way he makes me laugh, that causes me to completely forget how much I don't like other humans. I find myself getting sucked into ridiculously enjoyable conversations that leave me looking forward to the next one, which is one-hundred percent against my beliefs.

He's almost finished the master bedroom and en suite, which means the new flooring can finally be installed. I've decided on a light taupe carpet to replace the scruffy old green one that currently fills all the bedrooms, the staircase, the living room and dining area. The dining area and kitchen will have hardwood that matches the finish of the floor in the office, and the bathrooms will have ivory porcelain tiles. Once those are all in, this will feel a lot more like a home and less like a flophouse. I won't be sleeping on a double mattress on the floor, but will have my new queen bed to snuggle up in at night. For my fortieth, I've splurged on a cabin-chic bedding set with a light gray and ivory plaid pattern, and a throw pillow with a moose silhouette for a touch of fun. I'm going to have a pillow-top mattress to sink into for the first time in my life, now that I don't live with a man who insists the firmer the better. I found a reclaimed wood headboard at the same store where I bought the chairs. It's sitting in the garage waiting to be unpacked and set up.

The paint fumes are gone from my office, and every time I walk past it, my gut clenches. I need to start making money instead of spending it. Each morning starts with the best of intentions. I promise myself I'll sit down and write after breakfast, but inevitably, something more urgent pops up, like a flowerbed I really should tackle while it's nice out or a wall I could paint myself instead of paying Liam to do it. I'll write after lunch. Then after supper, but I can't very well leave a sink full of dirty dishes, now can I? By the time I turn out the light above the sink, I'm so tired from another day of working in the sunshine and fresh air, I walk right past my little office without looking, on my way upstairs. Then I read until I'm sleepy, which takes all of about four minutes.

Isaac doesn't appear in my dreams, or if he does, I sleep too soundly to know he was there. When I woke this morning, the realization slapped me over the head. I can't remember the last conversation we had. The thought has tortured me since I got out of bed even though I try to convince myself it's only because I'm sleeping so soundly. I haven't lost him. He's still here.

But what if he isn't?

My mood grows worse when I receive an email from Lauren which includes a link to a Publisher's Weekly article titled: Barrington Publishing Announces New Historical Romance Division. The subject line is "Just Sayin' ..." and in the body, she wishes me a happy b-day and says she'll call later when she gets a chance. Abby three years ago would have been super excited to talk to her about the possibility of working with Barrington. Abby today deletes the email and promptly tries to erase it, along with the accompanying sense of nausea, from her mind.

I then go in search of today's excuse, which arrives in a FedEx van. Ooh! What if it's a big birthday gift from someone who loves me?

I slide my Crocs on and hurry out to greet the deliveryman, who has just opened the back of the truck. He's shockingly pale and has wild black hair that makes his head look far too big for his painfully thin body. I stare for a second, a little taken aback as it occurs to me he resembles a Q-Tip that's just been used to wipe off heavy eyeliner.

He smiles down at me. "Are you Abigail Carson?"

"Yes," I say, giving him a friendly smile. *What is it? What do you have in there? Something fun for me?*

He snaps his fingers as a look of recognition crosses his face. "You're that American widow from New York, right?"

My smile fades, and I consider bursting into tears just to fuck with him. But I don't. Instead, I nod and say, "Mmm-hmm."

"Cool. I have a delivery of greenhouse windows for you."

Oh. Windows. Great.

The top half of his body disappears into the truck, and he pulls out a cardboard box. "Where would you like it?"

"Here is fine," I say, pointing to the ground.

He sets it down, then says, "Nine more to go."

"Okay, super."

I watch as he stacks the next two boxes on top of the first. "You ever replaced greenhouse windows before?"

Awesome. Another person who can't just quietly do his job and leave. "No."

Grabbing another box, he starts a new stack on the grass. "It's not too hard, but it's better if you have an extra set of hands."

"Well, I just have the two, so ..."

He looks confused for a second, then says, "Ha! I heard you were funny. I meant you should ask Colton to help. He and his dad replaced theirs last year."

"Okay, thanks for the tip."

"My great aunt is a widow, too. Do you like to play bridge?"

"Not really."

"Oh, too bad, because she has a bridge club with a few other retired ladies," he says.

He disappears into the truck again, which is fortunate for him because he can't see the intense rage on my face right now.

"There's also bingo night every Friday at the seniors' center. That might be fun for you."

"I just turned forty." Like, a few minutes ago.

He freezes mid-stride. "Seriously? That's sad."

"Is it?" I ask through clenched teeth.

"Well, yeah. You're kind of young to not have your husband anymore. My great-uncle died when he was eighty-four, so we were all expecting it."

"How many more boxes are there?"

"Four, I think."

"I left something on the stove. Do you need me to sign for this?"

"Nah, I trust you."

I storm into the house, bumping into Liam's chest.

"Whoa! You okay?" he asks, as I bounce off him.

"Fine. Sorry. I didn't see you there." I let out a long sigh. "How old would you say I am?"

"Oh, I don't like this game. There are no winners here," Liam says.

"Seriously. I need to know."

"Twenty-nine?" he asks, raising his eyebrows and giving me a hopeful smile.

I glare until he says, "Okay, listen, I'm *really* bad at guessing ages. Height and weight too. And honestly, I won't know if you look fat in that new dress, I mean should you buy one and ask me my opinion. I'll just tell you that you look great, and that'll be the God's honest truth."

"You do realize the longer you stall, the older I'll think I look."

He swallows hard. "Oh, Christ." Looking deep into my eyes, he says, "Old enough to know better but too young to care?"

"Men." I cut around him to the kitchen to crack open a can of Coke.

He appears around the corner, scratching his chin. "This feels a little like being married. I know I've fucked up, but I honestly don't know how."

I chuckle and shake my head. "It's not you. I'm just having a day."

"Anything you want to talk about?"

"No. Nothing worth discussing."

"You sure? I'm a reasonably good listener, for a man, that is. I know enough to not offer you a solution. I mostly just nod and gasp when I think it's appropriate."

"Wow, I really must look old because you have gone to a lot of trouble to avoid a very simple question."

"Forty-two."

My 'what the fuck' expression must be hard to miss because he looks panicked again. "But only because you lost your husband, so I figure you must be older than you look. In actuality, you only look thirty-six."

I turn and walk to the back door, his voice following me.

"Thirty-two? No, you're thirty-one."

I let the door slam behind me, and stalk over to the wheelbarrow, then huff and puff my way to the front to load up the boxes, muttering under my breath the whole way. "Forty-two. *Pffft*. My great aunt has a bridge club you could join."

By the time I bring all the boxes to the backyard and slice them open, I've added uncomfortably hot to my cranky mood. Walt, who is sitting on the small deck at the back of the house, meows at me like he does when I get too far outside his reach. He hasn't adjusted the way I'd hoped, shattering my image of him returning to his wild roots when given the chance. Instead, he refuses to step foot on the grass to explore. Something about the sight of him there irritates me, but I suppose everything is going to have that affect on me today. If I was smart, I'd just hop in my car and go for a long drive. But I won't. I'll just stay here and get this shitty job done. Happy fucking birthday to me.

Colton arrives just as I'm trying to figure out how to remove the first broken windowpane. "The windows finally came, eh?" he asks.

"Mm-hmm, and I hear you're a pro at putting these up."

He screws up his face in confusion, then says, "Tall, skinny FedEx guy?"

"Yup."

"That's Spooner. I went to school with him."

"Want to hear something creepy? He somehow knew I was single, from New York, and am replacing my greenhouse windows."

Shrugging, Colton says, "Don't worry about Spooner. He's a good guy. He just gets all the gossip because of his job."

"How does one avoid being the subject of said gossip around here?" I ask.

"Move somewhere else," he says in a matter-of-fact tone.

"Unfortunately, all my money is tied up in this place, so I'm afraid I'm stuck here for a while." I point to the windowpanes. "So, do you seriously know how to replace these?"

He nods. "It's really easy. They're clip-ons."

"Will you help me?"

"Gladly. I'm so sick of pulling weeds, I could throw up."

"Well, let's avoid that, shall we?"

Colton smiles back and we get to work. We remove the broken windows without talking. I can't think of anything to say to a guy who's just barely out of his teens, and I'm sure he feels the same way about the weird old lady next to him. The more progress we make, the less irked I am at the clueless delivery guy, and the more grateful I am to be working with someone who keeps his opinions to himself.

Out of the blue, Colton says, "I can't wait to get out of here."

"Oh, do you have something important going on? Because if you do, don't feel like you have to stay."

"No, I meant out of South Haven. It's so boring I could die."

"I remember that feeling when I was your age," I say. "That horrible restlessness."

"Exactly," he says, looking me straight in the eye. "Can I tell you something?"

"I guess so," I answer, feeling more than a little concerned about what he's about to say.

"I'm saving up to move to California."

"Really?" I wonder if his parents know that's what he's going to do with their money. "What do you want to do there?"

His eyes light up. "I'm going to live in a mansion with a bunch of other gamers. I just need a thousand dollars to buy-in, plus I need a few more followers on Twitch. Then they'll let me move in."

My expression must not convey the level of excitement he was hoping for because his face falls. "You probably think that sounds stupid."

"No, no," I lie. "That sounds ... awesome. I just don't really know what a Twitch is."

Colton bursts out laughing, then covers his mouth and tries to stop himself. "Sorry. I shouldn't laugh. It's not *a* twitch. It's just Twitch. It's a streaming platform gamers use."

I *am* an old lady. "To do what?" I ask.

"To stream your games."

Ah, that explains it. I raise one eyebrow and just stare.

"I play online games, mostly Fortnite but sometimes Apex Legends, and people watch me."

Wrinkling up my nose, I say, "Why?"

"Because it's fun," he answers, looking every bit as flabbergasted as I am. "Also, I don't want to brag or anything, but I'm pretty good. I have four-thousand followers."

"And you can make a living at this?"

"Yeah, the top gamers make a few mill a year."

"Seriously? I may be in the wrong business."

Colton gives me a blank stare.

"I'm just kidding. I know I'm not going to make it as a gamer."

Relaxing his shoulders, he says, "Good, because you'd probably suck balls at it." His eyes grow wide, and he says, "Sorry. I didn't mean to say it like that. I just meant ... it's a skill you need to learn when you're young." He gasps. "Not that you're old or something. Shit."

I stare at him with the same look I gave Isaac the time he left the toilet seat up and I soaked my ass in the middle of the night.

Shrinking a little, he says, "Sorry. I didn't mean ... you're actually pretty for someone your age."

"Oh, am I?" I ask, oozing sarcasm.

"I'll stop talking now."

"That would be good."

The sun is at its strongest now, so the more windows we put up, the hotter and more humid it gets in the small building. Sweat trickles down my back and my mouth throbs at the thought of a tall glass of water, but I keep going, wanting to get this done before the temperature goes up any more than it already has.

We're almost finished when he gives me a thoughtful look. "Can I ask you a question?"

"Yes, but you'd be wise to use caution."

"Right, yeah," he says, giving me a little grin.

He thinks I'm joking. How cute.

"Umm, you're from New York, right?"

"Not originally, but I lived there for most of my adult life," I say, using the back of my forearm to wipe off my damp forehead.

"Okay, so why would anyone who lived somewhere like New York move *here*?"

"Fair question," I say, even though I'm growing more emphatically against answering personal questions by the day. "It's cheap, safe, quiet, and I was under the misguided notion that I'd be left alone to write."

He steps out of the greenhouse, then comes back with two window-panes, one for each of us. "You're a writer?"

"Yup."

"Like books and stuff?"

"Yes, books," I say as I accidentally catch the pad of my thumb in between the windowpane and the clip. "Son of a bitch," I mutter, shaking my hand.

Colton doesn't seem to know how to read the room, so he continues with his interrogation. "Are you like, rich or something?"

"What?" I ask, examining the blood blister that's already popped up on my thumb.

"I mean, I've been here a lot over the last few weeks and you're always out here working in your yard. Are you rich enough that you don't have to write anymore?"

"No, I'm definitely not rich," I say, an angry fever taking over now. "In fact, I should probably be working, but I ..." *I what? I'm worried I can't remember how to write? I'm terrified I was never any good at it in the first place, and without Isaac, I'll never be able to do it again?* "You know what? I'd rather not talk about it," I snap.

"Okay, sorry. I was just wondering," he says, sounding hurt. "I didn't mean to pry ... I hate it when people do that."

"That's okay, you come by it honestly," I answer, my irritation from everything that happened since I woke up bubbling to the surface again.

"What?" he asks, narrowing his eyes.

"There's no way a person could be raised here and not grow up to be nosy."

I regret the words as soon as they leave my mouth, but I don't have time to smooth things over because Nettie has sneaked up on us and is now standing in the open doorway to the greenhouse. "Hello, you two! Workin' hard or hardly workin'?"

Oh, God.

In her hands is a tray of some sort of baking. "I couldn't help but notice you're fixing up the greenhouse, so I figured I'd pop over with some of my freshly baked scones and an offer of free dirt to fill your troughs."

"Hi, Nettie," Colton says, eying the scones.

"Hello, young lad. How's your family?" she waltzes into the greenhouse as though she's been invited, then holds the tray out to him.

"Good," he says, taking a scone. "Thanks."

Nettie turns to me. "And you, Abby? You must be hungry after taking down all these windows. Eat up!"

Defiance stirs up the dust in my soul and I set my jaw. I am done being talked into things by these people. "No, thanks. I'm still full from breakfast."

"Oh, come on now," she says with a smile. "They're fresh from the oven."

"Really, I'm fine," I say, sharpening my tone.

She points at one of the scones. "Just take that wee one then."

"No, thank you," I say, raising my voice to a pitch that shocks us all.

Nettie pulls the tray back, looking offended. "All right, then. I'll just leave them here and you can have them when you get hungry."

"I won't, but if Colton wants them, he can have 'em."

They exchange a questioning look, then Nettie looks back at me. "Are you okay, love? You don't seem quite like yourself today."

"You actually don't know me, Nettie. We're pretty much strangers and I think it's best if we keep it that way." I soften my tone some. "I'm not a people person."

She gives me a long, hard look, then says, "Okay, then. I'll go. We've got a big pile of dirt at the back of our property. You're welcome to it if you like. You can just come get it. You don't need to talk to us or anything awful like that."

"I'm probably going to leave the planters empty this year. I'm really busy, so I shouldn't be *wasting my time* trying to grow my own vegetables." She understands the meaning of my words—the vegetables aren't the only things I consider a waste of time.

Hurt fills her eyes, but she smiles anyway, making me feel like a complete bitch. "All right, Abby. If you change your mind, you know where to find the dirt." Turning to Colton, she reaches out and gives his arm a little squeeze. "Please say hello to your folks for me."

"I will." He nods and smiles at her, demonstrating how grown-ups are supposed to act. "Thanks for the scone. It was delicious."

I say nothing as Nettie leaves, totally unsure of what to say after having been so awful to her. All she's done is be completely welcoming since I met her, and yet, I might as well have just told her to fuck off. I quickly get back to the windows even though I know every time I look at this damn greenhouse, I'll be filled with shame.

An awkward silence hangs in the thick air as we finish the job, neither of us saying a word. When we're done, I walk around the yard, loading the empty boxes into the wheelbarrow to take to the bin in the front yard. Colton slides on his headphones, picks up his weeding tool, and goes to the far side of the lawn. I go in the house to take a shower, but hear Liam upstairs in my bedroom, whistling away without a care in the world. Must be nice.

My stomach growls and I realize its long past lunchtime. Grabbing my purse off the kitchen counter, I stalk out the front door. Then, I get in my car, start up the engine, and take off, blasting the air conditioning. This forty-year-old needs a big greasy cheeseburger, fries, and a huge-ass chocolate milkshake.

I return two hours later, cooled off but sick from all the grease I've just ingested. I crouch down a little in my seat when I pass by Nettie and Peter's, which is sort of the adult equivalent of a preschooler closing her eyes so she won't be seen. My gut churns when I park and look around the yard for Colton's bike. I'm torn between wanting to see him so I can apologize and hoping I never see him again. His bike is gone, leaving me both relieved and disappointed. It also means my peace-offering of a milkshake and fries won't be made today. Liam's truck is gone as well, and I remember he had to leave early for a doctor's appointment.

I toss the not-so-fast food into the bin, saving myself from making a mistake later on, then go inside. Walt, who is clawing at a felt mouse, looks up at me, then turns back to his job of leaping on top of it with every bit of gusto he's got. "Go get him, Walt."

For once, my house is quiet. No pounding, smashing, sawing, sanding, or whistling. I'm finally alone, as I make my way to the fridge for a swig of Pepto Bismol. I should be delighted, but now that I'm standing in my empty kitchen, it feels ... empty. I could have used a distraction because now I can't avoid facing who I was earlier this afternoon. I do not like that woman, not one little bit.

I spot Nettie's container on the kitchen counter. The scones are gone, and if I had to guess, I'd say Liam brought it inside for me before he left. I fill the sink with some water and soap, then wash it, and force myself to go next door and apologize. When I walk into the pub, it's quiet. Only two patrons sit at a table in the corner opposite the bar. Nettie is setting up cutlery for the dinner service that will start soon. She looks up and gives me a little nod, but her eyes don't brighten the way they normally do. Glancing at the container, she says, "You can leave it on the bar."

I trudge over and set it down just as Peter comes out of the kitchen. His face falls when he sees me, and I know Nettie must have told him what happened. I scratch my forehead, then sigh, wishing the right words would pour out of my mouth right now, but finding myself sorely disappointed. Nettie comes around behind the bar and starts loading her tray again.

"Nettie, I want to—" I start but she raises one hand without looking up.

"No need. You tried to warn me, but I didn't listen."

Peter picks up a rag and starts wiping the clean bar top. "We didn't think you were serious about all that 'wanting to be left alone' stuff, but clearly you are so we'll let you be. You're always welcome here, but we won't be stopping by at your place again."

I close my eyes for a second, regret vibrating through my bones. "I didn't mean ... no, well I *did* mean ... I was mean."

They both stop and stare at me.

"I was rude to you earlier and there's no excuse for it."

Shaking her head, Nettie says, "No, I get it. You're busy. I have to stop mothering everybody." Her voice cracks when she says this, then she turns abruptly and disappears into the kitchen, the door swinging behind her.

Peter closes his eyes for a second, looking pained, and I suddenly have the idea that this isn't all about their bitchy neighbor.

"Peter, is she okay?

Shaking his head, he says, "Did you ever wonder why we don't have children?"

"I just assumed you didn't want any."

He tilts his head a little, then says, "We did. Very much, especially my dear wife. After four miscarriages—the last one at seven months along—we decided to find a different way to make a home for someone."

"Shit," I whisper.

"Yeah, she's doesn't mean to meddle. She just needs people to take care of," he says, tapping his fingers on the bar. "I think she figured since you're alone and all..."

Nettie walks back in with a large bag of napkins. She walks past me, straight to the nearest table to refill the metal napkin holder.

I walk over, grab the holder from the next table and start to fill it. "I'm sorry, Nettie. All you've done since I met you is be welcoming and kind. And I ... haven't treated you the way I should have."

"Nope, that's fine. I'm too nosy for my own good." She moves on to the next table and I follow her.

"The thing is, for a long time, I've gotten used to being on my own and it's become very comfortable for me. And today was just sort of bad because a lot of little things happened that added up to me being in a terrible mood—which was in no way your fault."

"What happened?" Nettie asks, her face filling with concern.

"Oh, it's all so stupid," I say, glancing out the window and reaching for Isaac's ring. "I turned forty today, and I feel really old even though I know I'm not. And it just made me miss my husband because he would have made it a really special day, you know?"

"Oh, love," Nettie says, her facing crumpling. "Of course you'd be in a pissy mood today. No one likes turning forty. It's the absolute worst."

"It is," Peter adds.

"And you've got no one to celebrate with." She pulls me in for a big hug, and this time, I don't recoil. I accept, knowing it's for both of us.

When it's over, she pulls out a chair for me, then takes a seat. "Come sit and tell me what your husband would've done to make it special." I sit down and start talking, first about Isaac, then I move onto the other petty little things that upset me this morning—the email from

Lauren, the FedEx guy, Colton making me face the fact that I'm not writing, and my fear that I never had any talent in the first place. By the time I unload it all, I feel much lighter. "I mean, if even *Colton* can see I should be writing, I probably should be writing."

"Yes," Peter, who joined us at the table sometime around me complaining about Liam thinking I'm forty-two, says, "You probably should."

Nettie slaps his arm. "It's not that simple, you dolt. She's scared that she's no good at it."

"Well, sitting here crying in her soup isn't going to help, is it?" he asks her. Turning to me, he says, "There's really only one way to find out."

"It's her fortieth birthday! Quit nagging her, for God's sake," Nettie says. Turning to me, she smiles. "How about you stay here for a nice supper on the house? We can sing to you and ..." Her voice trails off, then she says, "And you would hate every minute."

"But just the thought is so sweet of you, really."

"Tell you what, I'll pack you a supper to go and some cake. You get home and get your arse to work."

I nod. "Okay, that sounds perfect."

A few minutes later, Peter comes out of the kitchen with a large brown paper bag. "Now, get going and don't come back 'til you've written something you're proud of," he says as he hands me the bag. "Oh, unless you need something. Then call or stop by."

"Or if you're hungry," Nettie says.

"Or it's Thursday night and you could use a break and some good music," Peter adds.

I chuckle. "Okay. Thank you, both." Looking at Nettie, I swallow, guilt still eating at my insides. "I really am sorry about this afternoon."

She waves her hand. "Think nothing of it. It's our first row as neighbors and we're over it now."

"Good to just get it over with. It would have happened sooner or later anyway," Peter says, gesturing with his head toward Nettie. "Especially with *this* one."

"Arsehole."

"Cruel wench."

"You're both lovely," I say. "And I'm lucky to live next door to you."

Peter narrows his eyes, but the smile never leaves his face. "Are you still here? I thought I told you to get going."

When I get home, I flop down onto my bed and draft a text to Colton. *I'm sorry I was such a grouch today. I didn't mean what I said about you being nosy. You're not. You were just curious, and there's nothing wrong with that.*

I read it over a few times before I send it. Then I wait. A minute later I get back a message from him. *No worries. Everybody has their bad days. I'll see you tomorrow.*

CHAPTER FOURTEEN

> **Happiness is having a large, loving, caring, close-knit family in another city.**
>
> ~ George Burns

It's been weeks since I've spoken to my mother. I let her call to me on my birthday go to voicemail, for fear of saying something I meant. Later that night, I texted a lame excuse that my cell phone battery had died and thanks for the message. We haven't really spoken since I 'up and moved to Canada' instead of coming home so she could bake cookies for me and pretend she's sorry Isaac died. This isn't the longest we've gone without speaking. Our first cold war took place when I told them I was madly in love and was about to move in with a much older man. The second was right after Isaac's death. My parents assumed I'd return to Portland with them and went as far as making arrangements while I was still picking out photos for his memorial. They were shocked when I told them I wasn't coming home. An ugly scene took place in the lobby of my building when we returned from the service. I screamed that there was no way I could live with them while I grieved for a man they both hated. It wasn't entirely fair, but it wasn't entirely wrong either. But today I have to make peace. It is my mother's sixty-fifth birthday, and if I don't call, it would be the equivalent of unlocking the case on the red button.

And I really should do it now while I have some privacy. Although things have been going smoothly since the dreaded day of the greenhouse, Colton isn't coming by to work on the yard for the rest of the week. He texted late last night to say he was super sorry (how Canadian), but 'something important came up that he has to deal with.' He must have forgotten he told me the new season of Fortnite comes out today, and they were going to 'destroy the map' and create a whole new one. Whatever the hell that means. Liam is upstairs laying the tile for my bathroom floor, so I should just get this call over with before I have any witnesses.

I sit down on one of my new black wooden kitchen chairs and dial her number. When her phone starts ringing, I take a deep breath, telling myself to be patient and let things slide, no matter what she says.

"Hello?"

I muster as much enthusiasm as I can. "Hi, Mom, happy birthday!"

"Oh, Abigail. I was wondering if you'd remember."

Here we go. First shot across the bow. "Of course I'd remember your birthday. Did you get the flowers?"

"Yes, they're lovely. Thank you."

"Good. I'm glad you like them. How are you?"

"All right. I've been getting migraines again, and the doctor doesn't seem to know why they're coming on so frequently. Your father said it's stress-related. He's probably right."

Stress caused by their only daughter moving so far away, no doubt. "That doesn't sound good. Has he referred you to a specialist?"

"No. He wanted to, but I told him not to bother. I'm sure it's just because I worry so much."

I suppress a sigh. "What are you worried about?"

"Oh, you know, lots of things. Mothers worry. That's just what we do from the moment we find out we're going to be blessed with a child. The worrying starts, and it doesn't stop until we die."

Neither does the guilt trip. "Is something wrong with Chad? Because I'm fine. Really."

"There's nothing wrong with your brother. He's here where we can help if he needs us."

It's her birthday. It's her birthday. "I know it's hard for you to have me so far away."

"I don't think you can possibly know what it's like to have one of your children ..." She stops herself. "It's just hard not knowing where your daughter lives."

"You and Dad should come see for yourselves. The house isn't quite ready for guests, but there's a lovely bed and breakfast next door."

"Oh no, there's no way we can get away. Who would watch the dogs for us? Plus, we need to be here for Grandma."

"Well, you could kennel the dogs and Uncle Jay can check in on Grandma for a couple of weeks, can't he?"

"No. He's completely useless. He'd say he'll look after her, but there's just too much he doesn't know. What if she ran out of one of her meds?"

"I'm sure you can refill them before you leave. Besides, she's doing well, isn't she?"

"Compared to other people her age, maybe. But honestly, Abigail, anything could happen." She gives an audible sigh that sounds almost like a moan. "You should really come and see her before it's too late."

Oh wow, she's really going for it today. "You're right. I should."

"Are you doing okay there?"

"I'm all right. Better than I was doing in New York. It's hard, though. Everything new is something I wish Isaac could experience."

"Well, he had a lot of experiences before he met you. Nearly two decades of them before you were even born." There it is. Don't feel sorry for him. He had his life.

"Why don't you just tell me what you really want to say?"

"I have nothing to say that you'll listen to."

She's not wrong. I can't remember the last piece of advice I took from her. When I was a teenager, she once told me that indigo was my color and I've never worn it since. "Go for it. It's your birthday. I promise I won't fight back."

There is a long pause, and I know she's considering it. "I just wish you had listened to your father and me. You wouldn't be alone right now. You could be happily married to someone closer to your own age, probably with a few kids."

I screw up my face and clench my teeth together to suppress the scream inside me. Then I take a deep breath and force my voice to be calm. "Young men die too, Mom. Life offers no guarantees."

"Well, the older they get, the closer they are to death. That's just a fact."

"Yup. You got me there. You win."

"It's not a game, Abigail, and if it were, it's not one I ever would've agreed to play."

"I just meant you were right. I thought Isaac and I would grow old together, but it didn't work out." I close my eyes while I talk. "He loved me, Mom. He was an amazingly supportive and encouraging partner to me for over fifteen years, and I would never have given any of it up, even if I had known how things would end. It was the best part of my life."

"You say that like you're never going to have anything good again."

"That's because I won't."

"You don't know that. You're still young. You can move on."

I close my eyes and slump down in my chair. "Oh, God, Mom, can you stop?"

"What happened to listening and not fighting back?" Her tone is clipped.

"Sorry, I tried." I let out a long sigh. "I'll let you go. I'm just upsetting you, which is the last thing I wanted to do today."

"This conversation isn't what's got me upset, Abigail." Her voice becomes quiet as she speaks. "It's the distance between us. And I'm not talking about the miles of land."

My heart aches at her words. No matter how crazy we drive each other, she'll always be the only mom I'll ever have. I try to look out the window, but my sight has grown blurry. "I love you. You know that."

"But?"

"But I wish you could accept my choices. It's not like I moved to the big city and became a stripper or something. I got my masters, found a wonderful husband, and became a reasonably successful writer. Maybe my dreams weren't the ones you and Dad had for me when I was a little girl, but I wish you could be proud of me anyway. For being strong enough to go against the tide and do what I was meant to."

She's crying now, and I know I've done it. She'll probably spend the rest of the day in bed, and tomorrow, my brother, the perfect son with the perfect family, will send me an angry text about upsetting her on her birthday.

She sniffles, then she finally speaks. "Of course I'm proud of you. I just wish I still knew you. I used to know everything about you, and now you're like a stranger to me. Do you know how hard that is? To be a stranger to your own child?"

It's her birthday. Let her win today. "Okay, Mom," I say with a sigh. "You're right. I need to make a better effort. I'll come home for a visit as soon as I can."

"Promise?"

I resent the doubt in her voice until I realize who put it there. "Promise."

After I hang up, my skin crawls as swirls of guilt and anger course through me. I go outside, letting the screen door slam behind me. I stand on the wood deck for a moment, breathing in long, deep breaths. Then I walk over to the still-untouched, overgrown garden and start yanking weeds, not bothering to get my hat or gloves first. Frustration fuels my body as I choose the tallest, toughest weeds to tug on, tossing them into a pile behind me as I go. The sun grows hot and my hands hurt but I continue, working furiously until I hear the screen door creak.

I straighten up, slapping my dirty hands on my jeans and turn in time to see Liam settling himself on the steps with his lunch pail and a thermos of coffee. Walt has come out with Liam and is sitting next to him, watching me intently.

Liam surveys the garden, then says, "You look like a woman on a mission."

"Impromptu weeding session brought on by an irritating phone call," I say, wiping the sweat off my forehead with the back of my arm.

Nodding, he says, "Anything you want to talk about?"

I shake my head. "Only to say there's a reason I live on the opposite coast from my mother."

"Gotcha. I'm a healthy distance from my family as well," Liam says, unwrapping his sandwich. "Do you want to stop for some lunch, or do you still have some rage to work out?"

I let my shoulders drop, realizing my anger has led to aching muscles and an empty stomach. "I think I'm about done. I'll just get cleaned up."

A few minutes later, I join Liam on the steps, with clean hands and a pre-made quinoa salad. I sit next to him and sigh, a sense of calm coming over me. Walt trots over and settles himself between us, then watches as a robin hops along the grass in search of food. His black ears prick up and he juts his head forward, but he doesn't spring into action.

"Your cat's not much of a hunter," Liam says.

"He's used to eating Fancy Feast on fine china. He'd never lower himself to eating a live bird." I pat Walt on the head. "I think he's scared actually. I thought he'd love having the freedom of a big yard, but so far he hasn't left the deck."

"He'll come around when he's ready. Won't you, buddy?" Liam scratches him behind the ears and is rewarded by Walt rubbing his head against his leg.

We sit in comfortable silence for a few minutes, Liam eating his second sandwich, and me, my salad. A slight breeze kicks up, cooling my feverish skin. I stare at the mess of weeds tossed around the garden, dreading the idea of bagging them.

Liam speaks up out of the blue. "My daughter, Olive, is a lot like your Walt. She doesn't rush into things. Her grandparents think she's too scared of new things, but I don't think that's it at all. She takes the time to properly assess a situation before deciding what she's going to do."

"She sounds smart."

He smiles, his pride obvious. "She is. She's just like her mother. Thoughtful and intelligent. Sarah was an artist. She painted and sculpted."

I'm not sure how to respond, so I just nod my head and wait for him to say more.

Instead of sharing more about himself, he brings the conversation back to me. "What did your husband do?"

"He was an English professor and a freelance editor."

"So, he wasn't exactly a dullard."

I chuckle a bit. "Not exactly. He was very well-spoken and well-read."

Liam nods, and I realize it feels nice to talk about Isaac with someone who didn't know him. It's almost like I can rediscover him again for myself. "Isaac was always the first person to read anything I wrote. He had a way of asking me just the right questions to uncover the hidden potential in each of my stories. Then I would dive back in, and when I was done with the second draft, it would be so much better than the first."

"Who reads for you now? Since he's been gone?"

"There's been nothing to read."

Liam makes a little 'hmm' sound that is neither dismissive nor judgmental. "You'll get back to it when you're ready."

Gratitude fills me at not having been told to 'get back on that horse.' "I hope so. I really love it."

He gives me a thoughtful look. "If you love it, what keeps you from writing again?"

"Guilt." The word pops out of my mouth before I have time to process or censor it.

"That you're alive and he isn't." Liam takes a sip of his coffee.

"Yes," I say, doing my best to keep my voice steady. "I take it you feel like that sometimes, too."

"Every damn day." His words are thick with emotion. "She's missing it all, and she would have loved being Olive's mom. Malcolm's too."

I blink hard to keep the tears at bay. "Do you ever think maybe she's watching somehow?"

"I have to believe she is." He shakes his head. "I don't think I could do it if I thought otherwise. The pain of being separated from your child is ..." His voice trails off, then he says, "Indescribable."

The word hangs there for a moment, then he says, "What about you? Do you think there's something else after all this?"

I sigh for a moment, considering the question. "I never used to, but now, I don't know. I dream about him a lot. Long conversations about things I'm going through, decisions I have to make. He always knew what to do, and somehow he still does." I suddenly feel naked, having shared something with Liam I have told no one else. "That probably makes me sound like an insane person."

He shakes his head. "Not to me. Sarah comes to me in my dreams sometimes too. We talk about Olive. I tell her all about what's happening, and she gives me her advice in that same gentle way she did when she was alive. It used to be all the time, but the last few years, it's only when something big is about to happen." Turning to me, he says, "Now who sounds crazy?"

I chuckle a little. "We probably shouldn't tell this to anyone else."

"Agreed," he says with a sad smile.

I turn away from his gaze and stare out at the blue water in the distance. There's a lump in my throat now, and I know there's no point in taking another bite because it'll be a long while before I can swallow. Walt seems to know I need him, and he climbs onto my lap, reaching his head up to rub it against my chin.

Liam speaks up. "It's hard being the one left behind, isn't it? So many questions unanswered. So many 'if onlys' and 'what ifs' and 'I should haves.'"

I nod. "Does any of that go away?"

"I don't think so. People believe you should grieve for a period of time—and I've noticed that most seem to think the appropriate amount is about three months—then you're expected to get over it and move on." His tone is matter of fact when it could be bitter.

"I've actually had people ask which stage of grief I'm in and how long it'll be until I've reached acceptance," I say, rolling my eyes. "As though I have it penciled in on my calendar or something."

"It's because we were more fun before and they want the old version of us back."

"As if *we* don't want things to be how they used to be." We exchange a look that shows we both understand the absurdity of it.

Liam stares out at the water. "Then they start pushing for you to find someone new. There isn't a person I know who hasn't either set me up on a date or suggested I get back in the game. Not one."

"Except me," I say, bumping his arm with my shoulder.

He chuckles and turns to me. "True. You've been a breath of fresh air, Abby."

Oh my, that felt nice to hear. I clear my throat and put on a formal voice. "I, Abigail Carson, hereby promise to never try to set you up with anyone."

"And I, you," he says with a nod.

We stare at each other for a moment too long, erasing the words we've just said and opening the door of possibility. He glances at my lips, then back up into my eyes and I feel a pull from somewhere deep inside to lean toward him. Instead, I quickly stand, shocked at myself for even considering whatever I was about to consider. Clearing my throat, I say, "I better clean up that mess I made."

The sun has almost set, and I sit on the deck, sipping a glass of chardonnay. Walt sits next to me, his body pushed up against my leg while I rub the top of his head and listen to the waves lap against the shore. I haven't been able to get the conversation with Liam out of my mind since it happened. I'm confused by what I feel for him—this horrible attraction that shouldn't be there. Shaking my head, I look down at Walt and say, "It's not real. It's just the result of feeling understood on such a deep level. And the fact that he's a man and I'm a woman, which makes friendship somewhat complicated."

There. Now that I've said it out loud, it's true.

I sit for a while longer, still unable to put my finger on what's bothering me. Then suddenly, it pops into my mind. His words about the pain of being separated from your child. I sigh, thinking of my mom, knowing I've caused her pain I never intended. Picking my phone up off the step, I send her a text. *I'm sorry I upset you on your birthday. I know you've always wanted me to be happy and you deserve better than to spend your days worrying about me. I'm getting stronger—I promise. I love you and I'll call you every Sunday from now on.*

CHAPTER FIFTEEN

Liam and I are setting up my new bed in my newly renovated, lovely bedroom. To look at us, we could be in a commercial for a mortgage broker—two casually dressed happy people sharing lots of inside jokes while we set up our bed for later (eyebrow raise here). At some point, probably sometime around the mattress going onto the box spring, things started to feel a little awkward because now this is a bed and he's a man and I'm a woman, and I really shouldn't have an attractive man in my bedroom. Not if I don't want to get confused.

Actually, now that I think about it, mounting the headboard to the wall was sort of intimate, requiring us to stand so close together, our shoulders were touching for a minute, followed by him on his knees, screwing it into the wall next to my thigh. Neither of us has said a word for a full five minutes, and I can't help but wonder if he's finding this as weird as I am.

Finally, he thinks of something to say. "I thought I'd move on to the roof since we're supposed to have several days without rain."

"Sure," I say, holding the box for my nightstand still while he lifts it out.

God, he smells good for a guy who's been working all day. *Nope, Abby. Just nope.*

"It'll get real noisy, so you may want to work somewhere else for a few hours each day. Also, you won't want to be doing any gardening near the house because you might get hit with a nail or an errant shingle."

I open the second box while he carries the first night table over to the side of the bed. "If this keeps up, I'll have you out of my hair by Halloween."

He winces and for a second, I worry that I've offended him.

"About that, I'm afraid I might have to slow down a bit. The woman who watches Olive after school called last night. Her mother is sick, so she wants to leave for Newfoundland right away to go look after her. It means I'll have to shorten my days by quite a bit until I can find another sitter."

Damn. That does not fit with my plans. "What if she comes here until you can find someone? I know there isn't much to do, but if she can keep herself amused, it could work out."

Liam tilts his head, his expression both surprised and relieved, and I can't help noticing those blue eyes of his are sparkling a bit. "Are you sure?"

"Sure, I'm sure," I say, looking down at the box so as not to gawk at him so close up. "The hermit of the sea needs to get you the hell out of here as soon as possible," I say with a grin.

"Hermit of the sea *rock*," he answers, grinning at me as he removes the Styrofoam from the nightstand. "Anyway, thanks. I'm sure it won't take long to find somewhere else she can go. In the meantime, she won't be any trouble. She loves to read and draw. She'd probably spend her time here with a sketch pad on her lap. Or Walt, if he'd put up with her. She loves anything soft and furry."

"Well, I don't know if he likes kids or not, but we can give it a try."

We both stand on opposite sides of the bed, staring at each other until my face heats up. Then, at the same moment, we both start cleaning up the boxes and plastic.

Once everything is in a manageable pile, he picks it up, glancing at the bed again. "You need any help with the sheets?"

"I don't think that was part of your estimate," I say with a half grin.

"That's why I like to be vague. So I can do what needs doing." A panicked look comes over him and he says, "Not like that. I only meant I like helping people."

"Sure, buddy," I say, pretending I don't believe him.

"No, seriously, Abby. That would have been creepy, if I meant it like that."

I shrug and make a *tsk*ing sound. "I know what I heard."

He picks up the garbage and shakes his head while he walks out the door. "Okay, very funny."

I call after him, "Is that what you meant by a jack of all trades?"

"Hilarious!" he shouts up the stairs.

I hurry to the hall and yell, "Is that the thing you do a little of or a lot of?"

The next day, Liam leaves at three o'clock to pick up Olive from school. As I wait for them to come back, a sense of anxiousness overcomes me. I have absolutely no experience with children. Other than having been one a long time ago, and having spent a few hours here and there with my brother's kids, I really don't know what to say to a child. I know enough not to treat her like a baby, but that's about it. I try to think back to what I was like as a young girl. I remember that after school, I was tired and cranky and starving.

By the time I hear Liam's truck pull up, I have a spread of sliced apples, some Camembert, and water crackers set out for my new guest. I place a napkin and a cheese knife next to it. It's just the sort of snack Isaac and I would offer company. "Perfect."

I hear the door open and Liam's voice. "Abigail, we're here."

I peer around the corner while I wipe my hands on a dishtowel and take in the sight of a waif of a girl with unruly long brown curls that look like they might just spring right off her head at any moment. She's standing slightly behind her dad, holding his hand and looking up at me with huge blue eyes behind a pair of red-rimmed glasses. I now get what he meant about her looking like she lives alone in the woods. She's wearing a denim dress with striped green and yellow leggings under it that look like they're two sizes too small, on account of how high up they come on her skinny legs.

Liam looks down at his daughter, then back at me. "Olive, this is Ms. Carson."

I cross the room and hold out my hand to her. "Nice to meet you, Olive. Please call me Abby." I look at Liam. "Oh, that's if it's okay with you."

"That's fine. I don't get too fussed about being formal," he says. "Say hello, Olive."

She takes my hand, and we shake. Her fingers feel so light in my palm, it's hard to believe she's an actual human being. "Hello, Abby." She gives me a tentative smile, and I can see she gets her smile from her dad. And her eyes. But the rest of her—the mass of thick curls and the slight frame—must be her mother.

"Are you hungry? I made you a snack."

Her eyes light up, and she gives a quick nod.

"You didn't have to do that, Abby," Liam says.

"It was no trouble. I just remember being really hungry after school when I was growing up."

"Well, that's very kind of you." Liam puts his hand on Olive's shoulder. "I'll show her where the bathroom is so she can get washed up."

A minute later, she follows Liam into the kitchen. I watch from my position in front of the sink as she slides into the chair in front of the fruit plate. "Do you like camembert and crackers?" I ask.

She stares at it blankly. "I don't know."

I see Liam eying the plate and the two of them exchanging a look. I may have overshot the whole snack thing. Perhaps peanut butter and jelly would have been better. "I have orange juice, water, milk, or Guinness. What would you like?"

She gives me a surprised look, then seems to understand that I was joking and smiles. "Milk, please."

Liam watches her for a moment, then seems to decide she'll be all right with me. "I'm going to be up on the roof if you need anything. Just call from down here though. I don't want you on the ladder."

"Okay, Dad."

"And remember what I told you on the way here. Abby is a very busy person, so you'll need to sit quietly and color so she can get her work done."

"I remember," she says, glancing at me nervously.

Guilt tugs at my chest for reasons I don't understand. "I have a bit of time this afternoon, so why don't I hang out with you a bit, since it's a new place for you?"

"Okay."

I smile reassuringly at Liam as I cross the room with a glass of milk. I'm too busy feeling smug about how naturally good I am with children to watch where I'm going. This results in me stubbing my toe on the table leg which causes the cold milk to splash all over my gray T-shirt, soaking me in the process. I follow it up with, "Oh, shit on a stick!" for good measure.

Olive's eyes grow wide, and she erupts in a fit of giggles behind both hands.

"Oh, sorry! I shouldn't have said that. I meant crap on a stick." My face grows hot and I look at Liam. "That's not much better, is it? Now you're going to think I'm a bad influence. Which, to be honest, I probably am."

Liam's trying not to laugh as he stares at me.

"Crap on a stick," Olive says, then bursts out laughing again. What a cute sound. I think I could listen to it for days. Her laughing, I mean. Not her saying 'crap.'

"All right, Olive. Mind your manners." He gives her a stern dad look, but I can see by her response that she's not going to stop being amused by the clumsy American lady.

"Okay, let's try this again." I walk back to the fridge to retrieve more milk. This time, I make it to the table without incident. I hand her the glass and sit down across from her. "I probably should change, but I'm covered with dirt from the garden anyway, so what's a little milk?"

She quietly munches on her snack, careful not to touch the camembert. I sip my tea and watch her. A shell necklace catches my eye. It looks like something from a booth at a music festival or a farmer's market. The shell is white with light purple swirls and is attached to a braided hemp string.

"I like your necklace. It's very beautiful."

Olive smiles and touches the shell with one hand. "It belonged to a mermaid." She says it like she's telling me the greatest secret ever told.

"Really?" I hope she can't tell that I have an urge to laugh.

She nods. "Yes. My dad found it on the shore up on Seal Island. That's where all the mermaids on the hot days, so it must have belonged to one of them."

She's so sincere that if I didn't know better, I'd grab my phone and Google it. "Are you serious?"

"Completely." Her eyes are wide open behind the thick lenses. "Mercedes at school says there's no such thing as mermaids, but she's doesn't know anything. She didn't even know that if you mix blue and red, it makes purple."

"Oh, well, then ..." I offer, as though she has just provided ironclad proof.

She gives me a knowing look, and we're immediately co-conspirators.

"How old are you, Olive?"

"Seven and three quarters."

Her answer instantly reminds me of how badly I wanted to grow up when I was her age. "So you're basically eight already."

She nods, and the grin she gives me shows that she's happy I get how important those extra months are.

"What grade are you in?"

"Grade three."

"How do you like school?" *How many boring questions can I ask in a row?*

"I like it all right," she shrugs.

"What's your favorite subject?" *Apparently quite a few.*

"Art class. Oh, but I also *adore* science." She selects a cracker and bites the tiniest bit off the corner.

"I liked those classes too." I look out the window for a minute. I have no idea what else to say to her. "Do you play any sports?"

"Not really."

"Me neither." I stare at her for a moment. "Grown-ups ask the worst questions, don't we?"

She nods at this universal truth, and we both laugh together at the acknowledgment of it.

I imitate myself. "What grade are you in? How old are you? Do you like school?"

She seems to like this and is now covering her mouth with one hand while she giggles away. "You're funny."

I blush a little, surprised by how good it feels to be on the receiving end of this small compliment.

"Would you like to meet my cat, Walt Whitman?"

She nods, her eyes lighting up.

I gesture for her to come stand by me, then wait while she slides off the kitchen chair. I crouch down near the end of the table and point, lowering my voice. "He's hiding on that chair."

She crouches too, then whispers, "Is he scared?"

"Maybe. He's never met a child before."

"Never in his whole life?" she asks, clearly shocked by this revelation.

"Not even one time."

Tilting her head so they can see each other, Olive uses a gentle voice. "Hi Walt. I'm Olive Wright and I'm what you call a child. Some kids—oh, that's another word for child—some of us are really loud and rough, mostly boys, but not me. If you want to play with me, I'll be very careful, and I promise I won't touch your eyes."

Looking up at me, she says, "My grandma's neighbor has a cat, Pickles, and one time my cousin poked him right in the eye with a stick. And Pickles didn't like that one bit."

"I would guess not."

"My cousin's a goofball." She looks back at Walt. "Will he come out and play?"

"Tell you what, if we get him some treats and a couple of toys, he may just decide he's not scared anymore."

Olive stands and gives me a confident smile. "That would totally work on me."

"Me too. Except with beer and Cheetos."

CHAPTER SIXTEEN

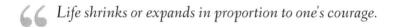 *Life shrinks or expands in proportion to one's courage.*

~ Anais Nin

Who knew I would like kids? Well, *one* anyway. Olive has come over four times now, and as far as I can tell, she's nearly as good as a cat. She expects almost nothing from me, doesn't poke her cute little nose in my business, and she's actually kind of fun. Even Walt has taken to her and seems to have an almost dog-like manner when she's around—wanting to play from the moment she arrives until they leave. When it comes to holding a feather stick toy for him, she has a much longer attention span than I do. She also bounces it at just the right ratio of challenging-to-satisfying to keep him interested.

And I shouldn't admit this because it sounds pathetic, but she's quite good for my ego. She laughs at all my jokes, and yesterday she said I have "beautiful smooth brown hair like a princess." She also asked me if I had fake eyelashes, which I don't, obviously, because that sort of maintenance is *way* too much effort for me. But apparently, I don't need them anyway because I already look like I have lash extensions. Well, according to a seven-year-old.

So, when Liam showed up this morning and told me he found a new sitter, and that today would be the last day I'd "have her underfoot," I felt surprisingly disappointed. I should be thrilled since it's one less person around, but instead, I'm kind of mopey. Not for my sake as much as for Walt's. He's going to miss her.

There's a terrifying bang on the roof and I flinch just as I'm topping up my coffee. I spill some on the counter, then glare up at the ceiling. It's the third day that Liam and Colton have been working up there, and I have to say, I'm at the point where I'd gladly just throw a tarp over the house permanently to avoid all this racket. It's been the worst part of the renovation so far because you can't get away from the sound. Yesterday, I worked on a flowerbed in the farthest corner of the backyard (to avoid falling nails and shingles), but it's even louder out there.

Finally, it's three o'clock, and Liam leaves to pick up Olive. I take my coffee and go to my office in case inspiration hits, then busy myself checking my email and seeing how many minutes I can go without glancing at the clock. So far, my longest run is two minutes.

When they finally return, I go outside into the bright sun to greet them. Colton, who has been lying in the shade of a maple tree with his headphones on and his eyes closed, sits up when the truck pulls into the yard. He takes off his headphones and hangs them around his neck.

Olive gets out of the truck, her head hanging down as she pulls her backpack onto her shoulders. Her feet shuffle as she walks toward me.

"Hey, Olive!" I say. "You okay?"

She shrugs and nods a few times without making eye contact. I glance at Liam. He waves his hand as though saying everything's fine, then lowers his voice. "She's a little sad that I found a new sitter."

Oh, well that is just heartbreaking.

"She's gotten really attached to Walt," Liam says.

135

"And Abby!" Olive spits out, using the sharpest tone I've heard from her.

I glance at Colton, who looks as though he's as surprised as I am to see an angry Olive.

I stand by, feeling helpless as she trudges past me and through the open front door. "Hi, Abby."

Turning to Liam, I wince, but he shakes his head. "She'll be fine."

Then he tells Colton he'll be right out. Once the three of us are inside, Olive lets her backpack slide off her skinny shoulders and drop to the floor.

"Oh, come on now, Olive. Chin up. The Wrights aren't pouters. We make the best of even the worst situation."

She gives him a look that is most definitely a preview to her teenage years. "I just don't understand why I can't keep coming here."

"Remember, I told you this would only be for a few days?" Liam asks, sounding slightly exasperated. He gets no response because Walt has chosen this moment to trot over to his daughter and rub against her leg.

Liam continues. "You're going to love it at the O'Brien's house. She has two other kids from your school who go there. Plus, Mrs. O'Brien bakes her own bread."

Olive sinks to her knees in a way that is so dramatic, I almost want to laugh. She rubs her face against Walt's head. "You mean Mrs. No Brien?"

"What? Who calls her that?"

"Seth in grade four goes to her house after school. He told me Mrs. *No Brien* says no to everything and that the bread she bakes isn't for the kids she babysits. It's for her and her fat husband."

"Olive! I'm shocked at you," Liam says, raising his voice.

"What? I'm just repeating what Seth said."

"Well, don't repeat things that ... aren't worth repeating."

Walt has curled up on her lap now, right on the entryway floor, and starts purring, oblivious of the building conflict.

"They don't even have a cat," Olive says. "And you can't get to the lake from their house!"

Liam sighs and shakes his head. "We'll talk about this later. I have to get back on the roof."

With that, he walks out the front door. A minute later, the thumping starts up again.

"Can I get you a snack?" I ask Olive.

"No, thank you. I'm too sad to eat," she says.

And I don't know if I'm just a total sucker, but I believe her.

I stand and watch her scratching Walt behind his ears with both of her little hands. His eyes are closed and he's clearly in cat heaven. A loud bang shakes the house and Walt darts off her lap and under my new armchair, leaving Olive with her arms stretched out and empty.

I'm suddenly desperate to fix things for her. "Do you think your dad would mind if we go for a walk? I can't take another minute of that awful racket. Plus, I haven't tried the ice cream at the Eighty-One Flavors Shack down on the beach."

She springs up onto her feet, a wide grin spread across her face. "He'll definitely say yes."

A few minutes later, we've obtained permission from Liam and are on our way through the backyard to the beach. Olive skips ahead of me, revived by the thought of a bubble gum ice cream cone. We're almost out of the yard when Liam hollers, "Olive! You stay away from the cliffs!"

She spins around and shouts, "Okay, Dad!"

"I'm serious, Olive. If you fall in, I won't be there to fish you out."

"I know!" she calls, then she reaches for my hand as we continue on down the dirt path to the beachfront.

I feel a bit awkward and don't quite know how tightly to hold on, but she grips hard enough for both of us. "You'd save me, wouldn't you, Abby? If I fell in?"

I make a little clicking sound with my tongue. "Don't think so, kiddo. I'm not exactly hero material. I'm also not exactly a strong swimmer."

She looks up at me with her face scrunched up. "What? I thought you had to learn to swim before you could be a grown-up."

"Who said I'm a grown-up?"

She purses her lips together and stares at me over her glasses.

"All right, fine. I do know how to swim. But it's been about a hundred years since I've done it," I say, giving her hand a light squeeze. "So let's promise each other to steer clear of the cliffs, okay?"

"Okay. That's not where you find the mermaid tears anyway."

"Mermaid tears?"

"Yup, they're on the sand part of the beach. Not the rocky part." She points farther inland, away from where Bras d'Or Lake meets the Atlantic. "Can we go there after we get our ice cream? I want to see if my mom left me some of her tears today."

"Is that something she does often?" I ask, wondering if Liam would mind me entertaining this notion.

Olive nods. "Uh-huh. All the time. 'Cept in the winter because it's too cold, so all the merfolks have to stay down at the deep part of the lake. Otherwise, their fins would freeze off."

"Oh, I didn't know that."

"It's true," she says. "Hey! I bet your husband left you some too."

Her words are jarring to me and, although it's against my better judgment, part of me needs to find out more. "Were all the mermaids humans before?"

"Yup. Well, they're not *all* mermaids. Some are mermen," she says, skipping while she holds my hand.

"Oh, I see."

"That's why they leave their tears on the shore—so the humans they love know they're thinking of them."

I will not cry. This is all just nonsense.

"Oh," Olive says, her eyes lighting up. "If you see a very beautiful mermaid with a big floppy ponytail and a baby boy, that's my mom and my brother Malcolm. Hey, I wonder if they know your husband? I bet they do. What was his name?"

"Isaac," I say, my voice wavering.

Olive looks up at me. "Don't worry, Abby. He's okay. They're all

138

happy down there under the water. It's the most wonderful place ever. No one has to go to school or work, and there's the most beautiful music because lots of them play harps and fiddles, and they all sing. And they dance, except it's so much better than our dancing because they can twirl so fast without getting dizzy." She lets go of my hand and twirls around with her arms stretched out to the side. "Isaac is probably dancing right now."

I press my lips together as hard as I can, but there's no stopping it. My eyes sting and my vision blurs. His face appears in my mind's eye—happy and young and free. A sudden sense of desperation comes over me. I need this to be true.

She stops twirling and puts her hand on my forearm. "Are you crying?"

"No, no," I say, faking a smile. "I just ... have allergies."

"Oh yeah," she says, "My dad gets those sometimes too when he's sad."

It's evening now and I'm sitting outside at my new wrought-iron table sipping some chilled chardonnay. After Olive and Liam left today, I needed to get out of the house for a while, so I went for a drive to the liquor store. The table was waiting for me in front of McDavid's Hardware with a thirty percent off sign on top of it. So I made a quick U-turn and an impulse buy to make me feel better.

The wine is kicking in as the last of the oranges and pinks disappear into the water, and the stars are lit one by one. A white salad plate sits in the center of the table. It has a handful of mermaid tears on it—or, as people who aren't Olive call them, sea glass. Most of the pieces we found this afternoon are brown, a few are green, but there is one tiny blue one that catches my eye. Olive is sure it belongs to Malcolm because only the youngest merfolk cry blue tears. I pluck it off the plate, then hold the round, pleasing object in my palm.

I know it's nothing more than a shard of a broken bottle, but somehow it seems like much more. I can see why Olive believes what she does. It seems almost magical that only time and the tide are required to smooth away all the sharp edges so we can safely hold broken glass in our hands. Maybe grief can be buffed in the same way, until our memories can't hurt us anymore.

Without thinking, I pick up my phone and text Liam.

Hey, can you back out on Mrs. No Brien? Walt's really choked up that Olive won't be coming over anymore.

A minute later, my phone rings. "Hello, Abby's Babysitting Service, where bread isn't just for fat grown-ups. Abby speaking."

"Abby, I know Olive was pulling out all the stops today," Liam says in a quiet tone, "But I promise you she'll be fine at the O'Brien's. They're nice people despite what that boy said."

"Yeah, but Walt just won't stop giving me the huge sad eyes. I can't take it anymore," I say. "What if it's a business proposition? You take babysitting fees off my bill? At least then I'll be making some money for a change."

"You *do* realize what happens at the end of the month? Summer holidays. That means all day, five days a week for the entire summer. That's a lot of days."

I hear her voice in the background and it tugs at my cold heart.

Liam's voice sounds far away when he says, "I'll be right back inside. You get on with your reading." Then he comes back to me. "It's over *two months*."

"I know how long summer holidays are. Please? I want to do this."

He sighs, so I keep going. "Come on, you and I both know that No Brien hordes all the homemade bread. What kind of sadist does that?"

That finally breaks him because he starts to laugh. "And you're sure about this?"

"Am I ever *not* sure?"

"Right. I keep forgetting." He pauses, then says, "All right, then."

"Really?" I ask, feeling almost giddy.

"Sure."

"Walt will be thrilled."

CHAPTER SEVENTEEN

Now that it's almost July, instead of *Bachelor* Tuesday, Lauren and I have *Pride and Prejudice* Wednesdays. PBS is showing the entire BBC mini-series, one hour at a time, over the next six weeks. We're getting caught up before the show starts and I've just been telling her about my new side hustle.

"So, let me get this straight. You're now babysitting your contractor's kids for him?" Lauren asks.

"Kid. Singular."

"And this doesn't seem odd to you?" she says. "Your contractor brings his child to the work-site and leaves you to deal with her."

"She's actually a cool little thing. Plus, I'm getting paid, so ..."

"But, have you forgotten you don't like kids?"

"That's not true. I like my niece and nephews."

"You mean the ones you once referred to as the tyrants of Portland?"

"Okay, they're a little wild for me, but Olive is ... more like a tiny grown-up. She likes to draw and color, and she has surprisingly good taste in music. She's a huge Beatles fan. In fact, she knows almost every word on The White Album."

"But you don't like The Beatles."

"I do, actually. I forgot about them after college, but now that I've heard them again, I'm right back into their music." I pour some salt and pepper chips into a bowl and walk into my living room. "In other news, I can officially watch Mr. Darcy on my television in my living room, which is now fully carpeted and furnished with a sleek but oh-so-comfy couch, armchair, and coffee table."

"Sweet. Send pics," she says. "Now, back to you, your hot contractor, and his adorable daughter."

"I never said he was hot."

"You never said he wasn't, so I filled in the blank on that one."

I laugh. "And, how exactly would you come to that conclusion? Maybe he's hideous and I just didn't want to be cruel."

"Is he?"

"No."

"I know. I could tell the first time you mentioned him. You tried to sound overly disinterested but there was this almost giddy quality to your voice that is a dead giveaway."

"I have never sounded giddy in my entire adult life," I say, indignation rising in my chest.

"Umm, yeah, Angelo from the art department?"

"Okay, Angelo is a very special case. Even Isaac was giddy when he met him. With that accent and the muscles and the fitted dress shirts and the whole hand-kissing thing? He's like a walking pheromone factory. It's ridiculous."

"Exactly. And you get that same tone when you start with the

'Liam said the funniest thing today,' or 'I was having the worst morning, and Liam just swooped in and fixed it.'"

"You are dead wrong. I've only talked about him because he's been in my space all day long for months. Nothing is going to happen between us. We're just friends, if that. It's mainly a business thing."

"The lady doth protest too much, methinks."

"Seriously, quoting Shakespeare to make your point? You're grasping and you know it."

"It's okay to like him, Abby. Let yourself have some fun for once."

"Well, Liam and I are not about to have that kind of fun. He's still in love with his wife, and my heart will always belong to Isaac. End of story." Before she can continue badgering me, I say, "Show's starting."

An hour later, I shut the TV off and yawn, then notice the green stains on my fingers. Olive and I made playdough, which I almost think I enjoyed more than she did. Lauren is updating me on another writer of hers who's been going all man-diva on her lately. As I listen, I pick at the green cuticle on my thumb, finding it hard to believe the different ways I'm filling up my time these days.

"... Drew thinks I should fire him, but I don't know. I'd feel so bad."

"I don't know how you do what you do. Most writers are slightly to moderately insane."

She sighs. "Some more than others. Speaking of crazy authors, how's your big comeback novel coming along?"

Urgh. I was hoping to avoid this. "Good. Slow. I mean, it's hard with the renos going on around me and the massive amount of yard work to get done before winter, but it's starting to come."

"Really? That's great!" She sounds excited. Shit.

"Mmm-hmm, it feels great."

Walt, who's been sleeping for the last hour, sits up on the bed and stares at me, then shakes his head, almost as if he's disgusted by the lies coming out of his food source's mouth.

"What are you working on?"

"It's really in the first stages, so I'm not ready to talk about it just yet." Oh, the guilt. Tell her the truth, Abby. She's your best friend. But she's also your agent.

"Well, that's just excellent." Her voice brightens. "I cannot tell you how thrilled I am to hear that."

"Yup. The words have been pouring out." How far can I stretch the truth? Quite far it seems ...

"Great! Just great. When you're ready, I'm always around to talk plots or give feedback, or whatever you need."

"I know. I'll definitely take you up on that when I get stuck." I wince at the hollow sound in my voice and pray she doesn't notice.

"Listen, Abby, I just wanted to say that I was wrong about your move. It was clearly the right choice for you. Every time we talk, you sound better. More like yourself."

"I feel better." That part, at least, is true.

"It's such a relief, honestly. You've given yourself a fresh start. You're gardening and writing and exploring." She sighs happily. "I mean, I still wish you were doing all those things about fifteen hours closer to me. I miss you every day, but I'm just so happy you're doing any of those things at all. I'm proud of you."

"Aww, thanks, Mom."

"Take the compliment, Abby. I'm serious. You should be proud of what you've done."

Ugh, that makes me feel so much worse. "Okay, Lauren. Thank you."

She yawns loudly. "Okay, that's it for me tonight. I need to get my beauty sleep."

"Me too. Good night, my friend."

"Good night."

I hang up and glance over at Walt, whose eyes follow me as I get up to go brush my teeth. "All right, quit judging me. I wasn't lying. I was just talking about what I am going to do. In the future. Starting tomorrow. Possibly."

The next day, we get an unexpected rainstorm which annoys Liam to no end because he and Colton only have about two more hours of work up on the roof. Colton stayed home and is likely in front of his computer at the moment. Liam's working on the main floor bathroom, which shares a wall with the den. I can tell it's not going well because every few minutes I hear a thump, followed by a loud curse word. I'm actually sitting at my desk, but since the thought of writing an actual book makes me want to throw up, I've undertaken the monumental task of answering the over three-thousand emails that have been patiently waiting for several months now.

I have just written a long reply to a fan who has sent me a very terse note admonishing me for not writing a book about the Duchess of Wiltshire yet. Apparently, I'm ruining her life and letting down readers everywhere, who are *all* going to lose faith in historical romance writers around the globe. My lengthy, rather nasty reply—designed to make her feel roughly the height of an ant—outlined in cruel detail Isaac's illness and last few days, followed by my numb and grief-filled existence since his death.

As soon as I signed it off, I promptly deleted it and started the second draft—a much shorter reply, including a quick acknowledgment of the pain of waiting for something you truly enjoy, a brief overview of what has happened in my life, and a thank you for reading my work and taking the time to reach out. I ended by stating my sincere wish to get back to work soon.

The moment I hit send, I see Liam carrying the old toilet out to the front door. I get up and hurry to open it for him, but he's somehow managed it with one hand by the time I get there. I watch as he lifts it into the bin, then turns to the house, his hair and shirt already drenched.

"Finally got it?"

"Yup. That was one stubborn old bastard of a toilet." He wipes his face with his forearm. "Just like me, I suppose."

"Stubborn bastard, maybe, but you're not old."

He chuckles. "Tell that to Olive. She thinks I'm ancient."

"Yeah, but for kids, anyone over seventeen is basically the same age."

"True."

I return to my desk and look up to find Liam leaning on the doorframe. "How's the writing going?"

"To be honest, I'm not off to a great start."

"Too much racket?"

"No, just my own stuff. I write historical romance. I used to anyway. Now that I know every happily ever after ends in the agonizing pain of losing your will to live, I may have to switch genres."

Liam nods and breathes in a "Yeah, yeah, yeah."

"Which is problematic, because as you pointed out when we first met, I better figure it out soon, or this house will leave me homeless."

He walks over to the bookshelf and pulls one of my novels down. "What's it like to be a writer?"

"I'm not sure anymore. It's been so long since I've done it."

He looks at me from under his eyebrows and takes a more serious tone. "What's it like to be a writer?"

I let out a long sigh. "Oh, it's so many things—terrifying, gratifying, exciting, boring, tedious, and lonely."

"All that in one job, eh?"

"All that in one day."

"Tell me about this book." He holds up *The Duchess and the Doctor*. The cover has a woman in a pale pink silk Mantua gown. "What's it about?"

I hate it when men ask me about my romance novels. They either find the whole genre silly or assume I'm totally oversexed. "That was my third novel. It's about a duchess and a doctor."

"I got that from the title." He comes around to the front of my desk and props himself up on the corner, still holding the book. "What happens with them?"

An uncomfortably warm feeling comes over me, like I'm doing something wrong, even though I haven't done anything. I look down at my laptop to make it go away. "You're welcome to take it home and read it if you're absolutely dying to know."

"Come on, Abigail. You let millions of strangers read your books—"

"Thousands."

"So thousands then. But you *know* me. I'd think you could at least tell me a little about your work." He flips it over and looks at the back. "Is it steamy?"

"Not Fifty Shades-steamy, but I did once get a review from Publisher's Monthly that said I was 'particularly adept at writing love scenes that work.'" *Why did I say that? Stupid, Abby!*

His mouth curves up in an impressed smile. "Particularly adept, eh?"

I purse my lips together. "You see? This is why I don't like talking about my books."

"You're the one who brought up how adept you are. A man can't help but have some follow-up questions on that."

"Yeah, well, trust me, the answers aren't going to be as thrilling as you may think."

His face drops. "No?"

"No." I set my attention to the terrifyingly blank word document labeled 'Write a Book, Stupid.' "I will tell you one thing, though. Romance writers are forever being asked about their sex lives, whereas I doubt anyone ever asks Stephen King how many people he murders when he's not at his desk."

Liam chuckles at the comparison. "It's probably because sex is more fun to talk about."

"I wouldn't know. It's another thing I only have vague memories of."

When I risk a glance at him, his expression is unreadable, but those ridiculously blue eyes of his are intense in their gaze. I clear my throat. "Anyway, I should get back at it."

"I'm going to take you up on your offer, you know."

Dear Lord, what offer does he think I just made?

"I'm going to read your books. All of them."

"Knock yourself out."

The next morning, Liam arrives with *The Duchess and the Doctor* in one hand and his toolbox in the other. He holds up the book, looking defeated.

"Let me guess, too much lace and not enough action. Couldn't get through it?"

"Couldn't put it down. I was up 'til two this morning, reading. I needed to know if they'd end up together."

I fold my lips in between my teeth, trying not to laugh.

"That damned Tabitha. What a wench she turned out to be."

He walks into my den and returns the book to its spot. "This the next one?" He pulls out *The Duke and the Dressmaker* and flips it over.

"It is."

"Oh! It's about her brother?"

"William, yes."

"Good. He needs a happy ending after everything he's been through."

He leaves the room, then pops his head back in and says, "You know, Abby, maybe you should read them again. You might be surprised at how good they are."

With that, he disappears, leaving me to think about what he just said. I stare at the shelf of books, realizing I appreciate what he didn't say so much more. He didn't tell me he knows I have another book in me, or that it would be a shame if I gave it up. He must know that's too much for me to face. But reading one of my books would be like dipping my toe in the shallow end of the pool. Safe and informative. I'll know the temperature before I'm all the way in to my nether regions.

I shut my laptop, walk over to the shelf, take down *The Duchess and the Doctor*, and then sit back down at my desk to read.

CHAPTER EIGHTEEN

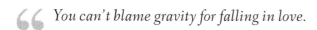 *You can't blame gravity for falling in love.*

~ Albert Einstein

School let out yesterday, which means today is the official start of my first full-time job since I was waiting tables at Gino's on the Lower East Side. Not that I didn't work full-time as a writer, but this job has set hours and real people to whom I'll be accountable. When I was on my second glass of wine the other night, this all seemed like it would be so easy, but now I'm a little worried.

What if Olive's been lulling me into a false sense of security, and she's actually an evil genius who will make my life a living hell? Or what if it turns out too much time together will make us despise each other? Is that even possible? Can you hate a child? Or what if I run out of ideas for fun stuff to do by the end of the day, then we just sit and stare at each other for eight long weeks?

Isaac was wonderful in this type of situation. Not with children—he was actually quite awkward around them—but he was terrific at helping me rein in the runaway horses of anxiety that pound away in my brain from time to time. If he were here, he'd tell me to take it one day at a time. He'd also say I really only have to worry about the next eight hours because tomorrow is the start of a long weekend. This means I'll have three days to scour the Internet for fun activities. Actually four, now that I think about it. Liam and Olive are going to New Brunswick to see his family, so I won't see them until Wednesday morning.

I take a deep breath. Okay, that's fine. I can handle one day, then a four-day break.

My cell phone pings just as I'm hurrying down the stairs to make coffee. It's an email from Lauren titled, *I don't want to rush you, but ...*

My heart sinks as I open it.

Erica and I had a breakfast meeting. She's absolutely thrilled to hear you're writing again! Any idea when you may be ready to share?

The horses in my stomach instantly morph into a guilt bowling ball. I've sat at my computer several times since our call. One evening, I wrote a few paragraphs about a woman who was trapped in a grocery store overnight. But then I promptly realized I had forgotten to eat supper and deleted them. That's it. This weekend is do or die time. Or in my case, write or upset my dearest friend when I admit to being a total liar.

The doorbell rings and when I open it, Olive is there in an Elsa nightgown and flip-flops. Her brown curls are jutting out at all sorts of odd angles and she's sporting a huge grin. The overall effect would be what Lauren and I would call mental-hospital chic, if she were an adult. I almost want to grab my phone so I can send a pic to her, but then I remember. Oh, Lauren, I'm sorry to be the shittiest friend of all time.

Liam stands behind Olive, holding her backpack. "I hope you don't mind me bringing her over in her jammies. I let her stay up late last night, so I had some trouble getting her out of bed. She's got a change of clothes and her brush in her backpack."

"It's all good. We take it pretty casual here at Abby's Babysitting Service." I say, stepping aside to let them in. "Happy first day of summer break."

Olive enters the house like a bunny rabbit with three giant hops. "Thanks, Abby!"

"You look excited."

"Yup, I am. Especially because I'm not stuck at Mrs. No Brien's all summer." She kicks off her flip-flops and drops to all fours, crawling across the rug in the living room to Walt, who immediately switches from fast asleep into play mode.

Looking over at Olive, Liam says, "Mrs. O'Brien. Now, Olive, I want you to run that brush through your hair. And I'll know if you just smooth it down with your hands, so you *really* have to do it this time. There's a change of clothes for you in your bag, as well as a couple of books and your sketching stuff. At some point today, Abby's going to be busy writing or doing whatever else she needs to do, and I expect you to entertain yourself."

"I'll just play with Walt."

Liam follows me into the kitchen, and I pour us each a coffee, trying to keep my distance. The last few days, I've noticed a subtle shift —nothing I can name, but an energy of some sort between us. I'm not sure if it's because we've both been reading my saucy books, or if it's just what happens when two single people of the opposite sex spend too much time together, but something is different, and I want it to go back to the way it was. I think.

And that's the problem.

"Sweet Jesus," Liam says quietly. "You won't believe this."

"What?" I ask, turning to see him looking at his cell phone.

"Remember when I suggested hiring Colton to help with the roof and you said—"

"—What's the worst that could happen?"

Liam nods and comes to stand beside me at the counter, holding his phone so we can both look at it. *Thanks for the e-transfer. I just used it for a one-way ticket to California. I leave tomorrow. Please don't mention it to anyone. I don't want my parents to know yet.*

"Urgh, that's not good," I say.

"Do you think this is my fault?" he asks.

"God, you're Canadian. You gave him a job. You're not responsible for how he spent the money."

He gives me a slightly irritated look, then glances back down at his phone. "Why a one-way ticket?"

"I think because he wants to be a pro gamer. Apparently, there's some mansion down in LA where a bunch of gamers live."

"June is not going to like this," he says, shaking his head.

"Well, at least he didn't fall off the roof and bag himself." The two of us snicker quietly.

We're standing so close together that my shoulder is brushing against his chest. I could move away from him, but I don't. Instead, I tilt my head to get a very close-up look at his eyes. His irises have bright blue rings around them that resemble the calm, warm waters of the Caribbean. They fade to a blue so light, it reminds me of the spot where the water meets the sand in St. Lucia. And the look they are giving me right now is one I haven't seen in a man's eyes in so long, I'd forgotten how it can turn you to butter.

I'm dumbstruck for a moment, and it's almost as though we've both stepped over the line in unison for absolutely no reason at all, and there's a shift in the mood that has taken us both off-guard. I want to ask him if this is because he's been reading my books, but I also don't want either of us to notice what's happening, for fear one of us will come to our senses. Instead, I try to think of something to say, then remember what we were talking about. "Don't tell my parents," I murmur, sounding exactly like a total idiot.

But Liam doesn't seem to mind. In fact, from this proximity, I'm able to watch as his pupils swallow up most of the sea. A slow smile crosses his face and his eyes flick down to my lips and then back up. "What don't you want your parents to know?"

Warmth spreads through me, starting at my chest and working its way up and down, around and out until I'm sure every inch of my skin is flushed. "I meant it like a question. About the guy with the roof and the plane ticket."

Grinning, Liam moves his face closer to mine. "You mean Colton Nickerson?"

I nod slowly. "Yes, him. It can't be all bad, can it? I mean, he's an adult, so it just seems a little pathetic that he's running away from home, instead of just being upfront about it."

"You only think that because you've never seen June when she's mad," he says in a low tone.

I lean toward him, a fraction of an inch closer, so the length of my arm presses up against his hard chest. There are two conversations going on between us now—one using words and one using our bodies. I swallow, then say, "Does she have a really bad temper or something?"

"What are you doing?" Olive asks. Her voice shocks us both out of whatever insane, lusty trance we were in. Liam backs off and I take a giant side-step, hitting my hip on the counter.

"Just having a coffee," Liam says at the same time I say, "Your dad was showing me something on his phone."

She narrows her eyes and tilts her head up at us. "What were you showing her?" she asks, obviously suspicious of us.

"None of your beeswax, young lady. Some things are for kids and other things are for grown-ups." His tone, although not harsh, clearly signals the end of the discussion. He clears his throat and turns to me. "Before I forget, I thought I'd let you know all the shops close on Canada Day. So if you need groceries, you may want to go today."

He's gazing again and I find myself doing it right back. "Good tip, thanks."

"You know who's a good shopper?" He asks, blinking and seeming to transform back into my good buddy, Liam. He points over his shoulder with his thumb at his daughter. "This one here."

"It's true," Olive says, her back straightening. "I like to push the cart and I'm excellent at spotting sale stickers."

Liam cups the side of his mouth with one hand. "And anything with enough sugar to rot all your teeth at once."

He stares at me an instant too long, then sighs and says, "Well, I better get at it."

With that, he makes his way outside, leaving me with a little brunette Elsa while I try to process what the hell just happened. I smile down at her. "So, tell me more about these sugary treats."

It turns out there was no need to worry about how to fill the time while babysitting. In my entire life, I never would have guessed how long it takes to get out the door with an unmotivated child. And I know it's my fault for saying, "No rush, my dear. We've got all day," but dear lord, that girl found a million things to distract herself from getting ready to leave. First, she was sure Walt had lost his favorite catnip toy under the couch, and she didn't want to leave him alone without having it for comfort. This led to a search for a flashlight, followed by hunting down some batteries, then finally, looking for the toy itself—which, it turns out, was *on* the couch the whole time, under a decorative pillow. Then, she wanted to draw a picture of Walt because the light was just right.

Next, it seriously took us over twenty minutes to brush the knots out of her hair. I ended up digging around in my medicine cabinet to find some detangler spray (and I'm definitely not leaving the grocery store without getting her some to take home). By the time she was dressed in her pineapple tank top and cropped jeggings, she was hungry for lunch, which then led to a trip to the bathroom that lasted nearly half an hour. I could hear her telling herself what sounded like a very exciting epic saga while I waited in the kitchen. I'm so desperate for plotlines, I almost put a glass against the door so I could rip off her ideas.

Finally, after two hours, we're about to get in the car. Except now, I hear Nettie's voice. "Hello, ladies," she says, walking up the driveway. (Over the past month, instead of popping by through the trees, she has taken to going the long way, and I'm assuming it's because this is her version of being neighborly without being intrusive.)

When she gets closer, Nettie grins down at Olive. "I baked you some 'happy first day of summer' scones. I thought you and your dad could use them on your big road trip."

Olive rushes over and gives her a big hug. "Thanks so much." She takes the container and tries to peer through the opaque plastic. "Is it the raspberry white chocolate chip ones?"

"What else would I make but my favorite girl's favorite scones?" Nettie answers before shifting her focus to me. "No pressure, but we're having our annual Canada Day barbecue for our guests, friends, and neighbors tomorrow night. After dinner, we'll have a few drinks and watch the fireworks from our back deck."

"That's so kind of you to invite me. I wish I could come," I say, surprised to discover I actually mean it. "But you'll be pleased to know I'm going to spend the entire weekend writing."

"Are you now? Good for you, Abby." Nettie reaches out and gives my elbow a light squeeze. "I knew you could do it."

I smile, even though on the inside, the bowling ball is spinning again.

I sit down at my desk as soon as Liam and Olive go home. Well, not right after—more like after spending way too long thinking about the look on his face when he said goodbye to me. It was that same look he had in the kitchen this morning—like he wanted to throw me over his shoulder and take me upstairs, not that this sort of behavior is acceptable these days (or ever was, for that matter). But just as a way of describing his expression.

I pour myself a glass of wine, get straight to work, and this time, the words come flying out as fast as I can type. I don't notice the sun setting outside, or remember to eat dinner, or see the moon passing the window. I only see what's happening in my mind's eye as a new story comes pouring out of me.

It's not part of my world of duchesses and dukes, but instead, comes forward in time a hundred years in London, England, during the Industrial Revolution. I know I'll need to go back and do a lot of research later, but for now, there's a strong, but secretly lonely, heroine named Beatrice Tisdale, who has fallen from grace. And now, considered unmarriageable, she runs an orphanage on the edge of the city. Our hero is Ian McIntyre, a carpenter who has a shop near the orphanage, who comes to her aid when a fire ravages the old building.

I don't think, don't worry, don't second-guess. Only type one word, quickly followed by another. At some point, long after bedtime, Walt walks across my desk and stops in front of me, flicking his tail and staring at me.

I crane my neck to see the screen over him. "Just a few more minutes, okay?"

A few more minutes turn into hours. Walt's long given up on me by the time I look up from the screen again. I stretch my hands, roll my neck, and then get right back to work, euphoric in my pursuit. The sky is light by the time I stop. I let out a long, satisfied sigh. I'm beyond exhausted as I drag myself up the stairs, but I am happy in a way that I haven't been in a long time. When I get to my bedroom, I see Walt curled up on a pillow.

I collapse into bed without bothering to take my clothes off. "I did it. I finally did it."

The next day, I have eggs sunny side up, toast, and an entire pint of raspberries to fill my ravenous appetite, then go straight back to my desk. I'm there all day and late into the evening, with passing thoughts of where those astronauts buy space diapers. Finally, when my fingers are too sore to continue, I quit. I make myself some macaroni from a box, crack open a beer, then go sit on my deck to eat my dinner directly from the pot.

I can hear people laughing and chatting in Peter and Nettie's backyard. I can imagine they've got trays of sweet and savory food set out for their guests, and plenty of chairs in case anyone else stops by. I can hear the crackle of a fire and can see a hint of the flames through the trees.

Part of me wants to wander over to join in the fun and see if they've got some lemon tarts left, but I won't. I don't need people the way some do. I'm happy here at my table with Walt asleep under my chair. I'm reveling in eating macaroni straight from the pot. I can open a second beer, or even a third, with no one here to judge me but myself.

I'm exhausted but feel better than I have in years. I finally believe I'm a writer again. I wish I could phone Lauren and share my exciting news, but I obviously can't do that without admitting the truth. And today is too happy a day to disappoint my best friend. I will do it, but not right now.

I consider calling Liam to tell him he'll have another book to read soon, but he's on holiday and I don't want to disturb him. Besides, it would be a little odd to call my contractor because I have exciting news. What sort of signal would that send to him? Or to me, for that matter ...

I've been doing my best to forget what happened yesterday morning in the kitchen—the gazing and the chemistry and the wanting to kiss him. Those thoughts and feelings do not belong in my brain, or in any other part of me. I do not gaze longingly at men. I do not speak in a breathy tone or bat my eyelashes or wonder what it would feel like to ... do anything I'm not going to do.

I avoid all of that because I'm one of the few enlightened people who know the truth. Hormones and ancient biological urges ruin your life. I know this by heart, and because I do, I'll distract myself from all of it until a certain rugged, handsome guy finishes doing a little of this and a lot of that around here. Then, the worst will be over, and I can sit by and let time turn us into little more than acquaintances. And when that happens, I'll be safe again.

For now, though, I'll use my work to keep my mind occupied. Beatrice can be the one with the lusty longings. She can wander through the meadow, letting her fingertips touch the tall grasses while she imagines what it would feel like if Ian finally kissed her. Yes, that is the smartest way I can handle this whole mess.

A bang thunders across the water and through the air, then the sky is lit up as the first of the fireworks go off. In the distance, I hear 'oohs' and 'aahs,' and they make me wish Isaac was sitting here next to me, taking it all in. A chill runs through me and I wrap my arms across my chest, not wanting to go inside for my sweater. This is one of those moments when I'd ask him to go, and he'd pretend to be annoyed (or maybe he really would be) but he'd go anyway, returning with my sweater and another drink for each of us.

I'm suddenly bored of the fireworks, so I get up, gather my things, and go inside. Some things just aren't the same when you're alone. And those things must be avoided.

CHAPTER NINETEEN

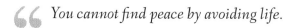 *You cannot find peace by avoiding life.*

~ Virginia Woolfe

Liam and Olive come by first thing on Wednesday morning. She's in a narwhal short-and-tee sleep set, and looks like she's just been on the seven-year-old's equivalent of a bender, sunglasses and all. She walks in the door, slips her bare feet out of her flip-flops, then makes a beeline for the couch. "Hey Abby, I am *wiped*. Those boys are insane. I'm so glad they don't live closer."

Liam rolls his eyes at me. "She means her cousins. They're good kids. There's just a lot of them."

Walt springs up onto the cushion beside Olive, then bats at her hand with his paw. Olive pets him while she also lifts her head and looks at me. "Believe me, four boys is about four too many."

I do my best to stifle a laugh while Liam grimaces. "She got that line from my mother." Raising his voice so it reaches his intended target, he adds, "It wasn't very nice when Gran said it, and it's still not nice now."

Olive holds up one hand. "Can you lower your voice, Liam? I have a splitting headache."

I laugh silently, my entire body shaking.

Liam, however, is not amused. "It's *Dad* to you, young lady. And that'll be enough sass for one lifetime, thank you very much. And get those sunglasses off. You're not Angelina Jolie."

"Who's that? Is she on Insta?" Olive asks, flipping her sunglass clips up.

Liam sighs and shakes his head. "My sister's eldest is a thirteen-year-old girl. You can see she's had quite an impact on her cousin."

"Yes, I can."

He looks at me with dead eyes and mutters, "Is it September yet?"

"Not quite."

"All right, I better get to work. Good luck," he says, before disappearing out to the garage.

As soon as he's gone, I walk over to the couch. "Did you eat breakfast already or should I make you something?"

"No breakfast for me. I'm intermediate fasting," she says. "Thanks though, hon."

"Do you mean intermittent fasting?"

"Right. That's the one," she says, looking a little sheepish.

"Hmph. Too bad you're fasting because I was going to make some special Independence Day pancakes."

She perks up, but then quickly recovers, remembering she's too cool for pancakes.

"You probably already know about Independence Day," I say.

"I think so, but why don't you tell me, anyway."

"It's like Canada Day but for the United States."

"Oh, lovely!" she says.

"I'm kind of missing home today and was hoping you'd help me celebrate."

"Okay," she answers, suddenly seeming very much like the Olive that left here on Friday. "What kind of pancakes?"

"Buttermilk with blueberries and cream." I hold out my hand and she takes it, then I help pull her up.

"I suppose I can fast another day."

As we make our way to the kitchen, I say, "Yeah, or not, because you're basically perfect the way you are."

By late morning, Olive is Olive again. Gone is the tiny teenager, and in her place is the little artist I've come to know and like. She's dressed now in some bright blue shorts and a unicorn T-shirt, and is currently sitting on a blanket under the oak tree, drawing in her sketchbook. I am outside, trimming a hedge (and by trimming, I mean doing a total hatchet job because I have no idea what I'm doing). I pause to adjust the Velcro closure of my glove and see Walt, who is sitting alone, meowing at her and looking forlorn.

Olive looks up at him and her face crumples. "Poor boy. Maybe I should go sit with him."

"Your dad said he wanted you to stay in the shade for a while. Besides, maybe Walt will finally get sick of sitting there alone and he'll come to you."

"I hope so because he's breaking my freaking heart."

Oh, I see there are still remnants of her cousin left. "What are you drawing?"

She smiles, then quickly stands and hurries over to me with her sketchbook. "These are the mermaids that live in the lake. See?"

I tug my gardening gloves off my hands and take the pad from her. "Oh, wow. This is excellent. Incredibly detailed."

"Thanks. This one is Arietta. She's a princess, and these are her sisters. There are seven of them. This little one is my baby brother, Malcolm, and that's my mom holding him."

161

I look at the largest mermaid on the page. She has the floppy pony-tail that Olive told me about. "She reminds me of you, very beautiful."

She smiles, looking slightly embarrassed. "Thanks, Abby."

"And this is Isaac," she says pointing to a merman with glasses and short, gray hair. "I hope you don't mind, I copied that from the photo in your office."

I swallow my emotions. "I don't mind a bit. It looks just like him."

She points to three people standing on the shore on the far right of the picture. "That's you, me, and my dad. We're saying hello to the merfolk."

I stare at her version of me. One of my arms is much longer than the other one, but otherwise, she's managed to capture me. She's in between Liam and me, and we're each holding one of her hands. I look closer at Liam. He has blue eyes but his head is perfectly round and white. "Did you forget to add your dad's hair?"

Shaking her head, she says, "That was when he was bald. I drew him that way because I like the feel of his smooth head."

"Bald? Really? You mean he shaved his head?"

She shrugs. "I guess so."

"But why? He has such nice thick hair."

Olive looks up at me, blinking quickly in a surprisingly astute way. "Do you like my dad, like a boyfriend?"

"No," I say, shaking my head while my face heats up. "I ... we're ... no. He's my good friend. You know what? You should get out of the sun now."

She giggles, then takes off back over to the tree and settles herself so she's lying on her stomach. Walt meows at her and Olive glances up from her book. "Well, come on, you silly boy. I promise nothing bad will happen."

Walt stops his complaining and stares at her as though trying to decide. I put down the hedge trimmer and watch him as he touches the grass with one paw, then retracts it.

"Come on, Walt. It's all right." Olive sits up and pats the blanket with her hand. "When you want something, you can't just sit there and cry about it. You have to be brave."

Hmm, I wonder where she's heard that before?

Walt presses his paw to the grass again. When nothing bad happens, he takes one step forward.

"You can do this." She smiles at him.

Walt takes three more steps. Now all four feet are firmly in the grass. He freezes in place, then decides to make a break for it and darts toward her. When he reaches the blanket, he launches himself onto the refuge of her lap.

I cheer and so does Olive, and for some dumb reason, I have tears in my eyes.

"He did it!" She grins at me.

I nod and find my voice. "He did, and on Independence Day, too. What a perfect day for an American cat to do something brave."

I walk over and give him a scratch on his head. "Well done, Mr. Whitman. And well done, Ms. Wright. I don't think he would have tried if he didn't have you cheering him on."

Olive beams.

And somehow the sight of my cat making a leap like that gives me the courage to do the same. I'm not sure what I'll do, but I feel ready to take the next risk that comes my way.

CHAPTER TWENTY

> *Courage doesn't happen when you have all the answers. It happens when you are ready to face the questions you have been avoiding your whole life.*

~ Shannon L. Alder

I've been having such a busy and emotionally draining day, I completely forgot it's *Pride and Prejudice* Wednesday. At a quarter to eight, I get a text from Lauren. *Ready?*

I stare at the word 'ready' for a moment. For a small word, it can be the cause of irreversible change. In this case, I know it means I have to fess up and tell Lauren that I've been a very bad friend lately.

I pick up my phone and text back: *Yes.*

Then, I close one eye, using the other to watch for her name to appear on my screen. Shit. There she is. "Hey you, how's July in New York?"

"Oh, you know, horribly humid and filled with sweaty tourists blocking the sidewalks and asking for directions. How's July in 1940 going?"

"Good," I say as my pulse quickens. "Actually, not that good. I have something to tell you and I think it's going to make you happy, then really super pissed at me—which you'll have every right to be."

"Oh," she says, dread filling her voice. "That doesn't sound promising."

"It's not, so let me preface this by saying you are my very best friend in the entire world and I love you no matter what. And I hope you can do the same."

"Abby, you're scaring me," she says.

"I know, I'm scaring me too." I take a deep breath and then let it all spill out. "So the past six days I've been writing a new book. It's not in my regular series, in fact it's set in the 1800s. But I think there's a chance it'll be passably decent when I'm done."

"Okkaay. Do you think I'll be mad you're not working on your Duchess series?"

"You won't believe how tempted I am to say yes to that."

"Woman up, Abby." Lauren's tone is sharp.

"Okay. I think you'll be disappointed in me when you find out I've been lying to you." My throat feels thick. I swallow hard, which doesn't help, then continue, "I've been pretending I was writing, but until this past Friday night, I hadn't written a word."

There's a long pause, and I shut my eyes, knowing what's about to come. She'll ask why I would lie like that, then move on to my lack of faith in her. I'll explain it wasn't about *her*, but my own desire not to disappoint her. She's going to tell me she is disappointed, and where it'll go from there is anybody's guess.

But instead, all she says is, "I know."

"What?" She *knew*? My brain is so far down that other road, it has to slam on the brakes and reverse about thirty seconds.

"Of course I knew you were lying," she says, sounding far too calm.

"Really? Why didn't you call me on it?" I ask, standing and wandering to the living room.

165

"Because you always lie, Abby."

Her words hang between us until I feel my entire body go numb. Only my heart is moving, and it's doing that so fast it feels like it could thump right out onto the floor.

"That's not true," I say doing my best to keep my voice steady.

"I'm afraid it is. You lie all the time," she answers, with no emotion whatsoever. "You've always been the type of person who uses humor to protect yourself, which I used to find endearing, but since Isaac died, I don't think you even know when you're telling the truth or when you're lying. I know this probably hurts to hear, but it needs to be said, and I think you're finally strong enough to hear it."

"What are you talking about? I am a *very honest* person. Sometimes, too honest." I add a frustrated chuckle for good measure. "In fact, I'm so honest, I make people very uncomfortable sometimes."

"Is that what you think?" she says, riding the line of sarcasm. "Allow me to help you understand how other people view your 'honesty.'"

"Are you doing air quotes on the word honesty, right now?"

"Yes, I am. Please don't interrupt me, because I have something you need to hear. and until now, I didn't think you could handle it." She pauses and I do as I'm told, knowing I'm the one who fucked up in the first place. "You spent over a year locked up in your apartment pretending to be totally fine, when in truth, you were so depressed, you couldn't even function. Who did you think you were fooling? Me? Your mom? The delivery guy from A Taste of Curry?"

"Sanjay repeatedly told me I was his most fun customer!"

"But you know what he probably told his wife when he got home each night? 'I delivered dinner to that sad widow again tonight.' And his wife probably said, 'She needs help, not more naan bread.'"

"Why are you being so cruel right now?" Tears cloud my vision, and I lower myself onto the couch.

"Because I've had enough. I'm just tired of it," she says. "You pretend you're so fucking tough that nothing could ever hurt you, when the truth is *everything* does—bad reviews, dirty looks from a stranger, never getting your parents' approval, that time Drew and I went with Erica and Jim to Vegas and you weren't invited. That one *really* upset you. You said you didn't care but, oh my God, it rocked your world to miss out on that trip."

The memory of it stings and I lash out. "Well, can you blame me? You guys just cut us out like we were a couple of tumors on your ass."

"You just made my point for me."

"You're welcome."

Lauren scoffs. "There you go again. That's why I never said anything. It's because you can't help it."

"I can help it. I can. I see what you're saying, and I'll work on it."

"Forgive me if I think you're just saying that to get me to stop, when really you have no intention of changing."

"That's not true, and to prove it, go on. Give me more examples. I can take it."

"Okay." She says it like we're playing a high stakes game of Truth or Dare and she knows she's going to win. "You used to pretend you didn't mind when Isaac would flirt with his students—"

"—he *never* flirted—"

"—spoke too highly of the pretty ones, then. Whatever you want to call it—that thing he did that drove you insane with jealousy but instead of admitting to such a lowly human emotion, you acted like it was fine. And you know where that got you? With a husband who wouldn't shut up about his young, pretty students."

"What the hell, Lauren?" I ask, my voice shaking with indignant anger. "Why are you attacking me like this? And Isaac?"

"I thought you just said you could take it. See? More lies."

Her words are like kicks to my face and I'm torn between not letting her know she's getting to me and fighting back. I shout into the phone. "What do you want from me, Lauren?"

"For *once in your life*, Abby," she yells back. "I want the truth!"

Jesus, she sounds just like Tom Cruise in *A Few Good Men*. I kind of want to make fun of her, but somehow it seems like the wrong move.

Before I can say anything, she says, "And don't you dare do your

Jack Nicholson impression and tell me I can't handle the truth, because I know you, Abby, and I know that's *exactly* what you were about to do."

Fuck me. I was.

"Because that's what you do. You deflect, you joke, and you lie whenever life gets too serious for you."

My stomach hardens and I feel dizzy and nauseous at the same time. "Wow, I don't even know what to say."

"I'm sorry. I know I'm being mean here, but I'm just so done pretending everything is what it isn't," she says with a loud sigh. "Just tell me one thing because I need to know there's a shred of hope here."

"What?"

"Was I right? Were you about to go Jack Nicholson on me?"

"Yeah, I was," I say in a tiny voice.

When she speaks again, her voice wavers. "Tell me something else because I really don't want to give up on you."

"Anything."

"Why can't you be honest with me at least? I'm your *best friend*. I just want you to have a great life, Abby, and I've never hurt you. Not once."

"Well, actually you've been pretty nasty this evening ..."

"Christ almighty," she sighs.

"And also, when you went to Vegas with Erica," I add.

Letting out a long groan, Lauren says, "Abby ..."

"Sorry. Bad habit."

"It's exhausting to be your friend sometimes. Friends are supposed to be honest with each other."

"You're also my agent, Lauren. And it's not necessarily the wisest thing to admit to your agent when you haven't been working."

"See what you did there? You said, 'it's not the wisest thing' when what you really mean to say is that you're scared."

"I'm not—"

"Stop fucking lying to me, Abby. Seriously." Lauren's voice wavers and I know I've pushed her to the edge of our friendship. "If your intention was to apologize for lying, then apologize for lying and stop doing it. Otherwise, let's just carry on like we always have, with you lying and me acting like I don't know."

I press my tongue against my top molars as hard as I can, my nose prickling. Instead of trying to change her mind, I just sit and wipe the stream of tears off my cheeks, feeling shocked, confused, and hurt.

"I'm sorry," Lauren says, her tone gentle now. "I didn't mean to upset you. It's just hard to keep going like we have been."

"Well, you did upset me," I answer, my voice rising two octaves. "How do you think it feels to have your best friend tell you you're some sort of pathological liar? I mean, why are you even my friend then?"

"Because I love you anyway, Abby, which is what friends do. We see each other's flaws, but we love each other anyway."

I let out a couple of sobs, then finally manage to say, "You're so easy to love, Lauren. You're basically perfect. You're smart and sophisticated and tall ... and hard-working and super successful ..."

"Don't change the subject."

"And it's sort of awful to be the one who's a mess all the time. I want to be the one who knows exactly what to say and can pull off a full-length, camel-hair coat."

"What?"

"I want to be the one who has her shit together."

Lauren sniffs and I know she's crying too. "That may be the first honest thing I've heard come out of your mouth since Isaac died."

We both sniffle and I hear Lauren blow her nose. "Actually, this conversation is a relief in a way, because I was starting to give up hope."

I glance at the clock, needing to think of something else before my brain explodes. "It's a little after eight."

"Jane Bennett has probably ridden to Netherfield in the rain already. The dumb twat."

I laugh a little, loving Lauren for trying to make everything okay again. Then, I let out a slow, shaky breath. "I'll understand if you don't want to watch it with me. If I'm being honest, I don't know if I want to watch it with you either."

"In that case, let's do it anyway."

We sit on the line for the next hour, neither of us saying anything. We don't say our favorite lines along with the TV, like we normally do. We don't make fun of Elizabeth's mother. But we don't hang up either. My mind rolls through the last two years of my life as I begin to process Lauren's accusations. When the closing credits roll, I shut off my TV and I can hear that she's done the same. Unable to think of anything intelligent to say, I ask her if she's still there.

"Yes," she says, the hurt between us returning. "Look, you've been through so much. I can't even imagine what it's been like. And I don't want to be hard on you. And I certainly don't want to ruin something we should be celebrating. You're writing again and that's huge and wonderful and shiny, and good for you."

"You're not the one that ruined it."

"How about we call this one a draw?"

"You're too easy on me."

"That's because things are about to get incredibly hard for you. Here's the thing, you've got a choice to make. You can start being honest in your life—and obviously I want you to do that—"

"—I want me to do that, too."

"Good. But, go in knowing that being honest makes you vulnerable, and I know how you feel about being vulnerable. And I also understand why. So, if your honesty tonight turns out to be a one-off, it's okay. I'll understand. I'll be here for you either way."

Tears spring from my eyes and I whisper, "Thanks. Sorry I've been such an ass."

"That's okay. Nobody's perfect, not even me in my camel-hair coat. Just please let me know which way you decide to go because it's only fair."

"Yup, I will. I should let you get some sleep. We've been talking about my shit for years now."

"I'm tired, but I'm not done."

"Thank you," I whisper. Then I say, "Hugs and shit." I don't dare to breathe while I wait for her answer.

"Hugs and shit back."

I let out a sigh of relief, then lower my phone to hang up, but change my mind. "Lauren?"

"Yeah?"

"It's going to be really hard, isn't it? To be honest, I don't know if I can do it."

"That's a little ironic, no?"

I laugh through my tears. "Very."

"You're right. It won't be easy, but it will be so much better for you," she says, and I find myself wishing she were here so I could hug her for real. "There's this whole amazing world waiting for you. You just have to be willing to get real with people and open yourself up to it."

"Do you promise?"

"I do. And I'm really smart, so ..."

Chuckling again, I say, "How's this for honest? I love you, my friend."

"That's a great start. I love you too."

CHAPTER TWENTY-ONE

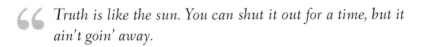 *Truth is like the sun. You can shut it out for a time, but it ain't goin' away.*

~ Elvis Presley

The next morning, I wake to a text from Lauren. *Just checking in to see how you are.*

Raw. Sorry. Ashamed.

I was worried about that. You want to talk?

No, but thank you, my friend. I'm sure you have a client waiting and I need to face myself alone.

Promise you won't stay alone with this too long? And you'll call if you need me, no matter what time of day or night?

Yes to both.

Okay, then. Get on with it. Take a day to say goodbye to that scared liar and usher in a brave new era of Abby.

I laugh, then cry a little, then text her back. *The next time you see me, I'll have a cape and a lasso of truth—but I'll only use it on myself. ;)*

I cannot wait.

Even though it's Thursday, Liam and Olive won't be coming. Liam has to go to Halifax for some kind of appointment, which will take the entire day. Olive is at her grandparents' until tomorrow night. I'm grateful for the time on my own. I need to think and sleep and think some more. I woke up around two o'clock with the entire ugly conversation playing on a loop in my mind.

How did I get to be this old without knowing myself at all? My ability to bullshit everyone, even myself, is almost terrifying. I start the day with a long soak in the bath, then sit at my desk for a while, only to find that I'm too emotionally raw to write the next chapter of my book—Beatrice and Ian's first kiss. After wandering around the house, I go out and pull some weeds in the front flower beds, needing something mindless to do.

I'm not out long before I hear the sound of tires crunching on my driveway. When I look up, I see Colton riding up on his bicycle. I stop what I'm doing and stand.

"Hey, Abby," he says as casually as if he were just here yesterday.

"Hi. I thought you were down in sunny California?"

Shrugging, he says, "Didn't work out. Turns out it was kind of a scam." He stops his bike near me and puts one foot down to balance himself. "Yeah, yeah, yeah, California was a bad idea."

My shoulders drop. "I'm sorry to hear that."

"Not as sorry as I am. All the money I made is gone, plus I owe my parents for my flight home."

"Well, that's shitty," I say.

Colton laughs, looking a little shocked, then his face falls again. "It really is. I thought those guys were my friends, you know? I played with them for like, over a year."

"Do you want to talk about it?"

"Okay," he says, getting off his bike and planting himself on the grass.

I do my best to hide my surprise, then sit down next to him and wait.

"It's just so fucking embarrassing, you know?" he says, then he looks up. "Sorry, I hope you don't mind if I say fuck."

"I said shitty, so ..."

"That's what I thought," he answers. "Anyway, they told me they had one roommate skip out without paying his rent for June, and if I got there fast enough and paid up what he owed, they'd let me stay."

"And in reality, there was no room at the mansion?" I ask, assuming he'll miss the hidden reference.

He gives me a knowing smile. "Yup, call me baby Jesus."

We both laugh for a second, then I say, "People can be the worst, right?"

"Tell me about it," he answers, sounding utterly dejected. Then he tilts his head and says, "Not most people. Just a few here and there. Most people are kind."

Instead of spewing more of my opinions about the human race, I tug at a blade of grass until it comes loose.

"I know you don't really think so, but I do."

"Even after what you just went through?"

Nodding, Colton says, "Yeah. Definitely. I met this lady down there—not like a hot chick or something—like a middle-aged woman—"

"So, like California Abby?"

Colton lets out another laugh. "Sort of. I didn't have the cash to get to the airport, so she gave me a lift. She didn't even want anything in return. I offered to send her money when I got home but she said no."

"Hmm. That *is* nice."

"I find most people are. Anyway, I see you're doing some yard work today?"

"You looking for a job?"

"Yeah, but this time you'd have to pay me yourself because my parents won't do it."

I wince and cover my face with one hand. "Sorry about that. It was too good an offer to pass up. But the money for the roof really did come from me."

"I know."

"How did you figure out what was going on?"

"I'm not blind, and it's not exactly like you and my dad were discreet."

We both start laughing and he says, "He'd literally hand you the money in front of me, then you'd put in your pocket and take it out again, like, not even a second later."

I laugh until my cheeks hurt. "I think somehow we both thought you couldn't see because of the headphones."

Colton nods, still laughing. "Yeah, 'cause that makes sense!"

When we both calm down, I sigh, then pat him on the arm in a motherly way. "I owe you an apology, Colton. That was both dishonest of me and condescending."

"That's okay," he says.

"No, it's not really. We treated you like a child, but you're not one."

"Thanks, I appreciate that." He digs into the large front pocket of his hoodie and pulls out a rolled-up piece of paper. Handing it to me, he says, "Speaking of adulting, I'm actually starting my own yard maintenance service. Mowing, weeding, and landscaping all spring, summer, and fall, then clearing snow in the winter. Now that I've had a taste of freedom ..."

"You'd like to have the whole meal?" I ask.

He gives me a blank look. "I just meant I'd like to get my own place." He rubs the back of his neck. "Meals too, I guess."

I bite the inside of my cheek so I can maintain a serious expression. Then I look over his flyer, noticing a couple of typos but managing to resist the urge to go in search of a red pen. "These look like very reasonable rates. And it's quite a comprehensive service package."

"Yeah," he says, pointing to the monthly service plans at the bottom. "I figured it would be easier for me and for my clients. This way, all you have to do is pick one, then your whole yard takes care of itself and you never have to think of it again. Well, other than paying the bill, of course."

"You have got yourself a client."

"Really?" His eyes light up.

Nodding, I say, "Absolutely. When can you start?"

"If you need me to start today, I could, but my plan was to spend the next couple of days biking around trying to drum up business."

"You should do that, then."

"Should we say Monday? Your grass is getting a little long, so I should definitely come back by then."

"Monday, it is."

After Colton leaves, I get back to pulling weeds while I think about him. He may be young, but in some ways, he's got a lot more wisdom than I do. He's got a plan and he's going for it, even though it means explaining to every person in this entire village what happened in California. He's going to get all the humiliation over with at once and move on with his life, free and clear. What a relief that would be.

For the rest of the day, I add up the many ways I sidestepped embarrassment, and what that has cost me. How many things did I keep from my husband for that reason? Dozens? Hundreds? I never told him I didn't like going to the symphony because I needed him to believe I was every bit as sophisticated as he was. I never admitted to loving Pink or Lady Gaga or Gossip Girls. I never told him I hated scotch—the smell, the taste, and the endless conversations about it.

I let him believe I was someone I'm not and never will be. I tucked away who I was and morphed into the perfect wife—the one I thought he wanted. The sad part is, I never even bothered to ask. I just assumed I knew who he wanted, then went on pretending. I wonder what our marriage would have been, had I told him everything that was in my heart.

Stronger? More fun? Over?

No wonder I never want to fall in love again. Losing your husband isn't the worst part. It's losing yourself first.

CHAPTER TWENTY-TWO

> *Life is a succession of lessons which must be lived to be understood.*

~ Helen Keller

August has arrived, which means it's been a month since Liam and I had our 'moment' in the kitchen. Since then we've both managed to maintain a more appropriate sense of decorum. It's almost like he came to the same conclusion as I did as soon as it was over. Thank God we didn't act on it because that would have been a hot mess of a situation, especially given how tangled up our lives are for now.

Our easy friendship has returned, aided by Olive, who we're both more than happy to focus on. Things are so comfortable that I've accepted an invitation to go out with them for the day on their boat.

They've made it their mission to see a new spot every Saturday this summer, and yesterday, they invited me to join them. We'll head out to the sea and lunch on a tiny uninhabited island. It all sounds so exotic, and I find myself so excited I can't sleep. Instead, I get up ridiculously early to make a picnic lunch and get myself ready to go.

Good thing I'm up early because choosing the right outfit proves difficult. Today, I'm in the mood to be sophisticated Abby—well, as sophisticated as I get. I select a striped boat neck (obviously) with three-quarter-length sleeves, and some capris. I hold the pants in my hand for a moment before I risk trying them on. It's been over a year since I could fit into them, and although I know I've lost some weight after months of cleaning and weeding and babysitting, I'm not confident that it will be enough.

Have courage, I tell myself. Then I laugh because trying on pants isn't exactly a triumph of the human spirit.

When I pull them on, I'm delighted that they make it past my hips. They're a bit too tight, but I fasten the button on the front of the waistband knowing they stretch out while I'm wearing them. I put on some makeup—nothing heavy, just a little mascara and a dab of CC cream with sunscreen in it.

Smiling at the woman in the mirror, I say, "Not horrible, Abby."

I pop on my white Toms because they are the closest thing to boat shoes I own, then hurry out the door.

It takes me exactly six minutes to get to the docks, then another two to find a spot along the road to park. The water gleams in the early morning sun, and I am welcomed by the call of a few seagulls. The ocean has that slightly gray look that will turn to a deep blue once the sun is angled a little higher in the sky.

I load my arms with a bag containing lunch and another containing sunscreen, towels, and my swimsuit. As much as I don't love the idea of wearing it in front of them, I brought it anyway, deciding it's part of the new honest me, because cellulite, while not pretty, is real.

I walk down the sidewalk to the pier marked 'Slips 11–20' and step onto it. It bobs a little. I steady myself as I continue along. Tied to number seventeen is an older, good-sized yacht that Olive has told me is called a motor sailor. When I asked her what that meant, she said, "Well, Abby, you can either sail it or use the motor." I grin at the memory. She can be surprisingly condescending for a not-quite-eight-year-old.

Liam told me that when the boat went up for sale, it was in such rough shape, he got it for a song. But now it sparkles and speaks of the glamour of the 1920s. The mahogany cabin has been polished to a shine, and it bears the name "Sarah's and Olive's" in flowery letters. It tugs at my heart, but I don't have time to feel the full weight of it because Olive is standing on the deck, squealing.

"She's here, Dad! Abby's here!" I'm sure she could wake the whole neighborhood with the news, but she's so cute, I bet no one would even mind.

I wave to her and watch as she climbs down the ladder, her arms and legs a blur. She hops onto the dock and runs to me with her arms out. A few seconds later, Olive crashes into my legs, and I'm on the receiving end of a fierce hug, with her head tucked in just under my chest as she clings to me with abandon.

Was I ever this carefree when I expressed affection? I think I may have been, but somewhere along the way, I learned a self-restraint that somehow seems pointless to me as I take in the glorious feeling of her little arms around me.

She pulls back and takes my hand. "Abby, these are the tomato plants I was telling you about. See? They're nearly ready to eat!"

She directs my attention to a tiny garden wedged into the space directly in front of the boat. Liam has made a yard for her out of faded green wooden planks and some dirt. In addition to the two tomato plants, there are four bright pink geraniums in full bloom and violet wave petunias spilling over the sides.

"This is lovely!" I remark, letting her lead me to the planter.

She points, her voice an excited whisper. "Look. It's my secret fairy garden."

I crouch next to her and peek under one of the geraniums. There is a tiny wooden house with blue shutters and an open yellow door. I turn to her and gasp. "Does a real fairy live here?"

"Yes! Dad says she must have a sweet tooth because I found a candy wrapper in front of the house yesterday!"

"Are you serious?" I do my best to look shocked, and Olive gives me a proud nod.

"Well, this place is a little bit magic," Olive says. "Have you ever seen a fairy?"

"No, I'm afraid not."

"Me neither. They're very tricky, but I will someday," she says with a confident nod.

A shadow falls on the planter, and I look up to see Liam standing above us on the deck of the boat. "Hello, Abby. Welcome!"

I straighten up and give my eyes a moment to adjust to the sight of him. He looks very relaxed in a pair of shorts and a T-shirt instead of his usual work clothes. I can tell by his expression that he is thinking I look different as well, and I find myself hoping he thinks it's a good change. But only because he's a friend, and it's perfectly okay to want to impress our friends.

"Hi, Liam."

"Ready for an adventure?"

"I am. I was honestly so excited that I've been up since five-thirty."

"This one here shares your enthusiasm, I'm afraid. She was up at the crack of dawn."

I pick up the bags, and Olive leads me to the ladder. After I hand everything up to Liam, I climb up, feeling a little awkward, then stand back and watch while Liam and Olive make the final preparations to set off. He's a whir of activity, and Olive seems thrilled to have me see her as his most capable first mate. He calls out for her to check the something and the other thing, which she quickly does, then hollers to him once the job is done. It occurs to me no matter how young we are, we all long to feel needed.

Liam is now behind the large wheel, while Olive plucks a captain's hat off a hook and brings it to him. It has gold braiding circling it and an anchor on the front, above the blue brim. She tells me she bought it for her dad with her own money. I can see how proud she is, and when I glance up at him, he doesn't have even a trace of embarrassment as he dons the white and blue cap.

"Thank you, my love," he says, as he ruffles her hair. "Go get your sunglass clips, okay?"

Olive's shoulders slump a little and Liam gives her a knowing smile. "You were hoping your old dad would forget, weren't you?"

"Nuts," she says, snapping her fingers before disappearing into the cabin.

I take a seat on the bench to the right of the wheel and stare out into the horizon. The sea is calm, and the sun is up enough that the gray is gone from the water.

"Abby, over there." Liam points to the other side of the boat.

I stand in time to see a small pod of what look to be black dolphins making their way along the shore. I shield my eyes with one hand so I can watch them as they cut quickly through the water. The sight is such a delightful surprise that I find myself laughing. "What are they called?"

"Pilot whales. They're looking for breakfast," Liam says. "Probably a nice school of mackerel right around here. Maybe some squid."

They all disappear under the surface, their tails flicking the air as they propel themselves down.

"Looks like they found something."

I glance at Liam as he draws a deep breath and turns the shiny chrome wheel slightly to the left. He's handsome in his cap and sunglasses, looking relaxed and content and somehow younger than when he's working. I notice that he's clean shaven and decide that must be the difference.

He turns to me and smiles. "Glad you decided to join us."

"Me too."

"Olive is certainly taken with you. She talks about you nonstop. 'Abby told me the funniest story today,' or 'Abby had two dogs when she was a girl,' or 'Abby likes blueberries the most out of any berry.' I know more about you than I do myself."

I grin at him. "I really love spending time with her. She has such a special little soul."

"That she does."

"I hope you don't mind me saying, but I think you're doing a wonderful job with her."

Liam narrows his eyes in confusion. "Now, why would I mind you paying me a compliment?"

"I don't know. Because I don't have kids."

"Anyone can tell the difference between a well-behaved child and bratty one." He's quiet for a moment, then he says, "To be honest, parenting is kind of like sailing. You bob along with the waves, hoping you're aiming in the right direction. Except with children, there aren't any checkpoints to follow, so you have to guess and hope you're going the right way."

"Well, from an outsider's perspective, it look like you're right on course. She's a lucky girl to have you for a dad."

He shrugs off my compliment. "I'm the lucky one. She's an easy child to raise."

"She didn't get that way by accident. You had a hand in that." I can tell by his expression that he's about to rebuff the praise again, so I hold up a finger and give him a stern look to stop him. "Ah! Just accept the compliment, Liam."

"Bossy." He says, narrowing his eyes so he looks annoyed. "I don't know why I'm surprised by that, though. I should have figured it out the first time I met you and you bit my head off for trying to sit beside you."

I laugh and feel heat creep up my neck. "Correction, the first time you saw me, I was sitting at the bar with a beer foam moustache."

"Oh, right. I forgot about that." He lets out a loud laugh. "The best part was when you swiveled the stool so hard, you snapped back like a rubber band and planted your hand in your dessert."

We're still laughing when the door slides open, and Olive appears, looking frustrated. "Dad, I can't find my sunglass clips."

His expression changes from jovial to stern in an instant. "That's because you left them by your fairy garden last night, so I hid them in the bread bin."

"Dad!"

"Don't you 'Dad' me, young lady. You need to learn to take better care of your things." He softens his expression to let her off the hook. "Now, go get them, and I'll let you be captain for a bit."

———

Two hours later, we find a place along the rocky shore of a tiny island to anchor the boat. It's small enough to see the width of it without turning my head. Liam stands knee-deep in the water, and we hand him what we'll need—folding beach chairs, a blanket, the food, and some drinks. Olive slings on her backpack, telling me it's her explorer's bag. She has been on the lookout for mermaids since we left the pier, and she's certain that even if we don't see any actual merfolk today, we will most definitely find evidence of them.

She's all business as she tallies the contents of the bag for me. "I've got binoculars, a magnifying glass, specimen jars, and a notepad and pencils to record my findings."

"Impressive. I had no idea you were a serious scientist on the weekends."

She gives a slight nod at the acknowledgment. "Well, it's true, Abby. I am a very serious scientist."

She climbs down the ladder while Liam and I exchange 'my God, wasn't that adorable' grins. A moment later, it's my turn. I take off my shoes, as my hosts have done, and toss them onto the beach. I then make my way down the ladder.

Liam holds out his hand to help me navigate the small leap from the boat to the beach. His palm is rough and warm against mine, and I find myself wanting to continue holding it after I've landed safely on the shore. Instead, I let it go quickly and collect my Toms. Olive is scrambling up the bank, like a puppy who has just been released from a crate, and the sight of it warms me as much as the sun ever has.

Liam and I set up a small picnic site, facing the shore from which we just came. It's wonderfully strange to be in a place inhabited only by crabs and insects and shorebirds. It feels like a trip to prehistoric times before humans arrived and changed everything to suit ourselves.

When lunch is set out, Liam calls Olive to come back, then the three of us sit on the picnic blanket to eat. I've made a pizza sub for her, and turkey on rye for the adults. Small plastic bowls containing berries and cut-up apples bring a delightful array of color to the faded orange blanket that serves as our buffet table.

Olive is too excited to sit still, having discovered a small tidepool that is in immediate need of a thorough scientific investigation.

"Go on, you can take your sandwich with you," Liam says, "But stay clear of the open water."

We sit in a comfortable silence, watching her for a few minutes. Suddenly, she turns. "Dad! I've made an exciting discovery!"

He gets up and makes his way to the shore, and I see him examine whatever it is she's put in her jar. He tucks a piece of hair behind her ear, and she grins up at him. The sight tugs at my heart and I feel unexpected tears behind my eyes.

I want this.

Through my blurry vision, Liam has become Isaac, and Olive has become our child. And for a moment, I feel a beautiful sense of contentment as he picks her up and swings her around. I imagine that they'll come running back to me to show me what they found, then he'll lie beside me, propped up on one elbow while we watch her go off again.

But that won't happen.

I reach up and play with Isaac's ring while a profound sense of loss sweeps over me. Why didn't we do this? I remind myself it was because we never wanted children. Except that suddenly I'm not so sure. The decision was made so long ago, I can't remember which one of us was more adamant about it. I know it was Isaac's suggestion, but he was only voicing what I wanted, wasn't he?

I wipe my eyes, and they are Liam and Olive again. Liam is walking toward me with a perplexed look on his face. He sits on the low beach chair next to mine. "You all right?"

I nod and swallow, trying for a happy smile. Then I hear myself say, "No."

"What's wrong?"

I put on a carefree air. "Oh, you know, women, never wanting something until we can't have it."

"Don't do that." His voice is quiet.

"Do what?"

"You have a habit of making a joke when what you really need to do is cry." I feel his eyes on me, but I refuse to look at him.

He puts his hand on mine. "You don't have to pretend around me. I can handle sad."

Fresh tears spring out of my eyes. I let out a shaky breath before I find my voice again. "I just realized I may have missed out on something really beautiful." I gesture with my head toward Olive and tears spill down my cheeks again.

He slips his fingers through mine and gives them a gentle squeeze without saying anything. He doesn't tell me it'll be okay or that I could always adopt. He doesn't pretend having children isn't so great anyway. He just sits and lets me cry, and it's exactly what I need.

The sun is setting when we reach slip number seventeen. I don't give more than a glance to the vibrant show the sky is putting on. Instead, I watch Olive, who is asleep with her head on my lap, tired out from the fresh air and exploring. She is more of a marvel to me than the sky could ever be, with her bright, fresh mind and her big ideas. We are on the bench seat near the steering wheel, the breeze still warming us as the day draws to an end. My fingertips trace her hairline, and I'm happy to have her here, even though she's become heavy against my leg. Her palm has opened, and I stare at the single green mermaid tear she's been holding onto for the duration of the trip home.

Liam glances over at his daughter, his eyes full of love. He's taken his sunglasses off and no longer wears his hat. He docks the boat and jumps down onto the pier to tether it in place. I wait for him, not wanting to wake her. When he appears a few moments later, he opens the door to the cabin, then takes her from me, easily lifting her into his strong arms. She shifts into his chest while I whisper, "Good night, Olive."

Once they're inside, I collect my things, hating that it's time to go home to my empty house, but not wanting to embarrass myself by over-staying my welcome.

Liam returns carrying two bottles of beer. "If you're not sick of me yet, maybe you could stay for a drink."

Relief washes over me, and I nod and smile, dropping my bags on the bench.

He sets up a table for two that has been neatly tucked away for our trip. I help unfold the chairs and soon we're sitting together, listening to the gentle tide lap against the boat. I'm awakened by the cold, malty drink as it slides along my tongue and down my throat.

"What a lovely day," I remark. "I hope I didn't ruin it earlier."

"Of course you didn't. Not every minute has to be filled with laughter in order for it to add up to a good day." He stares out at the last wisp of pink in the sky.

"Can I tell you something?"

"Of course you can."

"When I first heard about your ... loss, I thought I was the lucky one because I didn't have a child to look after through all this grieving. But now, I'm not so sure."

Liam nods. "When I first met you, I felt blessed that I wasn't as alone as you."

The realization makes us both smile sadly. "I guess you make the most of what you've got, right?"

"That you do, Abby. That you do."

"How did you manage ... when it all happened?"

"My mom took over for a few weeks so I could fall apart. But eventually, it was time for her to go and for me to get on with living."

"A few weeks? You amaze me, Liam. I fell apart for over a year."

"I'm not amazing. I just did what was required of me." He sips his beer. "I have this theory that when you face hardship, there's a time when you do what you have to and no more. I had a two-year-old, so I had to do a lot."

"Whereas I have a cat, so I could do almost nothing."

His expression is warm and understanding. "There were days when it felt like too much. There still are, but I've learned to put off my grief until Olive is away at school or at her grandparents' place for the night. I put on a pretty decent show for her most of the time. I hope."

We sit in silence, sipping our drinks as we let the conversation digest. I can make out the sound of a folksong in the distance.

"Can I ask you a personal question?" His voice is quiet.

"Sure."

"Why didn't you and Isaac have a family?" This is usually the type of question that would irritate me, but from him, there is no judgment, only curiosity.

I sigh. "I was twenty-two when we met. I was a teaching assistant at a university, and he was one of the professors there. He was close to forty when we started dating and I think that time had already passed for him." I pause for a second, then go on, trying to figure it out for myself. "It's hard to remember exactly how we decided it. It's not like it was a big fight or anything. I think maybe it was because he was too old to want children and I was too young to understand what that choice really meant." I stare down at my shoes for a moment. "I seem to recall fleeting thoughts of parenthood somewhere in the middle of our time together, but I dismissed it as my biological clock. There was no way I would allow myself to be a slave to something so primitive."

"Primitive." He repeats the word, sounding just the faintest bit offended.

I shake my head. "No, I don't mean it that way. I believed I was taking the road less traveled by not having children. I never wanted to be predictable. I wanted to be interesting."

"Oh, I see."

"That wasn't better, was it?" I ask, then have a couple of gulps of beer. "Let me try that again. As some of my friends became parents, they didn't want to talk about anything other than their children. 'Why isn't he walking?' or 'she said her first word' or they'd spend all their time complaining about how they never slept and didn't have sex anymore."

The words spill out quickly now, loosened by the alcohol. "They stopped caring about things like politics and world events and became completely absorbed in their little lives. Isaac and I used to congratulate ourselves for our mutual wisdom to remain carefree. It was all very easy with no one to look after but ourselves. I could stay up and write until the early morning hours and sleep all day if inspiration struck. We could take off on a whim for the weekend or for the entire summer, even. No way you can do that if you have a child."

He stares at me while I talk. "Well, then ... "

"I've offended you, haven't I?" I wince, feeling like shit for what I've said.

"Not really. What you've said is true. Most parents do start to lose track of the outside world. We don't get to sleep as much or have as much sex as we'd like, and we certainly can't drop everything and get on a flight to Paris. We're also fascinated by our little people. They hold our hearts and minds hostage, pretty much forever."

His words squeeze at my chest, and I can almost imagine the depths of the love I would have had for my own child. "I can see that now, after spending time with you and Olive. For the first time, the whole thing makes sense."

That night, as I climb into bed, I am grateful the long day has worn me out. I know I'll sleep well despite the twisting and churning of my heart. I feel as though I'm going to start the grieving process all over again, this time for a family that never existed.

CHAPTER TWENTY-THREE

 It serves me right for putting all my eggs in one bastard.

~ Dorothy Parker, *You Might as Well Live: The Life and Times of*
Dorothy Parker

It's just after midnight on Sunday evening, and I have been alone all day. I took a long walk this morning and had a most wonderfully refreshing swim before spending the afternoon curled up with my laptop, trying to distract myself. Other than words I have spoken to Walt, my tongue has had no exercise today. I feel restlessness bear down on me as soon as I finish the chapter I've been working on.

It suddenly occurs to me I was supposed to make my Sunday call to my mom already today. I grab my phone and call her number, hoping she's still awake.

After three rings, she picks up. "Abigail? What's wrong?"

"Nothing. I just remembered it was Sunday. Well, it was until five minutes ago."

"It's still Sunday here for another three hours, so close enough." She sounds old to me. When did her voice start sounding like an old lady's?

"What's wrong?" she asks again.

"Nothing." I consider steering the conversation to something trivial but decide against it. "Can you remember a time when I wanted children?" My voice cracks. Yup. I'm a mess again.

She sighs. "Of course I remember. Don't you? You used to play with your dolls all the time as a little girl. Changing diapers and giving them bottles. You practically wore out the wheels on that red carriage."

"Yes, I know that. But what about when I was older? You know, a teenager or a young woman."

"No teenager wants to have children, Abby. And to be honest, after you moved to New York, I didn't really know what you wanted anymore." For once I don't hear a martyr in her voice. I hear my mother, who lost me a long time ago.

I gasp for air, and my exhale is loud.

"Are you crying, honey?"

I nod, then remember she can't see me. "Yes," I whisper.

I hear my dad's voice in the background. "What's wrong?"

"I'm talking to Abby. Go back to sleep."

"Were you in bed already, Mom?"

"Yes, but I was reading. Just a second." There is a long pause, then I hear her pick up the cordless phone in the kitchen. I hear her breathing as she walks back to her bedroom to hang up the phone in there. A few moments later, her recliner squeaks, and I can picture her settling herself into it, dressed in her fuzzy pink robe. "Abby, are you still there?"

"Yes." My voice is a bit stronger now.

"We were really scared when you met Isaac. He was so much older and so sure of what he wanted in life, while you were just beginning to figure it out. I had a horrible feeling that you'd end up living a life suited to a middle-aged man and not a young woman."

"I know, you've told me that before, but I thought it was just because you wanted me to move home and give you more grandkids to spoil."

"I hate that you always put that on me, as though my reasons were purely selfish. It was never about that." She sighs, then says, "Well, a little bit, maybe. But it's natural for a mother to want to be near her children." She seems to catch herself mid-lecture and stops. "Abigail, what a mother wants more than anything is to see her children live the fullest life possible. In your case, it may not have meant becoming a mother, but I never believed you explored that idea enough. When you married Isaac, I saw your future. And it made me so sad." She's crying now, and I hate that I've done this to her.

Sounds of sobs come from both sides of the continent, and I'm completely unaware of how long we stay like this. "I'm sorry, Mom. I know you tried to tell me. I just wish I had understood."

"Don't be sorry. You were so young. There's no way you could see it from my side."

"But I should have trusted that you just wanted the best for me, instead of deciding you were trying to control me."

"Oh, Abby, you did what young people do. You fell in love, you got caught up in it, and you set out to prove your parents wrong about everything. I did the same thing when I married your dad."

"Because of the whole religion thing?"

"Yup. And look how we turned out. Only two kids. My father's probably still rolling over in his grave about it."

I laugh for the first time in over twenty-four hours, and it comes as such a relief.

"Come home, sweetie, even just for a while. Let me help you get through this."

"Okay. I'll come as soon as the work is done on the house."

"Really?" Her tone suggests she doesn't quite want to let herself believe it.

"Really. It should be ready sometime in October. I'll come home then."

In my dream, I've been waiting for Isaac in front of our favorite café overlooking the Central Park Zoo and when he finally shows up, he's sauntering instead of running like he should be.

I start yelling as soon as I catch sight of him. "Do you know how long I've been waiting here? Three days!" I scream at him, not caring that I'm humiliating us both in front of all these people. "Where were you?"

"I had to go to Spain for some vino de Jerez."

"You flew all the way to Spain for some sherry we can buy five blocks from our house?"

He shrugs. "It was on sale."

"But we were going to have dinner together! You *told* me to meet you here!"

"Sorry, Abigail, but you're not the center of the universe, you know."

I wake myself up punching the air above my bed. Sitting up, I rub my eyes while my heart pounds out the tune of my rage. It's a little after four in the morning and there is no way I can fall back asleep at this point. I don't even want to, in case I go back to that fight.

Getting up, I wander through the empty house, which has taken on an inky gray tone. I'm both furious and restless. Without thinking, I slide on a pair of flip-flops, then walk out the back door. There is only the full moon and a distant streetlamp to light my way. The cool air runs over my skin, waking my body. By the time I've crossed through the wet grass of my yard, my feet are soaked and cold, but it doesn't put out the fire that burns inside me.

The wind whips my hair across my cheek as I walk through the maples and make my way along the path to the shore. Other than the waves lapping against the rocks, the world is still. The sun hasn't woken the birds yet, and I am glad for that. It means I can be alone with my anger.

I walk all the way to the ocean, then stand on a large, flat rock and stare out. My bathrobe flutters around my shins, but I do not tighten the sash to shield me from the chill.

Why am I so furious?

My dream comes flashing back into my mind. I see Isaac's face. I suddenly hate him. I hate him for leaving me. I hate him for loving me. I hate him for showing me a life I can no longer have. I hate the young woman sitting at that staffroom table thinking it would be deliciously fun to turn his head. I hate her for letting him make decisions that were mine to make. I hate the pitiful woman wallowing away in that apartment, wasting so many days. I hate her weakness, her self-pity.

I reach up and take hold of his ring. Some wild part of my mind believes the delicate gold chain around my neck is going to choke me. I have to get it off now or I will die. I give it a sharp tug and the chain snaps with the force of my rage. I pull my arm back and hurl it into the water, letting out a scream of pure hatred.

The moonlight reveals to me the exact spot in which the ring drops. I'm shocked. I'm relieved. I'm done.

I walk back to the house, strip off my wet clothes, climb under the covers, then drop into a deep sleep.

I wake with a start and reach for my necklace. It's gone. I actually threw Isaac's ring into the ocean.

I throw off the blankets, startling poor Walt, then dress quickly in my swimsuit, not bothering to brush my teeth. I run out the back door and down to the water where I scour the shore. I know I won't find it, but I wade into the ocean anyway, diving under, trying to feel my way along the rocky bottom below me. Rays of light shine through the water, but I can't keep my eyes open without the salt stinging them. I surface, take a deep breath, then close my eyes and grope around some more before giving up and returning to the shore, my teeth chattering with cold.

The sun is too weak to warm me as I sit on a rock, breathing hard and staring out to the water. It's too late. I can't undo it. I have thrown away the dearest thing of Isaac's that I had. The symbol of my undying love and fidelity. What kind of a horrible wife am I? I slump down and sob into my hands.

"Abby, is that you?"

I know that voice without looking up. "Hi, Eunice."

"What's wrong, dear?" I glance up in time to see her as she hurries over, dressed in a neon green tracksuit with matching sneakers. Her hair is up in a high ponytail that is probably meant to take a decade off her face.

"Nothing. I lost something."

"What was it? I can help you look."

"A ring. But it's gone. I can't find it."

"It must have been very special for you to be so upset." She sits next to me and pats my hand.

I nod and feel the sting of fresh tears. "It was."

"Hmph, but if I had to guess, I'd say it's not about the ring, though, is it?"

"You'd be right." I look over at her and finally see past all the hair and makeup and matchy-matchy clothes. I see a woman who wants to make the world a bit brighter. "Did you ever feel like maybe the life you built for yourself isn't necessarily the one you should be living?"

She looks up at the sky for a second before answering. "Do you mean because I married the wrong Beckham?"

I chuckle and watch her as her gaze follows a sailboat.

"I hope you know I'm only joking. Dennis is a good man, and I love him to death. But, yes, sometimes I feel like I should be living a different life."

"Doing what?"

"It sounds a little silly maybe, but when I finished high school, I wanted to move to New York and perform on Broadway. I was sure I was the next Liza Minnelli. I was already with Dennis by then, if you can imagine. He wanted to stay here and get into island politics."

"Did you ever think about going anyway? On your own?"

"I did. But I couldn't give up Dennis," Eunice sighs. "Besides, I never really was much of an actress."

We both laugh and she bumps her shoulder to mine. "Can't sing worth a darn either."

"No, I've heard you at the pub. You're very good."

"Good at pub music. Not Broadway tunes."

I stare at her for a second, trying to imagine her as a new graduate. "Do you ever wish you had tried?"

"Some days, in my grouchy, 'nobody appreciates me' moments that we all have from time to time. For the most part, though, I'm happy. I'm surrounded by family and friends. We have a good life. We're healthy. Plus, you know, I've managed to bring my own sense of flair to this little corner of the world, even if I've never lit up a stage in New York."

"You really have. If South Haven were a play, you'd definitely be one of the most memorable characters in the cast."

"Why, thank you, Abby. That's very kind of you."

"It's true."

She tilts her head and stares at me for a second. "I take it you're not living the life you wanted?"

I sigh. "Obviously if I could have my husband back, I would. But it's more than that. I'm scared that maybe the choices I made when I was younger aren't the ones I'd make again."

"You're like most people, then."

"I suppose I am. But in my case, there's no way to fix it. It's too late."

"Is it?" She gives me a skeptical look. "Did you know, for the last three years, I've played Mrs. Cratchit in the local production of *A Christmas Carol*?"

"Really?"

She pats me on the leg, then stands. "It's not Broadway, but it's a hell of a lot of fun."

CHAPTER TWENTY-FOUR

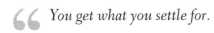 *You get what you settle for.*

~ Louise Sawyer, *Thelma and Louise*

For the next week, I am completely unsettled. Isaac doesn't come back to me in my sleep, and as batshit crazy as it sounds, I can't help but wonder if he knows what I did and he's so hurt, I'll never see him again. When I go to bed, I'm desperate to find him so I can tell him how sorry I am. And it's not just about the ring, and it's not just about how angry I was with him. It's about whatever it is I'm feeling for Liam.

I don't think I'm falling in love with him—at least I hope to hell and back I'm not. But there's a relentless pull to Liam that gets harder to fight each day. I look forward to seeing him each morning. I want to know his opinions on nearly every topic under the sky. I rush to him when I've written an especially good chapter because I want to share my excitement with him. He high fives me when I need to celebrate, and he gives me a shot in the arm when I'm losing my gusto.

But more than that, our friendship is the most honest one I've had, and I think it's because I started out with nothing to lose. Other than a brief second of sucking in my gut, I don't try to pretend I'm someone I'm not. I'm me—like it or leave it. And if I'm not mistaken, he seems to like me. Not me, as I present myself to the world, or me, as a woman trying to impress a man. Just me. Crying Abby. Angry Abby. Abby the Hermit.

And all of that is scaring the shit out of me. The old me would say 'we don't flirt, we joke around,' but the new, improved me can admit that we definitely flirt. A lot. And I like it. Which makes me feel absolutely fucking awful. Between the flirting and tossing my husband's wedding ring into the sea, I'm pretty sure I'm the world's worst wife.

Which is why every morning this week, I set my alarm for five a.m. and hurry down to search the beach before Liam and Olive arrive for the day. Then, I walk home empty-handed, the bright sunshine and blue sky mocking me.

Yesterday, I was so exhausted by the middle of the afternoon that I suggested Olive and I have a 'movie afternoon.' I turned on *Freaky Friday*, then promptly fell asleep on the couch, only to wake up to find her and Liam both staring at me. The movie had been over for a while, I guess, and it was already time for them to go home. I ended up telling Liam how I'd been spending the early morning hours and why. Even though he tried to sound supportive, I could tell by his expression he doesn't think I have a prayer, and I'm sure he's right.

But this morning, my feet propel me along in my search anyway, and I return just as they arrive. I can hear the front door opening as soon as I walk in the back.

"Walt? Where are you?" Olive calls. "There you are!"

I find her on the living room floor. "Good morning, you," I say, reaching down to ruffle her hair.

"Morning! Can we make play dough again today?"

197

"Sure thing. Give me a few minutes to make some coffee for the cranky old grown-ups first."

She grins up at me. "You're never cranky." Pointing to her dad, she says, "Him, though ..."

"Smart aleck," Liam says, as we walk into the kitchen.

"Any luck today?" he asks, even though I can see in his eyes he already knows.

I shake my head. "Not yet, but it's got to turn up eventually, right? It'll get washed onto the shore sooner or later."

He gives me a doubtful look. "From the sound of where you said it went in, I'd say it's not that likely."

"Thanks," I say sarcastically.

"I just don't want you to kill yourself looking," he answers. "Do you want some help? I have scuba gear, I could go for a dive."

I shake my head while I fill the carafe with water. "Thanks, but no."

"Penance?"

"Something like that," I say, turning to face him.

"Abby, throwing that ring doesn't make you a horrible wife." His face is full of a kindness I don't deserve.

The sight of it scratches at me like a pair of wool socks on the driest day of winter. Turning back to the coffeemaker, I say, "Doesn't exactly make me a good one, though."

"It makes you human."

I sigh and close my eyes. "I'm still going to find that ring."

"So long as you know that if you can't, it just means the tide moved it, or maybe a crab picked it up. It doesn't mean you didn't love him."

I turn and lean against the counter. "I blamed him, and I mean I really blamed him—a dead man who isn't here to defend himself," I say, letting my words tumble out as fast as my tongue can carry them. "He doesn't deserve that. It wasn't his fault we didn't have children. It was mine. If I wanted a different life, I needed to make that happen. I've been aiming my rage at him when really I should have turned the gun on myself."

Liam looks slightly shocked, so I hold up one hand. "I meant figuratively."

"I'm glad because that was quite the dark image." He softens his voice and walks over to me, placing both hands on my upper arms. "So, you're furious with a woman who was the ripe old age of twenty-two when she made a big decision. You know who else is roughly twenty-two?" he asks. "Colton Nickerson."

Rolling my eyes, I say, "I know where you're going with this analogy, but trust me, it's not the same thing."

"Why not?"

"Because he's a child, for God's sake. His mom still drives him around and does his laundry."

Liam leans toward me. "Did you know that the frontal lobe of the human brain isn't fully developed until the age of twenty-five?"

"No, Bill Nye, I didn't."

"Well, it's true," he says. "That means your higher-level decision-making wasn't all there yet. So stop beating yourself up over a decision you made almost two decades ago. Give young Abby a break. She did the best she could, just like still-young-but-slightly-wiser Abby is doing today."

I stare at him for a full ten seconds before I say anything. "I'm still going to look for that ring."

"I'm sure you will. But what if you made it more of a casual search instead of forcing yourself to get up at four in the morning every day?"

"Because I wasn't a casual wife."

"I know that. And I imagine so did Isaac."

"He said that?" Lauren asks, sounding as though she might fall for Liam.

"He did."

"Honestly, the bit about still-young-but-slightly-wiser Abby? Oh, wow," she says with a dreamy sigh. "That's like something out of one of your books."

I empty some salt and pepper chips into a salad bowl. "It's better."

"Okay, it is, but I didn't want to hurt your feelings."

We both laugh, then I groan loudly. "It is better, and that's the problem. I'm getting all confused and I don't like it."

"You mean you're falling for him and you're terrified," she says. "Oh, I forgot to tell you I'm your new emotions translator until you get used to being fully transparent."

"Thanks."

"No problem."

I take my snack to the living room and settle myself onto the couch. "Okay, I might be kind of terrified. The chemistry is definitely there."

"Really?" she asks, a smile in her voice.

"Yeah, and I'm pretty sure that's mutual."

"As chemistry should be," she says. "That sounds promising, if you ask me."

"It's not promising, it's terrible. I'm still married to Isaac, to whom I promised to remain faithful 'for all the days of my life.' Not some, not most, not as long as he was around. *All* the days of my life. So where does that leave me now?"

"Abby, come on. Of course you should find love again. Even Isaac, to whom you pledged your unending devotion, told you to find someone else."

"And I said I wouldn't," I snap. "So if I do, that means I was lying to him on his deathbed. And I know we've established I'm a total liar, but Jesus."

"He knew what you really meant, which was that you'd always love him. And you will. It's not like you'll forget about Isaac if you find a man who makes you happy again," she says. "Besides, if you'd have gone first, do you think he'd have gone the rest of his life without seeing anyone? Most men last, like, six months, tops. Drew's got someone picked out already if I go first."

My mouth drops open, then I say, "Are you serious?"

"Yes, she's a junior partner at his firm."

"Who?" I ask, suddenly furious on Lauren's behalf. "Have I met her?"

"Yes, at Drew's fortieth. Audra, the blond one."

Raising my voice, I say, "You mean Pollyanna with huge boobs?"

"That's the one," Lauren says, sounding like she couldn't care less.

"How are you still married?"

"Because Drew's got absolutely no game. There's no way he could land her, even if I was dead," she adds. "But my point is this—don't take yourself permanently off the market just because you would've wanted Isaac to."

I sit quietly for a minute, letting myself process all of this.

"Look, Isaac was a wonderful man and a loyal husband," Lauren says. "And I'm not trying to upset you."

"To be honest, what you're saying is kind of shitty. You're making all men sound ... shallow. Haven't you read *A Man Called Ove*?"

"Is that what you imagined Isaac would do if you died?" she asks, in a condescending tone. "Repeatedly attempt to off himself?"

"Maybe."

"Oh, hon, none of them do that. Nor should they. I mean, they should wait a respectable time, of course, not like Drew's dad." After nearly fifty years of marriage, Drew's dad lasted three whole months without his wife before hooking up with the divorcée next door. "All I'm saying is there should be a happy medium between my father-in-law and Ove. For you, it'll be two years soon."

"That's nothing after eighteen years together."

"It's *not* nothing. You've wept, Abby. You've grieved. Holy shit, did you grieve for him. In fact, if Isaac is somewhere looking down on you, he's probably sick of seeing you like this. He's probably up there saying, 'For God's sake, Abby, will you get laid already?'"

"I highly doubt that."

"Why?"

"First of all, he never would have used the word 'laid.'"

"And second?"

I think for a minute. "There is no second."

"Exactly."

"Okay, so let's say I could magically talk myself into not feeling guilty about it, there's a bigger issue. Olive."

"I thought you liked her?"

"And that's why I can't do anything with her dad. If Liam and I start knocking boots, but then something happens and we break up, it would devastate her. She is so attached to me, Lauren. I can't put her through that kind of pain."

Lauren sighs heavily.

"See how complicated this is?"

"Is it? Or are you just making it complicated because you're afraid?"

"Can't it be both?"

"Sure, but they're both crappy reasons not to try."

CHAPTER TWENTY-FIVE

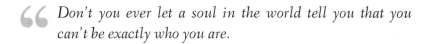 *Don't you ever let a soul in the world tell you that you can't be exactly who you are.*

~ Lady Gaga

I'm babysitting Olive from early morning to late this evening. Liam has gone out on the water for the day with a friend who has secured a bluefin tuna license, but finds himself down a man at the moment. It's been days since I admitted my feelings for Liam out loud, but since then I've done nothing other than to carefully observe them. Lauren's words keep coming back to me about how I'm making it more complicated than it has to be. But the truth is, there's no harm in waiting until I'm a thousand percent sure before I act. It's not like we're on a deadline or something. And when there's an innocent child involved, caution is the best way to protect her.

Waiting is also the smart move because he's not done with my house yet, so if I've misread the entire situation and his answer is a resounding no, it would make for several cringe-worthy weeks of bumping into each other around my house while trying to avoid eye-contact or speaking. This would prove especially awkward in the hallway or on the staircase where space is limited. And I know Lauren will be disgusted by my cowardice when we next speak, but I don't really care because it's not her house being renovated, or her heart being served up on a platter. It's mine. So while I'm not necessarily being honest with Liam about my feelings, I'll at least be honest with Lauren about the fact that I'm not being honest with Liam.

In the meantime, I'm going to wait and watch and think. And babysit Liam's daughter, too, I suppose. Olive and I have spent a most wonderful day together in the early autumn sun, walking along the beach searching for sea glass, and winding up at the Seaside Pizzeria for supper. I'm drinking in every moment with her because school starts in less than a week, and I'm going to miss our long, lazy days together.

Now we're back on their yacht. She's snuggled into her bed and I'm sitting on top of the covers, reading *Anne of Green Gables* to her. As I read, I think about how Olive can relate to Anne's longing for a mother. It squeezes my heart and I have to concentrate on the words on the page to get through it. I reach the end of the chapter, and as she hands me a bookmark, she yawns.

"Did you ever read this when you were a girl?"

"Oh yes, it was one of my favorites."

"Wow, so they had this one already back in the olden days."

I laugh, pretending to be offended. "Oh, very funny, young lady."

She's still giggling as I slide off her bed and replace the book on the shelf. I watch as she takes off her glasses, then carefully folds them and puts them into their case. She switches on a night light, then flips the switch on the wall to turn off the overhead light. Immediately the room is filled with the peaceful magic of thousands of stars glimmering against the walls and ceiling. We're transported to the world where she dreams of fairies fluttering over fields of tall grasses and mermaids twirling and leaping out of the sea.

"Abby, if you were my mom, what would you say when you tucked me in?"

The question guts me and I have to fight not to look emotional. I put off answering directly in hopes of getting myself together. "What do you mean, honey?"

"Well, I always imagined that if my mom were here, she would say something really lovely to me when she put me to bed. Or maybe she'd tell me some secret things I need to know about boys and being a woman and stuff."

"Oh, well, yes, I suppose my mother did that from time to time."

"You would do it *all* the time if you were a mom, I just know it." She looks up at me adoringly and I can't help but run my palm over her soft cheek.

She lays down and snuggles into her pillow while I tuck her quilt up around her neck.

"Abby, what do you think my mom said when she tucked me in? When I was little, and she was alive?"

I'm on the verge of tears and I pretend to be thinking as I look up at the low ceiling. "I bet she told you that you're perfect just the way you are, and that there is nothing she would ever want to change about you," I say, stopping just before my voice cracks.

Olive stares at me expectantly, and I assume she wants me to go on.

"And that she can't believe her luck to get you for a daughter."

"She definitely said that." Olive beams up at me. "I think I remember it, actually."

"I'm sure you do." I smile and cup her cheek with my hand. "It's late. Time to sleep." Then, I lean down and give her a kiss on her forehead.

When I straighten up, she grabs my hand before I can take it off her cheek. "Abby, can I tell you something?"

"Sure."

"You're my best friend. I wish you were my mom."

I wish I were too.

I tuck her hair behind her ear. "If I had a daughter, I would want

205

her to be exactly like you." I kiss her on the top of her head. "You better get some sleep now."

I walk out of her room and sit down on the small built-in couch to read. But instead of opening my book, I think about the little girl who probably fell asleep in about ten seconds flat. She is the best reason I can come up with to take things with Liam at a tortoise-slow pace. Yes, doing nothing is the best thing I can do for all three of us.

CHAPTER TWENTY-SIX

" *Man cannot discover new oceans unless he has the courage to lose sight of the shore.*

~ Andre Gide

I've been giving love a lot of thought lately, and I've come to some undeniable conclusions. For example, the difference between falling in love when you're twenty versus falling in love when you're forty is that when you're twenty, you're a lot more willing to compromise. You're so desperate to make it work, you'll do or give up almost anything. When you're forty, however, and you've been through what I have, you understand what giving up parts of yourself really means, and you're no longer willing to do it. It's got to be a 'here I am, take me or leave me' sort of thing for both parties. That way, if it doesn't work out, or your significant other doesn't happen to outlive you, you still know who you are and are happy to live with her.

At this age, you also understand the importance of using logic as well as lust to make your decision because you've given your heart away and lost it once already, so you know what that truly means. Now, I'm not saying I'm definitely in love with Liam, because I may not be, but on the other hand, I might be. So, if I am going to consider starting all over again, I'm going to do it right this time. Which, in my case, means knowing who I am, what I love, and precisely what I am unwilling to compromise.

To that end, I have started a list of things I love. This isn't one of those 'Must Have' lists in which any potential mate must either match up perfectly or he's out. It's more like things that I will unreservedly continue to enjoy after any type of commitments are made.

I like going to kitchen parties. I like the music, I like the desserts, I like the beer. So, instead of pretending I don't, I'm going to start going to them as often as possible (like tonight).

I have no idea what I am to Olive, technically, but I like her almost more than anyone else I know, and I want to do whatever I can to make her life better for as long as possible. (Total deal-breaker should Liam and I crash and burn, but remain friends, and I find someone else.)

I like Cheetos better than popcorn, and sometimes I like Cheetos for supper. (Actually, this one is a deal-breaker, so now that I think of it, this list may be one of those awful "Must Have' lists.)

I love to dance around the kitchen while listening to cheesy pop songs, folk music, up-tempo, classical, and the occasional jazz tune. (And I suppose this is a bit of a deal-breaker, because I want to be with someone who will dance along with me, or at the very least won't look at me like I've grown a third boob.)

I love Indian food—butter chicken, coconut rice, as much naan bread as I can get, and a nice cool mango lassie to wash it all down. (Not a deal-breaker because I can happily eat it alone.)

I love spending an entire day doing nothing but reading—especially when it rains, but also when it's too hot to do anything else. Or when it's bitterly cold outside and I have a mug of hot tea. Or when it's evening. I guess I just love to read. (Deal-breaker, but only if a man made a habit of interrupting me.)

I like the fact that I'm making a list because it means I love myself.

Liam will finish with the house at the end of this week, and although it's going to be a massive relief to have the entire place finished, it's also scary because it means that I may have to up the pace of 'finding Abby,' so as not to wait so long that I lose Liam in the process. There's such a thing as waiting too long, according to Lauren, who gave me the 'I knew you'd overthink this' speech, followed by the 'do you know how hard it is to find a good man when you're over forty?' speech. I told her that no, I didn't, but neither did she. That seemed to shut her up.

But she's not wrong about the fact that I don't have an endless amount of time to either make my move or forget about it forever. Because of this, it may be prudent to test the waters a little with my potential friends-to-lovers romance. And what better place to do that than at the pub?

As soon as I walk in, I spot Liam. His eyes light up and he points to the chair he's saving next to his. I walk over, not even bothering to hide my smile. As I wind my way through the crowd, I remember the first time we saw each other and how repulsed he seemed. Huh. That's not exactly what we in the romance industry would call a compelling 'lovers meet' scene. It would have been much better had he stared just a little too long, or had we actually spoken that evening, if he'd have mixed up his words or looked down at me with a sexy grin while he rubbed the back of his neck. But seeming to be horrified? That's not exactly a good sign.

Instead of immediately sitting with Liam, I give him the 'can I get you a drink' gesture. He shakes his head and points to the pint in front of him, so I head over to the bar, where Peter is preparing a tray of drinks

"Hey there, Abby! You finally decided to grace us with your presence," Peter says.

"I did. Turns out people aren't as bad as I thought," I answer with a grin.

"Beer?"

"Let's go with something stronger this evening. Long Island Iced Tea, please."

"Sure thing, I'll bring it over to you."

"That's okay. You're busy. I can wait here." I need a minute to possibly rethink the flirt test to see if the Liam waters are warm.

"It's my job. Now go sit down before someone else takes the spot Liam's been saving for you for the last twenty minutes." He gives me a wink.

Of course. I wind my way through the crowd at the bar, stopping to say hello to everyone I know, which allows me to stall, but doesn't allow me to think. Screw it, I'll have to wing it and see what happens. As long as I don't do or say anything irreversible, I'll be okay.

When I take my seat next to him, Liam says, "Finally. Do you know how many women I've had to fight off so you could sit here?"

"Like, one?" I ask with a grin.

"Okay, so that's a pretty accurate guess," he admits. "Eunice is here alone tonight."

"Where's the mayor?"

Leaning into my ear, Liam mutters, "Give it a minute, she'll tell you."

His breath tickles my neck and I laugh a little harder than I should.

Peter walks over with a tray of drinks. He puts mine down and waggles his thick eyebrows. "So? You two finally saw the light?"

I'm about to say no, but Liam answers. "Oh, yes. We've been going hot and heavy for ..." He turns to me and gives me a wink. "What is it, love, four weeks now?"

"Yup." I grin at him, then smile at Peter. "I can't get enough of this guy."

I feel more eyes around the table landing on us. Liam seems to be soaking in the attention as he puts an arm around me. "We can't keep our hands off each other. Probably leave early tonight so I can get her back into bed."

I nod, trying not to laugh. We turn to each other. "We should go right now, actually. It's been over two hours." I trail a finger down the front of his shirt, but only as far as the middle of his chest. I watch as his pupils grow large, feeling my skin warm up.

"Has it really been that long already?" He swivels his gaze back to Peter. "She's insatiable."

I force a grave expression on my face. "To be honest, I'm just using him for the sex."

Liam barks out a laugh, then gets it under control. "But don't feel bad for me, I don't really mind at all."

Peter narrows his eyes at us, obviously wise to us. "Couple of idiots, the pair of you. You should be shagging instead of sittin' here. It's like that saying about how youth is wasted on the young."

He walks away shaking his head, while Liam and I laugh. I try not to notice how disappointed I am when he takes his hand off my shoulder.

Liam leans in and speaks quietly in my ear. "Sorry. I hope you don't mind me bringing you in on that joke. I just couldn't help myself."

I turn, and now his face is so close to mine, our noses are almost touching. Giving him a conspiratorial smile, I say, "Don't be sorry. That was just plain fun."

He turns and picks up his beer. "Good. I would have felt bad if I'd made you uncomfortable."

"Not at all," I say, hoping he'll lean back in. When he doesn't, I have three very long sips of my iced tea. "Not a bit, really. Besides, all these Meddling Matildas deserve it."

He smiles, but it's more of a friendly smile this time. "Maybe it'll teach them to stay out of peoples' love lives for once."

"One can hope," I say, having another couple of gulps. "You know, if this were a romance novel, we'd have a fake relationship just to get everyone to leave us alone."

"Would we?" he asks.

"Mmm-hmm. In our case, it would be a whole opposites-attract angle—handsome, rugged Canadian fisherman-slash-contractor falls for uptown American writer."

"Handsome, eh?" he asks with a little smirk.

My face flushes so hot, I wonder if I'm starting menopause early. "I didn't mean you. I meant a character in a novel."

"A handsome, rugged character based on me ..."

"I didn't mean it. I meant if we were going to pretend to be a couple."

His blue eyes dance with laughter. "But you said it, and there's no one else listening, so ..."

"Oh, I get it. You're messing with me now, aren't you, you bastard?"

"It's hard not to, you're easy pickings."

"I am not easy, sir," I say, pretending to be offended.

"Is this our first fake fight?"

"Yes, but don't think we'll be having pretend makeup sex."

"What a shame. I think I'd like that," he says, shaking his head.

A high tone flickers out of a flute from the end of the table and Liam turns from me and lifts his violin to his chin. The moment is over, and I'm glad to have a second to gather my thoughts and catch my breath again. That definitely felt like real two-way flirting. Eunice, who is sitting on the opposite side of the horseshoe, gives me a knowing smile. Oh, I have a witness. She definitely saw it, too.

By the time the first set of songs is over, I've almost finished my second drink, which means nearly three ounces of alcohol have gone to my head. Liam is turned away from me talking to James Campbell, his part-time moving partner, and I find myself staring at his back and fighting the urge to reach out and touch it.

"Hey Abby," a male voice comes from the other side of me. I turn to see Colton, who has slid into the seat beside me. "How's it going?"

"Good. I thought kitchen parties were for old people."

Covering his mouth with his hand, he says, "I'm trying to find more clients. It's fall clean-up time, which means I could make a lot of scratch if I hustle."

"Excellent. So, you're enjoying the work then?"

He shakes his head. "No, I hate it. It's so boring, I want to shoot myself. But I still can't afford to move out of my parents' house."

"Bummer," I say, then finish my drink. "Say, if you hate landscaping, why don't you do something else?"

"I don't know what I want to do."

Suddenly, I turn into tipsy career-counselor Abby. "Well, what do you love?"

"Gaming. Streaming videos of me gaming. Watching other streamers."

"Anything else, in the non-gaming world?"

"Nope. Not really."

I tap my forefinger on my chin, trying to look wise. "You know what? When I was a teenager, the only thing I wanted to do was read."

"I don't really like reading."

"I'm going to pretend I didn't hear that," I say, swaying a little in my chair. "Now, back to me as a young woman. The only job I could have got reading was as an editor, and editing is the worst thing in life. So when I finished school, I decided, hey, if I can't make money reading, why not be a writer instead?"

I give him a satisfied smile which he exchanges for a blank look. I'm tempted to knock on his skull and ask if anyone is home, but instead, I help him follow the thread to the end of the brilliant idea. "Maybe you could write games instead of playing them? That way you'd always have games you wanted to play."

Colton grins and nods. "I think I'd like that."

"Good stuff. Glad I could help."

He glances across the room, then says, "Oh, I should catch Eunice before she leaves. They have a *huge* yard."

With that, he gets up, leaving me to feel smug at my helpfulness.

Two hours later, Liam walks me home. It's cold out and I'm very tipsy now. We've just bid good night to his friend Jake, the guy who gets the bluefin tuna license.

"God, I can't imagine fishing for tuna," I say. "I mean the smell alone must be awful."

He grins at me, and I see a twinkle in his eye. "There are more irritating things than a bad smell. You should try spending months renovating some nutty American lady's house."

"Oh, so I'm nutty now?"

"You're taking offense to me calling you nutty?" He feigns surprise. "The real insult in that sentence was when I called you American."

"Ouch!" I let my head snap back dramatically. "Hurtful. I thought you hosers were supposed to be so nice."

"Nah, we just pretend so we can get tourists to come spend a few bucks here." He looks up at the night sky. "And so no one invades us."

"Solid plan."

Liam tilts his head to the side. "It's worked so far. We've managed to get by all these years with a minuscule defense budget just by being polite and apologizing lots."

"Is that all there is to it? I should really take that idea straight to Washington."

"Could be hard to pull off at this point."

"Good point." I nod, trying to look very serious. "We'd need an entire rebranding from superpower to nice neighbors."

"You'll have to just study up and become a Canadian then."

"I just may have to. I'm assuming there are politeness exams ..."

"Yup. Every Tuesday night down at the school. They teach you all twenty-six different ways to say sorry, the top fifty situations that aren't your fault that you should apologize for, as well as phrases like, 'you go first,' and 'no that's fine, after you.'"

We both give up on pretending we're serious at the same time and have a quiet laugh together.

A chill runs up my back from the cold air. I shiver a little, and out of the corner of my eye, I see his jacket sliding off his arm, then he turns to me and places it on my shoulders.

I pull it tightly around me and thank him, my voice taking on a ridiculously sultry tone that causes me to clear my throat. The coat smells like Liam, and I have a fleeting wish that the scent will stay on me when I climb into bed soon.

"The nights are getting colder." He remarks as we saunter up my driveway.

"Yes, they are." I am hyper-aware of his proximity to me now, and I wonder if he's noticing it, too. He must feel it. But what if he doesn't? What if this is just how he is with his friends, and he really is physically repulsed by me? What the hell, might as well find out.

Swallowing hard, I say, "Liam, I've been wondering something. Have you ever heard of a meet-cute?"

"Can't say I have."

"Hmm, okay then. Do you think two people who meet, if one of them, say, finds the other one sort of repulsive, that he could later decide she's not actually that gross and that maybe she's attractive?"

By the time I'm done rambling, we've reached the front steps. I turn and look up at him, only to see a confused look on his face.

I touch him on the chest, and say, "Don't worry about it. I've had too much to drink. I'm not making any sense."

"No, you are," he says, nodding. "You're referring to the expression on my face the first time I saw you."

I blink a few times, glad I'm not sober.

"That wasn't repulsion, believe me," he says in a low tone.

"Then what was it?"

"Fear."

We both stand perfectly still, staring at each other, and I'm pretty sure my expression is saying, 'KISS ME DAMMIT.' A gust of wind kicks up and blows a lock of my hair into my mouth. I pull it out, then wince out of embarrassment. "That wasn't very sexy of me."

"I thought we were just going to be friends," he says, his face growing serious.

"I thought so too," I murmur, tilting my head up toward him.

He licks his lips, then seems to second guess what I think he was planning to do. Clearing his throat, he says, "*You* ... have had a lot to drink."

"Yes, I have."

"So, I will see you into your house, and bid you good night."

I grin, doing my best to cover up the disappointment that's weighing me down all of a sudden. He opens the screen door for me, then holds it while I unlock the door. I turn back to him with a toothy smile. "Okay, good night then."

"Good night."

I walk inside while he quickly descends the steps to the sidewalk. I'm just shutting the door when I hear, "Abby?"

Opening it, I see he's still down on the sidewalk, which means he is not about to kiss me. "Some things are best done sober."

My heart starts pattering about ten seconds before my brain figures out what he means. He means there's hope here.

CHAPTER TWENTY-SEVEN

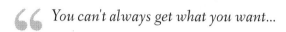 *You can't always get what you want...*

~ Mick Jagger (also, Every Mother Everywhere)

The next morning, I wake early with a dull headache but a happy heart. Some things are best done sober. Cryptic. And what did he mean by fear? I mean, it's so much better than repulsion obviously, but what was he afraid of? Was he *so* attracted to me it was terrifying? I want to call Lauren to dissect the entire conversation, but then I remember she's at work by now. Plus, we're not fifteen, so ...

I quickly get myself ready for the day, taking extra time for some mascara and a touch of bronzer. I don't want it to look like I'm trying too hard, but I definitely want to look a little better than normal, you know, just in case he comes over and we have 'the talk' which leads to ... oh, I can't even think that far ahead. I reach up to my neck to play with Isaac's ring, only to remember it's gone. I spot the framed photo of the two of us I have on my nightstand. It was taken in Paris on the Pont Alexandre III bridge that connects the Champs-Élysées quarter with that of the Eiffel Tower. I walk over and pick it up. It was a rainy spring morning and we're sharing a large black umbrella provided by the hotel. We look so happy. And we were.

"You won't hate it if I found someone who makes me happy, will you?" I ask. But he doesn't answer. And I don't suddenly have an overwhelming feeling that he's in the room and is giving me his blessing. There's just nothing but me and my own conscience to decide. I stare at him some more, then open the drawer and put the photo away. I quickly leave the room, then feel my entire body turn to jelly at the reason my favorite photo of us is now in a drawer beside my bed. "Nope. Not even close to ready for that." Spinning on one heel, I take it back out and put it where it was.

Walt and I are heading down the stairs when I receive a text from Liam. My heart speeds up as I slide the screen. Then it promptly drops. *Abby, I can't make it today. One of the toilets at my in-laws overflowed and flooded part of their basement. I'll be there all day and most of the weekend getting them sorted out. I'm sorry to skip out on you, but I promise I'll be back on Monday.*

What about Olive? Will she come here after school?

I thought I'd bring her back here instead to save time.

Okay, good luck with everything. See you next week.

Well, that certainly sucks. First, Liam says something that fills me with an abundance of hope, and then he decides to stomp all over that hope the next morning. Overflowing toilet. Yeah, right. That basement's not the only thing full of shit. He just doesn't want to lose his babysitter. Or maybe the thing that's best done sober is turning a woman down, because if she's been drinking, there's a higher chance she'll overreact.

I stew over it while I eat a bowl of Mini-Wheats and watch as the trees outside are blown around by a furious wind. Then I go into my office so I can use my own personal angst for Beatrice, who has just found out the reason Ian has been rebuilding the orphanage for free. It's not because he fancies her, but because he accidentally set the fire.

I spew out angry pages all day, breaking for lunch, then getting right back to it. After dinner, the wind and I both give out, and the world outside feels suddenly calm again. My mind refuses to distract itself from Liam, so I pull on a fleece hoodie and my Keds, and I go for a long walk, finding myself in front of the pier.

"I should just go home," I mutter. What exactly would I say if I went up to his boat right now? 'Hey there, I'm sober now, what's that thing you wanted to do to me?'

I stand, staring at his boat, then shake my head. "Screw it. Why *not* just say that?"

A light is on inside the cabin and I wonder if Olive is still awake. If she is, I'll just say hello, then walk back home. Hmm. This is a bit awkward. I can't exactly ring a doorbell, and once I'm up the ladder, it's basically the equivalent of letting myself in unannounced and uninvited. I pull my phone out of my pocket, then dial Liam's number and wait. I hear his cell phone ringing, then the sound of a light cough. He must be sitting outside on the deck.

He doesn't answer, and I consider turning back, but then for no good reason at all, I call to him. "Liam? It's me, Abby."

"I know." His voice is low and there is an unfamiliar quality to it.

"Can I come up?"

After a long pause, I hear a crashing sound. "Shit."

I start up the ladder, not caring that I am intruding, and tossing aside my original purpose in coming here. Something is very wrong.

When I get to the top, I see him stumble as he bends down to right the chair that must have been responsible for the crashing sound. I watch in silence as he gropes around behind him to find his seat again, and I'm alarmed at the considerable effort it takes him.

"Liam, is everything okay?" I walk cautiously toward him, finding it difficult to see in the dim light.

He shakes his head. "I need to be alone right now, Abby."

When I reach the table, I stand next to him and rest my fingers on his shoulder. "I just want to make sure you're okay. Then I'll go."

He won't look up at me, but from what I can make out, his eyes are blurry. There is an almost-empty bottle of scotch in front of him but no glass. He takes it and tips it back, then clicks his tongue and says, "Aah, yeah, yeah, yeah."

"Is Olive at her grandparents'?"

Finally, he looks at me. "Do you really think I'd do this with her here?" He's obviously insulted. Angry. Ready for a fight.

"No, I'd never think that of you. Is today an anniversary or did it hit you out of the blue?"

His head rolls back, and he looks up at me in surprise. Then he turns to face the floor. "The first one."

I pull up a chair next to him and sit down. I'll wait.

"He would've been six today." He hands me a photograph he's been clutching in his left hand. It's of Olive holding a tiny baby. The baby has the same dark curls she does and is looking up at her as she smiles at him. She is so little herself, with big chubby cheeks.

I feel a lump in my throat but swallow it. This is not my pain. I'm here for Liam. "He's beautiful." I place the photo on the table and put my hand on Liam's arm, gently rubbing it.

"He was." His eyes are full of tears, and even though he's looking at me, I know he's not seeing clearly. "I killed them. Nobody around here tells you that. They all act like I'm a fucking saint. But I'm no saint. Someday Olive's going to hate me. When I tell her the truth, she'll never look at me the same away again."

My hand stops moving on his arm, but I don't take it off.

He's crying now in violent sobs that erupt from his chest. "I should have driven them to the doctor. Malcolm had his booster shots that morning. He never slept. Colicky little thing, like his old man. Cried most of the time. Sarah was exhausted." He traces the baby's face with his finger. "I knew better. A little voice told me not to go, but I ignored it. I told myself they'd be fine, and I went off with Jake." His words slur together, and he shakes his head as if the thought is too much for him.

Tears fill my eyes now, and I'm grateful that the night sky hides my face from Liam. I force my breath to stay steady so he won't know.

"What kind of a man does that? Just goes off like that, to go fishing and drinking all day, when his wife and his babies need him home?" He waves his hand in the air wildly as he poses the impossible question to the night air.

I consider telling him it's not his fault, that he couldn't have known, but I don't. He needs to cry tonight. To get this awful pain out of his body. Besides, he knows the truth when he's not drowning in scotch and sorrow. This is the pain talking. Regret. The useless 'if onlys' that haunt the soul.

He's sobbing again, his arm folded on the table and his head resting on his forearm. I rub his back and feel a shift in the air as a slight chill moves in.

After a long while, he sits up and looks at me. His face is blotchy, and his eyes are red and puffed like he's gone ten rounds with a prize-fighter. In a way, he has.

"You're over the worst of it." My voice is gentle, like a nurse seeing a patient through a horrible bout of nausea.

"I should sleep now." He steadies himself with both hands on the arms of the chair as he rises. "Sorry I didn't make it today. They really did have a flood."

"It's okay. You don't need to apologize."

I stand and hover as he stumbles to the door. He manages to open it himself, then navigates the small ladder that leads into the cabin. I follow him, ready to help if he needs me. Liam makes his way to the back and slides open the door to his bedroom, then drops onto the bed.

I stand in the entrance to the tiny room for a minute. It's neat as a pin. Framed photos line the wall that tell a love story. Liam and Sarah at the beach, cheeks pressed together as they make funny faces. Their wedding day. Sarah laughing with baby Olive. Sarah holding both their children on her lap while she blows out birthday candles. It occurs to me that the pages in their book have been ripped out so near the beginning. The thought is like having my heart squeezed.

I look at Liam who is snoring lightly now. I take his shoes off and fold the quilt over him.

He mumbles, his words slurring together. "She'll be all alone."

"She'll always have you," I whisper, as I touch his hair.

This is how Liam falls apart. He makes sure Olive won't see, and he drinks until he can let himself cry. Then he keeps going.

I don't expect to hear from Liam today. In addition to helping his in-laws and being a dad again, I'm sure he must be hungover, raw, and maybe a little embarrassed even. In the aftermath of what I saw last night, my romantic notions toward Liam seem frivolous, although my feelings for him have deepened. I want to be there for all his bad days and nights. The good ones too.

All day, I have to resist the urge to call him, but around four in the afternoon, I get a call from his number. My heart leaps, then squeezes, and when I answer, it's Olive's voice I hear. "Abby? It's me, Olive."

"Hi, Olive, what's up? Is everything okay?"

"Yes. I'm calling because it's my class picture day on Monday and I was wondering if you know how to do a waterfall braid?"

"A what, sweetie?"

"A waterfall braid. All the girls in my class are going to have them, but my dad doesn't know how. I thought maybe you could do it?" Her voice is quiet, and I know this call was hard for her to make because even at her young age, she has already figured out that being a burden is not desirable.

"Sure I can. I haven't done it before, but I'll look it up on YouTube. Maybe see if your dad can drop you off here tomorrow for a while so I can practice."

"Really?" She sounds so thrilled at the possibility, and it breaks my heart on so many levels. "Okay. One second. I'll be right back."

I love her little Maritime accent. I'm not sure I've ever loved a voice as much as hers. I could listen to her talk all day long. I wonder if I should tell her that or if that would be weird.

I hear murmuring in the background, then Liam says, "Abby, hi."

"Hi, how's it going?" I ask, hoping to leave space for him to choose to pretend I didn't see him at his worst.

"All right" he says, his voice becoming much quieter. "Thanks for your help last night."

I aim for a breezy tone. "That's what friends do."

"Well, I appreciate it." There's a quick pause while Olive says something, then he's back on the line. "I didn't realize she was calling you about this braid thing. I'm sorry about that. We can take care of it."

"I'd be happy to help."

"No, I saw a video for this waterfall thing she wants. It looks really complicated. We can just put her hair in a ponytail. I'm good at those. It'll be fine."

"Liam, Olive doesn't ask for much. It's nothing for me to show up and play with her hair for a while."

He sighs. "Are you sure? Because you'd have to be at our place at seven-thirty on Monday morning."

"I can do that. Apparently, I'm an adult," I say, drawing on my ability to pretend everything's fine to get through this call.

"You sure?"

"Not about being an adult, but definitely about coming by to do Olive's hair."

He laughs, then says, "No. I'll do it."

"Good lord, Liam. She didn't ask for a kidney. She asked for some help so she can look like her little friends for picture day. Bring her over tomorrow so I can play with her hair for a while ... and maybe take her into Sydney to get her a chic outfit."

"No, that's too much. I can't ask you to do that."

"You didn't. Olive asked about the hair and I'm the one who wants to go shopping. It would be very satisfying for me to see her go to school looking like she owns the place."

"All right, that would be nice for her, actually, but I'm going to give you cash for the clothes. That's non-negotiable."

I can hear her squealing with delight in the background, then after a quick back and forth between her and Liam, she comes back on the phone.

"Thank you! Thank you! Thank you, Abby!"

"Anytime, sweetie." I wish I could hug her right now.

"Dad said he'll bring me over around eleven tomorrow, okay?"

"I'll be waiting."

She hangs up, and I can picture her bouncing around with a big grin, knowing that for once, she's going to look like the girls in her class, instead of a motherless child. The thought both breaks my heart and makes it sing. She needs this, and it's something I can do for her.

I get up and put the kettle on for some tea while I think about Olive. She's innocent and sweet and makes the best of any situation. And here I've been, moping around, feeling sorry for myself because the guy I have a crush on may or may not be blowing me off. While across town, a little girl who lives on a tiny boat with her dad is calling me because she doesn't have a mom who can make her hair look pretty for picture day. And if I say no, she won't complain. Not Olive. She'll say, 'okay' and go to school with whatever she and her dad can come up with, and she'll smile just as brightly as if she had the most beautiful hairdo in the world. I need to take a page out of her book.

My entire life, I've thought that children would be exhausting because you have to teach them everything about being an adult, when the truth is, they teach you about how we're supposed to live. Olive possesses a wisdom that is both jarring and beautiful. She's been a mirror for me, holding up who I am for my careful examination. This brings the odd glimpse of pride, like when she says I'm the funniest person she's met, but also moments like this, of deep shame. Maybe this is why I avoided children my entire life. Because some wise part of me knew they wield the power to force self-reflection, and it's just so much easier to go on ignoring one's shortcomings.

I may be broken-hearted, but I'm also exceedingly self-centered.

CHAPTER TWENTY-EIGHT

 Beauty is only skin deep, but ugly goes clean to the bone.

~ Dorothy Parker

It's Monday at seven a.m. as I hurry up the pier. I'm earlier than we had originally planned, but I'm worried I'll need extra time to make her look just right. The chilly autumn air nips at my skin as I shift the heavy bag of hair products and supplies looped over my arm. It's still dim out, and I can see the lights shining brightly inside the cabin as I approach the boat. I'm a bit of a nervous wreck about this entire thing. Somehow, I've decided that this is like a 'potential step-mom for my child' audition, even though I know Liam wouldn't think of it that way. I've been driving myself crazy all weekend thinking about everything that's happened (and hasn't happened) between Thursday night and now. I mean, that was some high-level flirting at the pub, but then after ... I don't know what the hell that was. Him being a gentleman? Him trying to put off the inevitable (which would be letting me down easy)? Him secretly being so in love with me he's been trying to forge an engagement ring in his spare time so he can present it to me in the mother of all proposals?

Okay, so that last one's not likely. I know that. He and I were very much 'business as usual,' on Saturday, not that there was an opportunity to talk. Maybe we should leave well enough alone. We can go on like this, with me being Olive's part-time caregiver and friend to both of them. It's better than nothing.

I lug my purse and my heavy bag up the ladder, then take a deep breath. *Relax, Abby. It's just hair.*

Liam opens the door, then takes my things so I can climb down into the cabin.

"Good morning," he says, in a warm tone that says, 'we're friends and that's that.' "I made you some tea."

"Oh great, thanks," I say, channeling my inner smooth, powerful Lauren.

Olive, who is already dressed in the black leggings and turquoise crocheted sweater we picked up, rushes around her dad to give me a huge hug. I hug her back and plant a kiss on top of her head. "Shall we get to work?"

She nods, her eyes wild with excitement. "I can't wait for everyone to see me with smooth, straight hair just like yours."

"Well, I love your curls, but I suppose I can miss them for today."

I set up the hair elastics, a comb, a brush, and my straightener on the kitchen table.

"I'm frying some eggs. Can I make you some?" Liam asks.

"Sure." *Thanks, buddy.*

"How do you like 'em?"

"Fertilized." I laugh. *Why did I say that? That was ridiculous.*

Olive looks up at me. "What does that mean?"

"Nothing. It's an old joke for old people," I answer. "However you're making the eggs is my favorite way to have them."

"Okay," he says, trying to sound like this isn't the most awkward moment ever.

Fertilized, Abby? You total moron.

I busy myself with the task at hand, glad that it allows us not to have to talk. For the next forty minutes, Olive does her best to sit still, which seems like torture because she's so excited. Finally, I stand back and survey the results. Not bad.

The waterfall braid cascades down the sides of her head, just like the girl in the video. I hold up a hand mirror for her and she bites her lip, smiling as she sees herself. We smile at each other and Olive gives me another big hug. "Thank you, Abby."

"You're most welcome. This was fun."

Liam takes out his phone. "Let me get a picture of you."

"Abby, too, okay?" she asks, wrapping her arms around my waist.

I smile past the phone and look directly at him, scanning for any clues to his feelings, but he is an enigma. Or I'm too blind to see the truth. "Can I drive Olive to school? Just in case her hair gets messed up on the way. I can do some last-minute touch-ups."

"Sure," he says. "Listen, I have to head back to Virgil and Fiona's again today. When I pulled up the carpet in the basement, I discovered the subfloor is rotten. I'll need the day to get it torn out, but I promise I'll be by to finish your place tomorrow."

Shrugging, I say, "Whenever."

———

I grin at Olive in the rear-view mirror as I wind my way through the village to the school. She is beaming, and I see her smoothing her hand over her hair each time I look back. It glistens in the early morning light. Shiny and healthy like her.

I find a spot across the road to park, and we get out. Olive slips her arms through the straps of her backpack, then takes my hand as we cross the road. I give her fingers a little squeeze of excitement as we walk, and the cold air cannot touch me through my cloak of happiness.

When we reach the front sidewalk of the school, she stops walking and turns to look up at me.

"Thank you so much, Abby." She lets go of my hand and grins again.

I lift my hands to the top of her head and let them glide down the length of her hair. "You're welcome, sweet girl. It was my pleasure." I give her a kiss on top of her head, and she is gone, racing to the door as the bell sounds. I stand watching, and my heart twists as I see her go in.

All day, I find myself restless and I can't seem to sit at my desk for more than a few minutes without getting up to do something. Throw in that load of whites or dust the shelves in my office, which show a thin layer of white in the morning sun—anything but sit still and write. I can't seem to return to Beatrice and her orphans. Instead, I've left her sitting in a tub full of warm water turning into a prune while I vacuum the entire house.

The house feels empty today with both Liam and Olive gone. Unable to face the quiet any longer, I go for a long walk along the beach, keeping my eye out for Isaac's ring, just in case it's somehow washed up onto the shore. After about twenty minutes, something shiny catches my eye. I hurry over and lean down. It's my necklace. Laughing with excitement, I dig furiously around it with both hands, my pulse quickening as the chain continues on, deeper down. But then, it ends. No ring. Just a broken chain. Pocketing it, I continue digging, then stand and kick at the sand anywhere nearby, just in case. I'm determined to find it. It's got to be here somewhere, if the chain is.

But it isn't. After what feels like hours, I give up and go home, but I don't give up hope because if I found the chain, there's always a chance I'll find the ring too.

After a long, hot shower, I sit back at my desk, checking the clock every few minutes and wondering if Olive will call to let me know how the day went. Finally, around two-thirty, I decide to pick up a few groceries. That way I can happen to be walking past the schoolhouse at three o'clock.

The next half hour is a steady climb in anticipation for me, as I peruse the aisles, keeping an eye on the time. It turns out, several moms use this as their chance to get groceries, and when I get to the checkout, I end up in a long line-up of women who know each other. They chat loudly, not seeming the least bit concerned about the time, while I tap my foot impatiently.

I walk out of the store just as the bell rings and see Liam pulling up in his truck. He gets out and gives me a confused expression until I hold up the bag. When I catch up with him, he's wearing a knowing smile. "Needed a few things at the store, eh?"

"I ran out of bananas."

"Want to come see how Olive's day went? You know, since you're here and all?"

"Oh, sure." I shrug, even though he's clearly on to me. "Might as well."

It only takes another minute for children to come pouring out the front of the school, like milk from an upturned jug. They chat and laugh with each other as my eyes wildly scan the crowd for Olive.

Finally, I see her. Her hair is no longer in the waterfall braid and my heart drops. I immediately assume that I've done such a poor job that it somehow came out. Large kinks jut out from the top of her head, and chunks of her hair are no longer straight but zigzagged. The only word I can think of to describe it is odd. She is looking at the ground, shoulders slumped.

"Oh dear," Liam murmurs. "Something's happened."

I say nothing, torn up by the sight of her. Her feet drag, and, as she walks in our direction, she gets bumped and jostled by the children in their hurry to get home and play video games. She takes no notice of them.

Liam and I wind our way through the crowd to her, and she stops when she sees his shoes in front of her. When she looks up, her face is stained with tears, her eyes are puffy behind her glasses. Liam puts his hands on her shoulders and crouches down to her. "What happened, my love?"

"None of the other girls wanted to look like me."

"What? What do you mean?"

"Mercedes Tanner told the other girls to wear headbands and big curls in their hair. She made them promise not to tell me."

"Oh love, that's awful. I'm sorry." Liam pulls her in for a big hug, and I see her frail body shaking.

Tears fill my eyes. This is the trick of the mean girl. They exist everywhere, at every age and stage in life, although I have no idea what their purpose is.

"They all made fun of me and said they were never going to wear waterfall braids in the first place and that they're for babies like me." Her voice hitches and she tries to catch her breath, but it's no use because she's sobbing so hard. "Mercedes said that if I had a mom, I wouldn't look so stupid all the time. I tried to take my hair out and wet it so my curls would come back, but it didn't work, so my pictures are all wrecked now."

"Oh, sweetheart, we can get retakes. It'll be okay," Liam says.

She shakes her head. "They don't do a retake of the class picture. Everyone is going to have a copy of me looking like a crazy bag lady." She sobs again, then says, "That's what Seth said I look like."

Anger is bubbling in my blood. How dare anyone make this perfect child feel any kind of pain? Not on my watch. I look around and spot a group of girls in headbands and curls. They are laughing together, surrounded by their mothers, who are very busy chatting about something most certainly useless, like their favorite brands of retinol when they should be teaching their awful girls to be kind.

I march over, not at all sure what I'm going to say, but I'm going to say it all right. I reach the group and stop. "Mercedes? Is one of you girls named Mercedes?"

The shortest one looks up at me sweetly and raises her hand. "I am." The look on her face says she thinks she's going to get a prize. I'll give her a fucking prize, all right.

"On what planet is it okay to make fun of someone because she doesn't have a mother? What if your mother died? Would that be your fault?"

A well-dressed, painfully thin woman gasps loudly. "Don't you talk to my daughter that way!"

I spin on her. "Oh, so Mercedes is your little cherub, is she? Are you aware that she told Olive that all the girls were wearing waterfall braids, but then she told all the girls to wear headbands and to promise not to tell her?"

The woman shrugs. "Mercedes would never do that. I'm sure she just forgot to tell Olive."

Another girl speaks up. "No, she made us promise not to tell her because she didn't want her to look like one of us."

I nod emphatically. The truth is out. "Thank you, Honest Girl. There is some hope for humanity after all."

I turn to the thin mom and fold my arms across my chest as I wait for her to be horrified to discover her daughter is a mean girl.

She gives her daughter a tilted head cutesy serious look. "Mercedes, that wasn't nice."

"Sorry, Mommy."

"Okay, then." She gives me a single nod, as though that will put the matter to rest. But it won't.

"Is that it? 'Okay, then?' You're not even going to make her apologize to Olive?" I'm leaning in toward her in a way that is probably very threatening. At least I hope it is.

"Okay, who are you even?" she asks, looking disgusted.

"I'm her G.D. babysitter," I say as though it's some super intimidating revelation that will have her shaking in her UGGs.

She snorts, then says, "Okay, well, it's really none of your business, so just back off."

Glaring at her for a second, I say, "Okay, sure. I'll back off. Because now I can see there's no point in bothering. I can see where Mercedes gets her lovely personality from. Congratulations on raising a horrible, hateful, shallow, cruel person. You'll have a lot in common by the time she's grown!" I'm so filled with rage that I shake my bag of bananas at her.

I feel an arm reach around from behind me and cover my upper chest, near my collarbone. It's Liam, and he's gently guiding me away from the fight. "Let's just go. They're not worth it."

"Olive's worth it." I bark at him. "Are you going to let these people get away with this?"

Liam looks at me. He's far too calm for my liking. He sighs, then looks at Mercedes. "I'm surprised at you, Mercedes. You used to be Olive's friend. You used to come to our place all the time to play. But now you seem to have decided that she doesn't fit in, and I can't for the life of me understand why. Especially when all she's wanted is to be your friend."

His tone is kind, which I cannot fathom right now. How could he be kind to this little shit? Hmm, the little shit seems to look genuinely upset now. Her bottom lip is actually quivering. Maybe his way isn't completely useless after all.

He looks at the moms, who are having trouble making eye contact with him at the moment. "Ladies."

With that, he turns, and I follow him. I see Olive has been right behind us this whole time, her eyes are wide with shock, and she looks like she isn't sure if she should laugh or cry. Liam picks her up and carries her, and I follow a few steps behind. I turn back to the women and glare at both Mercedes and her awful mother for good measure.

I lag a little as we cross the road, trying to calm down. The calmer I become, the more I am filled with regret. I really had no business going off like that, and now, I am horribly worried that I may have just inadvertently made Olive's life much harder.

Liam opens the door and flips the bench seat forward so she can climb in the back. Before she sits down, I hear him say, "They're just jealous because you're so beautiful and smart. You know that, don't you?"

She shakes her head but gives him a small smile. "No, I'm not. I'm weird."

Liam's eyes narrow. "You're not weird. Who told you you're weird?"

"All the kids. I'm not in dance or soccer or anything. I only like to draw and look for fairies and mermaids. That's why they don't want to look like me."

For the first time, I see him put on a very firm look when he addresses his daughter. He even wags his finger at her. "You listen to me. You're not weird. You're kind and thoughtful and smart, and you've got more imagination in your little finger than the rest of them have combined. Just because a few nincompoops decided to be mean doesn't mean the problem lies with you."

I stand, holding my bananas, feeling very out of place. When he's done, I lean my head into the truck as far as I can. "I'm so sorry, Olive. I shouldn't have lost my temper like that. I hope I didn't embarrass you."

She smiles a little. "I can't believe you called her all those names. Hateful, horrible, cruel and what was the other one?"

I slump a little. "Shallow."

"Right. What does that one mean?"

"Err—someone who cares more about how they look than how they act."

Her eyes grow wide. "Ooh, that's a great word!"

I take a long look at her. She's sitting there with wildly crazy hair, red eyes from crying, having been horribly rejected today by almost all the girls she knows, and yet she seems to be bouncing back already.

Finally daring to look at Liam, I say, "I'm really sorry. That was ... uncalled for."

"That was something, all right." He raises his eyebrows, looking nonplussed. "Abigail, I think I'm going to take Olive home. She's had quite the day."

"Oh, well, sure. That makes sense." I don't protest or tell him I was planning to see if they wanted to come over for celebratory spaghetti. I know he wants to get away from me and I completely understand his reasoning. He needs to get his daughter away from the insane woman who just yelled at an eight-year-old child she's never met before.

233

Liam climbs into the truck, and before he can close the door, Olive says, "Thank you for sticking up for me."

My shoulders slump. "I'm afraid I didn't handle that the way I should have. Grown-ups are supposed to be better at staying calm." I give her an apologetic look.

"Don't be sorry. It was the most awesome thing anyone's ever done for me." She gives me a wide grin, bordering on evil delight and I return it.

"Have a good night, beautiful girl."

"You too, beautiful lady."

I turn to Liam with an apologetic expression, but he doesn't let me off the hook. He just purses his lips, raises and lowers his eyebrows, then shuts the door, leaving me standing with my bananas swinging in the wind.

"So, now what do I do?" I ask Lauren, who's been listening to me pour out all the drama of the last few days, starting with Thursday night and ending with my tirade against the nasty eight-year-olds. She's cooking supper while I rant.

Lauren lets out a long breath. "Wow, Abby, that is ... wow."

"I know. I was awful. I just got so mad, I blew up."

"Urgh, that makes me feel all squishy inside just thinking about it," she says.

"Well, thanks for that," I say, hoping she can hear my eyes roll.

"One thing's for sure, you can never show your face at that school again."

"I know."

"And honestly, after the fertilized egg comment, I'm not even sure you should show your face around Liam either."

I groan, and flop onto my bed, covering my face with a decorative pillow. Walt hops up onto my bed and sniffs my ear, his whiskers tickling my cheek.

"That's it. I'm out. I can't be a part of this. I'm not built for emotional roller coasters," I say. "This is way too hard. And it's not the 'does he or doesn't he' thing that's the problem—although it sucks. It's watching a child you care about get her heart crushed and knowing you really can't do anything to make this world a less evil place for her. We were right not to bring children into this world."

"Umm, I think it's too late for you to just say 'peace out' to these people. The little girl clearly sees you as the mother she wishes she had. You can't just take off on her."

Banging my head on the mattress, I say, "I know. What was I thinking?"

"Well, who knows? Maybe Liam will decide it's for the best if you slowly taper off your relationship with them."

"Yeah, maybe. That would be for the best. I obviously don't know what the hell I'm doing in the parenting department. Not that I'm a parent, but you know ..."

"I knew what you meant. The truth is, you'd learn."

Shaking my head, I say, "I doubt it. I'm too late getting into the game." I sit up and look at myself in the mirror. "No, I can't do this. Tomorrow morning when he comes over, I'll just apologize and tell him we should just back things up a bit. See if he can find a new after-school sitter. It would be for the best."

"Well, you may be getting ahead of yourself here. I'm not sure he's going to think this is as big a deal as you do."

"You didn't see his face. He was mortified to be seen with me," I answer.

"Why don't you call him? Otherwise, you're going to drive yourself crazy."

"Yeah, I should do that."

"Okay, I'm sorry, sweetie," Lauren says, "I wish I could talk longer but we're about to sit down for dinner and it's the first time Drew and I have had a meal together since last week."

"Right, okay. Tell him I say hi."

"Will do."

Instead of phoning, I take the coward's way out and text. *Just checking to see how Olive is doing.*

A minute later, I get an answer. *She's surviving. We're snuggled up watching a movie. I'll see you in the morning.*

Well, if that wasn't Canadian for 'you've done enough. Leave us alone, psycho,' I don't know what is. I toss my phone onto the bed and run a nice hot bath.

CHAPTER TWENTY-NINE

It is not the strength of the body that counts, but the strength of the spirit.

~ J.R.R. Tolkien

The coffee goes cold while I wait for Liam to arrive. My stomach churns and my mind spins like it did all night. Should I tell him I might be in love with him, and that even though I know I'm far from perfect, I want to be there for him and Olive? Or tell him I can't do this, and we should back away for everyone's sake?

Now that his truck is pulling up, I still have no idea what to do. I just know the thought of pulling away from them feels like a loss I can't face right now, not when I finally feel strong again. But it's not about me, is it? Because the last thing they need is a woman who's barely hanging on asking them to keep her from falling.

My hand trembles slightly as I turn the doorknob. He's coming up the front steps, his hands jammed into the front pockets of his jeans.

I give him a small wave. "How is she this morning?"

Walking past me into the house, he shrugs. "She was all right until we got about a block from school. Then she had a bit of a cry."

My stomach rolls as I close the door. "I'm sorry. It must have been so hard to drop her off there."

He nods. "Parenting is the shits sometimes."

We walk to the kitchen and I pour him a coffee, then top mine up. We both know we need to talk and we both know it's going to be now.

Once we're seated at the table, I start. "I just want to say how sorry I am, Liam. I don't know what came over me. I was just overcome by this ... this fierce protectiveness."

I glance up at him, and his face is so serious I can't stand it. Instead, I stare down at my hands. "I really messed up, didn't I?"

"I appreciate what you were trying to do, Abby. I know your heart was in the right place, but good Lord, you really went after that little Mercedes and her mom." He shakes his head, then starts laughing. "I know I shouldn't find it funny, but the look on your face when you were yelling about being the G.D. babysitter ..."

I let a chuckle escape, relief flooding my veins. "Like that's supposed to scare anyone. Ooh, not the babysitter!"

When the moment passes, Liam says, "And that little brat had it coming."

Good, yes, let's focus on what Mercedes did wrong. So much easier. "She did, didn't she?" Then the image of Olive walking out of the school, her face stained with tears pops into my mind. "Olive shouldn't have to put up with that shit. She's been through enough."

He nods, running his finger over the handle of the white mug.

"Do you think they'll be extra awful to her today?"

Shrugging, he says, "Maybe, I don't know. That's the worst part of being a parent. You can't fix these things, you can't change the world, and you can't shield your child from it, no matter how much you wish you could."

"There's always homeschooling." I say it like it's a joke, but at this moment, I'd be willing to pull her out of school and become her full-time teacher.

Walt hops up on Liam's lap and he scratches under his chin. "But what happens after? Keep hiding them away their entire lives?"

"Yes."

He shakes his head. "They have to learn to fight their battles, and when they lose, how to get back up." Anger crosses over his face, then disappears. "The truth about parenting that nobody tells you is you spend most of it just feeling helpless."

Well, that's that, then. I don't do helpless, so this is going to have to be the start of a slow goodbye. I'll find them some amazing, strong woman who can handle all of it with poise. Someone who knows how to sew and can whip up a batch of chocolate cookies in under ten minutes.

He continues on, and I'm not sure who he's talking to at this point. "What kids really need is someone to hold them when they cry, and to help them pick themselves back up when they fall. And the whole fucking time you have to pretend it'll be all right." He's using both hands to pet Walt in long strokes over his ears and chest. "You tell them to get back out there and do their best, even though you know the game is rigged."

"That all sounds horrible to me."

Liam makes a sound that's halfway between a laugh and a cry. "It is." Then he laughs. "It's fucking shitty."

Reaching out, I take his hand and squeeze it. "And doing it alone must be so much harder."

He looks up at me, his eyes searching mine, and I'm sure he's wondering if that was an offer.

I pull my hand away and tuck it under my leg. "I'm sure Sarah would have known exactly what to do yesterday."

"Sarah would've done a lot worse than you," he says.

"No," I say, shaking my head.

"Christ, yeah. The temper on her when she saw something like that going down. I'm glad it was you there because I'd have been bailing her out of jail." Liam chuckles and shakes his head. "She was half bats, that one. But I loved her for it."

We sit in silence for a minute. He seems lost in his memory, and for my part, I don't know what to say or even think. Liam sighs, his frown returning. "It's my fault she doesn't fit in. It's got nothing to do with her hair or her clothes—well, maybe a little bit—but the truth is, I let her be different. All that stuff she believes about her mom and the baby being mermaids ... it puts people off, you know?"

"Well, that's their problem, not hers. I think it's beautiful. It gives her hope and it makes her happy. And for a child who's had so much sorrow, how could you take even a tiny bit of her happiness away?"

My insistent tone causes Walt to jump off Liam's lap and trot out of the room.

I watch him, then turn to Liam. "She's got more imagination than I'll ever have, and that's a rare gift. It's not something we should let the world take away from her."

He looks up at me. "You just said we."

"I'm sorry. I heard it as soon as it came out of my mouth. I'm over-stepping my bounds." I run both hands through my hair. "For someone who claims she never gets attached, I've certainly proven myself to be a liar."

Liam tilts his head, giving me an intense stare. "What are we doing here, Abby?"

"Having our morning site meeting?"

"Don't do that."

"I'm sorry." And I am. "It's just so hard to admit. I'm more me when I'm around the two of you than when I'm with anyone else in the world." Closing my eyes for a second, I can barely get the words out. "Even more than with Isaac. And I don't know if that's good or bad, but I love it. I love ... how I feel when I'm with you, *and* with Olive."

I risk a glance at those eyes of his, and feel my heart break, like I knew it would. "I also know it doesn't matter what I love because you need someone strong who always knows what to do. Someone who can keep her shit together, and that's not me. I just don't have it in me."

"What if you do but you don't know it yet?"

I start to shake my head, but the sound of his cell phone interrupts me. He glances at it, his eyebrows knitting together. "That's the school."

He stands and answers his phone, turning to the window. "She did what?"

There's a long pause, then he says, "No, of course I understand. I'll be right down."

When he hangs up, he looks at me. "I have to go pick up Olive. She's been suspended for punching Mercedes Tanner in the face."

"What?" I stand and follow him to the door, trying not to smile.

"She must have a hell of a right cross because she gave her a bloody nose." He opens the door, then looks at me, fighting a grin.

"You want me to come with—?" I start, then shake my head. "No, probably best if I wait here."

"Yeah, maybe."

Liam's demeanor has changed when he returns with Olive. He's in disappointed, don't-ever-do-it-again dad mode. Olive's face is red from crying and I can tell by his face he's had to give her a lecture he doesn't believe and he hates himself for it. I watch her pull off her backpack, her breath catching every few seconds, and I want to wrap my arms around her and hold her until it stops. Instead, I unzip her coat for her and put it on the bench by the front door, unsure if a hug would be the equivalent of saying it's okay to hit someone.

"You probably heard," she says. Her chest heaves as she chokes out, "I'm a big bully now."

I cover my mouth with one hand, trying not to laugh while at the same time, trying not to cry. "Oh, Olive. You're not a bully."

"I had to go to the principal's office and watch a video about violence and bullies." She burst into tears again. "Seth says my next stop will be juvie hall." Snot rolls out of her nose, but she takes no notice of it.

"Oh, sweetheart, you're a long way from juvie hall." I take her hand and walk her to the bathroom where I get some tissues and hold them up to her nose. "Blow."

She does as I said while the hiccups continue. Liam stands at the door to the bathroom and looks down at her with slumped shoulders.

"I have to go pee," she says, walking over to the toilet and starting to pull down her leggings.

"Whoop. I'll give you your privacy," I say, walking out and closing the door behind me.

Liam and I stand in the hall, wincing at each other. I put my hand on his arm and speak in a quiet voice. "This is awful. Don't you just want to tell her not to worry about it?"

He nods. "So badly it hurts. I'd take her out and buy her a pony if it wouldn't send the wrong message."

The toilet flushes and a second later the door opens.

Liam raises one eyebrow. "Did you wash your hands?"

She turns back and sobs out the words, "Sorry, Dad."

Clearing his throat, he says, "The principal said Olive may return to school tomorrow so long as she writes an apology to Mercedes and one for her teacher. Maybe she can get started on that now."

"Sure," I nod, holding my hand out to her and starting toward the kitchen. "Why don't I sit with you while you write it?"

She nods and sniffles. "Yes, please."

"I'll be down in the basement," he says, sighing while he watches her walk.

"Okay," I say.

Olive slides onto a chair while I go in search of the supplies she needs. When I come back, she has her arms crossed on the table and her head resting on them. I put down a pen and a few white sheets of paper, then rub her back. "Can I get you some water?"

"That would be nice."

I walk over to the cupboard. "You know, Olive, I got suspended once."

"You did?" she asks, perking up.

"Mmm-hmm. I was in seventh grade," I say, turning on the tap and filling the glass. "I had an extremely strict English teacher named Mrs. Butterfield."

Olive gives me a skeptical look while I walk back to the table.

"For real, that was her name." I put the glass in Olive's hand. "Drink up. She never did like me, but I have no idea why. One day, I was talking in class while she was trying to teach, and she'd had enough and kicked me out of class."

"You got suspended for talking?"

"No, it's what happened after," I say, holding up one finger. "And I want you to know I'm not proud of it. When I was walking out the door, she said, 'And before you come back, you need to drop the attitude.'

"So I said, 'Before I come back, you need to drop forty pounds of butt fat.'"

Olive slaps both hands over her mouth, her eyes as round as Walt's Fancy Feast plate.

"Yeah," I nod. "I said that. Horrible, right?"

"Why?"

"I honestly don't know why I said that. I didn't think she'd hear me, but I wasn't talking quietly enough. In fact, all the kids in the class heard it too," I add. "Actually, I was kind of shouting, now that I think about it. And suddenly it's pretty obvious why she never liked me."

I stare at Olive's shocked face for a second, a testament to the fact that I have no business being a role model of any sort. "I'm not sure I should have told you any of that. I'm definitely not condoning backtalk or umm ... fat shaming. The first one is cheeky and the second one is cruel. I guess what I'm trying to say is that everybody makes mistakes, and yours today feels like a big one, but someday, it won't feel as big. Does that make sense?"

She nods and sniffs again, then picks up the pencil.

"I'll shut up now so you can get your work done."

It takes her nearly an hour and almost all my blank paper to come up with the perfect apology letters. She's so sincere about it that she gives me hope for the future of humanity. And when she's done, Olive seems more like herself again while I make us peanut butter and jelly sandwiches and slice up an apple. I task her with pouring herself a milk and carrying my coffee over to the table for me, then we sit down together to eat.

"We only have three more sleeps on the boat." She hasn't finished chewing the bite of sandwich in her mouth when she comes out with this news, and I can see bits of food clinging to her teeth. Thankfully, she takes a sip of milk before she continues. "Dad's going to take the boat out of the water this weekend, so we have to spend the winter in our house."

"Do you like it there?"

She shrugs. "Sort of. I like having a yard and a bigger room and stuff. But my dad's happier on the boat, so it's better."

I don't say anything, but instead, pick up the napkin next to her plate and wipe a little lump of peanut butter off her cheek.

"It makes him sad because we're not on the water where my mom and baby Malcolm can see us."

"Oh, I see."

"They're sad too. So this year, I'm going to write a note for them to tell them where we're going so they won't worry. I think that'll make my dad feel better." She takes another bite of her sandwich. "Do you have a bottle I could use?"

"I'm sure I can find something."

After lunch, Olive gets straight to work on her note. I slip into the bathroom and splash my face with some cold water, trying not to let my sadness show. I must be in there a while because she comes to find me. "Abby, are you in there? I'm all done."

"Be right out." I take a deep breath, then another to convince myself that I can do this. When I open the door, she is standing with her coat zipped up, and a rolled-up paper in her hand. "Is your tummy feeling okay? You were in there for a long time."

My cheeks flush at her pointed question. "I'm fine."

I find a wine bottle with a screw top that had been rinsed out in preparation for recycling.

"I already told my dad we're going for a walk, so we can just go." She carefully slides the note into the bottle and then screws the lid on tight.

The world seems desolate today as we walk along the shore. It's dark and gray, and as a gust of wind whips my hair into my face, I feel the first hints of winter. Only the seagulls are out fighting against the wind today, searching for supper. There are no sailboats out, no seals, no other people strolling along while their dogs scamper down the beach seeking the perfect piece of driftwood for a game of fetch.

As we head out toward the open sea, the sandy beach gives way to rocky terrain. The water below drops off and soon, you can't see the spot where the water meets the cliff unless you're right on the edge. Olive scampers ahead, certain the mermaids come up to sun themselves on those rocks. She saw one there once. Her grandmother tried to tell her it was just a seal's tail disappearing below the surface, but she knows what she saw.

"This is the spot," she shouts. Clutching the bottle in one hand, she scrambles along to get closer to the edge of the cliff. It's steep, and she loses her footing, but then quickly recovers.

"Be careful!" I shout the useless piece of advice, and it disappears into the air behind me. Fear takes over my legs now, and I pick up my pace to a jog, even though I'm sure I'm overreacting. The tide has come in, slamming against the cliff, and my heart slams against my ribcage in response. "Olive, wait for me! It's not safe!"

But she doesn't hear me and keeps making her way down, tucking the bottle close to her while she uses her free hand to steady herself. A wave rolls toward her, and I see what happens two seconds before it takes place. The water rises above the rock, crushing down on her while I scream. It pulls her feet out from under her, taking her with it as it disappears under the edge of the cliff.

I scramble down the rocks, too terrified to breathe. My foot slips on the wet rock but I recover and force myself to move with a swiftness I forgot I had. My hair is whipped in front of my eyes just as her head bobs up. I scream her name and leap down to the rock just above her, then lie down and reach out my arms, trying to grab for her as the water rises again. I clutch at her hood, only managing to grasp it with the tips of my fingers. Another icy wave slams down on us, and I lose her. I try to call for her as water fills my lungs. *Please don't die. Please don't die.*

Without thinking, I push myself to a crouch, then launch my body into the next wave, reaching wildly around me as I go under. The air is squeezed out of my lungs and the cold shock on my skin feels like thousands of knives. I try to look around me, but the saltwater stings and my eyes shut automatically. *Where the hell are you, Olive?*

I bob up above the surface and take a deep breath, just before another wave envelops my body, lifting me and crashing me into the cliff. Pain tears through my back and legs, but when the wave pulls back, she is there. Just under the surface. I manage to get a hold of her hair with one hand, and my fingers grip hard. *Don't let her go. Don't let her die.*

She is spun by the next wave, and I see her eyes through her dark hair, wild with terror. She reaches for me, and as the wave moves us, it brings her tight to my body. My back slams against the rocks again, but the incredible relief of finding her outweighs the pain. I hold onto her with everything in me, using my legs to push us away from the cliff and toward the beach. But the tide is too strong, and it bashes me against the stone again, this time slamming my cheek and the side of my head. My ears pop from the impact and my eyes go dim, but I hold tight to Olive's little body, tucking her in as close to me as I can.

Our heads surface now, and I gulp the air and try to propel us to the left where it's safe. Violent sobs from Olive's chest shake us both as I try to swim toward a sandy break in the cliff. Out of the corner of my eye, I see another wave above us.

"Close your mouth!" We're taken under again, and I am disoriented by the time we resurface. I spin around, trying to find the shore, but my hair covers my face, choking me and blocking my eyes. The water is so cold it crushes my lungs, making it seem like I'll never take a full breath again. Olive clings to me, gripping my neck so hard I couldn't breathe even if there were air available. When we come back up, I try to scream for help, but my voice comes out strangled, and I know it will be lost against the rocks. We're being dragged to the cliff again, and I'm frozen with fear at what is about to come.

I lift her head above the water and hold her up while I fight the tide, trying to find a way to get us out of this. We are pushed to shore, then sucked down, then out to sea and back up again. I join forces with the rhythm. This time, I don't waste energy trying to fight the tide, but use it to my advantage, pushing off with one foot against the rocks when the tide starts to pull us out to sea.

I kick with every bit of strength I possess, and my legs cut through the water. My wet jeans and jacket are lead weighing me down, along with Olive's body. They slow my movements until I'm not sure if I've even made an inch of progress. It's all I can do to hold myself up, to get her head above the water. Somehow, I catch a piece of a wave headed for a sandy break in the rocks. If I can just hold onto her, if I can just keep moving toward the beach until my body gives up, we'll get there. *Keep going. Let the tide take you home.*

I spend the last of my strength to get us around the bend, and then let the waves carry us to the sandy shore, while I hold Olive up as best I can. I am unable to keep my head above the water now. There is nothing left in me but the thought of holding onto her. *Get her to the shore. Just get her there.*

I'm suddenly being pulled toward the beach, and through a sliver of light between my hair, I see hands gripping my jacket. I'm being dragged onto the sand as I clutch Olive with both hands, wild with terror. With each blink, my vision grows more dim. Then everything goes black.

The sound of shouting wakes me. I open my eyes and see a pair of boots next to me. I turn my head to the side, and water comes out of my lungs in violent sputters. I choke as it comes out of my nose and mouth. My body shakes violently as I try to stay awake long enough to know if Olive will be okay.

I hear Liam's voice as though it's through a tunnel, even though he's right beside me. He's crying and yelling. "Olive, I'm here." He shouts at her. "Dad's here."

I see her legs, limp and still, as she's flipped onto her side.

"Olive! Olive!"

Panic sets in. I choke and gasp. *Please don't let her die.*

I have to get to her, but when I try to sit up, my body is useless. I can only move my head, and when I do, pain shoots through me. I can only wait, pray, and silently beg.

I hear a strangled cough and liquid splashes the ground. Then I hear her wail. A loud, long cry that is the best sound I've ever heard in my life.

Each sob of relief is cut short by the pain in my back and chest.

"You're okay, my love. You're okay." He repeats it as though he's trying to convince himself, as much as comfort her. He sinks to his knees with her pressed against him. Sobs shake them both, and I know they are coming from Liam. "Thank Christ, you're okay."

Shock and ice cold rattle my bones. "I'm sorry," I whisper. "I should have stopped her."

He looks down at me, and I see rage. "Why the hell did you let her go down there at high tide?!"

"I'm sorry. I'm so sorry, Olive." I tremble with deep regret and the aftershocks of terror.

Liam turns from me and holds Olive's face in his big hands. "What were you doing? You could've gotten killed, Olive. You could have died just then!"

"I was bringing a message to Mom." She's crying so hard that her words aren't fully formed.

"What?"

"I wanted to let them know we'll be back at the house for the winter." She buries her head in his chest and cries. "I'm sorry, Dad. I never meant to fall in."

"Is this about the damn mermaids, Olive? I never should have—!" He's holding her upper arms, and his voice has grown to a yell now. "Your mom isn't a mermaid, Olive! She's dead! She died and so did the baby."

"No, she didn't! She's here! I know she's here!" Olive's body convulses with the force of her sobs.

Liam's eyes are crazed, and he shakes her once. "Stop it, Olive! Stop it! You're never going to find her. She's gone. They're both gone."

I watch them, although the world seems to be growing dim, as they both collapse onto each other, clutching and sobbing. When he speaks again, his voice is quiet. "She's gone, Olive, and trying to find her is only going to kill you."

CHAPTER THIRTY

 Dream as if you'll live forever. Live as if you'll die today.

~ James Dean

I'm on my side in a brightly lit hospital room. I'm numb and too hot at the same time. The pain in my back forces me to lie on my side. Every tiny movement of my face feels as though the skin on my left cheek will tear apart. I blink, trying to figure out what's wrong with me.

A nurse who reminds me of Nettie flicks at the tube at the bottom of a fresh bag of fluids. She glances down at me and smiles. "There you are. Don't try to move much, okay?"

"Okay," I say, and the effort of that one word makes my eyes shut. "What's wrong with me?" I whisper.

"You don't remember? You're at Northside General Hospital. Do you know how you got here, Abby?"

"In an ambulance."

She smiles. "That's right. You saved that little girl from drowning."

Tears spring to my eyes. "So she's okay?"

"She's fine—mild hypothermia and a few scrapes. They've been keeping her toasty warm and monitoring her for a few hours now, but she can go home tonight," she says, replacing the bag of fluid next to my bed. "I don't think I could have done what you did. Jumped in there like that during high tide. You must have nerves of steel, like Superman, only prettier." She glances at my cheek and I see an instant flick of concern before her bright smile returns.

I blow out a puff of air and sniffle. "Am I okay?"

"You will be. But for now, you have a bad concussion, your right arm is broken in two places, and five of your ribs are cracked pretty badly." She pauses, then looks at my cheek again.

"What?"

"I'm afraid your face was cut pretty bad. But you got lucky because one of the best plastic surgeons in the province happened to be here, so there's hope that the scar won't be too bad. He stitched up your back too. You've got over a hundred stitches ..."

She continues talking but I tune her out, not wanting to know any more.

"... But no matter, you're alive and that little girl is alive with barely a scratch on her." She pulls the blankets up to my neck and tucks them around me. "It's almost time for some more pain medication. I'll ask the doc if we can give you the good stuff so you can get a big sleep."

"Thanks," I say, but she's already gone.

My right ear is so plugged it throbs. Every cell in my body hurts. Tears roll across my temple and into my hair. I can't close my eyes because when I do, I see her under the water. I feel her jacket slip through my fingers. I hear the roar of the waves and feel the sharp rock as I'm slammed against it. Even though I know it can't, I find myself wishing the next set of pain meds will take away those jagged memories.

There is a knock at the door, and Liam comes in with Olive in his arms. She's dressed in a T-shirt and sweatpants that hang off her tiny frame. He swallows when he sees me, and his face screws up with emotion. Olive slides out of his arms and onto my bed.

"Be careful, love." His voice is gentle now. The fear has passed, and it took the rage with it.

Her little hand brushes the hair out of my face, and she tucks it behind my ear, just the way her dad does for her. "You're my hero, Abby."

I shake my head, feeling fresh tears fill my eyes. "I'm so glad you're okay."

Liam places his hand over mine. "She wouldn't have made it if you hadn't jumped in after her."

I shake my head as much as I am able. "She wouldn't have been down there if it wasn't for me."

"Don't say that." He gives me a sad smile.

There are not enough days in the year for him to convince me this wasn't my fault, and at the moment, I don't have the will to fight him about it. "How did you find us?"

Tears fill his eyes and he looks away for a second, shaking his head. "I just got this terrible feeling, and I started running."

He pauses and clears his throat, and I know it's all too fresh to talk about. When he looks back at me, he wipes his cheeks. "I'm so sorry I yelled at you."

"It's okay. I'd yell at me too."

He gives my hand a little squeeze and his face crumples again. "I almost lost you both."

Olive looks up at her dad. "But you didn't. We're here."

He picks her up and holds her tight to him. "I don't think I'm going to let you out of my sight for the next ten years."

She pulls back and smiles at him. "That's silly. What about when one of us has to poop?"

Liam and I both chuckle, but then I stop, because laughing and broken ribs don't pair well.

The nurse comes back in and clears her throat in a way that says it's time for them to leave.

Liam nods at her, then turns back to me. "We're going to head home, but I'll be back tomorrow, okay?"

"Oh, what about Walt?"

"Nettie already came and got him."

"Tell her thanks."

I look at Olive. "If you ever wanted a pony, kiddo, now's the time to ask your dad for one."

Relief fills Liam's eyes. "Thanks for that."

I try to grin at him, then at Olive. "Get me one too, while you're at it."

She lays her head beside mine and grins at me, touching my lips with her little fingers. "What color?"

"You pick."

"Okay, Olive, we have to go," Liam says.

"I love you, Abby," she whispers.

Tears fill my eyes. "I love you, too."

Liam runs his hand over my upper arm. "I'll be back as soon as I can."

Then he picks her up and carries her out of the room.

As soon as they leave, I'm overwhelmed by fear, but not of what we went through today. It's about what I almost lost and what I still might lose. The thought sends tremors through me because I've allowed myself to need them. I can deny it all I want, but I need them. I've allowed myself to love. And it could all be taken away in a heartbeat. In any number of ways, I could lose them both. He might not love me back. He might decide he doesn't want me in their lives anymore, or maybe I'll be too cowardly to tell him the truth, and eventually, this will all fade away.

CHAPTER THIRTY-ONE

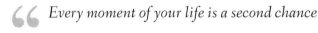 *Every moment of your life is a second chance*

~Rick Price

Early the next morning, Dr. McVicar comes by to see me. "How's my favorite cliff diver?"

I smile weakly and try to sit up, then stop myself when I realize sitting up isn't in the cards today.

"Oh, you won't want to do that. I'm afraid you'll be hurting for a few more days." She picks up the chart and flips through the pages.

"How long will I be in here?"

"Depends." She scribbles something and without looking up, asks, "Do you have anyone at home who can care for you?"

"No. I'm alone."

"In that case, your injuries suddenly look a lot more serious this morning, so we'll need to keep an eye on you for a few more days." She gives me a wink, then clicks her pen and replaces the chart to its holder.

"You know, you were very lucky, Abby. Most people would have drowned trying to do what you did. There's an involuntary gasping reflex in very cold water that causes people to try to breathe air into their lungs. We've all been talking about how you're a bit of a miracle."

I shake my head. "I'm not a miracle."

"To that little girl, you are."

She leaves me with those words ringing in my brain and I find myself completely overwhelmed at the reality of how close Liam came to burying another child. I say a silent prayer, my first since Isaac's death, thanking God for letting Olive live and for letting me live too.

The day floats by in a numb and lonely haze. I wait for Liam, but he does not come. Dusk falls as I stare out at the early evening sky over the ocean. Something about this time of day makes me melancholy, so I close my eyes and go back to sleep.

When I wake, it's dark out. Liam is sitting in a chair near the foot of the bed. He gives me a tired smile.

"Hi, have you been here long?"

"About an hour."

"You should have woke me up." I lift my head a little off the pillow and try to face him.

"Nah, you needed to sleep, and I needed to think." Liam stands and moves his chair so he's sitting beside me now.

"How's Olive?"

"Shaken up. But otherwise all right. My mother-in-law is with her now, feeding her some soup, and I'm sure as many cookies as she wants."

"Liam, I'm so sorry—"

"Stop." His voice is quiet, and he covers my hand with his. "You've got nothing to apologize for. I'm the one who screwed up. Letting her believe all this malarkey about mermaids and fairies."

"That's not true. You've given her hope and faith that there's more to life than what you can see."

"All I've really done is turn her into someone who doesn't fit into the world around her. The real one." He rubs a hand over the back of his neck. "She's got no friends. No mom. Other than you and her grandparents, she's got no one, really."

"She's got you."

His eyes fill with tears. He nods but there is a look of pain that crosses his face that is undeniable.

"Liam, you're the best father I've met. Olive doesn't have to wonder for even a second where her next meal is coming from or whether she's loved. She gets to go on adventures and see things other people only dream of. You've created a beautiful life for her."

"She needs more than just me. I'm—" His eyes take in the gash on my cheek, and he stops.

"You're what? Not enough? Because if that's what you were about to say, it's bullshit."

"Okay, thank you." He smiles, but it doesn't reach his eyes. "Yesterday kind of did me in. And you even more so. You don't need me going on about all of this right now."

"Why not? I'm not doing anything at the moment." I hope my light tone will encourage him to talk, but the bravado thing doesn't work on him. It never has.

He squeezes my hand. "You should be resting."

I lie awake for a long time after he leaves. It's dark outside, and I watch as the moon inches its way across the window. Tears pour down my cheeks as I finally allow myself to process what almost happened. Olive almost died. So did I. Another few minutes in that water and my parents would be arriving here to pack up my house and fly my body home. And Liam. Liam would be all alone in the world.

I sob at the thought of it. Sob for what we've already lost. Sob at the depth of my love for Olive and for Liam both. When I finally stop, I am worn out, but somehow stronger. I know what I must do. I need to take the leap again. I need to tell Liam that I'm in love with him. I am fully aware that it's quite possibly a knee-jerk reaction to a near-death experience, but there is an undeniable truth that when we are closest to death, we see life most clearly.

My heart pounds at the thought of telling him. If he were here right this moment, I know I would do it. I only hope my resolve is as strong tomorrow.

I wake to the sound of a familiar voice. "Abby. Abby, honey, I'm here."

"Mom?" I open my eyes and let them adjust to the light. There she is. Her hair has been highlighted, and she looks good, younger in spite of the way her face is pinched with concern right now.

"How did you—?"

"Your friend Liam called us. He went through the numbers on your phone and found ours." She's tearing up now, and I find myself doing the same. No matter what we've been through, no matter how far apart we've drifted, she's still my mom, who loves me and continues to worry about me, even though I'm grown and gone.

She rushes toward me and hugs me carefully. I get countless kisses on the forehead from her. And we both cry and laugh at ourselves for crying. My laughter makes me wince, which makes her wince as though she feels it too. And in a way, maybe she does. Maybe parents always feel the pain of their children.

"Chad found me the first flight here as soon as we heard. Dad wishes he could have come too, but he had to stay back for work, and to look after Grandma." She runs a hand over my hair, a familiar, comforting gesture to us both. "I can't believe you did that. Are you okay, honey?"

"I'm all right. Just sore." I sniff as she dabs my cheeks with a tissue.

Then she holds it over my nose. "Blow."

"No, that's okay, I can—"

"Blow."

So I do. What the hell? She came all this way.

CHAPTER THIRTY-TWO

66 *To share your weakness is to make yourself vulnerable; to make yourself vulnerable is to show your strength.*

~ Criss Jami

It has been a week since I returned home from the hospital. In that time, my mother has scoured the entire house, done a mountain of laundry I had no idea I even had, and filled my freezer with casseroles, lasagnas and what she calls 'meal starters,' which are portions of ground meats that have been precooked, spiced and are ready to use. I'm still very stiff, and my ribs ache when I move too much. The stitches on my back are itchy now, and I find myself eying Walt's scratching post longingly.

I've said nothing to Liam yet, although I've thought of little else. We haven't had time alone, and I doubt we will until my mother leaves. He's quieter this week, as he has been since his son's birthday, and I don't know if this is just one of those times when he has to grieve for a while, or if there is something else. As sure as I am about my feelings for him, I can't help but be terrified that he's guessed I'm in love with him, and that instead of this being a cause for happiness, he's filled with dread, knowing he's going to have to let me down soon. The possibilities of what might happen and how he may respond keep me awake half the night. It will either be a total rejection or one of the best moments of my life.

I look for clues when he's here. Signs that maybe he's feeling the same way I am. But there are no glances filled with meaning. No eye contact held a moment too long. Just normal, thoughtful, warm Liam. My dear friend. And the more I study him, the more I convince myself it was smart not to say anything immediately after the accident.

"Abby, I'm going to take off. It's almost three." Liam has poked his head around the corner into the kitchen.

I smile and tilt my head in his direction. "Oh, so soon?"

"Yup." He purses his lips together and raises his eyebrows. "Almost through with the basement. Couple more days, then I'll be out of your hair."

"No rush. I like you in my hair." *Dammit, Abby. Pull it together.* "I mean, it's fine. Take your time. Or not. Whatever suits you."

"Okay. Bye now." He looks thoroughly confused as he turns to leave. Not exactly the hallmark of a man in love.

I hear the front door close, and sit, staring out the kitchen window into the yard. The colors are glorious. The impossibly red maples blend with the brilliant yellow leaves of the birch, reminding me why autumn is my favorite season. The crisp air and the warmth of the sun bring new life to the world just before it falls into a cozy winter slumber.

My mom finally sits down to take a tea break. She pours herself a mug. "Did I tell you that Todd Blackwell got a divorce?"

"A couple of times, yes." I add a spoonful of honey to my tea and begin to stir it. "Also that he's a very successful dentist."

"Just want you to be happy, Abby."

"I know." I give her a mischievous grin that shows I don't even mind her trying. She's here, and even if she's pushing the wrong buttons, I know we need this time together. "I am happy."

"What about Liam? I've noticed the way you look at him."

"What are you ...?" My entire face flames and I will it to cool down. As much as I'm on the path to a more honest life, I can't test that out with my mom. At least not while she's here and has access to Liam. She's about as discreet as Eunice driving her Ford Fiesta around town. "We're just good friends."

"That's an excellent place to start if you ask me. He's a nice-looking fellow. Great father too ..."

"I already have a father, thanks." I take the spoon out of my tea and lick it, which I know will drive my mother nuts. But she's certainly not trying to avoid irritating me, so fair game in my books.

"So that's it then?" she huffs. "You're just going to give up on love?"

"I'm not ... yes, Mom. I am." Walt hops up on my lap and snuggles his forehead to my chin. I can see my mom is trying not to pull a face at having a cat so close to where we eat. I have to give her credit for that.

"You're never going to get married again?"

"That is correct."

"Abby, you're only forty."

"Forty and a quarter."

"Is this because of your cheek? Because it honestly doesn't look that bad, honey. Once the swelling and bruises are gone, you'll hardly notice it."

"It's not because of my cheek, but now that you've said that, maybe I should be worried about it."

She rolls her eyes.

"Mom, I know you want me to be happy, and for now, being happy to be alive is enough."

"So, you'll try to find someone in the future, then?"

"Probably not." I shrug. "I don't like how it ends."

She makes that little *tsking* sound that has gotten under my skin since I was a child. "No one does. Most people don't think about that part. They just get busy making a life with someone."

"I can't *not* think about that part, Mom. I've lived through it—just barely. I know how crushing it is."

"That doesn't mean you should give up on the best part of life."

"Are you talking about sex? Because if you are, a, yuck, and b, you don't have to be married to do that anymore."

"I'm talking about love. Obviously." She puts her mug down a little too hard, surprising us both as the liquid sloshes up and onto the table. Letting out a big sigh, she gets up and walks to the sink to retrieve a dishcloth. "You can't let what happened to Isaac stop you from falling in love again."

"Says the woman who's been with the same man since she was a teenager." I fix her with the icy stare I perfected when I was fourteen.

She ignores my dig and wipes the table. "You know, Abby, the way you spend each of your days adds up to your whole life."

"Well, thank you, Oprah. Is that one of the things you know for sure?"

"It won't work on me, you know."

"What won't?"

"The act. I see through you, Abby. And it's very clear that you have feelings for that man who just walked out the door."

I busy myself scrolling through my Pinterest feed. "Yes, it's called friendship."

"Don't waste your days wishing for Isaac to reappear. Let yourself have something wonderful again before it's too late."

With that, she gets up and walks out of the room. A moment later, I hear the washing machine start up downstairs. How the hell did she find more dirty clothes? I've been in the same pajamas for two days.

Over the next several days, I work on my novel, tweaking and cutting and smoothing it out so I can send it to Lauren for her notes. I can only manage to sit at my computer for an hour at a time and it's slow going with my right arm in a cast, but each hour is a mini-success. This morning I had a shower and actually put on real clothes, which, although normally wouldn't be considered note-worthy, felt like a victory for me.

Liam has gone to pick Olive up from school and I use the time to wrap up the final chapter of my book. I write a quick email to Lauren, and once I hit send, I stare at my inbox, happy but tired. I actually did it, even without my favorite editor to give me his notes.

The smell of chocolate chip cookies draws me into the kitchen where I find my mom at the sink scrubbing the baking sheet. She and Olive have become natural allies, having complementary needs— Olive's need to eat sweets, and my mom's need to feed people.

She glances up at me. "So? Did you get it done?"

"I did." I sit down in front of a large plate of warm cookies that have obviously been set out for Olive. Picking one up, I take a bite.

"Good for you," she says, crossing the room to give me a kiss on the top of my head. "Were you ever worried you'd never get it back?"

Nodding, I say, "For a long time, I was sure it would never happen."

"Yet it did." She gives me a meaningful look.

"It's not the same thing, Mom." My mouth is full of gooey good-ness, so I'm unable to properly form an argument.

The sound of the front door allows a nice, long pause in the conver-sation I don't want to have. My mom wipes her hands on a towel and hurries to greet Liam and Olive. I hear his voice, then Olive's as she shows my mother which of the feather toys is Walt's favorite and that 'this is how you bounce it just right for him.'

My heart speeds up when Liam appears at the entrance to the kitchen, and I instinctively cover my cheek. "Come have a celebratory cookie with me."

He smiles but I can see he looks worried about me as he crosses the room. "What are we celebrating?"

"I just sent my book to my agent."

Liam's face spreads into a huge grin and he leans toward me as though he might hug me, but then he straightens up. "Good for you, Abby."

"Now, the hard part—waiting to see if it's any good."

"It is," he says with a firm nod. "I can't wait to read it."

My face feels flushed as I realize he's likely to figure out who Ian is.

Two hours later, my mom and I watch Liam's truck back down the driveway. My mom sighs happily. "Oh, I think I'm in love."

"Poor Dad. He'll be devastated."

"Not Liam. Olive. What a dear, sweet child."

"I know. She's something else."

"Don't get me wrong. Liam's wonderful too." She gives me a sideways glance. "Better than Todd Blackwell even."

"The very successful dentist?" I pretend to be shocked. "Not possible."

She laughs. "I think it is possible. I feel like I really know Liam already. He's just such an open and warm man. Charming. Completely charming."

Unlike Isaac. She doesn't say it, but it's there. I give my mom a kiss on the cheek and swallow the snippy comment on my tongue. "Thank you for being here, Mom."

She gives me a serious look. "Abby—"

"Mom, don't. Please, let's just end the day on a high note. You're not going to change my mind."

"I know. You've pretty much ignored every piece of advice I've given you since you were twelve."

"High note, Mom. Please?"

"It's okay for you to figure out your own path, Abby. Really it is. Just so long as it's not fear steering you in the wrong direction."

My mom is leaving today. I'm still too sore to make the trip so Liam has offered to drive her to the airport in Sydney for me. I agreed to take him up on it, then spent the entire evening making my mother promise not to try any matchmaking on the way to the airport.

I stand at the doorway to the spare bedroom, watching as my mom packs. She's a whirlwind of activity, quickly deciding what goes in her carry-on and what will go in her over-sized suitcase. I've managed to make it to the local gift shop to send home some maple syrup and red mittens with Canadian flags for the kids, my dad, and my grandma. A feeling of sadness comes over me as my mom lays her favorite blue sweater on top of her clothes.

"Mom, I know I haven't exactly been easy since you got here."

"You're in pain. No one's at their best when they're in pain."

"I'm sorry I've been such a turd." My eyes fill with tears. "And I want you to know that I'm really just so grateful that you came all this way to look after me."

She crosses the room and wraps me in a deep hug. After a long, warm moment, she kisses my forehead like she used to do when I was a girl. "It's okay, Abby. I understand. You've had a hard time for quite a while, and I've been sticking my nose where it doesn't belong these last few days. But I know you love me, even when you're mad as hell at me."

"I do." I kiss her on her cheek. It's soft and smooth and full of comfort. "I'll try to come home for Christmas."

"Only if you're all healed up. I don't want you to push yourself."

"I'm sure I'll be fine by then."

She gives me another squeeze. "Good. Because it's just not the same without you."

That evening when I climb into bed, I see a note on my pillow. It's written in my mom's loopy, perfect handwriting.

Abby,

It's been wonderful to spend so much time with you these past couple of weeks. I realized this morning that this is the longest we've ever been alone together since you were born. Imagine that! I think we did pretty well, even if I did get on your nerves here and there.

No matter where you go or what you're doing, I'll be thinking of you and, likely, worrying. That's part of the job of mothering, and I'm afraid I can't change that. I hope someday you'll be able to accept that about me. I'm sure things will be a lot smoother if you can.

Don't forget to use the casseroles and lasagnas before they get freezer burn (they'll be best if you eat them in the next month or so). Thaw in fridge overnight. Bake at 375° F for an hour and serve with some salad so you'll get your greens. (Sorry, couldn't help that one.)

Please don't give up on love. If not Liam, then find someone else. I know Isaac wanted you to, and it's one of the few things he and I agreed on. You're young and talented and beautiful, and you deserve to have it all.

Love you forever,
Mom

CHAPTER THIRTY-THREE

> *Have enough courage to trust love one more time and always one more time.*
>
> ~ Maya Angelou

Gusts of wind have brought with them dark clouds. I sit at my desk listening as the rain starts to fall, first slowly, then with a determined roar. But nothing could ruin my good mood because I'm here in my cozy, bright office, and I've just received an email from Lauren titled 'Good News. Calling You in Five.' I get up and make myself some tea, then use a chopstick to scratch as deep as I can inside my cast. I glance at Walt, who is sitting on the floor watching me with great interest. "Ahhh, that's the stuff."

I answer the phone on the first ring, using the speakerphone so I can dunk the teabag in the water. "How good is the news?"

Lauren laughs. "How does mid-five figures sound, with an option on the next three in the series if you go ahead with more?"

"Yes!" I do a fist pump with my left arm. "That sounds amazing."

"Erica loved it. She said it's your most passionate work yet, and that nothing of this caliber has passed her desk in months."

I grin down at Walt. "Really? That's amazing, Lauren. Thank you."

"Don't thank me, you're the one who wrote it," she says. "How are you going to celebrate?"

"I'm going to buy a bottle of champagne and a carrot cake, and eat the entire thing, one slice at a time."

"You sure you might not want to share with Ian? I mean Liam?"

"Very funny."

"I thought so," she answers. "Speaking of Liam, have you womaned up yet and told him you're passionately in love with him?"

"No," I say, lifting the teabag out and letting it drip into the mug. "I haven't had a minute alone with him, but he'll be here soon."

"Really? Should I let you go so you can ladyscape?"

"No, obviously not. Nothing's going to happen today, even if he does confess his undying devotion to me," I say, picking up my phone and my tea and making my way to my office. "I'll have this ultra-sexy cast for another month. Plus, my face is still reminiscent of Frankenstein's monster."

"I'm sure it's not that bad," Lauren says. "Besides, if it's true love, he won't care."

"Still, I think I should wait until the bruises are gone and the scar isn't this angry red anymore."

"Abby, you got that scar saving his daughter's life. Surely, that won't be lost on him."

"It wouldn't be." I sit and watch the rain slide down the window. "He's not shallow."

"Which is why you love him."

My entire body hums with anticipation. "Just talking about this makes my heart feel like it's going to jump out of my body and beat its way out the door."

"Good for you. That means you're alive."

"It means I'm terrified." The sight of his truck pulling up makes my mouth go dry. "Oh, God. He just got here."

"Go! Meet your destiny, young woman," she says. "Call me the second he leaves."

"Okay," I say. "Hugs and shit."

"Hugs and shit to you. And good luck."

The front door opens just as I reach the hall. A cold blast of air precedes Liam, and when he walks in, his dark hair is damp, and he looks cold.

"That's quite the storm out there," I say.

"Yup. Another couple of weeks and it'll be snow." He takes off his light brown workwear jacket and hangs it on the hook to dry. "How are you feeling?"

Terrified. "Good, yeah. Stronger every day."

His eyes roam over my cheek and down to my cast, and when he looks back up into my eyes, he sighs. "I wish it would have been me."

"What? This?" I ask, pointing to my cheek. "Men dig scars. This is going to make me very popular down at the pub."

He doesn't laugh like I hoped he would, and I can tell whatever's been bothering him is still on his mind. He swallows hard, then says, "Abby, I think we should talk."

My entire body feels numb, but I smile anyway. "Sure, of course. You can tell me anything, Liam."

"Come here, I need to hold you for a minute," he says, his voice low as he steps toward me. He pulls me in for a long hug, resting his lips on my forehead and whispering, "Christ, you're perfect."

Perfect. I've never been called that before. The word wraps around my body and through to my bones, warming me. But when he pulls back, I see something is not right. I don't want to hear it, but I swallow my fear. "What is it, Liam? Whatever it is, we can figure it out together."

He closes his eyes for a second, then sighs. "Abby, let's go sit down for a minute, okay?"

I follow him to the couch and I sit down on it, while he sits on the coffee table facing me. His left knee is between mine, and he leans on his elbows and holds my hands, staring at them. "I have to tell you a story. It's going to end badly, and there's not much I can do about that part. It's the bit before the end that could maybe be a little bit amazing."

My mouth goes dry, and my palms start to sweat. Isn't that odd? How two parts of the same body have the opposite reaction when something horrible is about to happen?

"Abby, you're the best person I know. I've been in love with you for a long while now. I fell for you when we were on the way home from our first boat trip. Olive was asleep on your lap, and you were smiling down at her, and I just knew." The words are exactly what I've been needing to hear, but I can hardly hear them over the blood pumping in my ears.

He sighs and gives me a sad smile. "I love the way you speak and the sound of your laugh and how silly you can be. I love watching you put your hair up when you're heading out to the yard, or when you're about to cook. I love listening to you sing along at the pub, and how you go for it even if you don't know all the words."

He pauses and looks out the window. The rain is coming down in sheets now, the world has become a leaden blur. I'm glad he's stopped talking because I don't want him to tell me how the story ends. Whatever he's about to say, I don't want to know.

"To someone else, what I'm about to say would sound crazy, but I know it won't to you, which is exactly why you're so perfect for me, and for Olive. I think Olive was right that you were sent to us for a reason. But it's not the reason you may think."

Liam finally turns to me and looks into my eyes with a pained expression. I recognize it immediately because I've seen it once before.

CHAPTER THIRTY-FOUR

" *Home is the place where, when you have to go there, they have to take you in.*

~ Robert Frost

I stare out the thick plastic window of the plane. It is late evening and the lights of Portland are shining below. To an observer, I'm just a quiet woman with a broken arm who's slightly tired, perhaps from a long day of travel. On the inside, I'm raw with rage. My head and my heart are in a fierce, chaotic battle as they pull me apart with guilt, fear, and a deep sense of injustice that cuts me to my bones.

It's been three days since Liam told me the truth. Three days since I screamed in his face and called him a fucking liar and pushed on his chest to get him away from me. Three days since I told him to get the fuck out and never come back.

As soon as it was over, I was like a robot, acting out of pure logic— first a call to Eunice to tell her to come by and photograph the house because I'm leaving. Then booking an open-ended ticket home and texting Colton to offer him a job house-sitting. I didn't bother going next door to say goodbye to Nettie and Peter. They knew. The entire time, they knew. So fuck them too.

I am slow to get off the plane, letting people go ahead of me, although I'm not sure why I'm doing this. I know my parents will be anxiously waiting at the baggage claim and I want to see them and hug them. I do. But I'm also dreading the conversation that's coming. I don't want to answer why I'm showing up so suddenly, especially since I just spent two weeks with my mom. I don't want to cry while I spill out every detail. I don't want them to ask what I'm going to do now. I just want to forget.

I spot my parents as I'm coming down the escalator to the baggage area. They are both beaming and waving to me, and it brings tears to my eyes.

"Abby!" My dad calls, pulling me in for a long hug and a big kiss on my temple. I squeeze him tight, inhaling the scent of a little too much Polo cologne. "Oh, I missed you, my girl. You're finally home."

My mom rushes toward me and we hug. "You look a lot better. I can't believe how much your face has healed in just a few days."

I smile. "Yes, I'm almost starting to look like myself again."

When she lets me go, she looks at me as though she's trying to read my thoughts. I give her a look that says, 'I can't right now,' and she nods. "It's just so good to have you home again."

Today is Thanksgiving. We've been in the kitchen since early morning, chopping, washing, dicing, sautéing, and basting. She keeps checking the clock because my brother, Chad, his wife, Tammy, and their kids are due here around two in the afternoon, and she wants to make sure the appetizers and chocolate chip cookies will be set out before they arrive.

I have two nephews, Christopher, age fourteen, and Graham, age nine, and one niece, Kaitlyn, who is twelve. I haven't seen them in close to three years and my mom keeps mentioning how much they've grown and how much more fun she's having with them now that they've calmed down. I know she's saying it because I've always found them a lot to take, and each time she says it, I feel a pang of guilt for not being a better auntie.

When we hear the front door open, my mom practically runs to the small foyer to meet them while I wash the garlic off my hands and follow her, feeling a little nervous.

"There she is!" Chad gives me a brotherly hug, followed by ruffling my hair and I wonder if he'll still be doing this to me when we're old and gray. "Glad you didn't drown."

"Aww, thanks, bro, but try not to get too sentimental on me," I say as I smooth out my hair a bit. "You'll make me cry."

Tammy rolls her eyes at him, then gives me a big hug. "You look wonderful."

"You too. How's work?"

"Oh, you know, same old, same old. The patients never stop complaining and the doctors never stop ordering me around," she says, shrugging off her coat. "But more importantly, how are you doing after your accident?"

"I'm good. Really."

"And that girl you rescued, how is she?"

"She was over it about ten minutes after she was pulled out of the water."

"Kids are amazingly resilient, aren't they?" she asks before turning to her children. "Say hi to your auntie the hero."

I look at my nephews and niece, who are all taking off their winter wear while Chad says, "Hang those up, and don't leave your boots around blocking the entire floor."

When they finish, they all turn to me, looking as nervous as I feel.

"Hi Kaitlyn," I hold out my arms for my niece, who is now almost as tall as me, but with a lanky build under her oversized sweatshirt. Her dark blond hair is up in a high ponytail with at least four scrunchies in it.

She gives me a half-hearted hug and says, "Hi Aunt Abigail."

"I see you have braces."

"Unfortunately."

"Do you hate it? I hated them."

A surprised look crosses her face, and she nods enthusiastically. "Totally. They're the worst." She spits a little when she says worst, then slaps her forehead with her hand and rolls her eyes. "See? I can't stop spitting when I talk."

Graham bursts out laughing and points at her. "You're so gross."

Pulling him in for a quick hug, I say, "That'll be you in three years."

"No way. I'm never getting braces," he says, squirming away from me.

"I never used to spit when I had my braces," Christopher says, which gains loud protests from Kaitlyn and both his parents.

Lowering my voice, I say to Kaitlyn, "I used to spit all over the place. Once I spit right on the nose of a boy I had a huge crush on."

"Eww! That's, like, the worst thing that could ever happen!"

"I thought so too until my orthodontist made me wear headgear through all of grade eight."

"Shut up! He did not!"

"Swear to God, it actually happened. I bet Grandma has some pictures of it somewhere."

Her eyes grow wide suddenly, and she turns to her mom. "Oh my God! Am I going to have to wear headgear?"

"No. Not at school anyway."

Chad speaks up. "I'm going to demand it, if it'll keep the boys away."

"Dad!" she shrieks. "You wouldn't!"

Chad is laughing and nodding at her, "Oh, I will. You can count on it."

I watch the scene unfold, remembering how much he used to torture me when we were growing up.

Tammy shakes her head and gives him that exasperated look that doesn't register with him anymore. "Relax, Kaitlyn. It's not going to happen."

My mom decides we've had enough chitchat at the door and ushers us all toward the kitchen. "You kids must be starving. Grandma's got some chocolate chip cookies for you fresh out of the oven."

The kids clamor down the hall, fighting to get to the sweets first. Chad calls, "Relax! It's not like she only made two cookies. You'll all get some."

"One each or you'll spoil your dinner!" Tammy adds.

After a whole lot of snacking and chatting, my dad leaves to pick up my grandma. When they arrive, I go to the door to greet her. She looks so tiny and frail, and I suddenly see why my mom was so worried about her. Tears fill her eyes when she sees me, and she holds her arms out for a hug that I have to duck down to receive.

"There's my Abigail. Look how beautiful you are," she says, pulling back and holding my cheeks with her ice-cold hands. "So young and brave, saving that little girl from drowning. I'm driving everybody nuts at the seniors' center going on and on about how my granddaughter is a real-life hero. And a successful author, to boot!"

I blush and take her hands in mine to warm them up. "You're good for my ego, Gran."

"Well, I don't know about that, but I do know I'm proud of you."

My dad puts his hand on her shoulder. "That makes two of us. Can I get you some tea, Mom?"

"Oh, yes, that would be lovely, Bill."

An hour later, we finally cram ourselves in around the long table in the dining room that gets used exactly three times a year. It has the same gray carpet with the same red stain from the Christmas of 1995 when my dad had one too many rum and eggnogs before dinner and tipped over his glass of merlot. After that, my mom instituted the red wine moratorium that still stands. The turkey is carved, mashed pota-toes and brussels sprouts are dished up, gravy is poured, and cranberry sauce is tucked along the edges of plates.

Graham picks up a piece of turkey with his fingers and takes a bite, which earns him a quick poke on his side from Chad. "What are the two things you did wrong?"

Graham looks at him. "Fingers and ..." He pauses, looking confused.

Chad sighs. "We haven't said grace yet."

"But we never say grace at home."

My brother turns red and I burst out laughing. "Busted by the nine-year-old." Turning to Graham, I say, "Well played, young man."

My dad taps the side of his knife on his wineglass. "Let's get the praying done before the kids faint from hunger."

The room grows quiet and everyone bows their heads, waiting for my dad to say his usual grace. "Good bread, good meat, good God, let's eat."

"Amen."

Forks and knives clatter as the eating commences. I have a sip of my pinot grigio and sit back for a moment, trying not to think about how well Liam and Olive would fit in here in this room, or how much my grandma would love both of them. I try not to think of Liam winning Tammy over with his charm or Chad over with his quick wit. And I definitely don't think about having him sit next to me with our arms touching while we eat, or him leaning in to whisper some private joke in my ear at some point during the meal.

Instead, I watch my parents as they lovingly observe their youngest grandson and trade 'isn't he perfect' looks. I realize that this moment, right now—having us all in the house together—is probably the closest my parents ever get to pure bliss. They're both lit up with wonder and awe for all the things the kids are doing at school and the funny things they say, and they keep glancing around and beaming at each of us in turn.

Chad is to my left. He gives me a bump on the shoulder. "You look deep in thought."

I smile. "I was just thinking about how your children have managed to turn our parents into people I don't recognize. They're patient. And happy. Do you remember that from when we were kids?"

He laughs. "No, I do not. Last Sunday, Graham dropped an entire bowl of spaghetti on the white rug in the living room and when I got mad about it, Mom actually told me to 'take a chill pill, Chad. He's just a little boy.'"

"That didn't happen." I shake my head. "Not our mom."

"True story. She even gave him some ice cream to make him feel better about it."

"No, she didn't," I say.

"She did. Swear to God."

"Wow. It's like your children have literally cast a spell on them."

My dad narrows his eyes at us, meaning he must have picked up on bits of our conversation. "What are you two knuckleheads talking about?"

"How patient and kind you are since you became a grandfather," I answer.

Chad and I burst out laughing, and I'm glad to be home.

For the next week, my mom drags me to visit every family friend we've ever had, breaking only to stop at the outlet stores so I can 'update my wardrobe now that I'm almost thin again.' I don't even mind, actually. It keeps me too busy during the day to think about my fight with Liam, or the fact that when I go back to South Haven, it'll be to get Walt, pack my things, and spend the rest of my life pretending I was never there.

With any luck and a lot of time, I won't wonder if Liam is still alive, or worry what has become of Olive. They'll fade into the distance in my mind, two strangers I knew for a little while. As much as I wish I had it in me to be there for them, I know without a doubt it will kill me this time.

My mom and I have just left House of Vintage, my favorite clothing store outside New York. Our arms are loaded down with all our finds. We hurry outside into the cold, light rain, and drop everything into the trunk of my mom's Accord. She starts up the car, turns to me, and says, "We have a couple of hours before I need to get home and make dinner. Starbucks?"

"Sure."

I stare out the window as she winds her way through the busy streets. The entire world seems overcast, except for the Christmas lights that are already out in full force downtown.

"You're quiet today," she says.

"Oh," I say, giving her a relaxed smile. "Nothing a shot of caffeine won't cure."

"I don't think that's it," she says, signaling to indicate a left turn into the parking lot.

"I'm just a little tired. All that shopping."

"Please don't mistake my patience for stupidity. You suddenly show up with no explanation. You don't mention Liam or Olive even once," she says. "I was always good at math, Abigail."

"What is that supposed to mean?"

"I can add two and two."

"There was an irresistible seat sale and my mother taught me to never pass up a bargain."

"Abby," she says in a warning tone. Then, switching gears, she attempts to sound like we're just a couple of girlfriends out on the town. "I promise not to tell you what to do. I'll just listen."

"It's going to be awfully quiet then because there's nothing to say."

"Did you and Liam have a big fight or something?"

Tears spring to my eyes and I turn to face the window, trying to regain my composure. Sniffing, I say, "Not really. Well, sort of, I suppose. But the silver lining is we figured out we weren't right for each other before things got too complicated."

"Hmph." She finds a stall, turns in, and parks the car.

"I really don't want to talk about it, okay?"

"Okay, but I'm here to listen if you change your mind," she says, clearly restraining herself.

"I'm thinking of moving home, actually," I say, surprising both of us equally. "It would take a while to sell the house but there's nothing for me in Cape Breton and New York is too expensive." And even though I can't say it, I think I'd like to be closer to my family.

Turning to me, she smiles, her eyes filled with glassy hope. But she doesn't whip into planning mode or tell me she knows the perfect place. And she doesn't suggest I take over their basement or say she's glad I finally saw the light. Instead, she says, "Well, you'll figure it out. You always do."

"Yeah, I will." I nod, trying to reassure myself.

Her face grows serious, and she rests her fingers on my shoulder. "What happened, Abby? You seemed so perfect for each other—all three of you."

"Oh, fine." I sigh, closing my eyes for a second. "Four years ago, Liam had cancer—Non-Hodgkin's lymphoma. He thought he beat it, but ..." I shake my head, unable to get the words out.

"Oh, Abby!" she leans over to give me a hug which proves challenging, given the space.

I twist my body and cling to her anyway. Tears fill my eyes and for once, I have no desire to stop them. "It's come back, low-grade this time, which means he might be okay for a while. It could even be a few years, but then ..."

"I'm so sorry, sweetie," she says, when I finally let her go.

I sniffle and dab at my eyes. "Life is just so unfair."

"It is. It's fucking unfair," she says, her voice filled with anger.

My head snaps back and I look at her. "You just said the 'f' word."

"And I meant it. First, you lose Isaac, then you meet the perfect man, and now this. And poor Olive. Oh my God, that poor little thing. There's no justice in this world."

I nod, still too choked up to speak.

"And hasn't Liam been through enough? I can't even imagine how he's still standing after everything he's had to deal with. He doesn't deserve this," she says, her voice shaking with anger. "He's such a good man. A wonderful dad, and just so generous and thoughtful and full of life." Her voice cracks and now we're both crying.

"I know. I can't even ..."

She sighs heavily and her voice softens. "So this is why you came home."

Nodding, I say, "I just had to get out of there."

We're both silent for a minute, then she says, "So you are in love with him, then."

"What? No," I say. I mean to shake my head, but it nods instead. "Yes," I whisper. "But I can't, Mom. I just can't go through all of it again. The doctor's appointments and holding a bucket for him while he pukes and watching him lose his hair and waste away to nothing and get so weak, he can barely stand on his own." I suck in a shaky breath, and when I exhale, it comes out in stilted sobs. "And at the end, you're just so fucking empty you can't even breathe."

My mom's shoulders start shaking and now we're both sobbing so hard, I'm sure the car is moving. "I should have been there," she whispers. "I should have come. I could have helped. I could have propped you up when you felt like you couldn't take it anymore."

Shaking my head, I say, "I didn't want you to."

"But I'm your mom. I should never have let you go through that alone." She sniffles. "When I think about just leaving you to handle it all alone, I just ... I don't think I'll ever forgive myself."

"It's okay. Please don't blame yourself. I never would have let you be there for me."

"But then you just disappeared into this abyss. I was so scared I was going to lose you forever."

I nod, my face twisting with emotion. "I almost didn't make it. And that's why I can't ..."

"You don't have to explain. No one would blame you for not wanting to go through that hell again."

Closing my eyes, I finally understand why people compare relief to being let off the hook. But my reprieve only lasts for a fraction of a second before Olive's little face pops back into my mind. "I can't, but when I think of Olive ... fuck."

She digs around in her purse and takes out a packet of tissues, holding one out for me and using one to blow her nose. "She'll be okay. She must have grandparents or aunties and uncles who would take her in if the worst happens."

I close my eyes and shake my head. "Not really. Her mom's parents are going through their own tragedy—her grandpa has just been diagnosed with dementia."

"What about Liam's parents?"

"His dad's dead and his mom sounds like the least patient, loving person in the world. His sister already has five kids, and she doesn't sound much better than her mom."

"Well, someone will step up, I'm sure of it," my mom says, obviously needing to put it all out of her mind. "She's a sweet little girl and there's a village full of nice people there who would gladly take her in."

"Yeah, I'm sure you're right."

"And who knows? It seems like every week they come up with some new miracle drug. They might come up with something for him and he could be just fine." She starts up the car again and backs out of the stall.

"Aren't we going for coffee?"

"We need something much stronger than coffee. There's a bottle of tequila in the liquor cabinet with our names on it."

CHAPTER THIRTY-FIVE

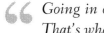 *Going in one more round when you don't think you can.*
That's what makes all the difference in your life.

~ Rocky Balboa

Neither of us bring up Liam over the next week. Instead, we carefully avoid the topic, preferring to talk about old times rather than the future. I keep expecting my mom to come to me with a listing of condos for sale, but she doesn't. Instead, she gives me the space I need, and I wonder if it's because we feel so close now that space doesn't hurt her anymore.

It's after supper and I'm at my brother's house. The kids have been teaching me to play Wii tennis and we've all been having a laugh at my pathetic attempts. I have to play left-handed which makes me less skilled and far more amusing to everyone. Somehow, the satisfaction of making my nephews and niece laugh is totally worth the humiliation. I'm sweaty and my face hurts from smiling, and I can't remember when

I was ever this silly.

Tammy comes to the rec room to find us when it's time for Graham and Kaitlyn to go upstairs to get ready for bed. They groan and beg for another half hour with Auntie Abby. I know their antics are irritating their poor mom, but I can't help secretly enjoying the fact that they want to be around me. They negotiate their way to an extra ten minutes, then the game resume.

When she returns, she's taken on an 'I mean business' tone, and the children accept their fate. Christopher, my oldest nephew, has been informed that he must finish his homework now, so the TV has to be shut off. His shoulders drop and he looks at me.

"Sorry. I have to do a stupid reflection essay about a field trip we went on today."

"That's no problem. We can pick up our game another time."

His face lights up. "Yeah?"

"Definitely. I'm here for another few days."

A slow smile spreads across his face. "Cool."

Cool. I'm cool Auntie Abby. I love that. I return the Wii remotes to the basket they're stored in and follow Christopher up the stairs.

When we reach the top, he says, "Hey, maybe I can come see you next summer? You know, stay for a couple of weeks or something."

I grin. "I would love that." Then I remember and my face falls. "But, actually, there's a chance I'll be moving."

"Oh," he says, his eyes shifting to the floor.

Crap, now he thinks I don't want him to come. "But wherever I end up, you should definitely come—"

My brother's voice booms from the top floor of the house. "Christopher, essay!"

"Okay! I'm going!" he shouts back. Then he looks up at me. "Do you think you could look at my essay for me? I suck at them, and thought maybe since you're such an amazing writer ..." He gives me a smile meant to win me over.

It works. "I would love to help you."

I help myself to a glass of water while he disappears into the mudroom to retrieve his homework. Upstairs, Kaitlyn and Graham argue about whose turn it is to brush their teeth first and Chad hollers, "Knock it off, you two!"

Chuckling, I mutter, "He got that line from your grandpa."

Christopher lowers his voice. "Did he also say, 'Keep going and I guarantee you won't like what happens next?'"

I laugh at the familiar phrase. "No, that was all Grandma."

"Really?"

"Yeah, she was a real harda— I mean tough bird."

Christopher's eyes grow wide. "I know what you were going to say!"

"No, I would never speak in such an unladylike fashion."

He grins at me, then squints his eyes a little. "Can I tell you something?"

I slide into a chair next to him at the table. "Sure. What's on your mind?"

"It's just that—I don't want to offend you or anything, because I'm trying to say something nice. And I don't want you to think I didn't like Uncle Isaac, because I did. He was always really nice and I'm sorry he died." He pauses and takes a breath finally. "I just ... I kind of like you more now. You're better. Kaitlyn and Graham think so too. We didn't know you were so fun, but you really are."

"Aww, thanks, buddy," I say, even though I'm sort of hurt.

"Yeah, before, you mostly hung out with our parents, and you didn't really seem to want to talk to us much. But now, you're like, playing Wii, and giving my dad a hard time, and you came to watch my basketball game."

"Thank you. You guys are really terrific human beings and it has been an absolute pleasure getting to know you."

My brother's heavy footsteps on the stairs have my nephew scrambling to open his binder. His words sit heavy in my brain and I try to recall the way things used to be. What was I like before? I'm not even sure I would like that person if I met her right now.

I fold my new jeans and drop them in my suitcase. In three hours, I'll be on an airplane, and another twelve hours and one connection after that, I'll be back in Cape Breton, where I'll have to face reality again, and face the man and little girl I'm about to abandon.

My dad knocks at the open door to my old bedroom. "Hey, Abby, you all packed up?"

I nod and stare at him for a moment, grateful he's still so young and healthy.

"Good stuff. We'll have to get going to the airport."

"I'll be ready in a couple minutes. How's Mom?"

"A little weepy." I can tell by his face that he didn't want to admit it at the risk of making me feel guilty.

"Me too, if you can believe it."

"It's sure been nice to have you home."

"It's been nice to be home." Nice. What a dull word for what we're trying to say. Yet, somehow it works perfectly when you're hoping to keep your emotions at arm's length.

"It feels like we finally got our daughter back this trip." His eyes glisten and he clears his throat. "Anyway, I'm really proud of you, Abby. I hope you know that. Not just your writing or saving that girl, but how you've managed to pick up the pieces this past year."

I walk over and wrap my arms around him, resting my cheek against his shoulder, and he hugs me back, the two of us trying to pack years' worth of hugs into this one. I'll always feel small and safe here, no matter how old I get.

He kisses me on the cheek and his voice cracks when he says, "I missed you, kiddo."

Apparently, I have an entourage to see me off. Chad, Tammy, and the kids showed up at the airport just after I checked in. The sight of them caused me to burst into tears, but lucky for me, Chad was quick to mock me, and I managed to pull it together before things got too out of hand.

Now we're sitting in the cafeteria at two tables that have been pushed together. Thankfully, the children are holding up the conversation for everyone as we sip our coffee and try to hold it together. My heart aches at the notion that I'll be so far away from them again and, depending on how long it takes to sell the house and find my way back home, the kids will have grown and changed by the time I return. I try to drink in my last few minutes with them, hoping to remember everything about this moment and telling myself I need to call them more often.

I look at my watch and sigh. "I better go."

We stand, our chairs scraping the tile floor. Chad collects the empty cups onto a tray and hands it to Christopher to dispose of, then we move the tables back into place. Soon there is no evidence of my little surprise party. I turn and walk out of the cafeteria, unable to bear the thought that it's already over.

When we reach the security checkpoint, I turn to them, unable to hold back my tears. "Thanks, everyone, for coming to see me off."

I run my hand over Kaitlyn's cheek and tell her to hang in there and that her braces will be off before she knows it.

I ruffle Graham's hair. "Don't go growing up on me before I get back. I like you this size."

"Too bad. I'm gonna be taller than Dad by the time I'm ten."

"Well, you'll need to eat your own vegetables from now on," I say with a sideways grin.

Christopher looks down at me. "Hey, maybe if you start eating your greens, you could grow some more."

"Very amusing, pal!" I give him a light punch on the shoulder. "Don't forget your transition statements when you do your next essay."

"Or I could email all my assignments to a certain famous writer I know who loves working on persuasive essays."

"Sure, I'd be happy to ..." I pause, glancing at his parents, then back at him. "...edit them for you. Wink wink."

Chad raises one eyebrow. "Not happening." Turning to me, he says, "Thank God you live on the other side of the continent. I had no idea what a terrible influence you'd be."

"Oh, don't worry," I say, giving him an evil grin. "I'll find a way to influence them from there."

The next minute is filled with kisses and hugs and tears and promises to call and assurances that we'll see each other soon. Then it's time for me to go. My throat is thick with sadness as I wind my way through the ropes to the security checkpoint. Once I'm on the other side, I turn back to see my mom leaning her head on my dad's shoulder, and him with his arm around her. The sight of it breaks my heart at the same time that it fills me with gratitude. I'm thankful they have each other. I'm thankful I now understand what I've been missing out on all these years. I'm thankful that I'll never be alone in this world as long as I have my family.

I'm almost to my gate when my cell phone rings. It's my mom calling. Doing my best to sound breezy, I answer with, "Miss me already?"

"Yes," she says, her voice cracking. "But, listen, Abby, I just had to say that if you change your mind, Dad and I will both be there with you every step of the way."

"Oh, Mom, please don't ..."

"I don't want to upset you and I'm not suggesting you should change your mind, but you know what? There are no guarantees, you know. What if he beats it? What if you two could have a long and happy life together? Wouldn't that be worth the risk?"

I close my eyes and hold the phone away from me for a second. When I bring it back to my ear, she's saying, "If you do, you won't be alone this time. I promise."

CHAPTER THIRTY-SIX

> *Love don't make things nice - it ruins everything. It breaks your heart. It makes things a mess. We aren't here to make things perfect. The snowflakes are perfect. The stars are perfect. Not us. Not us! We are here to ruin ourselves and to break our hearts and love the wrong people and die.*

> ~ Ronny Cammareri, Moonstruck

I'm driving back from the Sydney airport, my knuckles as white as the snow that blankets the island. The highway has been cleared, leaving treacherous patches of black ice. Each one reminds me of my mom's warning about the winter tires. CBC radio is providing the soundtrack to my drive, and the announcer informs me that we've had a record-breaking snowfall for November, and another big dump will arrive by midnight. In honor of that, he's decided to play Michael Bublé's "Winter Wonderland," and he hopes I sing along.

I glance at the frost-covered trees that sparkle when they're lit up by the headlights. It's both dangerous and incredibly beautiful at the same time. It's almost seven in the evening and even though I haven't eaten since breakfast, I'm too nervous to feel hungry. I've been riding an emotional roller coaster since I left Portland. Why did my mom have to ask me the 'what if' questions? It was all so much simpler in my mind before that. Now I can't help but wonder if I might be walking away from the most magical, beautiful thing life has ever offered me. Each passing mile wakes me up to what I'm really giving up if I leave.

A call from Lauren interrupts Michael Bublé, and I press the button on my steering wheel to answer it. We've spoken each week since I left. She's done a very good job of remaining neutral, and I love her for it.

"Hi, Lauren."

"Hey, just wanted to see if you made it home safely."

"Not yet. I'm currently being initiated into Canadian winter driving," I say, gripping the wheel tightly with my left hand as the tires swerve to the right. "Actually, it's more like a hazing."

"God, is it bad?"

"They've had about twenty-eight inches of snow today and this stupid cast isn't exactly making it easier."

"Good thing you'll be getting out of there soon." And I think I now know how Lauren really feels.

"Yup," I answer, the knot in my stomach twisting up even more than it already was.

"I know how hard this is going to be for you. You all right?"

Tears spring to my eyes. "Don't ask me that, okay?"

"I thought you might start second-guessing your decision."

"I am," I say, my voice wavering. "My mom said something this morning that really got to me."

"Uh-oh, Helen strikes again?"

I know she's being supportive, and she's working on years of me complaining about my mom, but after everything that's happened, it doesn't sit right with me. "Yeah, I have to give her one thing, Lauren. She knows me."

"What'd she say?"

"What if he beats it, and I'm walking away from a long and happy life with him?"

"Well, that's a real mind fuck." Lauren's tone is instantly angry, but she pauses, sounding overly calm. "Sorry, it's just that she didn't see how things were for you after Isaac died."

"No, I get it. You were there to see me fall apart. And this time, I wouldn't have the luxury of falling apart. I'd have a child to see through it." A semi-truck passes me, blowing snow across the windshield and blinding me for a second. My entire body tenses up in response. "I'm probably making the right decision. It's the safe choice."

"Does it feel like the right decision?"

"Logically, yes. It's the smart call."

"Forget logic. Does it *feel* like the right decision? Because you don't sound sure."

"Wait? Whose side are you on, because I thought you were sure I shouldn't do this."

"I'm on your side, Abby, and that means wanting you to be happy and healthy," she says. "So in my mind, the real question is, what's going to be best for you in the long run?"

"I guess the best thing for anyone in the long run is to live so they aren't filled with regret at the end of it all."

There's a long pause on the line. I speak up before Lauren can. "Here's the thing, Lauren. I could walk away and maybe years from now, I could convince myself none of this even happened. But I won't just be leaving behind two people who love me and need me. I'd be walking away from who I am when I'm with them."

"And who is that?"

"I'm alive. Like really alive, you know? I dance and sing and I'm silly and funny. I'm someone I forgot I could be, and I don't just love them. I love her. She's kind of awesome, really."

"You mean the person who disappeared when you lost Isaac?"

"No," I say. "The person I lost when I met him."

Lauren's voice cracks. "Then you know what you have to do, I guess."

Tears run down my cheeks as the *Welcome to South Haven* sign appears to my right, wet snow sticking to it.

"I guess I do."

When I finally turn onto Shore Lane, there is no 'for sale' sign swinging in the wind and I chuckle at the fact that Eunice hasn't done it yet. She knew. Cars are lined up in front of the B&B, and I can see it's lit up with Christmas lights. I signal and turn into my driveway, seeing that Colton has cleared the snow and left the front porch lights on for me. I texted him yesterday to tell him I'd be back, and he wrote back saying he was going to miss Walt and having his independence.

As soon as I shut off the engine, I let my shoulders and neck relax, wanting a hot bath, but knowing I have something much more important to do than soothing my sore muscles. My heart thumps when I think about it. I don't have the first clue what to say or how, and part of me is naïve enough to hope we won't need words, but that a meaningful look between us will be enough.

I don't bother with my luggage, but instead, hurry up the front steps and unlock the door. Walt is waiting on the floor in the hall. He meows loudly, complaining about me leaving.

Crouching, I reach out for him and lift him into my arms. "I'm sorry, Mr. Whitman. I shouldn't have left you for so long."

He immediately rubs his head against my neck, and I'm pretty sure he forgives me. I carry him through the house, turning on lights, and loving what I see. This is my home. Here in this little village. My cottage by the sea, which has been lovingly restored by the man I love. After a few minutes of snuggling Walt, I set him down on his favorite chair and I open the cupboard. I take a can of Fancy Feast out for him and give him some supper. "You eat. I have one more thing to do, okay?"

When I open the front door to the B&B, I'm greeted by the heat from the lobby fireplace. It crackles and spits and welcomes me as I stomp the snow off my boots. The smell of the wood burning blends with the strong pine scent of the garland swooping across the front of the desk. The sound of people talking draws me to the pub, and I take a deep breath, fear and hope and love all coursing through me. I hear Liam's laugh and my entire body goes numb as our last conversation plays out in my mind.

Swallowing hard, I force my feet to keep moving even though my legs are heavy with fear. A large fresh-cut tree sits in the corner of the pub with white lights twinkling against the frost-covered window.

I stop at the entrance to the pub and search for him among the crowd, my heart leaping at the sight of his face before my brain reminds me of how I left things. He's standing next to Peter at the bar, grinning over the beer in his hand. *Oh God, please let him love me back. Or at the very least, not hate me.*

Slowly, the conversation dies out as one by one, each of the sweater-clad people notices me. Liam stops and his smile fades as he stares at me. I stare back, hoping he already knows. But I can tell by the look in his eyes it's not going to be that easy. An awkward silence fills the space, but I force myself to speak, hoping to hell that whatever comes out of my mouth will be the start of a new life.

"Hello, everyone," I say, glancing around before fixing my gaze on the man I'm here to see. "For those of you who don't know me, I'm Abigail Carson. Some people know me as the resident New Yorker in the village. To others, I'm the hermit of the sea rock." I take one step into the room, then stop and clear my throat. "I'm glad you're all here because I have a confession to make. Several actually. I know it's been going around that I'm not interested in any type of romantic entanglement, but that's a lie. I actually started that rumor because I'm a coward and I like to take the easy way out."

Liam's expression is unreadable to me, so I keep going, my heart thumping at record speed while I try to keep my voice strong and steady. "But the thing about taking the easy way out is that it turns out it's the fastest way to a lonely, boring, horrible existence. And I don't want that anymore because it's not real. I want the magic and the mystery that comes with really living. I want to be with the one man who knows I'm crazy but might just love me anyway."

No one moves. No one speaks. And for one horrible moment, I'm certain I've made the biggest mistake of my life. I try to smile at Liam, but my face screws up with emotion instead. "I'm going to wait for you to say something because I'm so scared, my legs feel like they're about to give out and I'm fresh out of confessions."

Liam tilts his head and makes a little humph sound, then puts down his beer. "I thought once you made up your mind, you never changed it."

"Also a lie."

His eyes light up and he grins. "So are you saying you might be interested in a certain rugged, handsome Canadian?"

Relief washes over me. I shake my head and narrow my eyes at him. "I never should have called you that."

"But you did and now they'll all know you said it, so you can't take it back."

"Are you going to come over here and kiss me now?" I ask, holding back my tears. "Because I flew all this way and drove through a hell of a storm to tell you I'm in love with you."

And finally, he's moving toward me. I rush to him and he reaches out, pulling me to him with his strong, sure hands. I kiss him hard on the mouth and feel his lips on mine. Immediately I'm lifted to another world, bursting with love and passion, and I know he's there with me. He feels it too.

Applause and some random cheers fill the room but we both ignore it. His hands move up to my cheeks, and he holds my face as he tilts my head and, oh my, now we're really kissing. I had completely forgotten how this could feel. It's heaven right here in the pub and I'm pretty sure my heart is going to burst with happiness. He wraps his arms around my waist now and holds me up, and it's a good thing because my knees have turned to jelly.

Peter taps us both on the shoulders and clears his throat. "So, anyway, we should get back to the music now. If you'd like, the honeymoon suite is available. We'll give you fifty percent off."

Liam rests his forehead on mine and we both laugh. Then he says, "No thanks. We don't need you all listening in."

We make it into the house before Liam spins me to him and kisses me again. We strip off each other's winter coats and wool hats. Grinning at him, I say, "Canadian strip tease."

Liam laughs, then his smile fades, replaced by something much more serious we've been pretending isn't there. "It's going to be hard, Abby. So much harder than either of us can grasp right now."

"I know. And I'm okay with that, Liam." My eyes fill with tears, and I don't care to fight them. Tears are appropriate right now. "I'm hopelessly in love with you and I want to be with you, no matter what that means."

His eyes fill with tears too, and I kiss him again to let him know we're in this together. The feeling of his lips against mine feeds a craving deep within me, the part that yearns for the touch of another human being. The part that craves only him. I look up into his eyes, and I see love there. I want to be looked at this way every day for the rest of my life, but I know I'll have to settle for every day for the rest of his.

When we pull back, he says, "You're not scared?"

"Oh, no, I'm fucking terrified, but let's do it anyway."

He smiles, then kisses me again. This time it's slow and sweet and passionate. It's everything I need right now. It calms my fears and wakes parts of me that have been dormant for so long. The parts that let me know I am a woman. Our mouths move together, and it is utter perfection. We stay in this beautiful embrace so long I lose all track of time. And I forget about the future because I'm swept away by this perfect moment with this completely perfect man.

EPILOGUE

 The best thing to hold onto in life is each other.

~ Audrey Hepburn

"Are you ready?" Liam smiles at me, and his eyes are more brilliant than the shimmering water surrounding the boat. We've just left the safety of the harbor as we head out to sea.

I nod and smile. I'm frightened and excited and happy in a way I've never been. I wrap my arms around Liam's waist and give him a long kiss, thoroughly loving the taste of his mouth on mine. Olive has run back into the cabin to get Liam's captain's hat, and we have a moment alone on the deck together.

It's a beautiful Monday morning in late May. The sun is warm, and we are about to embark on the adventure of a lifetime. Our little family, Walt, Olive, Liam and me. Olive's been buzzing with exuberance since Thursday when we told her we were pulling her out of school a month early. We're going to sail all the way to the Bahamas and back over the next four months, stopping wherever we want, and at some point, when the moment is just right, we're going to have a tiny wedding ceremony on a beach somewhere. Just the three of us, two witnesses, and a minister. Maybe Walt, if he'll agree to get off the yacht by then.

We've agreed not to tell her what's coming until we get home. Liam doesn't want to taint this moment for her, or for us, and even though my hatred of what will come can be vicious at times, I'm doing my best to allow myself to just be in this achingly beautiful moment with them.

I'm determined to make these days the best he's known, because of anyone I've met, Liam deserves this. He deserves to be carefree and peaceful and happy. He deserves to bask in the sun and see new places and taste exotic foods. He deserves to be taken care of now, and that means setting aside my own fear and sadness, and exchanging it for moments of being truly alive with him.

Because he is here for now. He is real and alive, and I love him completely. I love him for who he is and how he loves. I love him for the oceans of compassion he has inside his soul. I love him for his music and the magic he brings to this world. And I won't ever stop loving him, even long after he's gone. And the pain of losing him will remind me that I am alive and that I chose to live fully for once, accepting the end, instead of hiding away and missing out on everything wonderful this life has to offer.

Olive's footsteps cause us to break our embrace. She says, "Gross!" but the grin on her face says she's happy to see her dad in love.

He squats down and she places the cap on top of his head, then gives it a solid pat before spinning in a circle with her arms spread wide. "I am the luckiest girl ever!"

Liam waits until she stops spinning to ruffle her hair and say, "Why's that?"

"Because instead of sitting in boring Mr. Peter's social studies class right now, I get four whole months off. In kid years, that's like an eternity."

Nodding, Liam says, "Damn straight it is. And we're going to drink in every precious drop of this life, my girl. Starting today."

I have to fight the urge to give in to sorrow, and instead, plunge myself into Olive's elation, focusing on her pure joy as she dances and spins in the breeze. I'll have to keep drawing on this moment, on her happiness and her wonder to see me through.

"Do you want to drive for a bit?" Liam asks her. Olive nods and slips between him and the wheel, taking hold of it firmly with a look of pure joy on her face.

I pick up the camera off the bench seat and focus on the two of them like this, as he covers her hands with his and helps her adjust our course. I quickly snap as many shots as I can before my eyes go all blurry again.

"That's it. Just like that. Keep her steady." Letting go of her hands, he puts the captain's hat on Olive's head. It falls down over her ears and pushes on her wild hair. "Here we go, love! We're off on our great adventure."

She cranes her neck to look up at him. "Dad. I was just thinking. Maybe we could keep going. Instead of coming back in time for grade five, we could just keep going for years and years and see the whole entire world!"

There's a twinge of pain in his face, but he recovers almost instantly in that way that only a parent can. "I'd love to, Olive. In fact, there's nothing I'd love more than to do just that. But I want to leave some parts of the world for you to discover on your own."

"But I don't want to explore without you and Abby."

"And that is a perfectly natural feeling for someone who's eight—"

"Eight and two-thirds."

"Them too. But the thing is, you get your start with your parents, then you're meant to go off and explore for yourself when you're all grown."

"That's stupid."

"No, it makes perfect sense. If you had all your adventures at the start of your life, there'd be nothing left for you to experience when you fall in love."

I can't hold back my tears now, and I turn back to the shore to hide my face. Cape Breton is growing smaller and I imagine myself leaving my sadness there, on a faraway dock. It will be there when we return. I let in a deep, shaky breath, then another, this time stronger.

I can do this. I know I can. I will be broken-hearted again, but today, I'm alive in a way I never have been. And so is Liam. When I turn back toward them, I hope my nose isn't a shade of giveaway-red, but from the look of understanding in Liam's eyes, I turned too soon.

"Olive, be a love and go check on Mr. Whitman," he says. "See if he's ready to come up on the deck yet."

"He's probably still curled up on my bed, the silly bean," she says, rolling her eyes even though she's clearly delighted to be Walt's favorite source of comfort.

She disappears into the cabin and Liam gestures for me to come in for a hug. I cross the deck and he wraps his arms around me, protecting me from the breeze as he kisses my forehead and holds me close. "You okay?"

"No."

"Me neither," he says, his voice cracking.

I pull back and look up at him, needing to make him feel better. "Kids have a way of cutting your heart up into pieces like a chef with a set of Ginsu knives."

Grinning down at me, he says, "Evil little creatures, aren't they?"

"Extremely. But we love them anyway." I lift myself up onto my toes and give him a lingering kiss, telling myself to remember this moment, like I do almost every moment we've shared in the past months. I spin around and take the wheel. "Where to?"

Liam presses himself against my back and intertwines his fingers over mine. "Anywhere the lady wants to go. Your wish is my command."

"Somewhere with really good French fries," I say. "Oh ... and thick milkshakes."

"God, you're high maintenance."

"What happened to my wish being your command?"

Nuzzling my neck, he says, "I was just trying to be romantic so I could get you into bed later."

Leaning back against him, I look up over my shoulder. "Well, then you better captain us all the way to a burger joint."

Chuckling, he asks, "So that's how it's going to be, then? No sex until you get what you want?"

"You know me, once I get my mind set on something, I almost never change it."

"*Almost* being the keyword," he says, leaning down and catching my mouth with his.

He turns me to him, and we smile through our kisses, soaking in the sunshine and freedom of this day.

I pull away suddenly. "Oh, I think I just came up with my next book. *The Captain and the Countess.*"

"So, I get to star in another one of your stories, then?" he asks with a smug smile.

"What do you mean *another one*?"

"You're trying to tell me Ian White wasn't a thinly veiled version of me?"

Shaking my head, I say, "I have no idea what you're talking about."

"Oh, I think you do."

"You know, I may be high maintenance, but you're awfully conceited, Mr. Wright."

"As one tends to be when romance writers base their heroes on them."

The cabin door slides open and Olive comes up, carrying Walt awkwardly in her arms. She sets him down on the deck and I expect him to dart back inside, but then she sits down next to him and crosses her legs, and he decides to curl up in her lap instead. Liam gestures toward them with his head and we both grin as Olive starts telling Walt all about where we're going and how much fun he's going to have and how she'll be right beside him if he ever gets scared or hurt or needs anything at all.

The sails flap as the wind pushes us south to warmer waters. I inhale the salty air deep into my lungs, filling them with all the possibilities that will open themselves to us along the way. These are the moments—the simple, precious moments that make up an entire life. And they make up for every ounce of pain that the tide washes in.

ABOUT THE AUTHOR

Melanie Summers lives in Edmonton, Canada, with her handsome husband, three sporty nerd children, their adorable one-eyed dog, and one tiny puppy with a cute little brown nose. When she's not writing, she loves reading (obviously), snuggling up on the couch with her family for movie night (which would not be complete without lots of popcorn and milkshakes), and long walks in the woods near her house. Melanie also spends a lot more time thinking about doing yoga than actually doing yoga, which is why most of her photos are taken 'from above'. She also loves shutting down restaurants with her girlfriends. Well, not literally shutting them down, like calling the health inspector or something. More like just staying until they turn the lights off.

If you'd like to find out about her upcoming releases, sign up for her newsletter on www.melaniesummersbooks.com.

ACKNOWLEDGMENTS

I am forever working at a ridiculously fast pace, which means I need a LOT of help to keep things flowing. Today, I need to stop and acknowledge the many people who have made this book possible, including:

-You, my dear reader, for giving me a reason to work each day,

-Nancy Smay, a most wonderful and supportive editor, who worked on this book with me day and night, on airplanes and beaches, while she was on what should have been a relaxing holiday,

-Kristi Yanta, the picky editor extraordinaire who took the shell of a story and helped me see what it could be,

-My amazing proofreading team— Melissa Martin, Kellie Porthe-Bagne, Janice Owens, Nikki Chiem, my Mom (Nevia Brudnicki), Brooke Lindenbusch, Laura Albert, Janice Owens, and Karen Boehle-Johnson. You all worked under an insane deadline at a crazy busy time of year (December), and I am truly grateful,

-Kelly Collins and Jenn Falls for always helping me when I get stuck and listening when I'm panicking about a book (which is most of the time),

-Tim Flanagan, my marketing genius who does what he can to help my work find new readers in this crowded book world,

- Ron Eckel at Cooke International who is making sure The After Wife will soon become an audiobook produced by Tantor Media,

-Nikki Chiem, who is always there for me no matter what,

-My mom, who helps out SO much around here so I can work, especially when I'm under the gun like I was with this book,

-My dad, who taught me to work hard and dream big. I miss you, Dad,

-My kids for saying, "You got this, Momola," and,

-My husband, Jeremy, (last but certainly not least), for taking over through the entire month of November so I could do this, and for always supporting me.

Thank you to all of you from the bottom, the top, and the middle of my heart!

You mean the world to me,

Melanie

Made in the USA
Columbia, SC
08 May 2020